LIPSI'S DAUGHTER

LIPSI'S DAUGHTER

Patty Apostolides

iUniverse, Inc.
New York Lincoln Shanghai

Lipsi's Daughter

iUniverse books may be ordered through booksellers or by contacting:

iUniverse
2021 Pine Lake Road, Suite 100
Lincoln, NE 68512
www.iuniverse.com
1-800-Authors (1-800-288-4677)

ISBN-13: 978-0-595-37572-1 (pbk)
ISBN-13: 978-0-595-81966-9 (ebk)
ISBN-10: 0-595-37572-3 (pbk)
ISBN-10: 0-595-81966-4 (ebk)

Printed in the United States of America

To my dearest husband, Tony,
Whose love and laughter,
Whose thoughtful words
And loving acts of kindness,
Inspire me to write.

ACKNOWLEDGEMENTS

I would like to thank all the wonderful people who helped make this book a reality: Alex Alexandrou, Matt Barrett (Athensguide), Jacqueline Freeman, Mary Jo Gileno, Linda Morelli, Marilyn Rouvelas, Mary Schaller, and Vivian Gilbert Zabel (Writing.com).

Special thanks go to my parents Christos and Anna Koumoundouros, who showed me love and support all through the years, and who gave me the gift of loving, and to all my sisters Rena, Manuella, Sylvia, and Helen, who through their loyalty and love, gave me the gift of sharing.

Last but not least, I give my heartfelt thanks to my family. To Tony, for all those times you read my manuscript into the night, giving constructive criticism, and Tony Jr., for all the times your bubbly personality made me laugh. You both showed me how blessed I am.

CHAPTER 1

August 1988
Did time stand still when first we met
As did my heart that saw you yet

The wind and rain pelted Tony mercilessly as he made his way to the Captain's steering room.

"Mr. Plakis! Thank God you came!" shouted Captain Haris, trying to steer the yacht. "We can no longer fight the storm! One of our engines is down."

"Where are we now?" shouted Tony. He battled with the door, trying to shut it. The yacht heaved itself headlong into the black night, while the howling winds and heavy rain pounded the ship with a vengeance.

"We are close to Lipsi Island. We will be safer if we dock there for the night!"

It was mid-day and the sky was a lucid blue with no clouds in sight. Ipatia stood in the courtyard, gazing at Lipsi's sun-splashed rolling hills and deep valleys. The vibrant greens of the cypress trees dotted the landscape, and the whitewashed houses, so pure in color, appeared almost saintly. Further ahead, the Aegean Sea seemed calm, deceivingly calm. She had learned a long time ago that the waters beyond Liendou's bay could easily turn treacherous.

"Come, Kitso. Grandfather wants us to go get bread before the bakery closes," she said, patting the donkey and straightening his red silk tie until it hung gracefully from his neck. "There, you're the handsomest donkey in town!"

The tie had become a part of him, identifying him from the other donkeys. She had mistakenly brought home the wrong donkey years ago and had solved that problem by giving Kitso her father's tie. At first, her grandfather grimaced at the gesture, but learned to accept it over time.

They ambled down the narrow stone path, down the hill past her grandfather's vegetable garden and olive orchards, past the open fields with stone boundaries.

Her thoughts turned towards the trip tomorrow. This was the first time she was going back to Piraeus where her aunt lived; to the house she grew up in. There, she planned to study at the university and get her degree. Her growing excitement had been dampened by the fact that she had not received a reply from her aunt. It wasn't like her aunt not to respond to her letters.

The sound of the donkey's plodding steps stopped. They were standing in front of the Tsatsikas house. The door appeared shut, indicating they were probably napping or gone. "You'll have to wait for your meal," Ipatia said, laughing and nudging him onward with her feet.

Her trips to town often included stopping in and having a chat with her *nona*, Mrs. Tsatsikas, who always had some juicy gossip to deliver over a cup of coffee and a *koulouraki*. There were also a few leftover morsels for Kitso, enough to make him smack his lips with satisfaction. But today they were running late.

They reached the bottom of the hill and turned on to the main road. It wasn't long before the magnificent domed church of The Virgin of Haron appeared. Ipatia reverently made the sign of the cross. Last week, thousands of tourists had come to this tiny island to witness the miracle of the Virgin Mary icon and join in the festivities that lasted several days. Today, it was eerily quiet.

A banging sound from the direction of the church interrupted her thoughts. She turned and looked. The door was wide open. She hopped off the donkey and ran up the ramp to the entrance. She peeked inside the church. "Hello?"

There appeared to be no one there. She shut the door firmly. The wind from last night's storm must have pried it loose.

"Come on, Kitso! I've got to get to the bakery before it closes," said Ipatia, guiding the donkey back on the road. Clucking loudly, she sped past the waist high walls made of rocks and stone that guarded the old almond trees with their knobby branches, olive orchards and fig trees. Up ahead was the village water basin. Kitso slowed considerably.

"We'll stop by on the way back," promised Ipatia, patting him reassuringly on the back.

They finally reached the outskirts of the town-square. She tied the donkey to a post, and briskly went up the steps of the alley. To her dismay, the door of the bakery was locked shut. Ipatia tapped loudly on the window, hoping someone would be inside. To her surprise, the door opened, smothering her with the scents of warm baked bread. Mrs. Poulos' wide, friendly face broke out into a grin, as she gestured her inside.

"Ipatia, come in. I was just closing up the shop."

Ipatia thankfully chose three loaves of warm crusty bread, placing them in her canvas bag. She then took the *drachmas* out of her skirt pocket and began counting the coins.

"No, no, my good girl! This is my farewell gift to you," said Mrs. Poulos, brushing off the proffered hand. She warmly hugged Ipatia, enveloping her in a soft cushion of human kindness.

"Thank you. I will miss you and your family," said Ipatia, feeling sad, as unexplained emotions surfaced. It had been a long time since anyone had hugged her.

Mrs. Poulos dabbed at the tears that had formed in her reddened eyes. "I remember when you used to play with my daughters. Although you were the youngest, you were the best behaved. When they married and left the island, I was sad. Now you are leaving us, and I am sad again."

"Don't worry, Mrs. Poulos, I'll come back and visit you some day."

On the way back, guilt feelings threatened to overwhelm her. *This island isn't so bad after all. At times, I felt sad because I missed my parents, but the kind people here have helped me in so many ways. And what about Grandfather? He is all I have, and I'll miss him dearly. Besides, he's getting on in years. He needs me here. Oh why, why do I want to leave?*

Her troubled thoughts continued for a few minutes longer. Then she remembered why she wanted to leave. "There's no future for me here except marriage," muttered Ipatia aloud. She sat up straight, her back like a rod, feeling more determined to leave the island than a few minutes ago. For some odd reason, that helped, for she began to feel cheerful. Was it because she would be in Piraeus tomorrow, one step closer to getting her degree?

It wasn't long before they reached the water basin. The donkey planted his feet firmly and sipped water under the shade of the tree.

"This might take awhile," said Ipatia aloud. She looked around. There was no one in sight. Impulsively, she hopped on the edge of the basin, then reached for the branch, pulling herself up. She settled against the crook of the tree. This would be the last time she would sit in her favorite, secluded resting-place.

She pulled out the slim English novel from her pocket and began reading it. It had been given to her as a present by her English tutor. Each sentence spoken aloud was followed by moments of complete absorption as she attempted to translate the text into Greek.

How is the heroine going to get out of her predicament this time? Within minutes, she got her answer. Her voice sounded loud and triumphant. The heroine in the novel was finally declaring her true feelings to the man that she loved!

Rustling sounds caused Ipatia to glance up from her reading. She froze. Just above her was a large black snake, and it was slowly slithering towards her. She scrambled blindly towards the lower branch, then jumped, expecting to hit the ground. Instead, she found herself floating in air. It took her a moment to realize what had happened. Her long skirt had caught on the branch and was holding her up! She flailed her arms and legs, crying out, "Help! Help! A snake!"

"Don't move," said Tony, intent on the snake. It must have sensed him, for it began to glide away in the opposite direction of the girl. Tony's first reaction had been to laugh at the comical scene in front of him, but the snake's presence had prevented him from doing so.

Ipatia peered at the handsome stranger who appeared out of nowhere. Before she could reply, he jumped on the basin, swiftly untangled her skirt and plucked her up off the branch. The feel of his strong arms holding her close to him sent shivers down her back.

"You are safe now," said Tony, gazing down at the girl, admiring her beauty.

How could you let this man hold you so close! The danger signal coursing through Ipatia's body gave her the strength reserved for emergencies. She pushed herself off the firm chest, toppling ungracefully on to the ground like a sack of potatoes.

"Ow!" sputtered Ipatia, scampering up, dusting the dirt off her face and arms.

Tony lost his balance from the force of her push, landing in the water with a splash. Trying to stand up, he faltered and slipped back into the water.

Ipatia stammered, "I, I thank you! I have to go!" She backed into the donkey, unable to tear her eyes away from the wet man.

"Wait! Wait just a minute!" said Tony, getting up.

Ipatia's heart started to race. He was coming towards her, and he seemed angry. She slapped the donkey in the rear, yelling "*Ante!*" That did the trick. Kitso broke into a trot, pulling her along with him. She ran until they reached a safe distance. Ipatia slowed to a walk, trying to catch her breath.

She scolded Kitso. "Why did you have to be so thirsty? If we hadn't stopped at the water basin for you to drink, then I wouldn't have gotten in this mess!"

The donkey's large, trusting eyes looked at her sideways. Feeling guilty, she patted him on the head and sighed. "I'm not really mad at you. I am mad at myself. I should have known better than to be climbing trees."

She went over the events in her mind. She pictured herself hanging from the tree like a bat, flapping her arms in the air. She started to giggle, while her fingers automatically pulled her long hair back into a braid. The stranger had shown up just in time! She was thankful that he rescued her, but he did not have to hold her that close! What would people say if they had seen her in his arms! Then she remembered the time she had fallen from the same tree and had sprained and cut her ankle. Her grandfather had scolded her and had prohibited her from climbing that tree again. Today her impulsiveness got the better of her, as it had done in the past.

She began daydreaming about being in the young man's arms. A part of her wanted to remain there, snuggling against him, while another part scolded her for being so bold. *Did you push yourself off because of Grandfather's strict rules about boys, or was it because you didn't trust your own feelings? Were you afraid that you would fall in love with him?*

"Ipatia Kouris, how could you stoop so low into thinking because someone saves you that you will fall in love with him?" Ipatia whispered fiercely, realizing her emotions were betraying her resolve not to engage in any relationship. *Yes, but this isn't just anyone. I've never been in a handsome young man's arms before.*

Tony stood there, silently watching the fleeing girl, as her long sun-kissed tresses streamed behind her. She reminded him of a frightened deer. His eyes searched the tree, but there was no evidence of the snake. He climbed slowly out of the basin, holding steadily on the side for support. His white cotton shirt and black cotton pants were drenched. He shook his legs to get rid of the water, then removed his shoes and poured the water out of them. He swore silently. Not only did she run away, she had the audacity to push him into the water.

Let's be honest. Your ego has been bruised. In all your twenty-nine years, your good looks always had girls flocking to you. Even your nanny adored you. This was the first time a girl ran away from you, and you didn't have a chance to talk to her.

His glance fell on something brown on the ground. It was a book. He picked it up, mindful of his wet hands. "An English novel," he said, somewhat surprised at the discovery. Curious, he opened the cover. On the inside it read, "*To Ipatia Kouris, May you enjoy this book. I wish you success and happiness all your life. Love, Mrs. Rodos.*"

He leafed through the pages, noticing the scribbling along the sides. A piece of paper fluttered out of the book. The large clumsy handwriting was evidently that of a child's. It was a poem titled "To My Father, Captain Manolis Kouris." Its simple stanzas revealed the admiration and love of a daughter for her father. Tony paused, deep in reflection. *Could this man be the Captain Kouris who had once worked for my father?*

He remembered being sad when he heard about the captain's untimely death. He had been even more shocked to find out his family had been with him on that trip. Could this elusive girl, this precocious, tall girl be the surviving daughter of Captain Kouris? The fact that she still wore black clothes even several years after their death was a sign she had not gotten over her mourning. There was an odd feeling in his chest, an unexplained yearning to see her again. Tony tucked the poem back in the book being careful not to get it wet. He checked his watch. He was to meet Michael in front of the yacht at five o'clock. His sightseeing for the day was over.

CHAPTER 2

Rolling hills and deep blue sky
The sea stood still so I could fly

Catching glimpses of the calm blue sea to his left, Tony made his way down a cobblestone path. He had made a good choice, for this led to the main road. The sun was beaming down on him and the breeze that ruffled his hair was doing a good job of drying his clothes. This beautiful island was such a different world from the classrooms of Oxford. Here was a magical world where people like Ipatia, who were once thought dead, came alive.

Tony was transported back in time, when as a teenager he met Captain Kouris who captained one of his father's cargo ships. Tony's father had plans for him to work in his shipping business, and eventually own the company. Tony had other dreams. He was determined to attend the university instead. His father threatened not to pay for his education unless he went on a voyage with one of his cargo ships. In a last attempt to appease his father, he had conceded to going on the trip. That trip was imprinted in his mind as if it happened yesterday.

He remembered the tall captain with his black mustache, charming manner, and zest for life. Captain Kouris encouraged Tony to help the crew, saying it was the only way he would find out if he liked this business or not. Tony submerged himself in the day to day operations of the ship, working alongside the men. The work was labor intensive and menial. It was not long before Tony became bored and began daydreaming about the university instead.

His boredom was alleviated whenever the captain invited him to play backgammon with him in the evenings. Tony looked forward to those visits, not just for the game, but for what happened afterwards. Tony would ask him to tell him about his travels. The good-natured captain would sit back in his chair smoking his pipe, thinking. Then he would inevitably prop his long legs up on the desk, signaling he had found a story. With a gleam in his eyes, he would weave a story so thick with adventure that oftentimes Tony secretly wondered if the captain was making it up. Nevertheless, he was an accomplished story-teller, causing Tony to escape for awhile, even if only for a few hours.

The day before they docked, the captain asked Tony how he liked the trip and if he planned to enter the shipping business like his father. That was when Tony confided in him, describing his plans for the university, and how his father tried to control his life. The captain listened quietly, with a sympathetic face, as if he understood. The advice from the captain was "Keep your doors open, because you never know when you will need them."

The most poignant image conveyed in Tony's mind was the next day, when the ship pulled in to the harbor. He stood by the captain's side watching him position the ship expertly. The captain was particularly happy that day, talking about his family, and how proud he was about his young daughter's accomplishments and her love for music.

Once docked, Tony wistfully watched from the deck, as Captain Kouris went on shore to greet his wife and daughter. Tony could still picture vividly the gusto with which the captain kissed his young wife and hugged his daughter. The girl was jumping all around him, laughing and singing. Then they walked away, and Tony remembered wishing he had such a family. His father, a businessman, had been too busy to notice Tony's accomplishments, and had used money as a way of pacifying him.

❦   ❦   ❦

Ipatia hiked up the stone path that led towards the Xilouris house. She needed to talk with Mrs. Xilouris about the trip tomorrow. The whitewashed house stood alone on the hill, exposed to the sun's searing rays. Kitso stopped abruptly, snorting loudly.

"What is it, Kitso?"

Ipatia got her answer. She jumped when she saw the scorpion. It was scurrying towards them with its tail up in the air. Ipatia's lithe body danced agilely out of the scorpion's path. Earlier today it was the snake, now the scorpion.

She remembered when she was eight years old. She had gone to visit Maria, her new found friend, and a huge centipede with thousands of legs had appeared out of nowhere, causing her to make haste towards the house. Maria had been waiting for her by the door, laughing at Ipatia's frantic dash for cover. The following day, Ipatia had learned that her parents had died at sea. Was this scorpion another omen?

Moments later, Ipatia knocked on the door, noticing how quiet it was. She was mildly surprised that the door was shut. There was always someone home at this time. She knocked more loudly.

"Ipatia, Ipatia! Hello, Ipatia!"

The sound of the shrill voice was coming from behind her. Mrs. Xilouris, a thin, sprightly woman, whose clothes hung limply on her body, was coming nervously up the path, pulling her young son along. She appeared distraught. Nick's arm was wrapped in a cloth and he appeared to have been crying.

"Mrs. Xilouris, what happened?"

Mrs. Xilouris' eyes darted around as she said anxiously, "I was looking for Doctor Thanassis, but he is not at the Clinic! My little Nick fell while playing, and cut his arm badly on a piece of broken glass."

"Can I see? I hope it wasn't a big cut," exclaimed Ipatia, concern written all over her face. Her hand trembled as she took the boy's arm and removed the stained cloth.

She was shocked to see a big gash right below the wrist. It was bleeding heavily. She swallowed hard trying to ignore the sudden nausea that threatened to overtake her. "I'm afraid that he will need to have stitches…but first we need to stop the bleeding." Recalling what she read in the medical textbook that Dr. Thanassis had lent her she applied firm pressure on the covered wound, then wrapped the cloth even more tightly. "There. Now keep your arm up." She gently lifted his arm towards his chest. "That's a good boy."

"I don't know what I should do! My husband is in Piraeus…and I have no one here to help me!" wailed Mrs. Xilouris.

"Doctor Thanassis might be down at the dock."

"Yes, that's where he probably is! We will go there," said Mrs. Xilouris nodding excitedly.

"Here, why don't you take Kitso? It will be better for little Nick if he didn't walk all that distance," said Ipatia, trying to reassure her. "If you like…I can come with you."

"Thank you, Ipatia! God must have sent you!" said Mrs. Xilouris, her face breaking out into a happy expression.

"Actually, the reason I stopped by was to see about the trip tomorrow."

Mrs. Xilouris must not have heard her, for she was busy lifting Nick onto the donkey. He seemed a little pale and frightened. Ipatia helped her with the task, patting his leg while his mother settled behind him on the donkey. She walked alongside the donkey, singing a favorite tune and trying to cheer them up.

"You'll be fine, little Nick. Just remember to keep your arm up. That's right," said Ipatia. "You know, I cut my leg not too long ago and the doctor took care of it. Everything is fine. See how I can run with it." She broke out into a short trot. When she returned, she was rewarded by his weak smile.

Mrs. Xilouris smiled at Ipatia's antics. Except for her tall height, Ipatia was becoming increasingly beautiful, just like her mother.

❦   ❦   ❦

Tony approached a small square, with alleys that fanned out from it like spokes. A coffee shop sat at a corner alley, its open door inviting him to stop. He had been touring the island since this morning and was feeling very thirsty. Small round tables and delicate chairs graced the small courtyard that flowed into the square. Painted ceramic flowerpots filled with beautiful red flowers lined the few stairs that led to the door. He noticed a large, unusual vase standing next to the door. Its geometric lines and black figures appeared to be telling a story. The vase cast a spell of another era, its beauty mesmerizing him. He would have to inquire about it.

A man with a potbelly and big bulging eyes came to the door. He yawned, scratching his stomach, looking as if he had just woken up.

"Excuse me for this request, but would it be too much trouble to get me a drink?" asked Tony.

"Certainly, certainly. Stellios Pericles at your service," said the man, bowing, displaying his shiny, bald head. He took the order and vanished into the shop.

Tony sat outside, flexing his fingers, studying the vase. The university courses he had taken on ancient Greece covered Greek art and the design of vases. If his memory proved right, the geometric style evident on this vase could prove to make it a very ancient vessel indeed. It was at least two thousand years old, if not older. It should be in a museum.

Stellios returned swiftly with the drink. "With all due respect, did you have an accident?" He was staring at Tony's damp clothes.

Tony had forgotten about his clothes. "Yes, they are almost dried."

"You are not from around here. Your accent tells me you are from Crete, am I right, Mr.?"

"Tony, Tony Plakis. Yes, I came with the yacht last night. We had to dock here because of the storm," said Tony, somewhat surprised at this man's acumen. Years at Oxford had blended the English with the Greek, and the resulting Greek was pronounced with a British clip. Peering at him with half-closed eyes, he ascertained this man looked sincere enough. Yet he had learned a long time ago not to give out personal information freely, especially when one was wealthy.

"Yes, the storm was a bad one," said Stellios, nodding his head. "We get those around this time of year."

"Excuse me, but would you happen to know of a person named Ipatia Kouris?" asked Tony. "I have something which belongs to her."

"Yes, yes, of course. I know everyone here. I have been here all my life," boasted Stellios. "You see that hill up there?" He was pointing towards a hill in the distance.

Tony nodded.

"She lives up there with her grandfather, Christos Rodakis. He comes down every morning and stops here for coffee."

"Is it easy enough to go up there?"

"You will need a horse or a donkey, and at least one hour to go and come back. Otherwise, it's a very long walk," said Mr. Pericles, shaking his head knowingly as he glanced down at the young man's shoes.

"Oh, I see," said Tony, noticing the glance. His curiosity was provoked once more when his eyes fell upon the vase. It was as if the vase was speaking to him. "Mr. Pericles, where did you get that vase?" He pointed to it.

"You can call me Stellios! Do you really want to know? It's a long story."

"That's all right, I'm very much interested."

"Well, it all began a couple of years ago. You see, I sell horses on the side, and Mr. Rodakis needed a horse. He's an old man, with limited means, and all he had was this vase to give me at the time. Since we are friends, we worked out a deal. The vase was used as collateral until he came up with the money."

"I guess he is still trying to come up with the money?"

Stellios laughed. "The horse was very old, as was the vase."

"What happened to the horse?"

"The horse died on him, and now I am stuck with the vase, which is good only for plants."

"The vase should be in a museum."

"We have a small museum here on the island," said Stellios, nodding. "The priest takes care of it and it holds quite a few interesting artifacts. He has shown interest in the vase, but I haven't gotten around to it."

"Is that right?" asked Tony. If he had more time on the island he could visit the museum. "How did Mr. Rodakis come across the vase?"

"His son-in-law, Captain Manolis Kouris, traveled all over the world and whenever he came, he would bring him presents. This vase was such a present. Now his daughter and son-in-law both are in the sea, God rest their souls." Stellios bowed reverently and made the sign of the cross.

Tony was silent for a moment, reflecting on what he had just heard. He stood up slowly and pulled out his wallet, placing a few bills on the table. He said quietly, "Thank you for your kind service."

"Wait, I will get you the change," said Mr. Pericles, picking up the large bills, his large eyes bulging from the amount.

"Keep the change. I will try to stop by tomorrow morning when Mr. Rodakis will be here. What time do you expect him?"

"He should be here around nine o'clock or so. Come by then, Mr. Tony. We will be more than happy to have you," said Stellios, beaming as he shook his hand. This gentleman had just paid him a very generous tip.

CHAPTER 3

The book which did belong to me
Did change my whole life's destiny

Ipatia spied the coffee shop up ahead. Mr. Pericles was standing outside and had his back turned to her. He appeared to be deep in conversation with someone. "Look! There's Mr. Pericles! Maybe he will know where the doctor is." She gave the reins to Mrs. Xilouris and ran ahead. "Mr. Pericles, Mr. Pericles!"

"Why Ipatia, hello! We were just talking about you and..."

"Little Nick Xilouris fell and cut himself!" interrupted Ipatia, not hearing him, pointing to the boy's arm.

Mr. Pericles hastened towards the boy and his mother. Ipatia watched him examine the boy's arm, then sensed someone's presence behind her. She turned to find a pair of warm, liquid brown eyes gazing at her. Her breath caught in her throat. He was the same man who saved her earlier from the snake. She blushed at the memory, embarrassed at seeing him again. She blindly fled towards the donkey, not knowing what to say. He also had not spoken.

Partially hidden behind the donkey, she quietly assessed the stranger. For the first time, she noticed his exceedingly handsome demeanor. It wasn't only that he was tall for a Greek, but he also had an athletic build of Olympian proportions. His fine noble nose and firm chin added to his handsome features. He was gazing intently at the injured child and his expressive eyes revealed a sadness that touched her inner being. Her knees became weak. It was the same look her father had given her, when as a child, she had injured herself. She brushed the tears from her eyes and focused on what Mrs. Xilouris was saying.

"Mr. Pericles, do you know where we can find Doctor Thanassis?" asked Mrs. Xilouris. "Little Nick has lost a lot of blood and I don't know what to do!"

"He was here this morning and said he was going to Patmos to get medical supplies," replied Mr. Pericles, gesturing first towards the sea, then scratching his head.

"Patmos?" wailed Mrs. Xilouris, wringing her hands. "What am I to do?"

"Madam, I know of a doctor who can help you. He came on the ship last night and is probably down at the dock. I am supposed to meet him there. I can take you to him," offered Tony.

Mrs. Xilouris looked at Mr. Pericles with a puzzled look. She didn't know who this man was that just spoke to her.

Mr. Pericles nodded his approval. "Mrs. Xilouris, this is Mr. Tony...he is a friend of mine. He will help you."

"Thank you very much!" said Mrs. Xilouris to Tony, her voice full of emotion.

They bid Mr. Pericles farewell and made their way down to the dock. Ipatia stayed on the donkey's left side, slightly hidden, while Mr. Tony walked on its right.

"Mrs. Xilouris, can you tell me a little bit about the island?" asked Tony, trying to steer the conversation away from the young boy's arm.

"In ancient times, this island, some claim, was called Calypso. It used to be much bigger than it is now. Divers have discovered part of the island sunk under water. There is a whole city underneath there," Mrs. Xilouris said, pointing towards the sea.

"Also, giant bones, this big, have been discovered on the island," blurted out Ipatia. She stretched out her arms to the length of two feet.

"Really?" Tony asked, looking amused. "Are they human bones?"

Ipatia nodded and said, "Oh yes! My father said they were from giants who once lived here! And they even found pirate's treasures, gold."

"Ipatia, let's not get carried away," laughed Mrs. Xilouris. "You know how rumors travel around here. Someone finds a gold coin, and suddenly it becomes a pirate's treasure."

"Hmm, it sounds interesting anyway," Tony said. "How many people live on the island?"

"Oh, close to seven hundred families, I guess," replied Mrs. Xilouris, scrunching up her nose as she tried counting everyone. "We have people coming and going here from other islands, like Patmos and Leros."

"How far are the other islands from here?"

"Patmos is northeast of here, and to our south is Leros," replied Mrs. Xilouris. "Captain John's boat makes it in thirty to forty minutes, depending on the weather. Most of our supplies come from those two islands, but in the wintertime, due to the weather, the amount of travel is very limited. That is why the supplies are so important now. They should last us the winter."

"I hear you also have a few Cretans living here?"

"Oh, yes. Ipatia's family is from there, and there are other families from Crete. Almost everyone here is related in some way or form, either through marriage or by birth."

"Do you get any tourists?"

"Dear, yes! In the summer, there are hundreds of them. Many are our own, visiting from abroad, while others are from Germany, Sweden, or from other countries. When the hotels are full, sometimes they come knocking on our door just to get a room."

They passed a small church. "For an island with so few families, it struck me odd that there are so many churches here," said Tony, gesturing towards it.

"There are close to forty churches," said Mrs. Xilouris proudly. "For several hundred years this island was under the rule of the monastery of Patmos. Patmos, as you know, is the island where St. John had his vision, and where the Book of Revelations was written. Anyway, monks from Patmos used to come here and use the land. They built churches, and since then, due to a number of reasons, many people here have also built their own churches."

"The main church, St. John, is located next to the Plaka. That is where the Sunday liturgy takes place, but not all the time," said Ipatia.

"Why not?" asked Tony, studying her lively expression. It seemed like she was enjoying herself.

"We have many churches, and several are named after saints. If a saint's name day happens to fall on a Sunday, then church service takes place at the designated church," offered Ipatia.

"Interesting," said Tony.

"There are a few churches so far away, we would leave the house two hours early just to make it in time for church service!"

"Two hours?" asked Tony, his eyebrows raised. "That is hard to believe."

"First of all, we only have one donkey, and I couldn't let Grandfather walk all that way," explained Ipatia. "So I walk alongside him. Besides, we want to get there early enough to witness the liturgy. The small churches get filled very quickly."

Tony combed his fingers through his wavy black hair. He was touched by the girl's respect for her grandfather and her strong faith. Should he mention that he visited the church of the Virgin of Haron earlier today? Instead, he pointed to some site in the distance and asked, "Where does that lead to?"

"All the way to the other side, which is Plati Yialo," Mrs. Xilouris said proudly. "There are no main roads, so one has to go by donkey. The water is shallow there, and it tends to be a favorite place for picnics. Often, we see tourists snorkeling there."

Mrs. Xilouris rambled on about the rest of the island, not needing any prompting from Tony. She covered the beaches at Liendou Bay, and when she started to talk about Katsaidia, located further away, she hesitated.

"What were you going to say about Katsaidia?" prompted Tony.

"There are two sides to everything, I'm afraid," said Mrs. Xilouris. "The same with this island. We may have the churches, but we also have the nudists! Katsaidia, for some reason, attracts tourists who like to swim without clothes!"

"I'm afraid your island doesn't have a monopoly on them!" laughed Tony heartily.

Ipatia blushed at what was being said, feeling it was improper for Mrs. Xilouris to discuss this kind of topic in front of a man, let alone a strange man. She sneaked a peek at him from the side of her lashes and was surprised to see him studying her. He flashed a smile at her. She looked down. She dare not, she could not smile back at this man. Beneath his wrinkled clothes, she sensed a raw power that defied everything she knew about men.

Nick moaned, and Mrs. Xilouris stopped her chatter, focusing her attention on him, talking to him in a soothing voice. Tony turned slightly towards them, lifting his hand to help. Ipatia's heart started to race when she saw the book he was holding. She slipped her hand into her skirt pocket desperately searching for her book, hoping it was there. But it wasn't. She must have dropped it in her haste to leave. He must have found it after she left. She grimaced at the idea of having to ask if that was her book.

He saw her staring at the book. He lifted the book up, revealing the title, taunting her. About to give it to her, he hesitated. Instead, with a twinkle in his eyes, he said, "I suppose you noticed by now the book I am carrying, Ipatia. I believe it is yours?"

His rich deep voice touched her inner being, causing her knees to shake. He had spoken in crisp English. Upset by her apparent show of weakness and his boldness, she retorted in English, "Yes, but how did you know my name, that I knew English, and that this was my book?"

"First of all, my darling girl, I happened to be walking down the road, when I overheard your beautiful voice speaking English from the tree. No actually, it was more like singing," he admitted. "I believe I heard the words "I love you with all my heart. Please take me away from this place!"

She was startled at the revelation.

"Of course I was intrigued by what I heard. So I came closer and discovered a girl dressed in black, sitting in the tree reading from a book. Little did I know you would need to be rescued from a snake!" He was goading her now, and he laughed heartily, enjoying her flushed cheeks and stormy eyes.

"There really was a snake!" she retorted. "Will you please give me back my book!"

"I'm afraid not. Where I come from, when people are rescued from snakes, it is customary to give the rescuer a gift. You see, I saved your life, and that is not a small thing."

She was silent. He was right. He did save her life.

"What gift would you like?" she asked timidly, afraid to hear the answer.

"I haven't decided yet, so until that time, I guess I'll have to keep the book as collateral."

She saw him deliberately place the book inside his shirt. Then he started whistling.

"Ipatia, please speak Greek! I don't understand a word you are saying," said Mrs. Xilouris sharply. She knew Christos Rodakis, and if word got around to him that his granddaughter was conversing so boldly with a man in English, he would have a fit.

Ipatia blushed at the reprimand. She was mortified at the idea that she had been speaking English all this time. It had happened so easily. She must remember to be more careful in the future. She kept silent for now. She couldn't get her book back, not while Mrs. Xilouris' sharp eyes were on her. She would have to wait.

CHAPTER 4

Whether by fate or by chance
I will now take a stance

The large dock was empty except for a young couple standing in front of the foreign yacht.

"That man over there is Dr. Michael Hatzis. The girl next to him is my sister, Melissa," Tony said, pointing to them. "Please wait here a minute." He left the group under the shade of a tree, then went towards the couple.

"Hi, Tony!" said Melissa.

"Sorry I'm late," said Tony, bending down to kiss his sister's cheek. He then patted Michael on the back.

"That's quite all right. Your little sister has been the perfect hostess. She has kept me company during your absence," said Michael, smiling.

Melissa's blushing confirmed Tony's suspicion that his younger sister had more than a crush on his best friend.

"Where are all the others?" asked Tony, looking around expectantly.

"We left the parents behind at the hotel. Bonnie and Chuck, I mean Mr. Daras, went ahead and are waiting for us at the taverna," explained Melissa.

"All right then, be a good hostess and go keep them company," replied Tony. "I need to borrow Michael for a medical emergency."

"I shall see you later at the taverna?" asked Melissa, her blue eyes focussed on Michael.

Michael nodded at her, while Tony remained silent.

"Don't be too long," said Melissa, tossing her head in a flirtatious manner as she walked off. She passed the group under the tree, pausing ever so slightly to witness the boy's bandaged arm. She caught Ipatia observing her. *So this island had its share of beauties and her brother didn't waste time in finding them.* Melissa had to speak to Bonnie.

Tony explained the boy's situation to Michael, ending with a request to help the young boy.

"For you, I would do anything!" replied Michael.

"Good. I knew I could count on you."

"Where is he?"

"Over there." Tony led Michael to the group. "Mrs. Xilouris, I spoke with Dr. Michael, and he said he could help little Nick."

"Very nice to meet you, Dr. Michael," said Mrs. Xilouris, bobbing her head up and down.

Michael nodded his greeting, then quickly discerned the boy's condition. "My medical bag is on the yacht. We need to take the boy inside…so I can treat him there."

"Ipatia, please come with me," whispered Mrs. Xilouris, holding Ipatia's arm tightly. "You know how everyone talks."

Ipatia silently agreed, knowing tongues would be wagging if they saw Mrs. Xilouris going to the yacht alone with this strange man.

"Here, don't be afraid. I will carry you inside so the good doctor can help you," said Tony, lifting Nick up gently.

Ipatia felt a strong sense of security just then, as if she was the one, and not Nick, held in this man's arms.

She tied Kitso to the tree, murmuring to him that she would be back shortly. Mrs. Xilouris held on to her arm as they followed the men up the ramp and into the yacht. Ipatia's eyes were big with wonder at the size and luxuriousness of it all. They entered a carpeted lounge. Large windows surrounded it on each side. There was a white leather couch with two matching loveseats, two round tables with chairs and a wet bar. They walked through the lounge and into the dining room. It had to be the dining room, because there was a large table with chairs that sat at least twelve people. It had oriental rugs, Chinese paintings, vases, and oriental furniture. She felt as if she were in another world. They went down a set of stairs and through a hallway with doors. Ipatia almost slipped on the shiny teak floor.

The doctor was standing in front of the Captain's cabin, holding his black medical bag. He gestured Tony into the cabin.

"You've been a brave boy," said Tony, placing the boy on the Captain's bed. "Dr. Michael is one of the best doctors around. He will take good care of you."

"Thank you for your help," said Mrs. Xilouris, entering the room with Ipatia.

"Don't worry about your son, Mrs. Xilouris. He will be fine," said Tony, standing up.

Ipatia couldn't help noticing how his tall frame filled the room.

Michael retrieved several items from his bag, then looked at the women. "It would be better if you both went outside. It might take awhile. I will call you as soon as I finish."

Mrs. Xilouris kissed her son on the forehead, whispering tearful endearments before leaving.

Ipatia followed her, quietly closing the door behind her. Mrs. Xilouris appeared distraught, clasping her hands together tightly as if she were praying. "How are Maria and Joanna doing in Crete?" asked Ipatia, feeling somewhat awkward, trying to change the subject. "I wrote to Maria, but haven't received a letter yet."

"Maria and Joanna? They are doing fine. My Maria is three months pregnant," said Mrs. Xilouris. "She probably didn't write to you because she's been having bouts of morning sickness and hasn't been feeling well. Joanna is helping her, though."

"She's pregnant! How wonderful!" exclaimed Ipatia. "Will you be going to visit them?"

"I'm afraid it's not so simple," said Mrs. Xilouris, sighing. "My husband Nick is in Piraeus, and he was expecting me on this trip...but now I'll have to wait until little Nick gets better. Then we'll see about visiting the girls."

"Oh, I was hoping you'd be able to go with me tomorrow," whispered Ipatia, realizing the impact of the woman's words. *I will have to travel to Piraeus alone then.*

"I'm sorry," said Mrs. Xilouris, touching Ipatia's arm apologetically. "Why don't you wait and we can go together later?"

"It's not so easy. I wrote to my aunt that I would be leaving tomorrow," said Ipatia firmly.

"Let me ask you a question, my girl. Why are you going to Piraeus? Don't you want to get married one day? There are some nice young men here, like Stamatis."

"Stamatis, the balloon?" blurted out Ipatia, remembering the nickname she used to give him when they were children.

"You should see him now," said Mrs. Xilouris proudly. "He just returned from his studies, and they hired him at the post office as a clerk. He's no longer the boy who used to tease you and pull your braids. If he weren't my nephew, I would have wished him for one of my girls."

Ipatia shook her head. "I know you mean well, but I'm not interested in getting married. When my parents died, I felt so much sadness and pain, that there were times when I had no desire to live. It took me a very long time to get over that. I don't ever want to feel so much pain again if someone I loved passed away."

"I understand, but you can't go through life feeling afraid," said Mrs. Xilouris gently. "Your parents are somewhere in heaven, a better place than here. God took them for a reason, although we don't always see it."

The clicking sound of a woman's heels interrupted their conversation. A glamorous looking woman, just like one of those models Ipatia used to see in the international fashion magazines in Rhodes, was approaching them. Her flawless skin was a golden hue and her straight, platinum blond hair bobbed perfectly to her shoulders. The low-cut turquoise summer dress revealed an abundant bosom and shapely legs.

"Is Tony here?" asked Bonnie, her pale blue eyes flashed at the two women.

Ipatia nodded, gesturing towards the closed door. "He is in there," she said meekly. She was curious as to who this woman was.

Bonnie walked boldly to the door and peeked inside. "*Yiasas,*" she purred her greeting.

"Bonnie?" asked Tony, looking surprised. "Is everything all right?"

"Yes, as a matter of fact. Melissa told me what had happened, and I came to see if you needed some help," said Bonnie, leaning against the doorway.

"Well, it depends on Michael here," replied Tony slowly, noticing her seductive pose.

"Thanks, but everything is under control," said Michael, looking up briefly. "I need to work fast before the anesthetic stops working. Tony, you are free to go."

"All right, Michael. Thanks for everything," replied Tony. He turned to the boy and saluted him. He walked out into the hallway with Bonnie.

Mrs. Xilouris extended her arm to Tony. "Again, thank you so much for your help, Mr. Tony. It will be remembered."

He smiled and shook her hand. "I am glad I could be of service, Mrs. Xilouris, but I didn't do much. It's the good doctor you should thank instead." His eyes rested on Ipatia.

Ipatia looked down shyly, unable to meet his intent look.

He was about to say something to her, when he was interrupted by Mrs. Xilouris' sharp cough. She was like a mother hen protecting her young.

"Goodbye!" Mrs. Xilouris pecked.

He nodded his farewell instead, feeling odd for leaving Ipatia there. A part of him wanted to remain behind, just to be with the girl and put a protecting arm around her. She still reminded him of a frightened deer.

Ipatia was almost tempted to follow him, for he had not said a word about returning her book. But the unexpected entrance of the woman had dampened her spirits. Besides, Mrs. Xilouris had been silently watching them like a hawk. After they left, she felt empty and cold, as if he took his warmth with him.

❦   ❦   ❦

Tony helped Bonnie off the ship and on to the dock. With mixed feelings, he gazed out into the calm water, his hands in his pockets. A strong gust of wind passed by just then, ruffling the water, causing the small boats docked there to bob up and down momentarily. The unsettling thought occurred to him that Bonnie was like this gust of wind, moving in and stirring things up.

Bonnie pressed lightly against him. "I hope you don't mind my coming and offering you help. I wanted an excuse to apologize for my outburst the other day," she said huskily. "We've got only a few days left before you go back to England, and I don't want to spend the rest of the time with hard feelings between us."

"I appreciate your thoughts and accept your apology," said Tony, bowing slightly. "By the way...the disagreement was because you were complaining about my going back to England. I am not going to another planet. England is only a few hours away by airplane."

"The way you've been avoiding me since our argument, Tony Plakis, sometimes I feel you are on another planet!" she retorted.

Tony winced at the reminder. It was hard to take back what happened two days ago. They had argued over his impending trip to England. She wanted him to remain in Greece, but he adamantly refused. That was when she broke down crying, and he placed his arm around her, trying to comfort her. He always had a weakness for females that cried. He told her he would come and visit her in Greece. That was his undoing, for Bonnie took the opportunity to kiss him, declaring her love for him. Tony, caught off guard by her affections, arose abruptly and left, confused and upset with the way things turned out. He hadn't talked to her since then, avoiding her.

"I think there has been a misunderstanding between us, Bonnie. When you were crying...I was only trying to comfort you...as a friend," he said. "You see, I don't like to see females cry."

Bonnie was quiet for a moment, her eyes lowered. "I guess you don't feel the same way about me as I do you."

Tony decided not to reply to her statement, not wanting to get into another argument. Instead, he asked politely, "Will you be going back to the taverna?"

"No," she said shakily. "I'm not very hungry...and besides, it seems as if Chuck and Melissa are doing fine without anyone else there."

"Oh?" asked Tony slowly. A wealthy shipowner in his early forties, Chuck Daras was a friend of his father, invited on the trip to discuss buying a ship from the Plakis Shipping company. Tony hadn't considered him a possible match for Melissa, since Melissa had been showing quite a bit of interest in Michael for some time. He wondered what his little sister was up to.

"What are your plans for tonight?"

"First, I need to see Father...then I need to take a shower and retire for the evening," he replied, gesturing at his wrinkled clothes.

"Do you mind if I join you?" she asked, taking his arm possessively.

They walked towards the hotel. Tony was silent, feeling mixed emotions about this woman, contemplating on what to say. He was keenly aware of her body leaning seductively against him. "So Bonnie, you never told me what made you become a fashion designer?" he asked, making small talk.

"I always liked clothes, ever since I was a young girl. When I finished my studies to become a fashion designer, I went to Paris. There, I modeled a bit, and worked at boutique shops," she said.

"Ahhh, did you like it?" he asked, prompted by her silence.

"Of course I did, you darling man," she said, pecking him lightly on the cheek. "You see this dress I am wearing? I designed it as a result of spending time in Paris," she finished proudly, lifting up her arms.

"It is becoming on you, but the neckline, isn't it a bit low?" he asked dryly.

"That's the style," she said, laughing flirtatiously, swinging her hair back. "I thought you liked low necklines."

He silently disagreed. Low necklines were not for public display.

They reached the hotel and Tony held the door open for her. Blinded by the darkness, he stopped and slowly looked around, regaining his vision. Irene, the Greek-American hotel manager, was behind the counter chatting with Christina, his stepmother. When his father married the thirty-eight year old heiress four years ago, Tony had been shocked. He had assumed his father would never remarry. He could never think of Christina as a mother.

"Hello, you two," said Christina, going over to meet them. "Tony, your father's been expecting you out on the balcony."

"Then I shall go to him," Tony said, politely excusing himself.

CHAPTER 5

What matter all the wealth
If one doesn't have one's health

Dr. Michael called loudly, "Mrs. Xilouris, can you please come in here?"

She ran inside the room. Ipatia peeked inside. Mrs. Xilouris held Nick, while the doctor stitched the wound. Ipatia stepped back outside, feeling nauseated.

In a matter of minutes Michael was done. He finished wrapping a bandage around the wound. He stood up, cleaning his spectacles. Mrs. Xilouris came to the doorway and gestured for Ipatia to come into the room.

"There is nothing to fear, Mrs. Xilouris. Although he lost some blood, he is on the road to recovery. He does need to see the doctor in a day or two, though," said Michael. Before putting his glasses on, he studied Ipatia with his cold blue eyes. "Are you his sister?"

"No, just a friend of the family," she said, her breath catching in her throat under his scrutiny. She was not used to being studied like some insect.

"I see," he said, smiling warmly. He put the spectacles back on. "The antibiotics I will give him are only enough for two days. We don't want him to get an infection. Please have him follow up with the island doctor in the next day or so."

"Thank you, Doctor," said Mrs. Xilouris, shaking his hand after he gave her the medicine. "I don't have any money with me to pay you! Can I bring it to you in a few days?"

"That's all right. We will be leaving tomorrow."

Upon hearing that, Ipatia quickly dipped her hand in her pocket and retrieved the coins left over from the bakery. They would surely be enough for his efforts.

"Here is the money for your work," she said proudly, firmly placing all the drachmas in his hand.

He took the coins. Although he did not need the money, it would be an insult not to take it. He nodded silently, admiring her pride. "Thank you young lady, and what was your name again?"

"Ipatia," she said shyly. He seemed to be staring at her. She blushed.

"Ipatia?" he asked, looking puzzled. "It's an unusual name. I believe it belonged to a famous female mathematician and philosopher. She lived in Alexandria, around the year 400 or so, am I right?"

Ipatia nodded silently, knowing the story. "Are Mr. Tony and his wife also leaving with you tomorrow?"

"Tony's not married!" laughed Michael, mildly surprised at the young girl's interest in Tony. "Actually, the woman who came by earlier is a good friend of Tony's sister. We will all be leaving together tomorrow."

"Mr. Tony has been very kind to us! We will never forget his helping our little Nick," said Mrs. Xilouris, beaming.

"Yes, he is a very good man. One of the best," said Michael, nodding. His friend also had a talent for charming the older women as well as the young ones.

Mrs. Xilouris bid the doctor farewell, thanking him several times. He smiled and watched as Ipatia helped Mrs. Xilouris with little Nick, walking slowly out into the hallway. Ipatia's naive question exposed her interest in Tony. It did not surprise Michael. Tony had a magnetic personality that charmed any woman he met. Michael smiled as he remembered even his own mother had been taken in by Tony.

Minutes later, Ipatia helped Nick and his mother settle back on Kitso. "Let's use the main road," said Ipatia. "I need to get home quickly, since it is getting late, and I have much explaining to do."

❦   ❦   ❦

Tony walked through the hotel lobby to the balcony where he found his father leaning against the handrail, listening intently to a man dressed in work clothes. Beyond the balcony, the blue waters of Liendou Bay shimmered like a Monet oil painting.

Gregory Plakis' observant eyes took in Tony's disheveled appearance. "Did everything go well with your tour of the island?" he asked, interrupting the man next to him.

Tony gave him a brief summary of the events that had occurred, mindful of the worker who was listening to their conversation. At that moment, the worker coughed politely.

Gregory pulled out his wallet and gave the man several bills, saying, "Here is payment for your labor and for the new part, Alex."

Alex thanked him profusely and left.

"Did they fix the problem?" asked Tony, sitting down in a chair.

"No," admitted Gregory. "Alex just told me the ship's engine was affected by the storm and requires a new part. It will take days before they can get the part."

"What about the other engine?"

"The other engine hasn't been working well, either. We have no other choice but to leave the yacht behind and travel back by ferry."

"I suppose no airplanes come by this way," said Tony dryly.

"Oh, no, no," said Gregory, shaking his head. "This is a very small island. It doesn't have that capacity. We'll take the ferry heading for Piraeus tomorrow afternoon."

"That'll do. I have to be in Athens by Tuesday to catch a flight back to England."

Gregory eyed his son skeptically. "Tony, why are you doing this to me? I don't want you to go to England. I need you by my side."

"You've done well all these years without me!" retorted Tony.

The words came out quickly, catching Tony by surprise. Although relevant to the discussion at hand, these words held a deeper meaning for him. His father had sent him away to boarding school when his mother had passed away. He had never taken the time to participate in Tony's school events and graduations because he had been too busy. He had sent money instead. This was the very same father who, when Tony had fallen ill, sent a nurse to take care of him, but never visited him in the hospital. Now, his father was not making a simple request. He was asking him to change his way of life.

"Let me be frank with you, son. I have not been doing well with my health lately," said Gregory, rubbing his head.

"What are you talking about?" asked Tony, perplexed. This was something new.

Gregory was quiet for a moment. "You remember when I fell down in the yacht's dining room a few days ago and you helped me up? I had given the excuse about tripping over something. That was not the truth. Lately, I've been having these spells, fainting spells, and I black out."

Tony looked at his father in a daze, feeling disbelief at what he had just heard. He had always assumed his omnipotent father would always be there, managing the family business. Now his father was pleading for help, pleading for forgiveness.

"Why didn't you tell me this sooner?" asked Tony, feeling helpless.

"I didn't think it was anything important at the time," replied Gregory, shrugging his shoulders. "I talked to Michael this morning because I had another spell. He thinks I should see a doctor he knows, as soon as we get back. He says these spells might be serious, like a brain tumor."

Tony was silent, shaken by the news. "So you will probably be undergoing tests?"

"That's right," replied Gregory tersely. "I will be too busy with the doctors to be managing the business. That is why I need you to fill in for me. The company needs a head and what better one than my own son."

"Whatever it takes, I will help you," said Tony, his voice full of emotion. In an unusual display of warmth, he went to his father and hugged him tightly, as tears threatened to spill out.

"Good. I knew you would pull through!" Gregory's voice shook as he patted his son on the back.

"My only concern is I don't have much experience with cargo ships," admitted Tony, after the show of emotion subsided.

"If only you had listened to me when you were young! I would have had you managing this business years ago. But you wanted to go and get your graduate degree in Economics from Oxford instead," said Gregory, shaking his head. "Anyway, you need not worry, for I will be giving you advice whenever I can. Also, there is plenty of help from others. Sarkalos, our fleet manager, who is like a brother to me, does most of the management. Spithas, our attorney, takes care of the legal papers, and several other people on our staff are experienced and knowledgeable. They will help you."

"Good," said Tony, nodding his head.

At that moment, Christina glided on to the balcony.

"Hello, honey," said Gregory, smiling fondly at her.

"Hello, dear," she said sweetly, kissing his cheek. "Shouldn't we join the others for dinner? It might do you some good to eat a little."

"Who's at the taverna?" asked Gregory.

"Bonnie just told me that Chuck Daras and Melissa were there," replied Christina.

"And where's Bonnie?" asked Gregory, looking around.

"She went to her room. She said she had a headache."

"Oh?" asked Gregory, surprised. "Tony, what did you say to her this time?"

Tony shrugged his shoulders. "Father, I told you before you invited her on the trip, that she's not my type! She is nice to look at, but all she talks about is herself and her clothes. You didn't listen to me."

"This is your chance to marry into a rich family, and the best you can do is say she's not your type!" complained Gregory.

"That's all you think about...marrying into a rich family!" retorted Tony sarcastically.

"Can you please stop this fussing," said Christina, trying to calm both men down.

"What's wrong with what I said?" asked Gregory. "It wouldn't be bad if Melissa decides to marry Chuck Daras, would it? He's told me he's interested in Melissa. Do you know he owns several ships and knows the shipping business very well?"

"As long as Michael is around, I don't think it will happen," said Tony dryly.

"Yes, I think you may be right," replied Gregory, looking skeptical.

"Tony, will you be joining us for dinner?" asked Christina.

"I'm afraid not. I feel quite exhausted by the events of today," he said wearily.

"Then go and get some rest. We will continue our conversation at another time," said Gregory, nodding.

"All right. Have a good time," said Tony. He watched the couple as they walked into the lobby and out the door. He turned and gazed at the sunset, thinking about his conversation with his father. He stood there for a long time.

Ipatia noticed they were approaching the fork in the road leading to the cottage. She stopped and said, "Mrs. Xilouris, you go on ahead without me. I'm going to take a shortcut through the fields. It's quicker that way."

"Thank you for all your help, and God bless you!" said Mrs. Xilouris, hugging her. "I'm sorry that we won't be going to Piraeus with you tomorrow."

"That's all right," said Ipatia. "Don't worry about me. You'll see, in no time Nick will be all right, and you'll be in Piraeus with your husband."

"What about your donkey?"

"Please send Kitso back to the house when you are done with him. He knows the way."

Ipatia untied the bag of loaves from the saddle and watched as the mother and son made their way back home on the donkey. Ipatia's agile, slim legs took her swiftly up the hill, off the main road. She ran through the fields, jumping over small stone walls, holding tightly to the bag of loaves. *I'm almost there.* She kept on running.

She reached the outskirts of their property in what seemed like record time. Her heavy breathing and tired legs were begging her to stop. She slowed down, walking the rest of the way, trying to catch her breath. The sun was setting, and everything around her was bathed in warm colors. Even the whitewashed homes nestled up on the hills appeared made of gold. The lazy sound of goat bells jingling in the distance was soothing to hear.

Up ahead, her grandfather's straw hat was bobbing up and down in the vegetable patch. He was working late today. She called out to him, waving at him. He stood up; peering out from under his hat he realized who it was and waved back.

As Ipatia approached her grandfather, the sun cast a strange, golden glow around him making his face look deceivingly pleasant, although she had anticipated his anger at her lateness.

"Come here, Ipatia. Tell me why you were so late," he demanded.

Ipatia swallowed before speaking. She had been right. Her grandfather was angry. His tone of voice and the scrunching of his bushy white eyebrows gave him away.

"Well, the good news is that Mrs. Poulos had saved three loaves of bread for us," she said, her voice trembling, as she tried to sound cheerful. She held up the bag of loaves. "She didn't take any money for them. She said they were a farewell gift."

"Hmm. Then what happened next?" he asked, slowly taking the bag from her. He studied her quietly, assessing the situation, waiting for her to continue.

Trying to phrase the next words carefully, she asked, "Remember the tree near the basin on the way to the bakery?"

He nodded impatiently.

"Well, on the way back Kitso was drinking from the basin, so I climbed the tree to rest in the shade. Then I saw a snake up on the branch above me. I was hurrying to get down and my skirt caught on a branch, and I was stuck there until a man came and saved me, and, and…" she babbled, then broke down crying.

"Now, now, that's all right. You are still young, Ipatia, and sometimes you do things without thinking. Let that be a lesson to you," he said, affected by her crying. He dug in his pocket and handed her a handkerchief. Patting her on the back clumsily, he thought about her impulsiveness. It had always been her weakness. He knew she had a good character that was as staunch and upright as her late mother's was, but he never remembered her mother being impulsive. It must come from her father's side. Ipatia needed a woman's touch to change her boyish ways. Running and climbing trees were not going to win her a husband. Maybe it wasn't such a bad idea after all that she was going to live with her aunt.

"You said a man came and saved you?" he asked.

She said softly, "Yes, and his name was Tony. He was a tourist from the yacht that came in last night."

"Oh?" he asked, wiping his hands and picking up the basket. This was becoming very interesting.

"Here, let me help you." She took hold of the heavy basket and they started walking towards the cottage.

"What else happened next?"

Ipatia rambled on, recounting the rest of the story, then finished by proudly saying, "Mrs. Xilouris said the Lord must have sent me."

"Although you did a good thing to help them out Ipatia, you must remember to slow down and think before you do things," scolded Christos "And one more thing, Ipatia Kouris, wherever you are in life and whatever you do, the one person you are always accountable to is God!" He pointed up to the sky.

She nodded, waiting for the sermon. Whenever she heard him call her by her full name, she knew he was going to preach. And preach he did, all the way up to the cottage. She kept silent as he talked about praying and how important it was, particularly when things did not go well, and even when things were going well. That was when the evil one made his entrance. He talked about the importance of knowing people and being aware of who one's friends were.

Ipatia's body was now beginning to ache. She was glad when they reached the cottage. They laid the big basket of vegetables on the countertop. Her grandfather excused himself and went to wash and change. Ipatia prepared their dinner, feeling very tired as well as hungry. She spooned the warm bean soup into the bowls. The wholesome smell of the fresh bread greeted her as she sliced it. Just then, there was knocking on the door.

CHAPTER 6

All of this I leave behind
To follow fate, what will I find?

Her grandfather went to the door, muttering, "Who could it be at this time?"

It was Katerina Tsatsikas and Thomas, her youngest son.

"How are you?" asked Katerina, greeting them with the customary kiss.

She was breathing heavily, and her cheeks felt cool against Ipatia's face. The chilly evening breeze caused Ipatia to shiver.

"You wouldn't believe this, but your donkey was standing in front of our house, so we fed him and brought him up this way. With this opportunity, I also brought some of Ipatia's favorite *tiropites*."

Katerina smiled broadly as she lifted up the bag of cheese pies. Some teeth were missing, and she was a large woman, but for all her unattractiveness, she made up for it with her kindness.

"Thank you, *Nona!*" said Ipatia, receiving the proffered bag from her god-mother. "Kitso always likes to stop in front of your house. He knows you take good care of him."

"This bag was tied to the saddle," said Thomas, handing it to Christos. "By the way, I already put Kitso in his stable."

Christos thanked him as he took the bag. Inside the bag were two, round *mizithras* and a note. He nodded his appreciation. These cheeses were well aged. He read the note aloud, "Thank you for everything, Ipatia. I hope you like the cheese. Again, I am sorry we could not go with you on the trip tomorrow. Regards to your grandfather, Mrs. Xilouris."

"I'm glad little Nick is all right," said Ipatia.

"What happened to him?" asked Katerina.

"He cut his hand and we took him to a doctor from the yacht to get it fixed," began Ipatia.

"*Koumbara*," said Christos apologetically. He knew about Katerina's insatiable curiosity and knack for gossip. "You know how people talk around here. Whatever Ipatia tells you, will you promise me it will remain here?"

"As I kiss the cross, you have my word on this!" Katerina exclaimed, making the sign of the cross with her thumb and finger, then kissing her two fingers, appearing flustered.

"Good. We were just going to have dinner. Would you like to join us?"

"Thank you. We already ate dinner. We will stay only a few minutes," replied Katerina.

They all filed into the cottage, filling the small kitchen.

"Sit down, sit down," said Christos Rodakis, pulling a chair for Katerina. The chair creaked as her large frame settled into it. Ipatia stifled a giggle, hoping the chair wouldn't break. There were only three chairs left, as Mrs. Tsatsikas had broken the fourth one on her last visit.

"Here, Thomas, please have a seat," said Ipatia, gesturing towards her chair.

"I'm fine," he said, shaking his head awkwardly. He remained standing.

Ipatia served her godmother a glass of water with a small dish of candied quince, a delicacy. Then she did the same to Thomas. He took them clumsily, almost spilling the glass of water.

Katerina eyed the dish, asking, "Did you hear about the yacht that came in last night? My oldest son, Alex, was called in this morning to see about helping to fix the engine on it."

"Who does the yacht belong to?" asked Christos, twisting his mustache.

"Mr. Praklis, or something like that. I hear he was traveling with his family from Crete, and that is not all. He is very rich! Besides owning the yacht, he also owns several large ships!" said Katerina, enjoying the attention she was getting from her rapt audience.

Ipatia leaned against the counter near the sink, listening quietly.

"I used to know a shipowner from Crete. What was the name again?" asked Christos, smoothing his mustache slowly. His fingers automatically formed a curl at each tip.

Then Thomas spoke, his Adam's apple moving up and down along his thin, scrawny neck, "Mr. Gregory Plakis is his name."

"Are you sure about that?" asked Christos, appearing very interested. "I knew a Gregory Plakis in Crete years ago! We almost went into the wine business together!"

"Yes, I'm sure. Alex was called in with two other men to work on one of the engines and I went down with them," replied Thomas. "I heard them speak his name."

"Who would have known, after all these years," said Christos, nodding thoughtfully. He was pleasantly surprised to hear Gregory was here with his family. This could turn out to be interesting.

"You should see the inside of the yacht!" said Thomas, his eyes shining brightly. "It's like a king's palace, with all the beautiful furniture and carpeting. I wish I had something like that one day."

"Thomas, you're fantasizing again! These people are in a different class from us altogether!" interrupted Mrs. Tsatsikas. She gripped the chair to steady herself. Then rose to leave. "Well, we must be going. You eat your dinner before it gets cold."

"Here, take a bottle of my best wine for you and your family," said Christos.

Katerina thanked him profusely and took the offering. She then turned and said, "Now that Mrs. Xilouris won't be going with you, Ipatia, you might want to reconsider about going to Piraeus. You know how people talk around here. What have you decided, *Koumbare*, will you let her go by herself?"

Christos winced. It was inevitable that his wife's cousin, who had been like a mother to Ipatia all these years and very protective of her, would be concerned.

Ipatia piped, "I'm old enough to take care of myself, *Nona*! I'll be eighteen in a few weeks, and when I traveled to and from Rhodes, I traveled by myself!"

"Oh, well. May the good Lord be with you during the trip," said her god-mother, making the sign of the cross.

Ipatia thanked her as she was gripped in a bear hug. Then, Thomas's turn came.

"Have a safe trip, little sister," he said affectionately, pecking her on the cheek.

"Yes, brother!" she replied smartly. He was two years older, and they had teased each other as far back as she could remember.

Katerina stood at the door; there were tears in her eyes. "Don't worry, Ipatia, we will take good care of your grandfather for you."

Ipatia nodded, as she wiped the tears from her own eyes. She waved to them, watching their bodies blend into the night. She was going to miss them. Her grandfather gently touched her on the shoulder, a reminder that dinner was waiting.

Afterwards, when she rested in bed, her thoughts churned over the events of the day. She had not had so much excitement packed in one day before. It took her a very long time to fall asleep that night.

❦   ❦   ❦

Ipatia felt the goose bumps rising on her thin arms as she finished buttoning her sweater in the early morning darkness. Was she shivering from the cold, or was it in anticipation for the trip? She eagerly went into the kitchen, locating the large pot. The crisp cold wind greeted her with a resounding smack as she closed the door behind her. Burying her face into the warm fold of her sweater, she ran down the path to the goat stall. The two mother goats were straining against the wooden fence, bleating loudly, complaining.

"Hello, my loves," she said, entering swiftly, shutting the gate behind her.

Their warm fuzzy faces nuzzled against her shivering body. She pulled the small stool towards her and sat down to milk the goats.

"Today I am going far away," said Ipatia in a soothing voice, rhythmically squirting the frothy warm milk into the pot. The dawn shed enough light for her to see, and for the first time, she noticed her hands. She bit her lips. Before she came to the island, her hands were soft and clean, used for light tasks, such as playing the piano or putting ribbons in her hair. Now, years of hard work and toil had made them rough as the bark on the trees, with jagged dark nails. Her fingers tightened. No more! She was going back to Piraeus where there was heat in the winter and people bathed often with warm water.

The goat responded by turning her head towards her, looking at her with a worried expression.

"Don't worry, I won't forget you. I'll come back after I get my degree, you'll see," laughed Ipatia, relaxing her hold. The goat seemed to understand, for she stood motionless, looking content. The second goat was equally still. Ipatia, satisfied with the results, shooed the goats to the next stall, where their baby goats were waiting. The kids sucked hungrily, reminding Ipatia of her own breakfast.

She quickly made her way back to the cottage. The heavy pot threatened to spill its contents, as the strain on her arms became unbearable. With a sigh of relief she watched the door magically open before her.

"There's my Ipatia…already here with the milk. You should have waited for me to do it!" her grandfather lightly scolded her. He lifted the offending pot from her aching arms as if it were a loaf of bread.

"That's all right, Grandfather. I just had to say good-bye to the goats!" replied Ipatia, removing her muddied shoes outside the door.

Christos Rodakis peered into the pot and nodded his appreciation. He said, "This will last quite awhile. You are a good girl. Just like your mother was."

He placed the pot of milk on the gas burner, and began stirring, while Ipatia sliced the bread into thick chunks, then the hardened Mizithra cheese.

"Bring the cups," ordered Grandfather, nodding towards the cupboard.

She watched in anticipation, as he maneuvered the spoon, skimming the froth off the creamy white surface. Satisfied, he poured the warm milk into the cups. Once seated, they bowed their heads and said the Lord's prayer.

The rooster crowed in the distance, a reminder of the new day ahead.

Ipatia looked at her grandfather impishly and said, "The rooster is tooting his horn again."

Her grandfather chuckled, wiping the milk off his mustache. "Yes, and I remember when you tooted your own horn outside the door not too long ago, and I ran outside, thinking the rooster had gotten loose."

With a twinkle in his eye, he went on to recount the number of mischievous acts she had performed throughout the years. They talked about the first time she put the red tie on the donkey without telling him, parading him in town. It had been the talk of the town. Then, about another time when she buried herself in the sand at the beach so that only her head was exposed. She had worn a large hat that covered her head. When the unsuspecting tourists came there to bathe, she moved her head around to look at them, causing the hat to turn also, alarming them. Laughter erupted in the small kitchen, making it cheerful.

After breakfast, Ipatia arose and started to clear the table. She began to hum a favorite tune as she moved rhythmically around the table. She hadn't felt this happy in a very long time.

"We need to talk about your trip, Ipatia," said Christos seriously, folding his arms and leaning back in his chair.

Ipatia stopped her humming, noticing her grandfather's stance. "Yes?"

"I am worried that your aunt hasn't replied yet, and now that Mrs. Xilouris isn't going, I have been having doubts about allowing you to go at all."

"We sent Aunt Sophia the letter over a month ago," said Ipatia hopefully. "She probably replied, but the mail tends to be slow this time of the year because of the weather."

"You are a very stubborn girl, Ipatia. When you put your head down to do something, no one can stop you!"

"I've been planning this trip the whole summer," she insisted. "Grandfather, everything will be all right, you'll see."

"You were just as stubborn to go to the school in Rhodes, even after I said no. You still went. You were fortunate that your cousins were kind enough to take you in. Now, you want to leave me once more."

"I want to go to the university, Grandfather, so that one day I can help people."

Christos was silent, lost in deep reflection. Ipatia was a month away from becoming eighteen, going on nineteen, which was a marriageable age on the island. "Remember, there's more to life than school," he said gruffly. "There are fine young men, like Tom Tsatsikas, ready to start a family. That is what the girls here your age do."

"Tom is like a brother to me," she said, sighing. It was no use. Her grandfather did not seem to understand she had other dreams. She wasn't meant to stay here, she just felt it in her veins. Her destiny was elsewhere.

"I'm getting on in years, and when I'm gone, I plan to leave all my land to you."

Ipatia knew about the land. He had mentioned it to her often. The land was decked with fruit orchards, one hundred olive trees, several dozen fig trees and lemon trees. Closer to the house was the vegetable patch, the chicken coop and goat stall.

"Grandfather, don't talk like that! You'll be here for many years!"

"Promise me this," he said sternly. "That one day, God willing, you marry. I want to die with the peace of mind that all of this will be passed on to your children." He stopped abruptly, breathing heavily, trying to catch his breath.

"Yes, Grandfather," she said meekly, knowing it was no use trying to change his mind. She had heard this speech several times before, and no matter what she would say, he wouldn't listen to her.

He arose slowly, partly due to old age, and partly due to sadness, and reached for his jacket hanging from the peg on the wall.

"Now I must go and see about the supplies. The ferryboat for Piraeus will be here in the afternoon," he said heavily, resigned to the fact that nothing was going to stop her from going. "Have you finished packing?"

"I am almost done," she said.

"Later, I will give you your legal papers and some things to take to your aunt," he said, his voice cracking midway. He silently wiped the moisture from his eyes.

"Please don't cry, Grandfather," said Ipatia, tears welling up in her eyes as she went and hugged him. "I don't have to leave. I can stay here, with you."

"It's too late now. I know this is important to you, and it will do you good to be with your aunt."

She followed him outside, helping him attach the small wagon to the donkey.

"Oh, I almost forgot!" exclaimed Ipatia. "Can you be sure to give Dr. Thanassis the medical book he lent me?"

"Don't worry about the book. Dr. Thanassis said you can keep it as a going away present."

"When did he say that?"

"Yesterday, when I saw him going down to catch the boat for Patmos. He stopped at the *cafenio* and told me."

"He is such a kind man!"

"Try and do as much as you can," he said before leaving.

The wagon ambled down the winding path and beyond, heading towards the sea.

CHAPTER 7

The gift that I do give to thee
When I am gone, remember me

Ipatia watched until her grandfather became a dark speck against the lime green landscape. It was turning out to be a sunny day. In the distance, the sea appeared calm. *Maybe the supply boat will be here today.*

It was still early, enough time to go light a candle in the church. She walked down the hill towards the Virgin Mary of Haron church, looking toward the horizon. She could see people working the Tsatsikas land. Her godmother's large frame stood out among the fruit trees, moving slowly.

Moments later, she entered the empty church. There was a faint scent of incense lingering in the air. Someone must have been there earlier. She went to the icons and made the sign of the cross, kissing them. Then she studied them. They suddenly looked more vivid, more lifelike, as if the saints on the icons were speaking to her, beckoning her to pray.

She lit a candle, then prepared the incense burner. Clouds of incense filled the air of the church with a sweet scent as she prayed.

"May the Lord bless my grandfather, and my deceased parents, my god-mother and her family, and my aunt," she said. "I also pray I get my book back, because Mrs. Rodos said it was a special present."

Ipatia stayed there, praying for awhile longer. "Help me to have a safe journey," she finished.

As she trekked up the road towards the cottage, a peaceful feeling descended upon her. She reached the courtyard and stood there, looking out at the serene view. The rays of the sun made the sea shimmer as if it were covered with millions of diamonds. Diamonds. Stones. *How about giving Mr. Tony the gemstone that Father gave me a long time ago, from one of his journeys? That would be a good present for the book.*

Ipatia took in deep breaths, pleased with herself, enjoying the fresh air. Then she noticed the pots of crimson colored geraniums lined up against the wall of the cottage. Their delicate red petals appeared exceptionally beautiful today, contrasting well with the white walls of the cottage. She watered them, then filled a bucket with water and went inside the cottage.

It was cool and dark in the cottage, as Ipatia washed the dishes. Afterwards, she went into her bedroom. A bright orange blanket lay on the small cot. Knitted by her mother, it added a welcome splash of color into the drab room. There was a water basin on the table, and next to it, a framed picture of her and her parents. She was around six years old in that picture. She opened the window, allowing a gentle breeze into the room.

On the wall was an icon of the Virgin Mary holding the baby Jesus. They were witnesses to Ipatia's many tears and sleepless nights. She went towards the trunk that stood against the wall. She unlocked it, smelling the strong scent of mothballs scattered inside. Everything that ever belonged to her, along with some of her parent's keepsakes, were here.

Her black blouse and long black skirt lay on top. She removed them from the trunk, intending to wear them on the trip. Although her grandfather had scolded her often for wearing the black clothes, she continued to wear them in memory of her parents. The medical textbook lay underneath several layers of clothes. She touched its brown cover, then retrieved it reverently. The book had inspired her to pursue an education in the health sciences. She placed it back gently.

"Where did I put the cat's eye stone?" she asked aloud. She searched for the treasure box her father had given her. Inside were several pieces of jewelry. Something glittered at the bottom of the box.

"Here it is!" she exclaimed. Her father had brought it back as a present for her from one of his long trips. She remembered how fascinated she had been when it had changed its color from a green during the day to a red in the evening. She placed it in her purse. *I must see Mr. Tony today before I leave. I will give it to him so I can get my book back.* She began daydreaming about him as she packed everything back into the trunk.

Then she remembered her hat and searched underneath the bed, looking for it. It was still in the hatbox. Her godmother had given it to her as a present to wear for the trip. As she pulled it towards her, it hit against something else, bringing it towards her. It turned out to be her photo album. She had forgotten all about it.

She sat on the bed, leafing through the photo album, gazing at the pictures. There was a black and white picture of her father standing in front of a large, majestic ship. He was wearing a uniform, looking handsome with his black mustache. She wiped back the tears. She remembered how she would eagerly look forward to his returns from his trips.

Another picture showed her standing with her parents and her Aunt Sophia, in front of the two-story house in Piraeus. This was the house where she had spent all of her eight years with her parents and Aunt Sophia. It must have been Sunday, for they were wearing their Sunday clothes, with their elegant hats and white gloves. Now she was going back there to stay with her aunt.

"My piano," she said softly, looking at the photo of herself wearing a pink dress and a large white bow atop her head, as she played the piano. She remembered her piano teacher, who always said encouraging words to her parents, patting her on the head and claiming she had much talent and should continue her lessons.

Ipatia was surprised to see a picture of her English tutor, the prim Mrs. Rodos. She was wearing those wire-rimmed spectacles, and was holding a book against her chest protectively, like a shield. Her teacher had given her the picture as a present along with the English novel for her eighth birthday.

Ipatia continued for awhile, gazing and reminiscing at the pictures. After what seemed a long time, she shut the album and placed it in the trunk, locking the trunk securely. She pulled the trunk towards the door.

Slipping into her work clothes, she caught her reflection in the mirror mounted on the wall. It was always fascinating to see the changing color of her eyes, depending on how much light there was in the room. Today, her large eyes were the color of green olives with specks of sliced almonds inside. She could almost see a bit of yellow in them. She pulled on one eye, trying to see how many yellow specks there were. She wondered what color they were the time Tony saw her.

She glanced down at her slim body. Although it was taking its time to fill out in certain places, her blouse had become quite snug. She tugged at her blouse, realizing that she could no longer ignore the fact that she was slowly but surely becoming a woman.

She went outside to feed the rooster and chickens. Then she rounded up all the linen and dirty clothes and began washing them in a large metal basin filled with well water. With a bar of soap she worked diligently, scrubbing the clothes, scrubbing her fingernails, scrubbing her life clean. She filled another bucket of well water and started to rinse the clothes, squeezing the water out of them, then hanging them to dry. At one point, she noticed her clean fingernails. They looked much better now. Later she should remember to put a little olive oil on them to soften them up. Washing always made them dry.

She pulled up her sleeves, feeling warm from the sun. She wiped her brow. *You are almost done.* She continued with renewed vigor.

The sound of bells jingled softly in the distance. At the bottom of the hill, she could see a shepherd with his flock of sheep, moving slowly. She searched the horizon for her grandfather. *Just like when you searched for your parents that summer when you were eight years old.* They were visiting her grandfather on Lipsi Island when her parents received the news that her other grandfather in Crete was deathly ill. They told her that they needed to go to him. They kissed her, promising they would be back soon to get her. She had cried, wanting to go with them. After that day, she faithfully stood outside each day, waiting for their return. As the days turned into weeks, her small body began to pace anxiously, hoping for a welcome glimpse of them.

It wasn't until a month had passed when the priest came on his donkey to pay them a visit. He had brought news with him. He gently told her that her parents were with the good Lord and would never come back to her. She had wailed in his arms, clenching her small hands angrily, not wanting to accept the news.

Ipatia wiped the sweat from her face, or was it tears? Squeezing the water out of the last shirt, she quickly hung it on the clothesline.

When she went inside, to her dismay, the kitchen floor had mud tracks all over it. Within minutes, she had a bucket of water and soap ready, and was on her hands and knees scrubbing the kitchen floor. She must not leave the house in this dirty condition.

Tony woke up early in the morning, and the peaceful stillness of the room seemed pleasing to him. He lay in bed, savoring the feel of the moment, his eyes trying to adjust to the hotel room. The clock showed it was only seven o'clock, too early for anything. He rolled over, adjusting the pillows, burying his head in them. Then an annoying thing happened. He could not go back to sleep. Instead, his head was filled with all kinds of thoughts.

Yesterday, for the first time in his life, he had seen his father with different eyes, feeling more compassionate and caring towards this person who had been cold and aloof to him all his life. Another thought contradicted that. *You know your father is shrewd and manipulative and that everything he did in the past was for Gregory Plakis alone and no one else. Don't assume because he is sick, that he will change overnight.*

Could it be possible that Father is using his illness to manipulate me to join the family business and marry Bonnie in order to bring in new money? He tightened up at the thought. *You can't go back on your word. Not now, Tony! No matter what your father's intentions are, you are his only son and it is your duty to help.*

Then he thought about Ipatia, the island girl, and her book. She had appeared so helpless hanging from the tree. He admitted when he held her in his arms, the temptation to kiss her had been very strong. Then he remembered her stormy green eyes when she found out he had her book. *It is obvious the girl wants her book back and you, Antonios Plakis, being a gentleman, should return it to her.*

An hour later, Tony slipped out of the hotel, feeling vibrantly alive and whistling softly. He was carrying the slim book in his right hand. He walked down the paved hill. To his right, below him, he could see a fisherman standing on a large boulder, beating an octopus against some large rocks to make it tender. It was an arduous task, yet well worth it. Next to him were a couple of young lads doing the same. The fisherman waved to him and he waved back.

Up ahead, he spotted his father's short, stout frame standing by the yacht, speaking to the captain. By the time Tony reached him, his father was standing alone, deep in thought.

"Good-morning. Why so early?" asked Gregory, patting his son affectionately on the back.

"Good-morning. I wanted to see more of the island, so I had an early start," replied Tony. "How are you feeling?"

"Fine, right now. The difficult part is I never know when it will hit me," said Gregory. He looked curiously at the book. "What do you have there?"

"I'm glad you asked. This book belongs to Ipatia Kouris, the daughter of the late Captain Kouris."

"Is that right?" asked Gregory, looking surprised. "How did you come by it?"

Tony explained the story, while his father chuckled.

"I'm planning to meet her grandfather, Christos Rodakis," admitted Tony. "Although he doesn't know I am. He supposedly goes to the coffee shop in the mornings and I'm hoping to catch him there."

"Christos Rodakis?" asked Gregory. "So he lives here! I knew him years ago, back in Crete, when he made the famous wine. He is the one who sent Captain Kouris to me. Tell him to come and see me. We have much to talk about."

"I will do that," said Tony.

"Oh, and don't forget, the ferryboat will be leaving at two."

"I know," replied Tony. "I'll be back before then. By the way, when would you like to get together to talk about the business?"

"We can talk about it on the way back to Piraeus," said Gregory, liking what he heard. He smiled, saying, "Now you go and enjoy yourself, because I promise you, it's going to get busy after today." Without notice, he teetered, losing his balance, almost falling into the water.

"Are you all right?" asked Tony, catching his father in time, steadying him. He studied his father's pale features. The aquiline nose was flared and his eyes were hidden under the fluttering of the eyelids.

"Yes, I'll be fine," said Gregory, standing upright shakily. He passed his hand over his eyes. "I've been getting these spells more regularly now."

"I think you should have someone with you all the time, now that you are experiencing these," said Tony sternly. "Why don't we head back to the hotel so Michael can take a look at you."

"I'll be fine, don't worry," said Gregory, having regained his balance.

"Father, I don't think you should be out here alone in case another spell comes along," insisted Tony.

"If it'll ease your mind, you can walk back to the hotel with me," replied Gregory. Although he tried not to let his anxiety show in his voice, he was shaken by the spell.

Tony conceded and walked with him slowly towards the direction of the hotel, holding his elbow. He saw Michael leaving the hotel and walking towards them. "There's Michael."

Tony told his friend what had happened.

"Here, Mr. Plakis, why don't you come with me," said Michael, taking his arm.

"Tony, I'll be fine with Michael," said Gregory, shooing him off. "Go finish with what you were doing."

Tony nodded silently, watching the two men walk slowly towards the hotel. He admired how his friend was able to make everything all right. When Tony asked Michael to join them on the trip, little did he know how much they would need him. He turned and resumed his journey.

CHAPTER 8

Searching for the proper way
To give her back her book today

Tony approached the coffee shop. Two older gentlemen were sitting outside, drinking coffee and talking. The younger of the two wore a black captain's hat and was noisily flicking a string of worry beads every few seconds. Mr. Pericles was leaning against the door talking to the gentlemen. It seemed as if he had just said something funny, for laughter erupted from the small table. He saw Tony and went eagerly to him, his large belly still shaking from the deep laugh.

"Good morning, Mr. Tony! I see you made it, my friend!" Stellios said, his wide grin and hearty handshake confirmed the words of friendship.

"Good morning, Mr. Pericles," replied Tony, grinning back. "I took your offer and decided to come by this morning to see Mr. Rodakis. Is he here?"

"Yes, come with me. I will introduce you to him. He's been waiting for you."

Mr. Pericles led him to the white-haired man, who at the time, was wiping his eyes with a handkerchief and still chuckling. He looked like he could be Ipatia's grandfather, with his large olive green eyes and firm chin.

As the introductions were made, Christos Rodakis stood up to shake the young man's hand, smiling. So this was the handsome young man Stellios had described to him this morning! He called himself Tony Plakis. How very interesting!

"Sit down, sit down and join us," said Christos, pulling a chair for him.

"Nick Kalogeorgos," said the other man, standing up and shaking hands with Tony.

"Stellios, a coffee for the gentleman!" said Christos, motioning to the shop owner. Nick was still standing. "Nick, aren't you going to stay awhile longer?"

"Barba Christos, you know my wife. If I don't leave now, she will surely come looking for me! She has been eager to get the supplies, you know. I just stopped to say a brief hello," he said. Then he turned to Tony and said, "I hope you enjoy the island during your stay. *Yiasou*, Barba Christos!" He slapped Christos heartily on the back, then left, flicking the worry beads expertly in his left hand.

Tony said, "Mr. Rodakis, I helped your granddaughter, Ipatia, yesterday when she was stuck in the tree trying to escape from a snake."

"Ah, so you are the Tony she talked about! You have my congratulations for helping her out of her delicate predicament!" said Christos, chuckling.

Tony laughed along with Christos, feeling comfortable with him. The coffee shop was beginning to get busy, as a few more people arrived. Rodakis greeted each newcomer with a hearty welcome. The Turkish coffee arrived shortly and Tony sipped the dark brew cautiously, savoring its sweet, delicious flavor.

"I came by to see you because I found a book belonging to your granddaughter. She dropped it in her haste to leave," said Tony. He handed the slim volume to Christos.

"Yes, thank you! Stellios had mentioned something about it. Ipatia has always liked to read, ever since she was a young girl. She reads whatever she can get her hands on. She even convinced Dr. Thanassis into borrowing his medical textbook, and she must have read the book at least ten times!" said Christos, leafing through the book. His shrewd mind was racing. He was curious what relationship, if any, this young man had with Gregory Plakis.

"It seems like you have a scholar on your hands," said Tony, smiling. The more he heard about Ipatia, the more intrigued he was.

"Yes, but a girl her age should be thinking about marriage, not about books!" scoffed Christos.

Tony decided to change the subject. "Mr. Rodakis, there's a favor I'd like to ask of you. I understand that vase sitting by the door was given by you to Mr. Pericles over the matter of a horse."

Tony pointed towards the object of interest.

Christos turned and looked at the vase. "Oh, that vase! Yes, it was a present from Ipatia's father, God bless his soul. But it is Stellios' vase now."

"I am interested in ancient vases. This one in particular," replied Tony. "I also understand one needs a horse to travel up the hill to your house?"

Christos turned to Stellios, who was now standing nearby listening, and asked, "Stellios, why do you tell nice people like this gentleman that one needs a horse to visit my home? Are you trying to sell him your infamous horse?" He winked and everyone laughed. He turned to Tony and said, "Our friend here has been trying to sell his horse for a long time now. But the price has been so high, no one would buy him!"

"Actually, I would be interested in making a deal with you. Is the horse here?" said Tony, looking at Stellios.

"Certainly, Mr. Tony!" said Stellios. His enthusiasm raised his voice to an even higher pitch. "Please come with me, my friend... the horse is in the back."

Tony followed him to the back, where a white horse was standing, tied to a pole. After looking him over carefully, Tony nodded his satisfaction at the horse's condition. He was young and healthy. Tony gently stroked the horse's mane, thinking for a moment, then turned to Mr. Pericles and made his offer. Mr. Pericles' happy nod confirmed it was more than a generous amount.

"Here is payment for both this horse and the vase in the front, the one near the door," said Tony, placing a wad of bills in Mr. Pericles' outstretched hand. Mr. Pericles thanked him profusely, then eagerly saddled the horse.

Christos was seated on his wagon when Tony and Stellios returned with the horse. He said, "I did not want to leave without saying good-bye to you. I see you both agreed upon the price. May you enjoy him in health!"

"Thank you, Mr. Rodakis. Are you leaving already?" asked Tony, mildly disappointed at the man's departure.

"Yes, I must be going back to the house. You see, my granddaughter will be leaving today on the ferry, and I still have to go and bring her down," explained Christos.

"Mr. Rodakis, before you leave, I wanted to tell you something. Did you know the vase you gave to Mr. Pericles was much more valuable than the old horse he gave to you? There are people in this world who would be willing to give lots of money for that vase."

"What do you mean?" replied Christos, somewhat puzzled. "How could an old vase like that one, which sat around collecting dust, have more value than a horse? Why, the horse could breed more horses, it could carry one everywhere he wants to go, and help carry his supplies. It could even help till the soil!"

"This white horse is much more suited to what the vase is actually worth," said Tony, handing the reins to the old gentleman.

"What is this?" said Mr. Rodakis, appearing surprised. "Won't you be needing the horse?"

"No. Actually, I will also be leaving today on the ferry going to Piraeus. I will be taking the vase with me, to place it in the museum in Athens, but this horse rightfully belongs to you," said Tony, a touch of firmness in his voice.

A speechless Christos Rodakis stared at him for a moment, realization dawning. Dismounting, he walked over and kissed Tony on both cheeks. This man's fairness and generosity had touched something deep inside him. It reminded him of his late son-in-law.

"A thousand thanks, Mr. Tony! You are a true *Leventi!*" exclaimed Christos, shaking Tony's hand vigorously. It wasn't often he coined this term reserved for the noblest of men. "How can I ever repay you?"

"If you can tell me where there is a good restaurant, that would do," laughed Tony. "I haven't eaten since yesterday morning, and I'm beginning to feel it."

"I know what! Why don't you join us for lunch? That is the least I can do to repay you," said Christos.

Tony hesitated.

"It would also be a good opportunity to return the book to Ipatia yourself," said Christos.

Something inside Tony spurred him to say, "Thank you, I will accept your gracious offer."

"Good, good," said Christos, slapping him playfully on the back. "Then it is settled. You just follow me with the horse."

Tony pulled Stellios over and said quietly, "Please prepare the vase for me and wrap it in cloth. I will return shortly for it."

Stellios nodded vigorously, his face still beaming from the man's generous payment, "Yes, my friend, don't worry! I'll have it ready for you when you get back!"

Tony mounted the horse and followed Christos down the narrow cobbled street, past the different shops, past the pedestrians. Several waved to Christos Rodakis. A couple of times, he stopped to talk with them. Once the introductions were made, Christos kept the conversation brief, and then moved on. Tony expected that by the end of the day, the whole town would have heard about him.

The road eventually led them outside the town and to the main road. Tony recognized the water basin from the day before. He smiled, remembering the scene.

Christos slowed down, turning to wait for Tony. "Here it is wide enough so that we can ride side by side."

"Mr. Christos, I've been meaning to tell you something. My father, Gregory Plakis, says he knows you from Crete. Is that true?"

"Ah-ha!" said Christos, looking smug. He shook his finger at Tony. "I thought there was some resemblance! The apple falls from the apple tree!"

Tony was surprised to hear this. People had often said he resembled his mother more than his father. "How did you meet my father?"

Christos Rodakis chuckled, "I've known your father for many years, even before he met your mother! We used to live in the same town called Herakleion. Ever since I was a boy, I helped my father with his wine business. He sold enough to feed the family and often gave wine to relatives and friends. Well, your father happened to taste our wine at a friendly gathering and asked who made it. Next, he came looking for us."

"Yes, that sounds like Father. Was he trying to start some business with you?" said Tony, smiling.

"You know him very well! He was single then, and interested in the way we made the wine. He almost convinced me to start a business with him, but I had other plans. Who knows, he may have ended up in the wine business rather than in the shipping business."

"What made you come here?"

"I was already engaged by the time I met your father. My fiance was from this island. She was a beautiful and virtuous girl. We had made plans to live here after our marriage. Her mother was a widow and too frail to live by herself. She didn't want to leave her."

"You must have loved her very much to leave Crete and come here," said Tony softly.

Christos nodded. "I did. She was one of a kind...beautiful, compassionate, always helping people. After we married, I bought the property next to her mother's house and started a grape orchard. Later, I added an olive orchard. My wife was a hard worker, working steadily by my side. We began making olive oil. I sold bottles of wine and oil, enough to make a living," he said, shrugging his shoulders. Then he remained silent after that confession.

They passed rows of fig and almond trees, their branches reaching out unto the road, forming sketchy shading over their heads.

"Whatever happened to your wife?" asked Tony.

"My wife died from pneumonia, God rest her soul. I went back to Crete for a visit shortly after that, to get away for awhile, but it wasn't the same. My parents were all gone by then. I have no brothers or sisters, just a cousin who had lived in our house all these years. He is a bachelor...older than I am...probably in his seventies by now. That was when I realized my home was now here. I have not gone back there since then," admitted Christos.

"How did your son-in-law happen to work for my father?"

"Manolis had a captain's license and was visiting here, when he set eyes upon my daughter, Irene. You see, she was very beautiful and he was eager to marry her. The problem was, he did not have a job at that time. I saw that Irene loved Manolis, so I decided to help."

"What did you do?"

"I knew about your father's shipping business, so I sent Manolis to him, with several bottles of my best wine. Your father remembered me, God bless him, and hired him on the spot. He became one of their best captains."

"I know. I met Captain Kouris," said Tony sadly. "We were very good friends."

"Oh yes, he was a very good man. I not only lost my daughter, but the best son-in-law I could ever ask for," said Christos. He took out a handkerchief and wiped his reddened eyes. "Now I'm also going to lose my Ipatia."

"What do you mean?" asked Tony. He was feeling an unexpressed sadness.

"Ipatia is leaving for Piraeus today, and God be with her on the trip. I don't want anything happening to the girl. She's all I have."

"Why is she going to Piraeus?"

"Her Aunt Sophia is there, and she wants to go to the university there. I have mixed feelings about that, and I will miss her."

"Is she traveling alone?"

"That's another problem. Mrs. Xilouris was to travel with her, and now she cannot go because of her son's condition. Ipatia is still young and to travel by herself is not good."

Tony silently listened, remembering the image of the girl swinging precariously from the tree. "I'll be taking the same ferry ride, Mr. Rodakis. If it's all right with you, I'll make sure she gets to her aunt."

"That's very kind of you, young man! Is your father traveling with you? For if he is, then I would love to give him some of my best wine!" said Christos, delicately using the excuse of the wine to ensure his granddaughter would be traveling with older chaperones.

"Yes, he is. Actually, he asked to see you before he left. He will be down at the dock. I can bring him to you," said Tony.

"Good, then it is settled!" said Christos heartily.

Their discourse continued on general topics, as they covered the history of Greece and its politics. Tony was impressed by Mr. Rodakis' knowledge. He was enjoying a lively discussion with Christos, when the topic switched to fishing.

"I am not a fisherman," admitted Christos. "I don't like traveling by boat. I get seasick. But I do go occasionally with friends if the sea is calm enough. You know, to keep them company. I like to fish for squid, though. You go in the early evening, just as the sun sets, and your boat just sits out there while you wait for the squid to bite. It's quite a feeling."

"I've never gone fishing for squid," said Tony, liking the idea.

The path finally led them to the house. Its simple white color, blue shutters and red flowers were inviting to the eye. The shady courtyard felt refreshingly cool after the warm trip. White trellises that lined its stone wall borders were laden with climbing grapevines. Ripened fruit hung heavily from the vines, a temptation for the thirsty traveler. Tony immediately liked it here.

Christos said, "Welcome to our humble home."

CHAPTER 9

My heart did lead me to your door
Your book to give and you adore

Ipatia was almost finished scrubbing the floor in the kitchen, humming a tune, when she heard knocking on the door.

"Ipatia, Ipatia!"

"Yes, Grandfather!" she sang out, standing up. She wiped her hands on her work clothes. "I'll be right there!"

She tiptoed on the mopped floor, opened the door and rushed outside to greet her grandfather. Caught off guard, she stopped in her tracks. Seated on a large white horse next to Grandfather, was Tony, the man who rescued her the other day. She was speechless, for she felt like she was reliving the dream she had the night before, of a knight coming to her seated on a white horse.

Christos observed his granddaughter's response, feeling an old familiar stirring inside his chest. She stood there, looking a little lost, yet just as beautiful as her mother used to be. Memories of his daughter clouded his mind. It was only yesterday when Christos had brought the young captain Manolis to the house to share with him his fine wine, just as he brought Tony today.

"Ipatia, my dear, I believe that you have already met our guest, Tony," said Christos, gently reminding her of her manners.

"Yes, I have. Good afternoon, Mr. Tony," said Ipatia, regaining her voice, nodding, but stopping after the greeting. She pulled back strands of loose hair from her face. This man made her feel tongue-tied.

"Hello, Ipatia!" said Tony, in a ringing voice. He dismounted lightly in one swift stroke. "You will be happy to know that I came to return your book to you," he continued, this time in English, bowing, so that she could not see the laughter that was ready to erupt. This odd girl made him feel happy in some mysterious way.

"Thank you!" she exclaimed, reaching out for the book that was in his outstretched hand. His fingers brushed hers lightly. She held her breath, stepping back, clutching the book close to her chest.

"It was my pleasure," Tony replied, smiling.

Christos, mindful of the time, gestured towards the door. "Please come in, where it is cool inside."

Tony followed him into the cottage. His tall height forced him to stoop as he entered the doorway.

"Grandfather, what will be done with the supplies?" asked Ipatia, trying to find an excuse not to go in right away. The young man exuded a powerful force that made her tremble slightly.

Christos peered outside the door and said gruffly, "They can wait. Mr. Plakis will be staying for lunch, so please come in to help."

She followed silently. Tony sat at the table, his tall frame making the room appear small. While he talked with her grandfather, she dutifully prepared the lunch, moving rhythmically with the chatter. She was constantly mindful of not bumping into Tony, as the kitchen was quite small. In a matter of minutes, the table was ready. There was a colorful display of black olives, stuffed grape leaves, and chunky slices of tomatoes drizzled with olive oil dressing. Then there were Mrs. Tsatsikas' cheese-pies and a fresh loaf of bread.

Christos went to the cupboard and got out the wine. "This is our simple house, Mr. Tony. It has weathered several years of storms and use, and has seen some very fine wine!"

He poured wine into three small glasses, handing one each to Tony and Ipatia. Then he lifted his glass up.

"Ahh, I am looking forward to trying your famous wine!" said Tony. He lifted his glass.

"A toast, for you, my kind man, who helped me bring our supplies up, and for the magnificent horse. We are indebted to you!" said Christos, saluting him.

They drank in silence.

Ipatia watched them drink, then touched the glass lightly with her lips as a token. She rarely drank wine. She wondered what her grandfather meant about a horse. Whatever it was, her grandfather was very happy.

"Yes, this is excellent wine," said Tony, appearing pleased.

"There's no greater joy than seeing a guest in my house enjoying my wine!" said Christos.

Ipatia sat down quietly, eating her lunch, observing the two men as they ate and talked.

"This tastes very good. Ipatia did you make this?" said Tony, pointing to the plate of stuffed grape leaves, having just finished eating one. The women he knew rarely cooked. Even his sister and stepmother didn't know how to cook.

Ipatia looked up, surprised. She rarely was complimented for her cooking. She nodded shyly.

"Yes, Ipatia has cooked since she was a young girl. All the girls here are taught to cook at a young age," said Christos matter-of-factly. Then he resumed the conversation. "We have about one hundred olive trees. Every year, starting in early November, I get a couple of the Tsatsikas boys and we pick the olives."

"I used to help also when I was young," piped Ipatia.

Christos was surprised to hear her talk. Typically, she would be quiet when they had visitors. "When Ipatia first visited the island during the summer with her parents, she was around five or six. So the little girl came up to me looking really important, tugging on my sleeve and confiding in me that there were a lot of olives on the ground and that maybe we should pick them up. When I looked down, I saw her pointing at a group of goat droppings!"

Everyone broke out laughing.

"Ipatia became my best helper," said Christos, wiping his eyes from the laughter.

"Is that right?" asked Tony, grinning at Ipatia.

She nodded shyly. Her grandfather continued, describing the preparations in making the olive oil. Ipatia was tempted to join in the conversation. She hesitated when she remembered Doctor Thanassis' visit a few months ago. She had eagerly jumped in to a discussion with him about medicine and her grandfather had reprimanded her afterwards. He said her time would come when she was married. Meanwhile, she was supposed to be quiet, or else she would be labeled a bold, vain girl.

After she finished her meal, her long fingers began tapping on her thighs. She had a habit of playing invisible notes whenever she was nervous. Then her grandfather turned towards her and said, "Ipatia, the ferryboat will be leaving today at two. Do you have your clothes packed?"

"Yes."

"Good. Tony will also be traveling on that boat. He and his family will see that you get to Piraeus safely."

Ipatia's eyes opened in wonder. That was the reason why her grandfather was friendly to this man! Her grandfather didn't think she could handle the trip alone, but needed assistance. Without noticing, her fingers found their way to the side of the chair and vigorously tapped on it, causing Tony to stop and stare at them. She immediately stopped, feeling flushed.

"Ipatia, why don't you go and get ready for the trip. Don't take too long, because we can't have Tony waiting here," said Christos, slightly annoyed at her mounting nervousness. That girl could not sit still for a minute. "We must be down there early enough to get the tickets."

Ipatia excused herself, then went nervously into the bedroom. She was feeling slightly remorseful. Her grandfather had talked to her as if she was a child, and here she was almost eighteen. She shut the door and stood there a moment, waiting until her heart slowed a bit. She had never felt this way before. She could hear them talking. Curious, she pushed the door slightly open so she could peek through. Tony's back was towards her, and to his right sat her grandfather.

Ipatia observed Tony, as she removed her work clothes and slipped into the black skirt and blouse. He talked confidently with her grandfather. His handsome features came alive, as he gestured while talking. Was it her imagination, or did the kitchen appear warmer and fuller, as it filled up with his vibrant voice ringing out in laughter.

Then, just as quickly, the conversation died. She shut the door in haste. She did not want them to notice her. She caught the last words her grandfather was saying. "I need to unload the supplies from the cart, so we can put Ipatia's trunk in it."

They must have gone outside, for it was quiet after that.

Ipatia finished dressing. She bundled her long hair briskly into a bun and secured it with two large pins. Checking the mirror, she placed the hat on her head. When Mrs. Tsatsikas had presented it to her, she had said knowingly that all women in Piraeus wore them. It was the fashion. Ipatia winced as it engulfed her head. She lifted it and perched it more carefully on top of the bun. That will do for now. She prayed there would be no wind.

She then checked her purse for the money and key for the trunk. Everything was there. Then she remembered the gemstone. She found it and held it up, cherishing its beauty. Her mind was racing as she carefully put it back in her purse.

The last thing she did was put on her black Sunday shoes. Her feet had out-grown them and they were beginning to pinch, but she had no other shoes. She walked around the room, trying not to wince. She will take them off as soon as she got on the boat, she promised herself.

She made sure the trunk was locked. Then she pulled it behind her, gingerly entering the kitchen, mindful of her tight shoes. The kitchen's door was open and the boxes of supplies had already been placed in the kitchen. Her slim arms were surprisingly strong and it did not take much of an effort for her to drag the trunk across the kitchen and into the courtyard.

"Ipatia, over here," said Tony, gesturing to her. He was standing next to Mr. Rodakis, who was busily arranging the wagon and donkey.

"I will be back with the wine," said Christos, heading for the storage place in the back where he kept the jugs.

Tony nodded, then watched the girl attempting to pull the trunk towards him. In a few strides, he was by her side.

Ipatia felt Tony's hand as he took the trunk from her, and when she looked up, her hat plopped down in her face. As she went to move it up, her purse slipped from her hand. She heard Tony's deep laughter as she tried to peer from under her hat. Then she stooped to pick up the purse, which caused her hat to fall off and her hair come tumbling down. *Oh the humiliation of it all! He is still laughing!*

Tony's laughter died, as he sensed her quiet desperation. She had her back turned to him, gathering her falling hair together back into a bun. He had done an ungentlemanly thing by laughing at her. Feeling a sense of guilt, he stooped down and retrieved her hat, shaking it. He waited until she finished placing her hair up.

"This is a very nice hat," he said solemnly, giving her the hat.

"Thank you!" she said, still smarting from his laughter. Trying to compose herself, she put her hat on more securely, pulling it all the way down to her eyes. She tried to peer from under it. Her grandfather was nowhere in sight.

"I'm sorry if I laughed. Everything happened all at once, you see," Tony said, gesturing comically.

This time, the girl surprised him, for she started giggling, and then her purse fell down a second time, causing them both to break out into laughter.

"This place of your grandfather's gives a beautiful view of the sea from here," said Tony, after the laughter had subsided and Ipatia resumed her composure. "Is it safe to swim in these waters, Ipatia?"

For some reason, he enjoyed listening to the sound of her name. He pointed towards the sea, lost in thought, realizing that this simple house was in a wonderful location, secluded up on a hill with a panoramic view of the water, even a better view than his own father's house.

"Yes, it is. We usually swim close to the beach anyway. Sometimes sharks have been seen further out."

"Dolphins are supposed to be good to have around," said Tony. "It is said that they help keep the sharks away."

"Once I saw a group of dolphins playing nearby," she said, brightening up at the memory. "It was the prettiest sight one could ever see. They were so playful. They looked as if they were having fun."

Tony smiled at her openness.

Then Ipatia remembered the stone. She dug inside her purse, clasping the smooth hard object in her hand. "I would like to give you something, as my way of saying thank you for everything you have done," she said, proudly placing it in his hand.

"That is very kind of you," he replied, touched by her gesture. He looked at the polished stone. It was the size of an almond and glittered intensely. "It has an interesting color."

"It was given to me by Father, from one of his trips to Russia. He called it the cat's eye. He said it reminded him of my eyes. It changes color from a green to a red, depending on how much light it gets."

"Ahh, can this be an Alexandrite stone?" said Tony, looking at it more closely, very much interested. "Do you know the story?"

"My father said that in Russia, when Alexander was coming of age in the 1830's, this stone was named after him," she said proudly.

"Very good, Ipatia," he said, nodding. "I'd like to thank you, but I don't know if I should accept this, since your father gave it to you."

"Oh, you should!" she blurted out. "I mean, I owe you so much for saving me and for bringing back my book! It's the least I could do. Please take it."

He thanked her, then placed it carefully inside his pocket. Her father evidently picked good souvenirs. First the ancient vase, and now this valuable stone. He would check into it, but he believed this type of stone was not common.

"Here is the box of wine for your father," said Christos, coughing slightly behind them. Tony smiled and lifted the box effortlessly on the wagon, pushing it to the side.

"I'll take that," Tony said firmly, taking the trunk from Christos' hands. He placed it effortlessly next to the box.

Ipatia skipped up into the wagon and settled herself on the small seat, keeping one hand on her hat, so it wouldn't fall off her head again.

They ambled down the small path, with Tony following them on the horse. When they reached the main road, Tony moved to the front and began talking with Christos, while Ipatia stayed quiet, absorbing everything around her, almost as if it would be the last time she would see this place.

CHAPTER 10

Life's cycles, one by one
Unfold like an onion

When they arrived at the coffee shop, Tony said, "Mr. Rodakis, I'll see you down at the dock. I have to stop and see about the vase."

Christos nodded, and they moved on. Ipatia spilled out all the questions she had bottled up inside her.

"Wait, wait," said Christos, laughing. "I'll answer them one at a time."

He took his time explaining everything to her, about Tony's visit in the morning to give back the book, about Tony buying the vase, and finally, about his giving them the horse. She was beginning to piece the puzzle together.

They stopped a short distance from the passenger boat. Her grandfather removed the trunk from the wagon, then handed her the canvas bag. "Wait here while I go and get your tickets."

Ipatia looked around. People were slowly arriving, gathering in small groups along the harbor. To her far left, the weathered fishermen sat on the ground, with their fishing nets spread about them like spider webs. They skillfully mended the nets, chatting to each other, while others, further down, were removing the fresh catch of the day from their boats. Her gaze rested on a group standing near the passenger boat. She recognized Tony's sister, Bonnie, and Dr. Michael. Tony approached the group, riding on the white horse, appearing very pleased. He was holding a large, wrapped object.

"Ipatia, guard these well. This one is for the passenger boat, and the other one is for the ferryboat," said Grandfather, interrupting her thoughts. He handed the tickets to her.

"Yes, Grandfather."

"What did you do with your money?"

"It's in my purse."

"Good. Now listen carefully. Here are the legal papers your aunt sent after your parents passed away. When you turn eighteen, you will take them to the bank in Piraeus, the one listed on the papers. Your father has placed money in a trust fund there and the papers have the account number on them. Guard these well!"

Ipatia carefully placed the papers in her purse.

"Look, Grandfather. Mr. Tony is coming here and he's bringing someone with him," she whispered, watching the two men approach. Mr. Tony was darker and much taller than the other man.

"Christos Rodakis! Old friend! How long has it been?" shouted Gregory, coming up to him, slapping him on the back, then shaking his hand vigorously.

"Gregory Plakis! It must be at least thirty years since I last saw you, and you haven't aged one bit!" exclaimed Christos, looking at him intently.

"Tony told me you were here and I couldn't leave without saying hello to an old friend," said Gregory. He stared curiously at the young woman.

"This is Ipatia, my granddaughter," said Christos proudly.

Ipatia smiled and extended her hand to Mr. Gregory. "How do you do?"

"She's Captain Kouris' daughter," explained Christos.

"Ah, yes, yes! I thought you looked familiar. You've grown into a beautiful young lady since I had last seen you," he said, first shaking, then holding on to her hand, admiring her beauty and height. Although the girl was tall like her father, her bone structure and delicate features bore a strong resemblance to her mother. He could never forget her mother's beauty.

"My father worked for you?" she asked timidly.

"Yes, thanks to your grandfather. Your father was one of my best and most courageous captains. A good man he was. We were very sorry to lose him."

Tony was surprised at his father's interest in the girl and his generous compliment about her beauty. The only other time he remembered hearing his father give that compliment, was to his mother years ago. Not even Christina had that privilege. He stared at the girl, but she had lowered her head even further, hiding her face underneath that colossal hat!

"Thank you, Gregory. But more important is her character. Beauty is only skin deep!" replied Christos, with a twinkle in his eye. "And now I'm going to be losing her. She will be traveling to Piraeus to stay with Sophia, her aunt."

"Not Sophia Kouris?" asked Gregory. "She was the best seamstress we ever had."

"Yes! That's my aunt!" Ipatia blurted out.

"You tell her Gregory Plakis said hello."

Ipatia nodded shyly, regretting her outburst.

"Tony was kind enough to offer to see that Ipatia gets there safely. Now that I know that you also will be going on the trip, I feel even more confident that my granddaughter will be in good hands."

"Yes, my son has always been one for helping people out. Don't worry, my friend, you can trust that she will get there safely," said Gregory, somewhat dryly, looking at Tony. Tony smiled back. It didn't surprise Gregory that his son would grab an opportunity to spend time with a lovely girl.

"Are you traveling with the rest of your family?" asked Christos.

"Yes, my wife Christina and daughter are over there with some friends of the family," said Gregory, gesturing towards the direction of the group.

Christos looked at the group and nodded appreciatively, saying, "You have a lovely family! Now look what I have for you, Gregory. Several jugs of my finest wine!" He proudly displayed the box filled with the wine.

"Thank you, my friend!" said Gregory, patting Christos on the back with gusto.

"It is my pleasure! I heard you visited Herakleion. How is life there?"

"Where shall I start? Although it was a wonderful trip, things are not the way they used to be."

They conversed for a little while, talking about the people they knew, the new buildings and roads that were built, the sad news of those who had died, and the good news of those whose children married.

Ipatia stood awkwardly nearby, listening. Tony was standing very close to her, tuned in to the conversation. She could feel his warmth emanating towards her, almost as if his arms were embracing her. Grandfather said that Tony was going to see that she got to Piraeus safely. She wondered what that meant. *Is he going to sit with you and keep an eye on you?* She liked the idea. *What if he has a cabin and asks you to go with him there? Ipatia, get those wicked thoughts out of your mind right now! I wouldn't go! I will stay in my seat!*

The sound of the ferryboat's horn was heard in the distance.

"The ferryboat has arrived!" said Ipatia. She pointed towards its direction. "I hope we are not too late!"

"Don't worry, the ferryboat won't leave until the passenger boat takes us over there," said Tony, looking down at her. All he could see beneath that hat was her full mouth, puckered up, ready to be kissed. It was so easy.

A woman's voice called out from a distance. "Tony, Tony!"

Tony looked around and saw Bonnie waving to him. Melissa was next to her, waving to him also. They were in the line of people that were beginning to board the passenger boat.

"Father, it is time to go. They are now boarding the passenger boat," said Tony.

Gregory shook Christos' hand one last time and said, "If you need anything, please don't hesitate to let me know!"

Tony then shook Christos' hand. "It was nice knowing you, Mr. Rodakis. Here is your horse. I'll be back for your grand-daughter."

"Thank you for everything, and God bless you!" replied Christos, taking the reins from Tony's hands. He led the horse to the wagon and tied him.

Tony picked up the box and said to Ipatia, "I'll be back for you." Then he whistled as he walked with his father towards Bonnie. She had remained behind after the rest of the group had already boarded the passenger boat.

Ipatia watched them secretly from beneath her hat, admiring the ease with which Tony carried the box. She knew it was heavy, for in the past, she used to help her grandfather pack and carry them. Tony went over to Bonnie, picked up her luggage with his other hand and walked with her up the ramp to the boat. Ipatia looked away, not wanting to see anymore. She and her grandfather slowly walked towards the passenger boat.

"My Ipatia, remember to write to me and let me know what happens."

"Don't worry, Grandfather. I will write you. You take good care of yourself," she said. They reached the ramp to the passenger boat. She hugged him tightly, the tears now flowing.

"It's all right, my dear, now don't you cry, or else I'll join you. We'll see each other soon, won't we? Now you go, before the boat leaves without you!" said Christos, patting her on the back. He then took out a handkerchief and began to wipe his eyes.

Tony loomed over them and said, "Don't worry, Mr. Christos. We'll make sure she gets to her aunt. Here, I can take her trunk."

"Thank you, Tony, for your reassuring words," said Christos.

Tony smiled as he lifted the trunk, then gently led Ipatia up the side ramp. As soon as she gave her ticket to the attendant, the ramp was removed and the boat began its short journey. They had been the last ones to board. The attendant led them to the back of the boat, and Tony followed her. There were few people here, as most of the others were at the front of the boat, including Tony's family.

Ipatia walked towards the handrail and leaned against it. She could see her grandfather in the distance and waved to him.

"Are you all right here? I can stay with you a bit, if you'd like," Tony said, placing the trunk down, feeling protective of her.

Tony's words were soothing to hear, and she smiled up at him. The boat chugged along, hitting some waves, causing Ipatia to grip the rail tightly. Beginning to feel nauseated, she sat down on her trunk. Tony sensed the girl's fear and held on to her arm, talking to her about different things. She didn't remember what he said, just that his warm touch felt good, and his pleasant voice was soothing to her ears.

He excused himself when he saw that she was stabilized and went to the front to check up on his family. Afterwards, Tony stood with the captain at the wheel, chatting about a number of things, including the island's history. As he was talking, his glance fell on the spot where Ipatia sat. She was bent over. It was evident that she had not inherited her father's sea legs.

When the boat stopped, Ipatia gave a sigh of relief. She stood up shakily, eager to get off. She knew the large ship did not rock like the passenger boat. Hope was strengthening her unsteady legs as she wobbled forward, pulling the trunk ever so slowly. Within minutes, she reached the ramp. Tony had finished helping his family's luggage on board the ferry, and spotting her, came over to help her.

"Ah, here you are! I see we don't have to carry you off the boat! Follow me," he said cheerfully, walking in front of her up the large ramp, carrying her trunk.

She followed him silently.

"How do you feel?" he asked, turning slightly towards her.

Ipatia blushed at the personal question. "I feel much better now that I'm getting off that boat!"

He laughed, saying, "The ferryboat is much bigger, and it won't rock as much."

As soon as they boarded, she looked around her. There were all kinds of people everywhere. It was a much larger ship than the one she used to travel to Rhodes with.

"Ipatia, do you have your ticket?" asked Tony.

She pulled out her ticket and handed it to him, feeling nervous. *Remember to stay with your plan, no matter how strong the temptation!*

He looked at the ticket and bit his lip. Her grandfather had gotten her a class C ticket, the lowest class seating. He thought quickly, then said to her, "Would you rather go into a cabin? It's not too late to get one for you."

"A cabin?" she asked, suddenly seeing red. *You were right! See how he tries to get you into a cabin!* "No, no, thank you. This ticket is fine."

Tony thought she was being polite, and he said once more, "No, really, it would be much better for you in the cabin."

"Would you be kind enough to give me back my ticket?" Ipatia said, almost shouting.

"All right then. I know where that is. Let's go this way," said Tony, noticing her stubborn look. He admired her resolve at not changing her seat for a cabin. The women he had known would have jumped at the chance to take advantage of his offer.

She followed him up the stairs. There were people coming down the stairs to her left, and some were men dressed smartly in white uniforms. They looked at her boldly. She quickly lowered her head, blushing and focusing on the steps instead.

They passed through a large lobby and made their way to an outside corridor. Tony whistled as they walked slowly down the corridor. Ipatia was beginning to relax, and glanced to her left where the island was. She could see the white boats bobbing up and down, embracing the dock like a coral necklace, while the sea all around them was at its most beautiful blue.

"Here we are," said Tony.

To their right was a very large room filled with rows of chairs, with people either sitting or standing everywhere.

Tony located a seat next to an old couple and placed her trunk on the side. "This looks like a good place for you. It is quieter here. Please stay in your seat so no one takes it. I will be downstairs in a cabin. I will try to stop by later and see if you need anything. Try and get some sleep if you can."

"Thank you," she said brightly, settling in the seat and looking up at him with large, trusting eyes, shining brilliantly like precious gemstones.

He blinked at her, realizing how beautiful she looked just then. She was just as comfortable here as Bonnie and the rest of them were in their cabins. He paused, tempted to stay, but he first had to talk to his father about the business. Maybe he would visit her later.

Ipatia watched him leave, feeling a sense of pride at being escorted there. When he reached the door, he looked back and waved at her. She nodded in return, embarrassed at being caught staring.

Ipatia settled in her seat. She looked around the room, noticing that the women did not wear hats. She immediately removed the offending object, wondering where her godmother got her notions. The tight shoes were the next things to come off.

The room was filling slowly with all types of people. To her right, the older couple was quietly discussing something, their voices lowered. People seated in front of her were arguing about politics, gesturing emphatically, trying to make their points. To her left, a group of college students, boys and girls, were joking and laughing, as if they had no care in the world. She focused on them, watching them in admiration. Maybe one day she would be a college student, traveling in a group like that. They appeared to be returning from some field trip. *Yes, but what makes you think Grandfather would let you travel with boys?*

In the front of the room were two musicians who appeared to be entertaining a small audience. One was playing a santouri and singing folksongs, while the other played a violin. As soon as the ship began its journey, the noise stabilized into a low hum.

After awhile, the woman next to her started a conversation with her. Ipatia learned her life story. She was going with her husband to Piraeus because his health was not doing too well. Ipatia related her own story to her. The woman promised Ipatia that she would let her know when they arrived in Piraeus. Just then, a uniformed man interrupted them, asking for their tickets. After he moved on to the next row, Ipatia continued her conversation with the woman.

It wasn't long before the room quieted down and the lights were subdued. Ipatia glanced at the older couple next to her. They had already fallen asleep. Ipatia shut her eyes, trying to sleep, thinking about what lay ahead for her.

CHAPTER 11

My dear sweet aunt did not appear
But you did care and drew me near

Tony sauntered into the ship's dining room with his family and guests. They sat around a large table, eating and talking.

Later, the group filtered off in different directions, and Tony stayed behind, talking with his father and making arrangements regarding the first plans of his transition into the family business.

"May I join you?"

Tony looked up. It was Chuck Daras.

"Of course!" said Gregory. "We were just discussing the shipping agency. You came just in time."

Chuck Daras thanked him and sat down. He removed a box of cigarettes from inside his shirt pocket and after offering it to them, lit a cigarette, puffing it slowly.

"Tony, I hear you are going to be your father's right arm," said Chuck.

Tony looked at him, surprised. "Yes. May I ask who told you?"

"Your little sister," said Chuck apologetically. "We were upstairs on the deck just now, before Michael interrupted us, discussing the shipping business. I admit she is very knowledgeable about the business. She almost sold me a ship."

"Hahahaha," laughed Gregory, slapping the table excitedly. "I tell you, that girl can run this business as well as any man!" He was shrewd enough to realize that it was more than a business deal that Daras was after. He expounded on Melissa's beauty and accomplishments, making her appear almost superhuman.

Tony listened quietly to his father's creation of an angelic Melissa, one who took care of stray animals and wanted to help others. His father was up to something.

"Melissa has not only been a good daughter, but a son to me," continued Gregory, nodding his head emphatically. "She has been more dedicated and devoted to the shipping business than Tony here. From the very beginning, he wanted nothing to do with ships, but instead, wanted to go to the university."

That is when Tony excused himself and went to his cabin. His father had said enough. The small room with the double bed was all that he needed to take a brief nap. His large frame sank into the soft mattress. He needed to calm down. *A few minutes before Chuck Daras showed up, Father was praising me about getting involved in the family business. As soon as Chuck showed interest in Melissa, Father was just as willing to cut me down so Melissa could look good in Chuck's eyes. Father has not changed. No matter how much I try to see him in a good light, he will always be a self-centered, thick-skinned man, thinking only about himself and his business.*

Afterwards, he strolled outside, appreciating the resplendent sunset, while lovers walked past him, hand in hand. Noisy sea gulls were combing the air above, following the ship. He gazed at the frothy water flowing out from the back of the ship. He felt as turbulent as the water.

There were so many thoughts that needed straightening out. He went over the plans he discussed with his father regarding the business. Everything appeared fine, until Chuck Daras showed up.

Tony stood there for an indefinite amount of time, mulling over the mixed feelings that were threatening to engulf him. This transitional period in his life was not going to be easy. Everything he worked for, his education, his freedom, was soon to be demolished by his father. His omnipotent father, close to impending death, was still trying to control his life. *Yet, it is your duty as the first born, to take over, Tony.*

Then he thought about Ipatia and he felt better. He remembered his promise to her that he would check up on her. He made his way to her floor. Side-stepping the people coming out of the large room, he finally entered. From where he stood, he could see that she was sleeping peacefully. He wasn't about to interrupt her sleep. He went through the lobby, heading towards the lounge, when he saw Melissa coming towards him.

"Where have you been, Tony? I have been looking all over for you! Look what I have on my hand!" Melissa exclaimed. She held out her hand proudly.

"What about your hand?"

"Can't you see the ring on it, you silly? Michael proposed to me. We're going to be married!"

"Congratulations, little sister! Does Father know?" asked Tony, surprised slightly at the timing. It wasn't like Michael to propose on a ship. He wondered if Michael had been pressured into marriage by his sister because of Chuck Daras' interest in her. He kissed his sister lightly on the cheek.

"Not yet! I wanted you to be the first to know! Now that I have your approval, I know Father would be just as pleased."

"Yes, and why shouldn't he? Michael is one of the best people I've ever known," he reassured her.

She beamed up at him.

"Where is the lucky bridegroom?" he asked, looking around expectantly.

"He went to the lounge. He's expecting you."

Tony found Michael in the lounge, seated at the bar. He appeared to be nursing a drink. Tony joined him, congratulating his old friend. Then he made a toast, raising his glass.

"This is for the happy couple. May you both have many, many years of happiness together!"

They drank and conversed into the night, reminiscing about the past and their friendship.

Ipatia rubbed her eyes and looked around. It was dark, but she could see people gathering their belongings and leaving, as new people were arriving. There seemed to be fewer people in the room. The couple next to her was still sleeping soundly. Ipatia stretched, and her stomach growled in return. Minutes later, she was munching on a cheese pie, thinking about her grandfather, Mrs. Tsatsikas, and what would be happening back on the island. After she finished, she realized she was very thirsty. She had forgotten to bring water with her.

She remembered the lobby she had passed on the way here. There should be some staff that could direct her to some water. She placed her bag on her seat and walked out into the hallway. The lobby was quiet, except for a man behind the counter, dressed in a white uniform. He pointed towards the direction of the lounge, and she thanked him, heading in that direction. She wondered what had happened to Tony. She got her answer as soon as she arrived at the doorway.

The place was empty except for Tony and Dr. Michael, who were standing at the bar, their backs to her. She could hear Dr. Michael clearly saying, "I've been wanting to ask you what your plans were for Bonnie. Melissa's told me the girl's in love with you."

Ipatia was ready to leave, suddenly feeling awkward, not knowing what to do. If she walked in, she would be intruding on the private conversation, and if she left, she would still be very thirsty! Something held her there a little while longer, listening in.

Tony replied, "I made it clear to Melissa that I'm not interested in a long term relationship with Bonnie. I am going to be busy dealing with my father's shipping business. Bonnie is a nice, attractive girl, and I can see her one day marrying someone very rich and making him happy. But I am not that man!"

That was when Michael raised his voice. "Tony, you've been a very good friend all these years, the best friend a guy could ever have. You've helped me a number of times when I needed it, and I appreciate it. But there's something you need to know about yourself. You see, you always seem to attract beautiful, wealthy women with your good looks, and there's nothing wrong with that, but…" He stopped, guzzling down his drink, as if to give him courage for what he was about to say.

"Go on," prompted Tony. He was curious where this discussion was leading. He wondered if his little sister had her hand in this pie also.

"Oh, you're the perfect gentleman, treating Melissa's friends like queens at first, with your undivided attention, your compliments, your smiles, always making them feel special. Just when they start falling in love with you, another girl comes into the picture, and you seem to lose interest in them. Then they run to Melissa for help…telling her all about it…then she comes to me, telling me what happened. You are probably doing that to Bonnie right now! She is not like the others, you know. She's got class and her father's so rich, he could buy your shipping business!"

Tony was disturbed at the description his friend gave of him. He heatedly said, "I did not treat Bonnie or any other of Melissa's friends like queens, as you say, and my compliments are not meant to make them fall in love with me! If it appears that I lose interest in them because another girl comes into the picture, it's because there was nothing there between us in the first place!"

"What about this new girl…what's her name…Ipatia? I saw how she looked at you the other day…and she looks like she could get hurt if you decided to dabble with her."

"Ipatia is not a topic for discussion! She's in a totally different class of people!" said Tony in a loud voice.

Ipatia quickly slipped back to her seat, trying to make sense out of all that she heard. She didn't know who to believe, Dr. Michael or Tony. One thing was clear; Tony's sister was in the middle of all of this.

Michael had never seen Tony so angry before. He quickly apologized. "Tony, I'm sorry if I offended you. I realize when I drink a little too much, I sometimes say things that may be offensive."

Tony forgave him instantly. He patted him on the back. "No, no, that's all right, Michael. I think I drank a little too much myself! We have been friends too long to let something like that get between us. Everything is all right. I think I'll call it a night."

Michael agreed with him, and the two separated on friendly terms. Tony went to his cabin and stayed there for the rest of the trip.

After some time, the horn sounded for Piraeus. Tony and his family were one of the first groups of people to get off the ferryboat. They were all tired and sleepy, and there wasn't much talking going on. Once on the dock, Tony obtained cabs for the group. The drivers began loading the luggage, with Tony's direction. Slowly, the members of the group disbanded. Mr. Daras was the first to leave. He appeared quiet, even upset about something. The next to leave was Bonnie, who looked sleepy and tired. She yawned as she waved to them. The third cab was busy getting the Plakis luggage into the trunk when Gregory pulled his son over to the side and talked quietly to him.

"Tony, what's the story with Christos' granddaughter?"

"I passed by earlier in the evening to see her, but she was sleeping. All I know is that she is in the third class and they haven't come out yet. I promised her grandfather to see her safely home."

Gregory appeared skeptical as he got into the taxicab. Christina and Melissa were already inside the cab, waiting for him. Christina peered out of the window and asked Tony if he was coming. He said he would come home later. He watched, as the cab sped onward, towards Kifissia. Michael stood next to him, silently waving to them as they left.

Tony said to Michael, "Now you better get home before your own family wonders about you!"

"Fine, fine. I'll be seeing you tomorrow then. Good-bye, good friend!"

After Michael left, Tony found a taxicab and began his search for Ipatia, driving around slowly, looking for a tall girl with a large, silly hat.

❦   ❦   ❦

The lady next to Ipatia nudged her, saying that they had arrived in Piraeus. Ipatia looked at her watch. It was already ten o'clock. She arose along with the couple and they stood in line with their belongings. There were several other people ahead of them, and many others more behind her, as they all waited for the door to open.

After what seemed like a long time, Ipatia finally stepped out of the doorway and into the cool, dark night, pulling the trunk behind her, feeling weak and tired. She had been standing for a long time in the line, waiting for the door to open. The shoes were pinching her feet, causing her to inch slowly down the narrow ramp. People behind her were pushing and juggling past her, making her lose her balance and fall forward.

"Watch out for the girl!" barked a man's voice. Several others clamored in unison.

Ipatia was caught by strong arms, and was forcefully lifted up and helped to walk down the rest of the ramp and over to the side, away from the crowd. Her trunk was placed next to her. She thanked the two men who helped her. They smiled back at her, asking her if she was all right. She nodded shyly, watching them go back to their families, disappearing into the dark night. The older couple, who had gone ahead, saw her and came to her side, asking her if she was all right. She thanked them, saying she was going to wait there for her aunt. They left in a taxicab after she assured them twice that she was all right.

Shivering from the cool evening, she slowly pulled the trunk away from the ship, away from the crowds of people. It would be easier to spot her aunt from a distance. She hugged herself as she sat on the trunk, looking around her, feeling somewhat lost. Her thirst, her tiredness were put aside as she began to concentrate on the people around her.

She strained her eyes, constantly searching for her aunt, trying to spot the tall, thin woman with a long face and short hair among the crowd. The flow of people continued to spew out of the ship, like a big tidal wave, going off in different directions. A big ramp resembling a mouth with wide jaws slowly opened. It was the avenue from which the cars and small trucks now drove out, one by one. She saw a taxicab roll to a stop in front of her, and Tony got out. Her heart started to beat faster. She thought he had already left. What should she do now?

"Ipatia, why are you still here? Wasn't your aunt supposed to come and pick you up?" asked Tony sharply. He didn't know whether to be happy or upset finding her there alone.

"I'm waiting for her. She is supposed to come and get me," she said, tightening up.

"It's late. I can take you to her house," he said, noticing her pale, drawn face. She looked so fragile, so young. He wanted to gather her in his arms and warm her. Yet there was determination stamped all over her face.

"No, thank you, for if she comes and I am not here, then she will be worried," she said, shaking her head.

Tony continued to insist that she leave with him, but she adamantly refused any assistance, explaining that her aunt was somewhere around there. He finally left her sitting stubbornly on her trunk, waiting. He shook his head. He had never seen a woman before turn him down like this. They always jumped at the chance to be with him. The girl was very stubborn, and that worried him. It could get in the way of her safety, particularly at this late hour. He began to think about what to do next. By the time he arrived home, he had a plan. He went directly to the small house adjacent to theirs, and pounded on the door. Tim, their chauffeur, had been with the family for over ten years. He would help him out.

❦   ❦   ❦

Ipatia's watch showed eleven o'clock. Maybe something had happened to her aunt. She was beginning to question if it was a good idea to have come without Mrs. Xilouris. *Maybe Grandfather was right after all. I should have stayed with him on the island. Now what am I going to do?* Sighing, she began to contemplate about getting a taxicab. At that moment, there was a tap on her shoulder.

"Are you Ipatia Kouris?"

She turned. It was a taxicab driver and his taxi was nearby. She nodded thankfully. Maybe her aunt had sent him.

"I am to take you to your Aunt Sophia," he said and briskly took her trunk, whisking it into the car. "Can you please give me her address?"

Ipatia dutifully produced the piece of paper with her aunt's address and read it aloud, thinking nothing of it. The driver nodded and they drove into the night. She settled in the cab, feeling relieved. Her aunt sent for her after all!

Finally, they stopped in front of her aunt's residence, the two-story house she used to live in.

The driver refused her money, saying it was already paid for. He followed her, remembering Mr. Tony's request not to leave until the girl had entered her aunt's house. She approached the door and knocked, but no one answered. She continued to knock, wondering why her aunt was not opening the door.

She thought for a moment and then turned to the cab-driver, her voice quavering, "Sir, who paid for this ride?"

Tim hesitated before answering. He had not expected her to ask.

"Mr. Tony Plakis, my boss," he finally admitted. "I am the chauffeur for the Plakis family, and Mr. Tony told me to come and pick you up and take you to your aunt's house."

"Oh!" Determined now, she dug inside her purse, pulling out some coins. "Sir, please take the money for the ride. I insist! And please tell your Mr. Tony that I can very well take care of myself!"

Tim took the money sheepishly. "Thank you, miss, but I have instructions to stay with you until you enter. I'm to help you with the trunk. Orders are orders."

He waited, while she continued to knock. After what seemed like several minutes of pounding, the door opened slightly. Ipatia cried out her aunt's name with joy and crumpled into her outstretched arms, having fainted from sheer exhaustion.

When Ipatia awoke, she was lying on a couch. She lifted herself up, then rubbed her eyes to see better. In front of her sat her aunt, talking quietly to the cab driver. Ipatia looked at her more carefully, realizing to her dismay that she was not her aunt.

"Is my aunt here?" asked Ipatia, looking around, wondering who this woman was.

"I'm sorry, dear child, but you see, she's not here. That is what I was explaining to the driver. I'm renting the downstairs apartment. My name is Marika. I know we look alike, and I understand how you mistook me for her, but please understand that she is not here."

"She's not here?" repeated Ipatia, feeling a rush of anxiety. Then without warning, she broke down, sobbing uncontrollably.

"Here, now don't cry, poor girl. Please don't cry," said Marika, wringing her hands together.

Ipatia's crying slowed down, and between sniffles, she asked, "How can I get a hold of her?"

"All I know is that she is in America and she'll be back in three weeks. She didn't mention that you were coming," replied Marika. "If it would help, you can stay here until she gets back."

"She's in America?" cried out Ipatia. Shocked at the news, she started sobbing again, not paying attention to what the woman was saying. A handkerchief was handed to her, and her tears slowly subsided.

"Miss, it will be all right. We will take care of you. My boss promised your grandfather that he would make sure you got safely to your aunt's, and he always keeps his promises!" replied Tim, taking responsibility for the girl.

Ipatia looked up at him, still in a daze. He helped her to her feet and down the stairs, back into the cab. She slept, as the cab sped along into the night.

"Miss, we are in Kifissia. We've arrived," announced Tim. Moments later, the car pulled to a stop.

Ipatia opened her eyes, seeing nothing but blackness all around her. She blinked, trying to refocus. Within moments she was able to decipher the white outline of a large villa. Yawning, she walked with Tim to the front door. Even through her tiredness, she could smell the soft scent of jasmine coming from somewhere. If only she could just sit down for a minute. She did not notice her legs giving way from under her and the ground rising up to meet her, for she had already faded away into a deep sleep.

CHAPTER 12

I sing with the birds a merry tune
Because I know I'll see you soon

Ipatia dreamt that her parents were alive and well, walking in a large, green pasture away from her and through an open door. She ran after them, but the door shut behind them. She tapped on the door and it opened, but instead of her parents, Tony was standing there, smiling down at her. Behind him was a room full of food, and the scent of warm bread. He was bending down to kiss her, when Ipatia awoke from the dream. Snuggling further in her bed, she buried her face into the pillow, trying to finish the dream, but to no avail. Tony had vanished, and she was left hugging the soft, fluffy pillow instead.

Her eyes fluttered open, greeted by the daylight.

"I'll be right there, Grandfather," she said, stretching lazily. There was no answer.

Suddenly realizing where she was, she bolted out of bed and lost her balance, landing on her left foot. She winced from the pain shooting up her foot, and sat down on the cold marble floor, rubbing her throbbing ankle. The Swiss cuckoo clock on the wall caught her attention as it chimed twelve o'clock. It took her a moment to realize that it was afternoon. Did she really sleep all this time?

She looked around and found the source of the scent. There was a small round table on the side of the room, laden with food. Someone must have just brought it in. The dream had been so real, as if Tony had been in the room just a minute ago, bending to kiss her. She blushed at the idea.

Her stomach growled in anticipation as she raised herself up, almost tripping on the large, white cotton nightgown she was wearing. She folded it around her body and limped towards the table.

There were thick slices of fresh bread, butter and jam, biscuits, two boiled eggs, cheese, and red plump grapes. A glass of milk also rested on the table, and nearby lay a folded note with her name on it. It was in English. "*Dear Ipatia, I hope you slept well. After you eat, please don't leave, for I wish to speak with you. Tony.*"

Her nervousness at seeing Tony again was overcome by her basic needs. She said her prayer, then gulped the warm milk down, her thirst overcoming her hunger. The breakfast was plentiful, as she ate it, thinking about what had happened last night. She drew a blank after she arrived at the Plakis house. Questions were beginning to form in her mind. Who undressed her and whose nightgown was she wearing? Who brought the food in this morning? Where was her aunt and why hadn't she written to let them know she was in America?

Afterwards, she found her trunk in front of the closet, with her purse lying on it. Then she picked up her black blouse and skirt. She wrinkled her nose. They needed a good wash. What else did she have to wear? She searched the trunk, pulling out a light blue silk dress her godmother had bought for her. She thought fondly of her godmother.

It was last year when Mrs. Tsatsikas asked her to go with her to Patmos, saying she needed help in deciding what to buy for a niece of hers. After they returned to the island, her godmother promptly gave it to her as a gift, saying that it was time for Ipatia to stop wearing black. Ipatia insisted that she should give it to her niece, but her godmother said that the dress was for her. She explained that she knew Ipatia would not have come if she had told her it was for her. Ipatia had agreed. The dress stayed in the trunk all this time, and even now, Ipatia had no inclination of wearing it.

But what else did she have to wear other than her work clothes? Everything else was too small on her! She looked at the dress once more, holding it up, stroking the fabric. She admitted it had a nice feel to it, and she remembered her godmother saying how well it fit her.

She needed to wash first. She looked around for the wash basin, but did not see any. It was probably in another room. Maybe they had a washroom, just like in Rhodes, where there were sinks and even bathtubs. She would have to venture outside of her room.

She attempted to put her shoes on. To her dismay, her shoe did not fit the now swollen foot. She searched in her trunk, and found a pair of sandals. That will do for now! Carrying her dress and clean underclothes in one arm, she opened her door and peeked out into the hallway. There was no one in sight. She decided to veer right, hobbling carefully down the grand hallway. There must be a washroom somewhere in this house! It was very quiet, except for the chiming of a clock coming from somewhere ahead.

"May I help you?"

Startled, she looked around and saw an older woman staring kindly at her from the well-lit kitchen. She was plump, with a blonde braid wrapped around her head, and was wearing an apron. She appeared to have been stirring something in a bowl.

"Hello. Who are you?" Ipatia asked.

There was a hearty chuckle, followed by a thick foreign accent. "I am Gilda, the housekeeper and this house belongs to the Plakis family. We were worried about you last night when you fainted, yah."

"I don't remember anything after I fainted."

"Yah, you fainted right there in front of the door, and the professor, I mean Mr. Tony, picked you up ever so gently and took you straight into my bedroom. As he was leaving, he asked me to take your clothes off and give you a nightgown. I hope you did not mind, but I had nothing to give you but one of my nightgowns. Miss Melissa was already asleep, so I couldn't ask her."

"Thank you, Gilda," said Ipatia, wrapping the nightgown around her body.

Gilda chuckled. "I know it is too big for you, but I had nothing smaller. Anyway, he also asked me to check you to make sure you didn't hurt yourself badly when you fell."

"Thank you for everything!"

"You are welcome, but I was only doing my job! You should thank the professor! He stayed up late just to make sure you arrived safely."

"Oh, that was kind of him! Is he here?" asked Ipatia, pulling her nightgown around her more protectively as she looked around. She didn't want to be seen in her nightgown.

"No, no, don't be afraid! He left a few minutes ago with Tim. He said he would not take long. There is no one else here but Miss Melissa, his sister, and she is upstairs in her room!"

"May I ask you something Gilda?"

"Yah!"

"Who made the breakfast"

"Why, was anything wrong?" asked Gilda, her eyes widening.

"Oh, no…everything was delicious!" said Ipatia, nervously. "Thank you very much for making it! I'm just not used to eating so much breakfast!"

"Yah, I did put a little more food on the tray because you looked like you could use it. There was a problem carrying it to your room. It was too heavy! So I asked the professor to help."

"What do you mean?"

"I asked him to carry it into your room."

"He did?" said Ipatia, feeling weak in the knees.

"Ah! Don't you worry! I knocked and checked to see if you were presentable first. You were still fast asleep when he brought the tray into your room," said Gilda, beaming broadly.

"Why is he called professor?"

"Oh, that's because he taught economics at the university in England!" said Gilda proudly. "Now his father wants him to manage the business because his father is too sick to do it himself." Her voice had dropped down to a whisper.

"His father is sick?" echoed Ipatia.

"Yah, I think it is serious, because today is Sunday and they usually go to church. This morning, I heard him tell Mrs. Christina that he wasn't feeling well, and they left immediately for the hospital in Athens," said Gilda, her eyes opening wide.

"Oh, I'm sorry to hear that," said Ipatia. She had rather liked Tony's father. "Who is this Mrs. Christina?"

"Why his second wife, of course," said Gilda. "Is there anything else that you will be needing?"

"Oh, yes. The only thing is that I need to wash."

"Why of course! How silly of me, talking to you like this and you standing there in nothing but a nightgown!" Gilda said. "Come, follow me to the study. That is the closest one here."

They went down the hallway, past several rooms, then stopped in front of two glass doors. Gilda opened the doors, and Ipatia immediately liked the large room. It was filled with sunlight, and had a beautiful Persian rug on the floor. Two tall windows with lace curtains allowed views of a flower garden and a glimpse of the verandah. In between the two windows stood a baby grand piano, filling her with a surge of happiness. A vase filled with cut flowers was on top of it. She wondered who played the piano in the family.

The wall to her left was lined with bookcases filled with all kinds of interesting looking books while the other wall boasted expensive oil paintings depicting different eras and different worlds. In the center of the room stood a large desk with a comfortable chair, and on the desk was a telephone.

Ipatia's eyes widened when she saw it. She knew that telephones were very difficult to come by, and people who requested them waited years to get one. She didn't know anyone else who had one in their homes, not even her aunt. There was only one telephone on the island. It was at the post office, and they charged a heavy price to use it. Maybe she could ask Mr. Tony if she could call her grandfather on the telephone.

Gilda pointed to a door on the right. "This is the washroom. I see you have your clothes with you, so feel free to take a bath. The towels are over there. I will have your other clothes washed later, but now I must get something out of the oven before it burns."

Ipatia thanked her, then stepped into the washroom. She looked around in awe, noticing that everything was white and spotless, even the alabaster white porcelain bathtub. It was almost as large as the bedroom she slept in last night. To her left, the entire wall was one large mirror. She turned on the water, then undressed. She stepped into the bathtub and slowly lowered herself into its inviting warmth. She shivered as she felt a breeze coming from somewhere. She looked up and saw a small window at the other end of the room, partially open. Oh well, she was not getting up to close it, not now!

She began humming, enjoying the warm, sudsy water. The humming turned into a song and she could hear the birds chirping outside, accompanying her. The water they used on the island was well water, and she could never get it warm enough like this.

Tony thanked Tim, then got out of the Mercedes. He had just returned from the hospital. He visited his father and talked with him briefly, then their conversation was interrupted by the nurses, who came in to see his father, so Tony didn't stay there long.

He walked out to the back of the house and sat out on the verandah, reading the newspaper. He heard someone singing from the house, and looked curiously in its direction. It couldn't be his sister. She never sang this cheerfully.

He stood up and walked slowly towards the house, trying to decipher where the song was coming from. His glance fell on the open window. He smiled. The music was coming from in there. Ipatia was awake. He stood quietly on the side, enjoying the gay music, enjoying the girl's infectious spirit. When the singing subsided, he strolled back to his chair and sat down, trying to resume his reading, but instead, his thoughts wandered towards the girl. He had spoken to his father about her and his father grudgingly said she could stay with them.

Ipatia stood up, gingerly stepping out of the bathtub. She dried her hair first, then her body vigorously with the large bath towel, humming softly. She studied herself in the mirror. She had never seen herself in a full-length mirror before. She smiled at her image. She was pleased to see that she was filling out nicely in all the right places. When she was done dressing, she looked at the mirror again, this time appreciating the dress, which made her look fuller and a little older. She touched the wet strands, combing her fingers through it. It would take awhile before it dried. Out in the hallway, she could hear female voices. She recognized Gilda's voice, but not the other woman's voice. That was probably Melissa.

Ipatia went to the piano and sat down on the bench, gazing out the window. A large jasmine bush faced the window. She opened the window, allowing the intoxicating sweet scent of the jasmine to fill the room. Then she sat on the bench, tapping her fingers gently on the keyboard. She didn't know what to do now. When was Mr. Tony coming back so they could talk? Hearing the sound of a car, she got up and looked out the window, trying to catch a glimpse. She could see Tim leaving with Melissa in the car. The house was quiet again.

The sun was pouring in from the open window, its warm rays inviting her to play. Content, she leafed through the sheets of music, picking a familiar Mozart piece. Her fingers played each note slowly at first. Within a few minutes, she had gained enough confidence to pick up speed and expertly weave the notes in a smooth succession. She was transported back in time to when she was seven years old again, happy and carefree. To a time when her parents were alive and she had felt loved. The last notes echoed in the room as her fingers rested on the keyboard. She was finally at peace.

CHAPTER 13

Love notes floated like the kiss
To plant themselves upon my lips

Ipatia searched through the sheets of music, looking for something else to play, when her keen ears picked up a movement behind her. She turned around and saw Tony sitting at the desk, studying her. She stood up quickly, knocking over the music.

"Ouch!" she exclaimed, wincing from the pain of her ankle. She sat back down on the bench.

"Sorry to have surprised you. The door was open and I couldn't resist coming in to see you play. Is everything all right with your foot?" asked Tony, standing up and coming towards her.

"I fell on it and it's a little swollen," she confessed, "but it will be fine."

He bent down to look, not noticing that she was blushing furiously. She had shapely legs, probably from all that running she did on the island. He touched her ankle gently.

She coughed slightly, almost giggling. "It's the other foot."

"Oh, yes, that's right," he said, slightly flushed. He stood up abruptly, standing very close to her. "It looks quite swollen. You probably should see a doctor. Meanwhile, you should stay off of it, if you can."

"Yes, sir," she said meekly, not knowing what to do, not able to tear her eyes away from his. Should she get up and leave, or sit there? She hadn't been used to being alone in a room with a young man before.

He picked up the music from the floor and placed it back on the piano, saying softly, "You play the piano very well, Ipatia. My congratulations on your fine performance."

"Thank you for the compliment," said Ipatia, smiling at his words of praise. It touched a deep chord when he said that. "Do you play?"

"I haven't played for a long time, but let me see now," he said, leafing through some music. "How about a little Beethoven. What do you say about Fur Elise?"

She nodded. "It's one of my favorite pieces."

He sat down on the bench next to her and rolled up his crisp white sleeves. Her playing had inspired something within him. He touched the keys softly at first, stroking them, caressing them, then more boldly he cruised through the music, his fingers moving fiercely.

Ipatia shut her eyes, enjoying the swelling and ebbing of the music. Her eyes fluttered open when she felt him touch her. He had leaned over, reaching for the low notes. The music ended, leaving the room filled with a fullness of spirit it didn't have before.

"Well, how did I do, maestro?" he asked huskily, his hands resting on the keyboard.

He gazed at her with an amused look, his half-closed eyes hiding his true feelings.

She stood up shakily, leaning against the wall. He was too close for comfort. Breaking the spell, she said impulsively, "You did very well except for the middle section. You need to practice it more often. It needs to flow, like ripples in the sea. My music teacher used to say that to me, for that is the most difficult passage in the piece."

He stood up, leaning towards her.

Ipatia tensed, for there was nowhere to go. He was blocking her path.

"It seems to me the most difficult passage has still to be lived," he whispered, before he planted a kiss on her lips. He lingered slightly, before moving back, enjoying it. *You can't run away this time, my Ipatia.*

She was caught off guard from the kiss. It was tender and soft, not demanding. It actually felt pleasant. *But it was not right! What am I to do now?*

"Why did you do that?" she managed to whisper, after she came back to earth.

He paused for a moment, battling with the idea of telling her the truth that she was beautiful, naïve, innocent, and adorable. That he wanted to kiss her from the very first moment, under the tree, when he held her close in his arms.

Instead, he studied her large, fascinating eyes. "I've been meaning to thank you for your beautiful gift, the cat's eye stone. The gemstone does change color, as you said. Ipatia, I can't help noticing, but your green eyes, they're a different color now, almost hazel."

"You didn't have to thank me with a kiss!" she scolded lightly. "I mean, you don't kiss men when you want to thank them, do you?"

He stepped back, laughing at her rebuttal. Then a thought occurred to him. "Ipatia, you have never been kissed by a man before, have you?"

She shook her head defiantly, fighting back the tears. He was treading too closely into her personal life.

"How old are you?"

Ipatia blinked. She wasn't used to men asking her this question. It was bold of him to ask! But then, this wasn't an ordinary man! She regained her courage, and straightening herself up, looked him squarely in the eyes. "First of all, thank you for the nice compliments, Mr. Tony. However, where I come from, it's considered impolite for a man to kiss a girl before they are engaged, and even more impolite to ask a girl her age!"

"Mia culpa!" he said. Stepping back further, he bowed his head slightly.

At that moment, Ipatia took the opportunity to move away from his reach, cautiously at first, then more boldly, limping away, limited by the soreness coming from her ankle. She wasn't about to stay around and fence with this man, for she felt herself dangerously lapsing further and further away from her upbringing every time she was near him.

"I don't know what that means, but I do think you are taking advantage of my situation!" she retorted.

"Ipatia, I assure you, my intentions up until now have been purely philan-thropic," he said, sensing she was slipping away from him again. He carefully chose his next words. "I apologize if I offended your sensitivities. In the future, you can rest assured that I will not get closer than a foot from you."

"Thank you!" she said, trembling now.

"Now, regarding your stay here," he said, pacing the room. "I understand your aunt is to return in three weeks?"

"Yes, that is what the renter said," she replied.

"I spoke with Father, and we agreed that you could stay here the three weeks," he said, stopping briefly at the window to gaze outside, his back to her. There was silence. He turned to look at her, waiting for her response

She paused. Before his kiss, she would have been eager to accept his offer. All she could picture now was having to fence daily with his affections. Could she maintain her distance? *But you have nowhere else to go!*

"Thank you," she managed to say. "Is your father here so I can thank him also?"

"Actually, he went to the hospital this morning because he wasn't feeling well," admitted Tony. "I just returned not too long ago from visiting him."

"Oh, I'm sorry to hear that he is in the hospital," said Ipatia, recalling Gilda's words earlier that morning. "I would like to speak with my grandfather first before I give you my answer."

"That will be fine. If there is a telephone on the island, we can call there," he said stiffly.

Ipatia said, "Yes, there is! Grandfather gave me the telephone number to the post office! I have it in my purse. I'll go get it!" With that, she quickly limped out the door.

Tony watched her leave the room. He wondered if he should have a doctor look at her foot first before they did anything else. He was curious about her age. Although she had the beginning signs of breasts and hips, she lacked the social graces of a young lady. She was impulsive, stubborn as a mule, and so shy, she blushed every time he talked to her! How many young ladies did he know who swung around in trees yelling for help, then ran away from their rescuer? *You're only upset because she asked you not to kiss her!*

Then he shook his head, smiling. She looked and acted young, yet there was a part of her that he had seen come shining through that showed glimpses of an older, gentler, kinder Ipatia. Besides, her grandfather did say she should be thinking about marriage and not about books.

Then he remembered how he felt like a schoolboy today, entering her bedroom with the food tray and going over to her bed, curious to get a glimpse of her. The image of her peaceful, angelic face with the golden curls billowing around her was still fresh in his memory. Enchanted by her beauty, he gazed down at her, tempted to steal a kiss, but when she stirred, he withdrew quickly. His own heart had raced as he left, for he thought he had heard her speak out his name.

From now on, you should be more careful around the girl. Let's face it, you are used to older, more sophisticated women, making the first moves, falling in love with you, encouraging your kisses. To them, it is just a game. You have no experience with young, naïve girls! To her, a kiss is probably just as good as a proposal for marriage!

❀   ❀   ❀

Ipatia returned shortly, handing him a piece of paper with the telephone number on it.

Tony read the number. "Why don't we go and make the call now?"

"He doesn't usually go down to the post office except in the mornings."

"Let's see now…how about we arrange for him to be there tomorrow morning…around nine thirty?"

"Yes, that's a good idea! I know he's down at Mr. Pericles' coffee shop by nine o'clock, so it wouldn't be much of an effort to go to the post office from there, and…" Ipatia stopped, appearing thoughtful. "I forgot to ask…how much will it cost?"

"Don't worry about it." Tony laughed as he dialed the telephone number. He talked to the person there, arranging for them to let Christos know about the telephone appointment. "Now that we've taken care of that, we can't do much until tomorrow. Would you mind joining me for a cup of coffee outside on the verandah? It's as pretty as the view you get from your home, I guarantee it," he ventured.

Ipatia was still feeling excited about the prospect of speaking to her grandfather and said impulsively, "Yes, I mean, I don't know! It all depends what you meant by mea copa…or whatever that was!"

"I thought you would ask," he said, chuckling, thoroughly amused. "But where I come from, it's impolite for a girl to ask!"

Ipatia blushed, realizing he was fencing again.

"No, seriously, Mia Culpa means my mistake, or in other words, forgive me," he replied.

"Oh!" she replied, liking the explanation.

She limped alongside him down the hallway. They had reached her room. "Will you excuse me for a moment? I have something to do first, then I will meet you in a little while outside."

He looked at her for a moment, then nodded graciously and left.

Ipatia slipped into her room, catching her breath. This man was going too fast for her! She clutched the slip of paper and sat down on the bed, thinking about everything that had happened. She wasn't used to spending so much time alone with a young man, and on top of it, being kissed! *Ipatia, you have not been heeding your grandfather's advice. The reason why this young man took these liberties is because you were talking too boldly with him there in the studio, encouraging his advances! Remember what Grandfather said about conversing with young men! You should be ashamed of yourself!*

❦   ❦   ❦

Tony stopped at the kitchen and looked inside. "Gilda? Oh…there you are. Can you please bring two coffees and a few pastries out to the verandah?"

"Yah, professor!" said Gilda, smiling broadly. "I want to let you know that Miss Melissa told me that she and Dr. Michael will be here for dinner at six o'clock."

"Thank you for telling me. Please make sure there is ample food and that the table is set."

"Will the young girl be joining you for dinner?"

"I assume she will. Go ahead and set an extra plate for her anyway. Also, chances are that Ipatia might be remaining here for three weeks, so you will also need to get her moved into the guest bedroom before you leave today."

"She is staying here? Oh no! Today I leave for my vacation! The new house-keeper will not be here until tomorrow. Who will take care of her until then? Miss Melissa will be leaving after dinner with Dr. Michael to go and visit his family. They plan to stay there overnight, and Mrs. Christina will be staying in the Athens hotel close to your father. There will be no one else here!"

"I forgot about your vacation," he said, rubbing his forehead. "I didn't know Melissa was going to Michael's home either."

"Besides, you are a single man, no? She is only a girl. It is not good for the girl to be alone here in this house with you. What if her parents find out?"

"She has no parents. She has only a grandfather who is living in Lipsi Island. So there is no one else for her right now. We are her family for the moment, until we figure out how to get her to her aunt."

"Oh, how sad! The poor girl has no family! Tsk, tsk," said Gilda. "Maybe I can see if my niece Olga can come and stay over tonight."

"Gilda, you are a gem!" said Tony, pecking her on the cheek. He whistled as he went out to the verandah.

Ipatia was sitting on her bed, when she heard a knock on the door. "Come in."

Gilda peeked in the room. "Miss Ipatia, the professor told me that you will be staying tonight. I will take you now to another room because the new housekeeper will be coming tomorrow and she will be staying in this room."

"A new housekeeper? Are you leaving?"

"Yah, I will be leaving for my trip tonight. I will be gone four weeks. I will ask my niece, Olga, to come and stay over for the night, in case you need anything. Please come with me, and don't worry about anything."

Ipatia followed her slowly down the hallway. They went past the kitchen and turned down into another hallway, going towards the entranceway. At the front lobby stood a great stairway that wound upstairs to the second floor. She looked around her in awe. There were marble floors and white columns in the doorways, and busts of Greek statues everywhere, and beautiful paintings on the walls. They continued down another hallway and finally they stopped in front of a door.

"Here we are. This is the guestroom and is even bigger and nicer than my room, Yah?" said Gilda, smiling, as she opened the door. A stream of sunlight met them, bathing the room in the early afternoon glow.

"It's very beautiful!" exclaimed Ipatia. She had never witnessed so much beauty and elegance in a bedroom before. There was even a private washroom!

"I heard you playing the piano. How nice it was having the house full of music again! And you play very well, too!" Gilda's face had a joyful expression as she clasped Ipatia's hands together.

"Thank you, Gilda," said Ipatia. The sound of the cuckoo clock chimed. It was four o'clock.

"There I go again, talking, and there is so much work to do!" said Gilda, shaking her head and waving her hands in the air. "Oh, Mr. Tony said to tell you that he is waiting for you outside. I will bring out some coffee and pastries in a minute."

Gilda left a breeze behind her as she swooshed out of the room, her plump body moving surprisingly swiftly down the hallway.

Ipatia was feeling better already. The room was cheerful and large, with elegant gold drapes over white lace curtains that graced the two large windows. A Persian rug covered the cool marble floor and there were paintings on the wall. A beautiful crystal vase, filled with flowers, sat atop a white dresser. The bed had a satin ivory bedspread on it with intricate embroidery that resembled two large, colorful birds.

She limped towards the window and looked outside. It overlooked the large verandah that boasted several pots of beautiful flowers and life-size, marble Greek statues. Beyond, she could see a glimpse of the sea. Tony was sitting to the side, appearing to be alone at the table, reading a newspaper. He looked like he was deep in thought.

She slowly made her way outside, following the path that led to the back verandah. She would have normally enjoyed the walk, savoring the scents and beautiful array of flowers, but her foot was hurting every time she pressed on it.

To her relief, Tony was still there. He looked up in surprise at her arrival.

"I thought you had changed your mind," he said, brightening up at her appearance.

Behind her came Gilda, carrying the tray and placing it on the table.

Ipatia said, "Gilda came and took me to the guest bedroom! It is a very beautiful room!"

"I'm glad you like it. I hope you can stay the three weeks so you can enjoy it more," said Tony, his eyes smiling.

"Thank you for your hospitality, but I do need to speak with Grandfather first, to see what he will say," she replied, suddenly feeling shy again.

CHAPTER 14

You talked about your life to me
It opened possibilities

Tony didn't say anything. Instead, he handed her a cup of warm coffee. She sipped it quietly, enjoying the chirping of the birds among the peaceful setting. Just behind Tony, she could see steps leading down to the large swimming pool area. Next to the pool was a tennis court. Tall cypress trees surrounded the pool and tennis area, providing a private setting. Beyond, the land sloped downward, lending a spectacular panoramic view of Athens.

Ipatia had resolved not to be the first to start a conversation with him, very much aware of and nervously anticipating, what the young man sitting across from her was going to say or do next.

Tony sensed the girl's nervousness and continued reading his newspaper, appearing absorbed in the news. *You must remember to maintain a respectable stance so she can feel comfortable with you.*

"I can't believe it!" he exclaimed unexpectedly. He just read about a possible merger between Chuck Daras and Meriklis, who was Bonnie's father. Meriklis was a supermarket tycoon. Wasn't Daras supposed to have worked some deal with his father? He would have to tell Father about this.

"What is it?" Ipatia asked, looking at the back of the paper, her curiosity piqued.

"What?" he asked. He folded the newspaper, trying to compose himself. He was upset at losing his temper in front of the girl. He typically did not overreact like this. *Is it because you want to talk to her but don't know what to say after that scene in the study?* Ipatia repeated her question.

"Oh, well, the news is always the same, either there is a scandal, or someone dies, or someone buys someone else's business," said Tony, more calmly. He leaned back against his chair, pondering on the news, then caught the girl staring at him.

"My grandfather used to say the same thing."

He smiled, struck by her innocent beauty. "Ipatia, let's talk about something more pleasant."

"What do you mean?" she asked, becoming nervous again.

"For one thing, where were you born, and how is it you ended up on that island with your grandfather?"

Ipatia's eyes moistened, as deep emotions, evoked from his question, came to the surface. Taking a moment to compose herself, forgetting her prior resolution not to speak, she said, "First of all, I was born in America."

"You were?" he asked, arching an eyebrow.

"Yes, it is a fact. My father had gone to America, to a city called Baltimore, on one of his trips, hauling cargo. My mother went with him. It was not unusual for her to travel with him, but this time, she was a little over seven months pregnant and my father thought it was not such a good idea for her to come. She insisted, saying she felt well enough for the trip. Somehow, something triggered her to start her labor pains the same time the ship was docking at the harbor in Baltimore. She was taken immediately to the hospital, where I was born two hours later. Because I was a premature baby, I had to remain in the hospital for more than six weeks there. I had to have special equipment to keep me alive."

"Is that so? How did you get back to Greece?" asked Tony, trying to picture this healthy looking girl as a tiny, premature baby.

"My father had to leave with his ship, so he left us behind until I was able to travel. My mother and I flew back to Greece by airplane." She continued her story, including the time when her father surprised her on her fifth birthday with a piano, and how she took piano lessons for three years, but they were stopped once she went to Lipsi island.

"Yes, I'm amazed at how well you played the piano," he said. He was about to say something, then hesitated. "Now what made you want to learn English?"

"My parents called me "Amerikanaki", which was a pet name they gave me for being born in America," she said, smiling fondly. "Because of that, I had a natural interest in learning English. When the opportunity came, I took it. Mrs. Rodos, a friend of the family, lived down the road from us in Piraeus and taught English. One day, when she was visiting our house, she saw that I was interested in learning English and offered to give me lessons. She is the one who gave me the English novel as a present."

Ipatia went on. When she was eight years old, they visited her grandfather on the island that summer. She had a wonderful time, playing with her friends and going to many picnics. They and several other families rode their donkeys to other parts of the island, spending the day swimming, playing, and eating.

Ipatia remembered when she had gone with her mother and a group of other women to look for sea urchins. The women laughed and joked, pulling up their skirts as they waded into the water, searching for the dark, spiky creatures, pulling them out and throwing them into the baskets. Ipatia's mother told her that the black sea urchin was the poisonous one, and to avoid them. She wrinkled her nose, preferring to sit on the side, reading a book instead.

Ipatia continued, "I also remembered the crowds of people that visited the island in late August, for the Theotokos holiday. They flocked to see the Virgin Mary's icon inside the church named Virgin of Haron and—."

"Many churches have such icons," interrupted Tony.

"Yes, but this one was different," replied Ipatia. "This icon shows the Virgin Mary holding Jesus on the Cross. It is the only one of its kind. Many years ago, around the 1940's, a young woman prayed to this icon and placed some lilies on the icon as a gift, and it remained there even after it lost its bloom. The following year, the withered flower blossomed and gave off a beautiful fragrance…it was during the third week in August, around the twenty-third day. My parents used to say it was a miracle. It continues to blossom every year on this day."

"Hmm, every year?" asked Tony, lifting his eyebrows, feeling amused. "Are you sure those are the same lilies?"

"It is true!" insisted Ipatia, unshaken by his teasing tone. "The lilies are encased within the glass of the icon, so they cannot be touched. If you would have come a week earlier to our island, you would have seen it for yourself!"

"Sorry that I missed it. I would like to see it sometime," said Tony, thoughtfully. She appeared to be quite serious about it. "What happened after that?"

"During the festivities, my father received news from a relative visiting from Crete. My father's father, who lived in Crete, had a severe stroke and was lying in bed on the verge of dying," she said. Her voice was beginning to tremble. "My parents left immediately for Crete, leaving me behind with Grandfather. They felt it best that I did not go along. I remember crying because my parents had left. A few weeks later we learned that their ship was caught in a storm at sea and had sunk…there were no survivors."

Ipatia stopped, suddenly feeling sad. She looked away, blinking back her tears. *There, you did it again. You talked too much! Yes, but this time he didn't take advantage of you.*

At that moment, there was the sound of heels clicking on the pavement. Ipatia turned and saw Melissa approaching them, behind her were Michael and Bonnie. Ipatia stood up quickly to leave. "I'm feeling somewhat tired. I'd like to go lie down for a little while."

"Please stay for a few minutes more. I want Michael to take a look at your foot, if that's all right with you," said Tony softly, touching her arm before standing up to greet the group.

"Hi, Tony!" said Melissa, kissing him lightly on the cheek. "We just came back from visiting Father. He's expecting you tonight. He said he had something to tell you. It's about business."

"Oh?" he replied quietly. "Hello, Michael! Hello, Bonnie."

Ipatia stood there, greeting them with a shy smile. She knew everyone in the group and was curious that no one seemed surprised to see her. Was it possible that Melissa, having learned the news about her from Gilda, wasted no time in telling it to Michael and Bonnie? Ipatia sat back down, while the group stood around talking.

Tony went inside and instructed Gilda to bring more drinks and refreshments outside. Then he called Michael into the house to help him bring more chairs out to the terrace.

"How is it going with Ipatia?" asked Michael curiously, as he picked up a chair.

Tony was surprised by his friend's question. It wasn't like him to show interest in women. "She fell on her foot today and it appears swollen. She hasn't seen a doctor yet."

"I shall take a look at it then," said Michael promptly. They approached the table and placed the chairs down.

"Ipatia, Dr. Michael knows about your swollen foot and would like to examine it," said Tony, making it a point to sit next to her.

She blushed, not feeling comfortable at being examined publicly She shifted herself to the side, exposing her foot as Dr. Michael bent down to take a look.

Michael picked up her swollen foot, making her wince as he examined it. "How did it happen?"

"When I woke this afternoon, I had forgotten where I was…and got up out of bed quickly, landing on my foot."

"I can't tell for sure if it is sprained or fractured," he said. "It has to be x-rayed, just in case." He slowly lowered her foot. "Melissa, is Tim available tomorrow?"

"Yes, my love, but I've already made plans for him to take me shopping tomorrow," said Melissa quickly.

Ipatia's ears perked up when she heard Melissa addressing Dr. Michael in that fashion. She looked at Melissa, then Dr. Michael. Yes, there seemed to be something more personal than a friendship here.

"Oh, well then, Tony, how about your car?" Michael asked.

"I suppose I can use it tomorrow, since it will be Monday. It's in the shop, though, so I'll need Tim to drop me off first thing in the morning. Is that all right, Melissa?" Tony asked, looking at Melissa with an amused expression.

"I'm sure he can squeeze some time in there," she remarked dryly.

Tony noticed the puzzled look on Ipatia's face. "Here, the general population can only drive on certain days of the week because of the air pollution. Michael, on the other hand, doesn't have that restriction...because as a doctor, he can drive any day of the week he chooses."

Michael smiled at Tony's friendly jab. "Good, then stop by the main hospital in Athens, first thing in the morning, and get the foot x-rayed. I'll have given the orders by then. Then come by my office afterwards."

Gilda arrived just then with another tray of refreshments, placing them down on the table.

"Meanwhile, it would help if you put some ice on it to take the swelling down. Try to stay off of it," said Dr. Michael.

"What time would you be able to see her tomorrow?" asked Tony, standing up.

"Anytime is fine with me," said Michael, also standing up.

Melissa crossed her arms, appearing upset. "My love, don't forget we need to shop for the engagement rings tomorrow."

"Oh, yes, I completely forgot," said Michael, wincing at the reminder. He turned towards Tony. "Why don't you have Ipatia come in the morning then?"

"She'll be there," said Tony, nodding.

"Thank you, Dr. Michael, Mr. Tony. Will you all please excuse me? My foot is hurting a little, and I'd like to go and rest it," said Ipatia, getting up to leave.

"Here, Miss Ipatia. Take my hand and I'll walk with you," said Gilda, protectively offering her arm. The two walked away slowly, entering the house. Gilda helped Ipatia settle in her bed. "You lie down and rest. The doctor said to put some ice on your foot, yah? I'll go and get some for you." She returned with a bowl of ice and a towel. She wrapped the ice in the towel and placed it on Ipatia's foot.

"Ahh, thank you, Gilda. That feels nice."

"Will you be joining them for dinner?"

"No, thank you. I just want to rest now."

"I will be leaving right after dinner. I am going on my vacation. My niece, Olga, said she could come by later and see if you need anything. I hope your foot gets better."

Gilda was gone before Ipatia could say anything.

🍁   🍁   🍁

Ipatia rested in bed, thinking about what happened today and how she felt being with Tony. She smiled at the picture of her sitting with him out on the verandah, talking about herself. He appeared interested, gazing at her with his large, chocolate-brown eyes and prompting her with questions. Without realizing it, she had disclosed so much of her life to him, feeling comfortable for the first time with him.

She arose to get writing paper from her trunk. She poured her thoughts into her writing, describing her feelings about Tony. When she was finished, she read the poems, enjoying the flow of feelings revealed in them. Tucking the papers carefully back in the trunk, she rested once more on the bed. The sun was setting and there was a rich glow in the room. She was beginning to feel drowsy and her eyes closed. She fell into a light sleep, feeling the breeze from the window and the sound of the birds chirping cheerfully outside. It felt so peaceful.

A knocking on the door aroused her, followed by a woman's voice. "Hello? Hello? I am Olga," she said, opening the door. She was a younger version of Gilda, except that her dark blonde hair was shoulder length.

"You are Gilda's niece?" Ipatia asked, watching her place a tray of food on the table.

"Yes, and you are Ipatia, the young lady that my aunt talked about," said Olga cheerfully, looking the girl over.

"Will you be staying here during the time your aunt is on vacation?"

"Oh, no! I am only here for tonight. Someone else is coming tomorrow," said Olga, shaking her head emphatically. "I work in a beauty salon, and have to be at work early tomorrow morning by seven thirty."

"You do? What do you do?"

"Oh, everything," began Olga, sounding important. She described the work she did as an apprentice, and how she had plans one day to open her own beauty salon.

"That is very interesting, Olga! I wish you the best of luck!"

"Thank you!"

Ipatia looked over at the tray. The roasted lamb and potatoes were making her feel hungry.

"Well, I will leave you then, so you can eat," Olga said going to the door.

"No, wait! Why don't you join me for dinner?" asked Ipatia, desperate for some company.

"Thank you, but I ate already. I can just sit here and keep you company, though."

Ipatia got up out of bed and hobbled to the small table. She said her prayer and began to eat.

Olga studied her quietly for a moment. "You know, Miss Ipatia, you could use a hair cut. The style now is much shorter, and although it'll make you look a little older, it will make you look more sophisticated."

"You think so?" asked Ipatia, remembering how Mrs. Tsatsikas had tried to convince her to cut her hair before the trip, but she had stubbornly resisted.

"Yes, I'm quite sure. I have my cutting shears with me. I can do it, if you'd like."

"Thank you, Olga, but you see…I've always had my hair long. I wouldn't know how to handle it if it was short!"

"Why not? It's less work and easier to comb. Even if you don't like it, it'll grow back again!"

So it was settled. Shortly after Ipatia's dinner, Olga went and retrieved her shears and comb and started snipping Ipatia's curls. In no time, Ipatia's long tresses were on the floor and Olga was finishing the last touches.

"There, I hope you like it," said Olga, giving her a mirror to look at.

Ipatia gazed at herself in the mirror with mixed feelings. She was used to her long hair, but on the other hand, Olga had been right, her short hair bobbed around her face, making her look older. She couldn't decide if she liked this haircut.

"In case you don't like it, I brought you a scarf that you can put on," said Olga, half-joking as she retrieved it from her pocket and gave it to her.

"That was very thoughtful of you," laughed Ipatia. She unfolded the scarf, admiring the bright colors "How can I repay you?"

"Don't you worry about that! If anyone asks you about your hair, send them to me," said Olga, taking the tray with her tools and going to the door. "Just to remind you, I will be staying in my aunt's room for the night, in case you need anything. The new housekeeper is supposed to arrive tomorrow morning. Otherwise, have a good night."

❦   ❦   ❦

That evening, right after dinner, Melissa and Michael excused themselves, intent on leaving.

"Melissa what are your plans for the night?" asked Tony.

"I'll be visiting Michael's family and should be back in the morning. Michael has appointments tomorrow and I have shopping to do."

Tony nodded, bidding the couple farewell as they left.

"I must be going also," said Bonnie. "Now that you will be staying here in Greece, I hope we'll be seeing more of each other."

Tony walked at a leisurely pace with her towards the entranceway of the house, his hands in his pockets, thinking about what to say to her. She was being sticky and he was beginning to feel annoyed with her. "Bonnie, the reason I decided to stay here is because my father is too ill to run the business."

Bonnie was silent as they walked outside. Tim got out of the family car and opened the car door for her. "My car is parked across the street," she explained to him. She turned and glared at Tony. "I hope your decision wasn't swayed by that island girl who is staying here!"

She was gone before Tony could reply, her heels clicking angrily down the driveway and out into the street. He stood there, staring at her retreating figure, stung by her toxic remark, yet admitting silently there was some truth in what she said. "Tim, I need you to drop me off at the hospital to visit Father." He got into the car, feeling miserable. In two days, two women had been cross with him. He was not used to this. It was getting to be too much to handle.

When he entered his father's room, he found him sleeping. Christina was sitting by his side, reading a magazine.

"How is everything with Father?" asked Tony. He pulled up a chair next to her.

"They gave him some medication to help him sleep. He's still been complaining of those spells," she said quietly.

"Do they know what is wrong with him?"

"No, not yet. They will be running a series of tests on him. He's supposed to have a needle biopsy done tomorrow to see what it is."

"Oh. So they still don't know what he has yet. Do you know how long he'll be here?"

"No, they haven't decided that either. I'd rather have him here for the time being, so he doesn't hurt himself," she said, shrugging.

"Good idea. Melissa said he was upset about something and wanted to see me?"

She paused. "He received a business call this morning, and did seem upset afterwards, but did not tell me anything about it."

"I can talk to him tomorrow when I visit him again."

"He'll be disappointed that you came and he was asleep. He did want to talk to you."

"That's all right, it's better that he gets well."

"When you come tomorrow, it would be best to come in the late morning, after they've done the biopsy. You can also talk to the doctors then if you have any questions."

Tony stayed awhile longer, hoping to speak with his father, but he did not wake up, so Tony returned home.

CHAPTER 15

Two gentlemen spent time with me
I wonder where all this will lead

The next morning, Ipatia woke up to the sound of birds chirping outside her window. She rubbed her eyes, then stretched. Her thoughts turned to yesterday's events. She smiled dreamily, remembering Tony's kiss. *Ipatia, you stop those thoughts right now! It was wrong of him to kiss you.* Then she straightened up and pulled the covers away from her body. She was about to get out of bed, then remembered her foot. It was still swollen, but not as much as yesterday. How foolish she had been to jump out of bed yesterday.

The knocking on the door interrupted her thoughts. Her heart jumped. What should she do if it was Tony bringing the tray? She did not want to be exposed. She scrambled under the covers and pulled them up to her chin. "Come in!"

"Good morning, Miss Ipatia. I am Soula, the cook, with your breakfast," said Soula. She was a friendly, middle-aged woman, with sturdy arms strong enough to carry the heavy breakfast tray into the room.

"Good morning, Soula."

"I hope I didn't wake you up, but Miss Olga told me before she left this morning that you would be wanting your meal early."

"Thank you," said Ipatia, smiling and sitting up in bed, feeling special. "Is anyone else awake?"

"Oh, you mean Mr. Tony? I think he left with Tim earlier this morning, and Miss Melissa still hasn't come back," said Mrs. Soula, as she left the room. "Enjoy your meal, Miss Ipatia!"

There was no note today on the tray. Ipatia felt slightly disappointed, secretly hoping Tony would have written again. She ate her breakfast, thinking about how she was going to call Grandfather if Tony didn't show up. Moments later, there was a knock on her door again.

Ipatia's heart started racing again. *It might be Mr. Tony.* But it wasn't. It was the new housekeeper, Mrs. Katina. She was a thin, nervous woman.

"Miss Ipatia, would you be needing anything?" she piped.

"No, thank you. Everything is fine."

Once Ipatia said that, Mrs. Katina appeared relieved and excused herself, saying she was very busy, since she was new and trying to get everything in order.

At nine thirty, Ipatia limped towards the study, wondering if Tony was going to show up. She found the double doors already open and peeked inside.

The study was empty. She perused the bookshelf, looking through books, waiting for Tony. Her grandfather would probably just have to wait for her call. She heard footsteps coming quickly down the hallway. She put the book back and went towards the desk.

"Good morning, Ipatia, sorry I'm late," said Tony, walking briskly into the study. "I had to pick up my car." He stopped in his tracks when he saw her, surprise written all over his face. "What happened to your hair?"

Ipatia touched her curls, remembering her haircut. "Oh, uh, Gilda's niece, Olga cut my hair. She said it was the style now."

"I liked it better long. You shouldn't be influenced so easily by other people," he said curtly.

She blushed. "We had an engagement to call my grandfather, didn't we?"

"Yes, we did," he said, clearing his throat. "Before you telephone him, I would like to remind you that you are more than welcome to stay here. Melissa will be back today, so you can tell that to your grandfather. Here, let me dial for you."

She handed him the paper with the telephone number on it.

After he finished dialing, he picked up a book from a shelf and walked out of the study.

"Hello, this is Ipatia Kouris. Is my grandfather there?"

"One minute, please," said a young man's voice.

"Ipatia, my girl…how are you?" asked her grandfather. His voice was shaky from emotion.

Ipatia was glad to hear his voice. She told him the news. When she finished, she asked him, "What should I do? Should I remain here?"

"I'm sorry that things turned out this way. If I had only known your aunt would not be there! How stupid of me to send you off without making sure she was there! Listen to me now and try to remember everything I say to you. There is a cousin of ours by the name of George Mastroyiannis. He lives in a suburb of Piraeus with his family—"

"Oh, yes! Isn't he the one who visited us a couple of times with his wife Paula? They had invited us to visit them, hadn't they?" she asked, interrupting her grandfather.

"Yes, and that's what you will try and do, my girl. I don't know if they will be there, though, because they travel a lot, but at least give it a try," he said. "Now, get a pen and paper, because I am going to give you their address. If they are willing to have you, gather your belongings and go and stay there until your aunt arrives."

She wrote down the address. "What if they aren't there or cannot take me in?"

"Then so be it. You will have to stay with the Plakis family," he said. "Let me know what happens. By the way, give my greetings to your cousins if you see them, and to Mr. Tony and his family."

"I will do that. How are things there?"

"Fine, fine. We all miss you, and everyone's been asking about you," he replied. His voice was beginning to soften.

They talked a few more minutes. Grandfather had seen Mrs. Xilouris and her son in church the other day. As far as he could see, the boy was doing very well, and she made it a point to stop and ask him about Ipatia. Mrs. Tsatsikas and her family were helping grandfather out, and often, he would find a plate of food, covered with a cloth, left at his doorstep. They all sent Ipatia their love. Her grandfather then sternly reminded her to behave like the good girl that she was and not to talk too much in the presence of Mr. Tony.

"We don't want them thinking our girls from the island are too bold," he said. "Now I must say good-bye because there are others here that need to use the telephone."

Ipatia made her tearful farewell. She went into the hallway and found Tony waiting there, leaning against the wall, reading the book.

"How did it go?" he asked, studying her closely.

"My grandfather has a cousin who lives somewhere in Piraeus and he gave me his address. I am to go and see if they could take me in," she said, trying to sound cheerful.

"Oh?" asked Tony. He looked somber. "Well, just know that you are always welcome to stay here. Meanwhile, don't forget, you have an appointment to see the doctor first."

"Yes. Is it possible to ask you one more favor?"

"What is it?"

"Can we stop afterwards and check on my cousins?"

"I think we can manage that."

As they drove down the road, Ipatia noticed a bus stopped ahead at a bus stop.

"Where does that bus go?" she asked curiously.

"It goes all the way to the docks in Piraeus," said Tony, pointing in the general direction. "Why?"

"I was just curious," she replied. She remained quiet after that, looking at the scenery, mindful of how masterfully he drove. She realized they had been quite high up on a hill, for the winding road led them slowly down its slope, past beautiful large villas with spacious properties.

Tony pointed towards the city of Athens below them. "We are going down there."

She gazed down at the famous city, with its cluttered tall buildings, busy streets and busy way of life, so different from Lipsi Island's slower pace. They went to the hospital in Athens first, to get her ankle x-rayed. Tony guided her to the right department. After what seemed like a long time, she was finally finished. He drove her to Dr. Michael's building next, not far away from the hospital. The lobby felt cool with its marble floors as they entered the building. The office was located on the first floor. Tony held the door open for her as she limped into the office.

Dr. Michael came out of the examining room and greeted them. "Ipatia's x-ray results have not been given to me yet. I hope you don't mind, but it might be awhile before the results are in."

"In that case, is it all right if I leave her here and come back later for her?" asked Tony. "Ipatia, can you call home when you are done here?"

"Yes, but I don't have the telephone number."

"Michael has the number," he said, before leaving. "I will have to excuse myself, for I need to do some errands."

After Tony left, Dr. Michael excused himself and went into his office, saying he needed to place some calls to patients. The waiting room was empty, and Ipatia caught herself yawning. She noticed several medical journals lined up on a bookshelf. She picked one up to read. Patients came and went as she continued her reading. Time passed, and she was beginning to feel hungry. Shortly thereafter, Dr. Michael came out into the waiting room and asked her to come into his office.

"I have good news, Ipatia. The films show you don't have any breaks in any of the bones in your foot," he said, smiling at her. "You'll be back to normal in no time."

"Dr. Michael, you don't know how happy that has made me!" she exclaimed, her face radiating with joy.

Michael smiled back at her in a whimsical manner. Her reaction was so much like that of a child, that he felt her happiness.

At that moment, a patient entered the waiting room.

Ipatia asked if she could call Tony. She followed Dr. Michael into his office, where he dialed the number for her. He excused himself before going out to examine the patient.

Katina, the new housekeeper, answered the telephone. She said that Mr. Tony was not there. Ipatia asked her to tell Mr. Tony to call her at the doctor's office when he arrived.

Ipatia went back into the waiting room, noticing that more patients had arrived. She sat and read some more magazines. Finally, the waiting room was empty.

Michael came out of his office and was surprised to see her there. "What happened to Tony?"

"When I called his house, Katina told me that he hadn't arrived yet," she replied.

"If you don't mind waiting, I can take you back to the house later in the day when I'm done seeing patients. I'll be going there anyway to see Melissa."

"It's not so easy. I have to go somewhere else after I finish here," she said, blushing at his invitation. She explained the situation leading up to her going to stay with her cousins.

"I know the Mastroyiannis family you are talking about!" exclaimed Michael, his blue eyes lighting up.

"You know them?"

"Yes. Last time I saw your cousin was a month ago and he mentioned they were going to Italy for a visit, but I don't remember when they were to go."

The telephone rang at that moment. Michael answered it. "Dr. Michael here." He gazed at Ipatia. "Oh, hello, Katina. Yes, she is waiting here for Tony. I will be sure to tell her. By the way, is Melissa there? Please let her know I wish to speak to her. Thank you."

Ipatia listened curiously to his conversation with Melissa. It seemed like his voice tightened slightly.

"Yes, we can go for the rings. I think we should try several places before we decide, don't you?" Michael hung up the telephone, then turned and said, "Tony telephoned the house not too long ago and told Katina he would be here around one o'clock or so, to pick you up. I just finished seeing my last patient. Why don't we have something to eat until he arrives?"

"Oh, I don't know," began Ipatia, blushing once more. Although she felt comfortable being with him, the idea of having lunch with him sounded too intimate.

"Don't be shy. I know your foot is not well yet, so I will go next door, get some souvlakia and bring them back here. Will that be all right with you?"

She nodded silently, wondering how in such a short time, she had been left alone with two single young men and it did not feel all that bad.

Within minutes, Michael returned with the wrapped food. The waiting room was filled with the savory aroma of the souvlakia. They sat down and ate their lunch. Ipatia asked him about his profession and he responded by relating his experiences in medicine. Ipatia was enraptured by what she heard, admiring the little miracles he performed on people, helping them to live. They were laughing over an incident he had with one of his patients, when the glass door to the office flew open.

"Hello you two! What have you been up to?" asked Tony cheerfully. He had never seen Michael look so boyishly happy. Was Ipatia infecting him also with her youthful cheerfulness?

"I was just telling Ipatia that story with the old man who had a hearing problem, remember that story?"

"Oh, yes, and you asked him to sit down and he dropped his pants down instead?"

"Yes," and with that the room erupted with laughter once more.

"How is your foot, Ipatia?" asked Tony, after the laughter died down.

"Very well, thank you. Dr. Michael said there are no fractures, and in a short while, I'll be back to normal."

Michael walked with Tony and Ipatia outside, heading towards Tony's red convertible sports car. "By the way, how is your father doing?"

"I just returned from the hospital. I had just missed him. The nurse told me he had gone to get some tests done and Christina had gone to the hotel. I waited awhile, hoping I would see him, but he did not show up by the time I left. I'll find out later when I go back in the afternoon."

Then Ipatia and Tony got into the car and Michael waved to them both as they drove away.

Tony looked at Ipatia. "Can you give me the address where we are going?"

She took the paper out of her purse and read it aloud.

"I know where it is," he said, smiling at her. "It's near my office."

"Oh, that's nice," she replied dreamily, then realized how it may have sounded, tried to explain her reply by saying, "I mean, it's nice that you know where they live."

He pulled down the top of the car. They rode through the busy streets, weaving in and out of the cars. It was slow going, but he was a smooth driver and Ipatia enjoyed the ride. Tony turned the radio on and started singing along with the music. His rich, baritone voice blended well with the song, drowning out the sounds of the noisy streets. The song he was singing was about a woman's hair and the seasons of life.

He would occasionally look in Ipatia's direction, making her blush and feel warm inside. She pushed the curls of hair from her face, conscious of how short her hair was, conscious of his remark earlier that morning. Then she remembered Olga's scarf and retrieved it from her purse. She tied it on, thankful for the gift. The hat Mrs. Tsatsikas had given her had been tucked away in the trunk indefinitely.

"Mr. Tony, I heard you speaking with Dr. Michael about your father," she began. "I hope it isn't an inconvenience having me stay at your house, now that he is ill."

"First of all, please call me Tony," he said. "Your visit isn't an inconvenience at all. My father often invites people to stay with us and besides, the house is large enough to accommodate several more guests."

It was not long before they arrived at her cousins' address. The building was a three-story building. They entered the courtyard. Her cousins lived on the first floor. Ipatia knocked on the door, but no one answered. She looked around and saw an older lady, dressed in black, sweeping the adjacent courtyard. She said to her, "Excuse me madam. Do you know if the Mastroyiannis family lives here?"

"Yes, they live downstairs, but they aren't here. They left two days ago on a trip and won't be back for a month."

"Thank you," said Ipatia.

"You're very welcome," replied the woman.

Ipatia then turned to Tony, looking at him expectantly, hopefully.

"Then it is settled. You stay with us for now!" he said, feeling a rush of unexplained happiness.

She felt a sense of relief as she got back into the car with Tony. "Thank you," she said simply, rewarded by his warm smile.

They pulled out into the main road and traveled a few blocks, entering an area that had shops and stores. When they stopped at the light, he pointed to a tall, modern looking building on the right hand side. "That is our office building."

"That's quite a large building!" exclaimed Ipatia.

"Yes, now that you mention it," he replied, nodding appreciatively. "We own the whole building. My office is on the third floor and we have close to thirty employees working there."

Tony turned a corner. "There's a place nearby where they make the best loukoumathes. Why don't we stop there and take some back for my father? I will be visiting him later at the hospital. It will perk him up. He goes crazy over loukoumathes."

Ipatia laughed along with him, liking his thoughtfulness for his father.

A few minutes later, they were sitting at a small table outside the loukoumathes shop, enjoying the sweet doughnut balls with their drinks under the shade of a tree. It was peaceful here. The sounds of birds chirping could be heard above them. Ipatia caught him glancing periodically at her, making her feel warm all over. She noticed he was not saying much today. It was a much more polite Tony than the day before. He was keeping his distance and she was beginning to relax.

"Hmmm. You were right, these are the best loukoumathes," she murmured, chewing one of the honey-dipped treats. "Thank you so much! They are wonderful!"

"You are welcome," was Tony's simple reply.

After they finished, Tony ordered a large batch of loukoumathes to take back with them. As he drove back home, he sang along with the radio, making the whole trip amusing and fun for Ipatia. She enjoyed listening to him. She was almost tempted to join him, but resisted when she remembered the consequences of being too liberal with him. Even her grandfather sternly reminded her this morning on how to behave in Tony's presence, as if he sensed she had already strayed from her upbringing.

Ipatia and Tony arrived back at the Plakis house around three thirty.

"I won't be coming in," said Tony, getting out and opening the door for her. "Father's been expecting me since this morning, and I need to see him."

"I hope I didn't make you too late."

"No, no, don't worry about it," he said, laughing and getting back into the car. He waved to her as he sped away.

She felt a surge of happiness as she strolled into the house. Tony had a way of making a woman feel special. Even her foot felt better. *Yes, but he treats all the girls like that. Remember his kiss the other day, and Dr. Michael's words on the ship!* More somberly, she removed her scarf and entered the hallway, going towards her room, almost bumping into Melissa.

"Hi, Melissa!" she chirped.

"Ipatia...was that my brother that just drove away?" asked Melissa somewhat abruptly.

"Yes, he was going to the hospital to visit your father."

"Hmmff," said Melissa, narrowing her eyes. "I wanted to speak with him first before he went to the hospital." She walked off towards the study, muttering to herself. She just got off the telephone with Michael. She had asked him if he had seen her brother and he told her he had left hours ago with the girl. So where had they been all these hours? She was going to call Father and have a talk with him.

Ipatia, sensing that things were not right, immediately went to her room. She lay on the bed. It wasn't long before she fell into a light sleep.

CHAPTER 16

I heard your family's wish for you
Goodbye for now, dare it be true?

Tony hiked up the hospital stairs to his father's floor and walked down the dimly lit corridor, sensitive to the rank smell of formaldehyde that seemed to be everywhere, permeating every corner, even settling on his own clothing. He gingerly carried the box of loukoumathes, appreciating their sweet scent, a nice reminder of another world that he had just come from.

He found Dr. Vaskanos speaking to the nurse in the hallway. He asked him about his father. He was led into a private room.

"Let me speak frankly, Dr. Plakis," began Dr. Vaskanos. "We are still obtaining results from the tests and cannot be one hundred percent sure until they are finalized. But so far, what I can tell you, is that, given your father's symptoms and what the films show…it does suggest strongly that he has a brain tumor in the lower base of the brain. We won't know for sure until the biopsy results are in."

Tony was disturbed with the news and asked several questions. He thanked the doctor, shaking his hand, slipping money into it.

He found his father sitting upright in his bed, alone and wide awake, wearing his reading glasses and reading the newspaper. Tony tried to be cheerful as he presented his father with the loukoumathes. "For you, Father."

His father grudgingly took them, then put them aside. "Can you explain yourself, Tony? You were supposed to come this morning and speak with the doctor. Instead, you were traipsing around town with an island girl half your age! You spent more time with that, that girl than with Bonnie!" Gregory took off his glasses and rubbed his eyes.

"I gather you spoke with Melissa," said Tony quietly.

"I just got off the telephone with her," grumbled Gregory. "She said you were gone all day with Ipatia."

"For your information, I dropped Ipatia off at Michael's office in the morning because of her swollen ankle and came immediately here, but was told you were getting tested and Dr. Vaskanos was not in yet. Then I went back to Michael's office and brought Ipatia to the house before coming here."

"And the loukoumathes?" demanded Gregory, knowing Tony's fondness for taking girls there.

"The loukoumathes were for you, since I know you like them."

"Hmmf. What did the doctor say? I've got a brain tumor, don't I?" grumbled Gregory, changing the subject.

"All the tests are not back, but given your symptoms and the spot on the x-ray film, he thinks that's a strong possibility," replied Tony, trying not to use the word "brain tumor".

"I knew it! When he kept stalling, I guessed right that there was something serious he was hiding from me," said Gregory, tightening his mouth. "Did he mention surgery?"

"Treatment does include surgery, if the tests come back positive, but he doesn't recommend you having it done here. Instead, he gave me the name of a top neurosurgeon in the United States. They have these surgical machines that are much more advanced there."

"I thought he would say something like that. I'm going to get a second opinion before I decide anything," muttered Gregory. "Sit down, I wish to speak to you."

"Yes?" asked Tony, making himself comfortable in the large armchair near the bed. This was a special purchase made by his father for Christina so she could sit comfortably by his side.

Gregory coughed nervously before he began speaking. "When I promised Christos Rodakis that my son was going to help his granddaughter to come to Piraeus, I kept my promise. I didn't realize however, that my son was going to make a fool of himself spending all day with her showing her around the town! Did you forget you are practically engaged to Bonnie!"

Tony waited until his father stopped his ranting. He quietly said, "I helped the girl, Ipatia, just as I would have helped anyone else needing my assistance…and for your information, Bonnie knows my true feelings about her."

"Melissa told me. She says Bonnie was crying to her on the telephone and had to take tranquilizers to calm down. It's obvious the girl's in love with you.

What's wrong with marrying Bonnie? She comes from a good, rich family, she's attractive, and she's a nice girl!"

"I didn't intend to hurt Bonnie's feelings," said Tony thoughtfully. "She is a lovely girl and has good characteristics. I'm simply not interested in marrying her…or anyone else!"

"You're going on thirty, son. That's a good marriageable age," said Gregory.

"Yes, but you didn't marry until you were thirty-three!" retorted Tony.

"Ah yes, and I remember my father pressuring me to marry a certain heiress when I was also thirty," recalled Gregory, chuckling. "I was stubborn then, like you are now, and didn't give in. I married the most beautiful woman on Crete."

"Yes, and she wasn't an heiress either."

"You got me on that one. I guess I can't force you to do something you don't want to do," replied Gregory. He turned and pointed to the folded newspaper. "Did you read the newspapers recently? Chuck Daras is playing games! He said he would consider signing a contract with us…and now he wants to do business with Meriklis, who has a supermarket empire! I think he did it once he learned about Melissa's engagement to Michael!"

"Who knows why he did it," said Tony, feeling exasperated. "Also, Bonnie's father is a shrewd man and won't make any deals with Chuck Daras unless he's sure he'll get a good bargain."

Gregory leaned back and placed his hand on his forehead. He shut his eyes.

"Should I call the nurse?" asked Tony, getting up.

"No, no, it'll pass," said Gregory, breathing deeply. "Don't leave yet. I have to speak to you about something else. I received a telephone call from the port of Thessaloniki. One of our cargo ships has been held there for questioning. I do not know the details, but I need you to go and investigate the problem. Typically, I would go, but as you can see, I'm in no shape to be traveling. Also, you may need to consult our attorney if the need arises."

"Oh?" said Tony, digesting the information. "When should I go?"

"Make arrangements to leave on the first airplane for Thessaloniki. We've already delayed a day, and every minute that passes by while that ship sits at the port is costing us money."

Christina came in at that moment, and after he talked with her regarding his father's health, Tony went to the travel agent's office and made the necessary arrangements for the trip. He was to leave the next morning.

❦   ❦   ❦

Ipatia awoke later that afternoon to the sound of voices coming from the hallway. It took her a moment to realize where she was. She arose, washed and dressed, then went and stood near the window. The sun was setting and everything was embraced by the orange glow of the sunset. There was something comforting about a sunset. She took out some papers from her trunk and began to write poetry.

Mrs. Soula came by after awhile, and told her dinner was being served. "I'll take you there, if you like."

Ipatia set aside her poems and followed her to the grand dining room. It was an elegant room with wine-colored velvet curtains and a large Persian rug. A big chandelier hung above the long dining room table. On one wall was a large, gold-framed mirror.

Melissa and Dr. Michael were the only ones seated there. Ipatia greeted them.

"I see you are walking better," said Dr. Michael, standing up, smiling at her.

Melissa sat quietly in her chair, staring at her.

Ipatia wasn't used to having all this attention focused on her and blushed, nodding silently.

The cook entered the room, pouring white wine into the crystal glasses. The dinner was then served, and consisted of fresh baked fish smothered with tomato sauce, baked potatoes, salad, and crusty bread.

"Where is Tony?" asked Michael, looking at Melissa.

"Tony couldn't make it for dinner," said Melissa, wiping her mouth with a napkin. "He is busy preparing for a business trip. Father's health is not the best these days, so Tony represents the company now."

Michael gave Melissa a puzzled look. She leaned over and whispered in his ear. "I'll tell you later."

Ipatia had looked forward to seeing Tony again and was somewhat disappointed. The dinner went by quickly, with Michael and Melissa doing most of the talking. It seemed they couldn't agree on a number of things regarding their wedding. Ipatia quietly ate her food, listening to the couple talk.

They were now having a heated discussion about the rings. Dr. Michael was content with a simple, gold ring, asking what was wrong with that, since he had spent a considerable amount on the engagement ring.

"The large diamond ring I set my heart on is the one I want," Melissa insisted.

"How much does it cost?" asked Michael.

When Ipatia heard the price of the diamond ring, it caused her to drop her fork. She apologized while the couple stopped to stare at her.

After dinner, the couple arose to leave and Ipatia excused herself, saying she needed to go and rest her foot.

Melissa said, "Come, Michael, let's stroll out into the verandah. I feel like going outside."

Michael grudgingly followed her, as she led him outside. He was still upset over their previous discussion, realizing this wedding was going to cost him a fortune. He didn't know how his parents would react to this. Besides the purchase of the diamond ring, Melissa wanted to travel around the world for their honeymoon. He preferred going to Paris, or one of the Greek islands for their honeymoon. She insisted on a world trip. She wouldn't have it any other way.

❧   ❧   ❧

Ipatia went into her bedroom and immediately felt the evening's cool breeze coming from the open window. She shivered as she went to close it. She stopped when she heard Michael's voice. He was outside, conversing with Melissa. Ipatia moved away from the window, but she could still hear their conversation.

"What do you mean Tony had a quarrel with your father?" asked Michael.

"Well, it wasn't quite a quarrel. I called Father shortly before dinner to see how he was doing, and he appeared quite upset that Tony spent the whole day with the island girl, you know. They had even gone to the loukoumathes shop and ate there, and Tony brought loukoumathes back for Father," said Melissa.

"What's wrong with that?" demanded Michael.

"Did you forget about Tony and Bonnie? Father wanted him to stay here not only to run the business for him, but because he wants him to be near Bonnie."

"Yes, but I don't think Tony is interested in Bonnie."

"How can it be? Bonnie told me Tony kissed her on the trip," said Melissa. "I know Tony. He doesn't kiss women unless he's really interested."

"Are you sure it wasn't Bonnie doing the kissing?"

"Anyway, Father says if Tony marries Bonnie, that marriage can bring much money into the family."

"I'm beginning to understand everything now," said Michael.

Ipatia had heard enough. She went into her washroom and shut the door, trying to close out the conversation. She didn't want Tony quarreling with his father over her. She was beginning to notice a different side to Mr. Plakis, and Melissa was just like her father, having an insatiable appetite for money.

Afterwards, she lay in bed, thinking about things, unable to sleep. She went over the couple's conversation several times in her mind. Each time she went through it, she ended up thinking the same thing. She must leave this place. She didn't feel comfortable staying here any longer.

If Tony's fate was to marry a rich girl, why should Ipatia get in the way of his destiny? Where could she go? Her cousins were away on a trip and her aunt was in America. Then the option presented itself. She sat up in bed, feeling excited.

She pictured the renter talking to her and telling her that her aunt was not there. She also remembered hearing her say that Ipatia could stay there. She replayed the scene over again in her mind, trying to convince herself that the renter had actually made that statement. The only way to be sure was to go and visit her.

Ipatia arose swiftly and began packing her clothes, making sure everything was ready, making sure she didn't leave anything behind. She retrieved a pen and a piece of paper from her purse. Sitting down at the little table, she mused for a moment, hesitating, wondering if this was the right thing to do. *You must let Tony know! Yes, but what if someone else found this letter? You can seal it.*

Without further thought, she began to write, *"Dear Mr. Tony, Thank you so much for all you have done for me, and in making my stay here a pleasant one. I will never forget it. I think it is better that I leave. Yours truly, Ipatia."*

She folded the note, then searched in her trunk for some envelopes. She had brought some along for writing to her grandfather. Finding what she was looking for, she inserted the note, then wrote Tony's name on the envelope and left it on the table. In bed, she tossed and turned, unable to sleep. It was way into the night when she finally did, with tears still wet on her cheeks.

Tony returned home late in the evening. He had spent the rest of the day purchasing his airplane tickets, then meeting with their attorney. The house was quiet, as he made his way upstairs to his bedroom. Inside his bedroom, he changed quietly, then lay on the bed, unable to sleep. Light filtered in from the moon, casting its magic glow into the dark bedroom.

Tony remembered the gemstone Ipatia had given him. He arose and went to get it, standing near the window, holding it up against the light from the moon. It glowed red in the dark room, just like Ipatia glowed in his own life. He smiled softly.

His little Ipatia had aroused deep emotions in him. He had truly felt happy when he heard her yesterday, first singing merrily, then playing the piano. The kiss was a spontaneous overflowing of those deep emotions. He didn't remember feeling this way towards a woman before. When she asked him not to kiss her again, he realized how much that comment meant to him. This girl had values! His happiness continued as he sang beside her in the car, then afterwards, when he saw her enjoying her loukoumathes. He felt as if he was a boy again, without a care in the world.

He had lived in a structured world for as long as he could remember where everything operated like clockwork. His classes, his schedules, his summer vacations all had a sense of ritual woven into their fabric. These rituals had choked out any feelings he had, replacing them with a boring complacency lacking spirit.

Within the last few days, all that had changed. Fate or a higher power had made their yacht run into bad weather, forcing them to land on the island. Was it so he could save the girl from the snake, or to help a young boy who cut his arm? Or was it to bring the girl to his house?

Now, fate again caused his father to fall ill, requiring Tony's help, forcing him to leave for Thessaloniki. He gazed at the stone again, wondering if a girl named Ipatia, who had a fondness for running away, was going to be there when he returned, or was she to become just a beautiful memory.

The next morning, Ipatia arose promptly at four thirty. She had been so used to getting up early to milk the goats, it was easy for her to move around in the dark. Everything had been packed the night before. As the clock in her room struck five, she stole out quietly, her heart racing at the thought that she might bump into somebody. She tiptoed down the hallway, quietly pulling the trunk behind her, stopping periodically to make sure no one was coming. It seemed forever before she reached the large front door. With relief, she found herself outside, carefully shutting the door quietly behind her.

By the time she reached the bus stop, she was breathing heavily and her foot was beginning to ache. She sat on the trunk and prayed the bus would not take too long, so no one would recognize her. After twenty minutes, the bus came. Ipatia, with the help of one of the passengers, boarded the bus with her trunk. She showed her aunt's address to the bus driver.

The bus driver nodded. "I'll let you know when we are near there."

❦   ❦   ❦

Six o'clock that morning Tony arose from a sleepless night. Ipatia had been on his mind all night. He was feeling guilty that he had invited her to stay at their house, and now he was leaving. As he washed and dressed, he toyed with the idea of writing her a note to explain his absence. That was the least he could do. He decided he wasn't going to let Melissa know his plans. She had been interfering in his life too much lately.

An hour later, he slipped the note underneath Ipatia's door before leaving for the airport.

CHAPTER 17

Life brought me back to Piraeus
To teach the English language

The bus pulled to an abrupt stop. "You get off here, miss," said the bus driver, opening the door. "A taxi can take you the rest of the way."

Ipatia gathered her belongings and arose. The trip had been a long one, and she had fallen asleep along the way, yet somehow she now felt refreshed. She noticed there were only a couple of people in the bus, and it appeared they also were sleeping. The bus driver placed her trunk on the pavement, then pointed towards the direction of the parked taxis. She thanked him, then walked across the street, pulling the trunk behind her. The bus turned the corner and was instantly out of sight.

She found a taxi, and the journey continued for awhile longer. It was quiet, and the early morning darkness was beginning to wane. They passed groups of children carrying their books, evidently going to school. At the top of the hill stood a small grocery store.

"We're almost there," said Ipatia excitedly, recognizing the store. "It's down the hill. There, where the playground is…you can drop me off there."

Moments later, she knocked on her aunt's door, wondering what she would find. To her delight, her aunt opened it. "Aunt Sophia!" exclaimed Ipatia, surprised to see her.

"Ipatia! I almost didn't recognize you!" said Aunt Sophia, as she hugged her niece with emotion. She wiped the tears of joy from her eyes. "I'm so glad you came back! I returned yesterday, and Miss Marika, the renter, told me all about your visit! But she wasn't sure where you were staying!"

"I'm sorry. I wasn't thinking clearly that night to tell her," admitted Ipatia sheepishly. "But I am so glad you are back!"

"That makes two of us!" said Aunt Sophia, her eyes moistening. Then she became businesslike. "Well now, let's get you settled first! Is this all you have?"

"Yes, Aunt, just me and my trunk! Oh…I almost forgot. Here is the wine that Grandfather made. It's for you," said Ipatia, retrieving the bottle from her handbag.

Her aunt thanked her and helped bring the trunk inside. The two-story house consisted of two living quarters. One suite was downstairs and another one upstairs.

"Marika, the tenant you met, is renting downstairs. So we will be living upstairs," said Aunt Sophia. "Here, can you help me carry this?"

Ipatia helped her with the trunk, going up the winding marble stairs, mindful of her sore ankle. She winced from the pain.

"The house is too big for just me, so throughout these last years, I've rented the downstairs whenever possible, and have resorted to living upstairs."

As her aunt unlocked the door, memories of Ipatia's youth came rushing in, overwhelming her. She stifled a cry, trying to compose her emotions. "I remember this so well," she said, excited. She eagerly followed her aunt into the living quarters. To the right of the entranceway was the kitchen, and to their left, was a small hallway that led to the sleeping quarters.

Ipatia followed her aunt into her parent's bedroom. She shivered in anticipation as she entered the room. She could almost smell her mother's perfume lingering in the air, a reminder of a time of leisure and prosperity, a reminder of her father's expensive gifts. The white dresser, imported from France, with the large mirror, still stood against the wall. Two porcelain female dolls, dressed in exotic clothes, sat on the bed. "Aunt Sophia, you kept my dolls! Thank you so much!" Ipatia rushed to the dolls and touched them fondly.

"I kept them so you can give them to your children one day."

Ipatia went to the dresser and saw the gold comb resting there. She picked it up and gazed at it with nostalgia. "This was my mother's comb. I would pester her to comb my hair with it when I was a child. I wanted to do and use everything she did."

"If you look around, you will see everything the way it was when your parents were last here," said Aunt Sophia, gesturing around sadly. "At one point, you will have to decide what you want to do with them. By the way, you will sleep here, and I will be in the other bedroom, the one that used to be your bedroom."

"Thank you, Aunt," said Ipatia. "Is it all right if I unpack?"

"Surely, just come out into the kitchen when you are done. I'll be fixing breakfast."

Ipatia unpacked, and reverently placed her parents' pictures on the dresser, then checked the contents of its drawers. They were filled with her parent's clothes. She carefully removed the contents of the drawers and replaced them with her clothes. The ache in her heart was becoming unbearable. What should she do with the rest of her parent's clothes?

"Ipatia, food's ready!"

"I'll be right there!" Ipatia hurriedly changed into other clothes, hung her Sunday dress in the closet, and joined her aunt in the kitchen. The round table held plates of food on it, while her aunt poured the coffee into the cups. They sat down to eat. Ipatia said a prayer, then began to eat.

"Ipatia, now tell me the news from the island. How is your grandfather, and your godmother?"

Ipatia obliged her aunt and chatted cheerfully about her grandfather, the people and life on the island.

"I feel bad I didn't visit you sooner, but you see, after your parents died, I was afraid to travel by boat," said Aunt Sophia. "I'm embarrassed to say that I still am!"

"I understand," said Ipatia, nodding her head emphatically. "I used to be terrified also whenever I traveled by boat to Rhodes, but I got over it. See, I even came here by ferryboat to stay with you!"

"Yes, you are a brave girl at that!"

"Did you get my letter?"

"Unfortunately I had left for America before your letter arrived. Marika forwarded all my mail to me. As soon as I received it, I made airplane arrangements to come back. She didn't know I was coming until a few days ago."

"Oh, that explains why she said it would take you three weeks," said Ipatia. "So what made you go to America?"

"Mostly boredom, I guess," replied Aunt Sophia, with a far away look. "We have cousins in Chicago who visit here quite often, and each time they visited, they kept inviting me to go there. Well, I finally accepted their offer and went this summer."

"Do I know the cousins?"

"I don't know if you know Antonios," said Aunt Sophia, noticing Ipatia shaking her head. "Well, his father and your grandfather were brothers. Anyway, Antonios is married to Stasoula, and they have two sons. They wanted me to meet someone there."

"Oh?" asked Ipatia.

"I didn't know either until I went there," said Aunt Sophia, chuckling. "Who would have thought that at my ripe age of forty-two, I would be meeting someone? Anyway, he is a good friend of Antonios and lives next door. He is Greek and a widower…with no children. He just celebrated his fiftieth birthday with a party. We were all invited and I went along."

"Do you like him?" blurted out Ipatia.

"How about I tell you some other time," replied Aunt Sophia, smiling fondly at her curious niece. Then she changed the subject. "Your grandfather stated in his letter that you wanted to further your education. Tell me about that, Ipatia."

Ipatia explained how her teachers pushed her to continue her studies at the university because she had done well in school.

"Just so you know, young lady, it's very difficult to enter the universities here in Greece. My friend's son took his entrance examinations last year and even though he received high marks, he was not accepted in any of the universities," said Aunt Sophia. "He is studying now in Italy."

"Really?" asked Ipatia, gulping her milk down nervously.

"Yes, but then again, Marika's niece made it to the university here, so one never knows."

"I hear the entrance examinations are given in late spring."

"Yes, sometime in June. We can get all that information before the time comes," remarked Aunt Sophia. "So tell me…was your trip a nice one?"

Ipatia nodded, describing the few days before the trip and her involvement with the Plakis family. "I went to their house in Kifissia," finished Ipatia.

"I happen to know the Plakis family!"

"That's right! Mr. Plakis said he knew you," exclaimed Ipatia, her eyes widening. "You were their seamstress, weren't you?"

"Yes, but first, why don't you finish your story."

Ipatia continued, finishing with the conversation she heard between Melissa and Michael outside her window.

"It seems as if Melissa is very loyal to her father and will do anything he says," said Aunt Sophia with insight. She was about to ask Ipatia what her feelings were for Tony, but refrained. Instead, she asked, "Do they know where you are now?"

"I left a farewell note, but didn't say where I was going."

Her aunt raised her eyebrows. "I think we need to place a call to the Plakis residence right away, and let them know where you are, young lady!"

"But how? You don't have a telephone."

"Don't you worry about that! There is one down at the corner, at the pharmacy. Come on, follow me."

"Can we also call Grandfather so he knows what has happened?" asked Ipatia, grabbing her purse with the telephone number in it.

Her aunt nodded. Their walk to the pharmacy was a pleasant one. They passed some residential buildings with pots of bright flowers lining their entrances. They crossed the street, and entered the two-story building located at the corner. The pharmacy was empty except for a young man standing behind the counter. He was wearing a white lab coat. A big clock on the wall showed twelve o'clock.

"*Yia*-sou Vassili. I need to use the telephone," said Aunt Sophia cheerfully.

"Over there, Miss Sophia," said Vassili, smiling and pointing to the telephone. "Pay me when you are done."

"Thank you." Aunt Sophia picked up the receiver. "Ipatia do you have the number?"

Ipatia handed her the paper with the telephone number on it. "This number is for the post office. We can leave a message with Mrs. Xilouris' nephew, who works there, to tell grandfather we will call back tomorrow morning at nine thirty."

Aunt Sophia nodded and proceeded to dial the number, leaving the message with the young man. She looked through the telephone directory, then dialed the Plakis residence. "Hello, I'm Sophia Kouris, Ipatia's aunt." She paused. "Oh, you are the new housekeeper? Is anyone from the Plakis family there? No? Then could you take a message and give it to the Plakis family, please? It is to let them know Ipatia has come home to her aunt safely and to thank them very much for having her stay there."

They walked quietly back to the apartment.

"So tell me, Aunt Sophia, how did you get to work for the Plakis family?"

"We go a long way back with that family. First, your grandfather knew Gregory Plakis back in Crete. Then your father worked for them as a captain, and he put in a good word for me. I ended up sewing clothes for the whole family and anyone else they referred me to."

"What about Mr. Plakis' first wife?"

"I never met her, but I did see pictures of her. She was a very beautiful woman. She passed away before I started working there. Tony resembled her more, with his dark looks, whereas Melissa resembled her father, short and fair. She was a mischievous one, though. There were many a time I could not find my threads or needles, for she often hid them," said Aunt Sophia, laughing.

"Was Tony mischievous also?"

"No, not like his sister. Actually, as a young boy, he was the perfect little gentleman, always saying thank you and helping me out. I remember thinking that with those handsome looks, he would probably break a lot of women's hearts one day," said Aunt Sophia, chuckling. She was about to continue, when she noticed a slight blush forming on the girl's face. Was it possible her niece had developed feelings for this young man?

"Really?" asked Ipatia, her heart racing at the memory of Tony's features. "Who took care of the children?"

"They had a nanny. Tony, the older of the two, went to a boarding school in England. His father wanted him to learn the English language because of the shipping business. Mr. Plakis kept saying his son was to take over the business one day. I never saw Tony after he left for the boarding school, but he used to write and ask about me once in awhile. I still sewed for the family and sometimes his nanny would tell me his news. I worked up to the time when your parents died," replied Aunt Sophia, sobering up. "After that, I was so much affected, that I couldn't work for almost a year. Mr. Plakis remarried soon thereafter and didn't request my services anymore."

"I'm sorry to hear that," said Ipatia. They had arrived at the house.

"Oh, things are much better now. I sew for a few good people and that's enough for me," said Aunt Sophia, going up the stairs and unlocking the door. "Here, let us go into the living room."

They went through a glass door that led into the living room. It had a large, comfortable sofa the color of ripe peaches, and across it were two, creamy white upholstered chairs. A glass coffee table with a small crystal bowl sat in the center of the room. On the wall were several framed pictures. She recognized her father in one of them.

Her aunt saw her looking at it, and nodded. "Yes, that was your father when he was twelve years old. I am that girl there. Can you believe it? I was eight years old then."

Ipatia studied the picture. Her aunt resembled a lanky boy with her cropped head of hair.

"There's something else in this room, Ipatia. Have you forgotten?" asked her aunt mischievously.

Ipatia looked around. There was the balcony at the other end of the room, with its door open. Behind the door, somewhat hidden, stood an upright piano. She ran to it. "The piano is still here!" She ran her fingers over the keys fondly.

"I knew this would make you happy. It took up a lot of space, but I have been saving it for you all these years, for I knew you would come back one day," Aunt Sophia said. She settled comfortably on the sofa, shooing her niece to play.

Ipatia did not need much encouragement. The room filled with lively notes that flowed in succession, transporting her back to another world where there were no cares, no worries, but beautiful feelings. When she finished playing, she was rewarded by the sound of clapping.

"Well done, Ipatia!" exclaimed Aunt Sophia. She arose to pat Ipatia on the back. "You bring back nice memories! How about having something light to eat? We can have it out on the balcony."

CHAPTER 18

Your search for me did make me start
A note you sent did touch my heart

Ipatia and her aunt sat outside on the balcony, enjoying the breeze and view. Rembetiko music was coming from a nearby residence. The heavy strains of the soulful song seemed to penetrate the open air, causing Ipatia to feel a sadness she could not shake off.

"There's old Mr. Damaskis playing his music again," said Aunt Sophia, tittering. "He lives in the building next door. He retired about a year ago and likes to play his bouzouki out on his balcony. The only music he plays now is Rembetika."

"It's sad music."

"He recently lost his wife and daughter in a car accident."

To her left, beyond the tops of the buildings, Ipatia saw a slice of blue. "That must be the Piraeus harbor," she said, pointing to it.

"Yes."

To her right, she had glimpses of the playground and open field, a reminder of her youth. There were a few small children running around. Their mothers stood nearby chatting.

"Aunt Sophia, how did you come to live here?"

"A young man from Piraeus is to blame," said Aunt Sophia, laughing. "You know you ask a lot of questions young lady!"

"I hope you don't mind."

"No, I was just teasing! I was quite young then, not much older than you," said Aunt Sophia. "He was my best friend's cousin, visiting Crete for the summer. He hung around us and we saw much of each other. He was a likable and charming young man. Then one thing led to another. We became engaged and he wanted me to go back to Piraeus with him at the end of the summer."

"You went with him?"

Aunt Sophia nodded her head emphatically. "My father saw how much in love I was, so he came with us to Piraeus. Manolis helped Father buy this house. The suite downstairs was mine, while this suite here was your father's. But at the last minute, my fiance decided he didn't want to get married."

"Oh dear, that must have been awful for you," said Ipatia. "You know Aunt Sophia, I don't think I want to get married."

"Don't be silly! Don't let an old maid like me influence you! If someone good comes along, you grab him, because those chances don't always come your way! I know!" retorted Aunt Sophia. Then she fell silent, as she thought about John Stavrakis, the man she met this summer. She had given up on romance a long time ago, so it had come as a surprise to her that she had fallen for him so quickly. He had seen her to the airport, promising he would visit her soon.

"I want to go to the university and get an education so that I can help people. Maybe it will be in nursing, or a health science. That's what I want to do in life."

"Haven't you considered marriage?"

"Yes, but I don't think I would make a good wife," said Ipatia, shaking her head. "Why, I'd be worried all the time that something might happen to him, and I can't live like that." Somehow, it didn't sound so appealing to Ipatia as she spoke her dreams aloud.

Aunt Sophia studied her niece with renewed eyes. It was obvious Ipatia had been deeply traumatized by her parents' death. She continued to wear all black, and she talked about helping people live. Ipatia needed a friend. "In nursing, you will have all kinds of sick people. Not all of them survive their illness, for one reason or another. Can you live with that?"

"I know...that is why I am interested in nursing...because I want to help people live longer!"

Aunt Sophia sighed. This girl was persistent, just like her father. "Yes, it is wonderful to want to help others live their lives as fully as they can. But there will come a day when you will notice that even the sick person is better off than you, when they have their family gathered all around them to show their love and support."

"That's good for the sick person!"

"Yes, but what about you?" asked Aunt Sophia. "You will go home tired from working all day, and who will be there to meet you, to love you, and let you rest your head on his shoulder? When that day arrives, then it may be too late to find the right man."

"Aunt Sophia, you would have made a good lawyer!" laughed Ipatia, breaking the somber atmosphere.

"No, thank you!" said Aunt Sophia, chuckling. "Ipatia, my girl, I'm going to take a nap now. You probably are dusty from the trip. Why don't you take a bath first before resting?"

Ipatia was directed to clean towels, soap, and a clean bathrobe. Moments later, as she sat in the warm water, her thoughts turned towards her future. She visualized herself helping people, which made her feel well disposed towards the idea. Then she remembered her aunt's words and shivered. She had never looked that far ahead before, but the picture of herself in her aunt's place, years from now, old and alone, was not an appealing picture.

❦   ❦   ❦

Tony arrived in Thessaloniki Tuesday morning and met with the captain of the ship. The captain complained that the ship was being held for no good reason by the port authorities.

When Tony went to check with the port officials, they were not around. He was told he would be contacted as soon as the officials were located. With nothing else to do but wait, he returned to the hotel later that morning.

It was around eleven thirty when he called his home. He found only the housekeeper there. Melissa was out and his father still in the hospital. He asked about Ipatia's whereabouts.

"I don't know, sir," said Katina. "I haven't seen her all morning, and today Soula has the day off."

"Can you go and check her room, please?"

Tony waited for a few minutes, then heard the sound of the receiver being picked up.

"Mr. Tony, the girl is not in her room. I found an envelope addressed to her laying on the floor near the door."

Tony was worried. That was the note he had left her. She must have left before he did. "I'd like to speak with Tim, the chauffeur."

The housekeeper appeared flustered, saying it might take a few minutes.

"I'll wait for him," replied Tony.

Tim came to the telephone.

Tony explained the situation to him. "She's my responsibility, as you well know, Tim. She disappeared without saying where she went to."

"If I may make a suggestion, sir."

"Yes?"

"Olga, our housekeeper's niece, may know something about Ipatia's disappearance."

"Good idea. By the way…why don't you also pass by Ipatia's aunt's house and check there, in case she decided to go there. Call me as soon as you find out any news."

"I will do that. Is there anything else you may be needing, sir?"

"Oh, I almost forgot…there is a letter addressed to Ipatia. It's in her room. Please see that she gets it."

"All right. Where can I reach you?"

Tony gave him the telephone number to his room. After he hung up, he dialed the hospital. He asked the nurse how his father was doing. She said he was still sleeping. Tony asked to speak to Christina.

"One minute, please," said the nurse.

"Hello, Christina. This is Tony. How is Father?"

"Your father is the same…just a little more irritable. Anyhow, they think they know what is wrong with him. He will tell you when you get back. Meanwhile, he will be discharged tomorrow to go back home until he decides what further action he wants to take."

Her voice sounded tired. Tony briefed her on his status. He planned to contact Spithas, their lawyer, as soon as he found out what the problem was. He didn't know when he would be returning to Kifissia, but if everything went well, he anticipated he should be returning the next day or so. After he hung up, he went downstairs to eat lunch at the restaurant across the street.

A clean and thoughtful Ipatia made her way to her bedroom. She noticed that her aunt's door was shut, indicating that she was napping. Ipatia combed her hair with her mother's comb, reminiscing of moments shared with her parents. After she dressed, she didn't feel sleepy, so she searched for something to read. She found the English novel given to her by Mrs. Rodos. She leafed through it, thinking about Tony, then about her English tutor. She would have to check with her aunt if she had any news about Mrs. Rodos. She took the book out on to the balcony and sat reading it, feeling the breeze running through her wet hair, escaping into another world.

A bell was ringing somewhere, startling Ipatia from her fascinated absorption with the story. The bell rang again. It was the doorbell. Ipatia arose to answer it, realizing her aunt was asleep.

She opened the door. To her surprise, it was Olga, Gilda's niece. "Olga, what are you doing here?"

"I am so glad to see you, Miss Ipatia! We were pounding the door for quite awhile before the lady downstairs let us in."

"That's Miss Marika. Who did you come with?"

"I came with Tim, the chauffeur. He drove me here," explained Olga, looking pleased. "He called me at work, you know, to tell me you had disappeared and if I knew anything about it. Of course I didn't, but since I felt responsible for you, I asked to come along. You see, he remembered your aunt's address."

At that moment, Tim came up the stairs and joined them.

"Hello, Miss Ipatia. We were so worried about you!" said Tim, taking his hat off and shaking her hand thankfully.

"Thank you for taking the trouble to look for me. I did leave a note for Mr. Tony, and we did call the house not too long ago, telling the housekeeper where I was."

"Oh, is that so? I didn't get the news. I may have already left by then," said Tim, scratching his head.

"Please, why don't you come in."

"Thank you, but we must be going. We only stopped by to see if you were all right," said Tim, hurriedly. "Oh, I almost forgot. This is from Mr. Tony."

Ipatia became flustered, thanking him as she took the envelope from his outstretched hand. Olga chatted with her for a few more minutes, reminding her that if she ever needed another haircut to let her know, before they bid her farewell.

After they left, Ipatia rushed to her bedroom, shutting her door. She opened the envelope with trembling fingers and read the note excitedly, feeling elated that Tony had written to her. The note read

"Dear Ipatia, I'm sorry I won't be able to see you today. I had to go away on a business trip. I don't know how long I will be gone. It was a pleasure hearing you play the music the other day. It brought back memories of my youth. In case you've already left for your aunt's by the time I return, good luck with everything, Tony."

She read it several times, then clutched it to her bosom. Her heart started racing at the thought that he cared enough to write her a note before he left for the trip. *How did he know I was going to go to my aunt's house? It's as if he could read my mind!* She was blissfully happy.

Then she remembered Melissa's conversation and suddenly her happiness didn't ring true. How could she be happy with a playboy, who went from one woman to another as if they were used clothes? *He had kissed Bonnie, just like he had kissed me. Now Bonnie was crying because she loved him, and he was spurning her to make me happy. How do I know one day he won't turn around and do the same thing to me, make me cry while making another woman happy?*

Ipatia's happiness turned into tears.

❧   ❧   ❧

Tony returned to the hotel late in the afternoon after meeting with the port officials. He telephoned his lawyer and told him the news. Their ship did not have authorization to be hauling the cargo that it carried, and there were stiff penalties involved. After a long conversation, he hung up the telephone. Spithas assured him that he would handle it from now on, and would keep him updated on the situation.

Tony took off his suit and tie and gazed out the window, thinking about everything that had transpired that day. At that moment, the telephone rang.

"Mr. Tony, Tim here," said Tim. He explained the situation to Tony. "The girl was at her aunt's house. Her aunt has come back from her trip."

"Did she say why she left?"

"No. She just said that she left you a note, and that they had telephoned the Plakis residence earlier today to let you know her whereabouts."

"Hmm. Can you make sure her note gets placed in my bedroom? I don't want to lose it."

Later that afternoon, Aunt Sophia had arisen from her nap and found Ipatia sitting out on the balcony, reading her book.

"Oh, there you are," said Aunt Sophia, stifling a yawn. "Ever since I came back from the trip, I find myself sleeping during the day and less at night! I think it may be caused by the jet lag." She sat down next to her.

Ipatia told her about the incident with Tim and Olga.

"That's strange that the housekeeper didn't tell them," said Aunt Sophia.

"Tim said he had probably left before we called."

"Yes, that may be the case."

The sound of Ipatia's book dropping to the floor startled her. It had slipped out of her lap.

"What were you reading?" asked Aunt Sophia, looking curiously at the book.

"An English novel given to me by Mrs. Rodos years ago. It is quite good. The heroine ends up with the man she loves."

"That sounds like a nice story," said Aunt Sophia. "You were always interested in books, Ipatia, ever since you were a young child! How is it you read love stories, yet you won't think about falling in love and getting married yourself?"

Ipatia laughed. "It's much easier to experience this through a book than to actually live it!"

"By the way, I bumped into Mrs. Rodos before I left for America, and she asked about you."

"How nice of her. I would really like to see her again," said Ipatia wistfully.

"Why don't we go visit her now! She would be very happy to see you," said Aunt Sophia impulsively, feeling young again.

Ipatia eagerly jumped up and hugged her aunt once more. They left shortly after that, stopping at the bakery.

"We would like one of these," said Aunt Sophia, pointing to a chocolate torte. "Ipatia, why don't you choose the wrapping?"

Ipatia chose the wrapping paper with the bright red roses splashed all over the white paper. She watched the clerk wrap the box, then tie it with a gold ribbon.

As they approached Mrs. Rodos' street, Ipatia recognized a building with Greek columns at its entrance. "I remember this building," she said excitedly. "I used to pass by here everyday for school. And over there, that's the house with the twins. They used to walk to school with me. Just beyond that is Mrs. Rodos' house." She pointed at the house. A few minutes later, they rang Mrs. Rodos' doorbell.

Mrs. Rodos came at the door wearing the same gray dress she always wore. Ipatia smiled. She had always thought of her as Mrs. Gray. Everything about her was gray. Her gown was gray, and there were gray hairs on her head. Her keen gray eyes peered at them through her silver rimmed spectacles.

"Greetings, Mrs. Rodos. Look who I have brought to see you," said Aunt Sophia, proudly moving Ipatia forward.

It took Mrs. Rodos a moment to realize who it was. Then she exclaimed, "Ipatia Kouris! I can't believe it. After all these years, you have finally come to visit me! Come here, my girl!"

They hugged and after their warm greetings, they were led inside.

They sat in the parlor, the very same room in which she had taken her lessons. Ipatia looked around her, soaking in the familiar musty smell of the books, while her aunt and Mrs. Rodos conversed in small talk. There were books everywhere. Nothing had changed here. She felt that only she had changed.

"Excuse me for a moment. I'll go make some tea. Would you like some honey in it? We can have it with some of your delicious pastry," said Mrs. Rodos. She was gone before they could resist.

Ipatia sipped the tea. It was just right, a little sweet, with a hint of lemon in it. Mrs. Rodos was the only person she knew that drank tea instead of coffee. She then sampled a small slice of the torte. It proved to be a delicious selection.

"I am so glad that you are back with us," said Mrs. Rodos with her British accent.

"Thank you," replied Ipatia. "I am glad to be here."

"Tell me, Ipatia, have you finished school yet?" asked Mrs. Rodos. She was sitting upright, her back straight like a poker, which came from years of teaching students.

Ipatia nodded, recounting her story of having done well in school, and having gone to Rhodes Island to finish her schooling. Something held her back from saying anything about her goals for a higher education.

Mrs. Rodos took a sip, then placed the cup gingerly on the coffee table and wiped the ends of her mouth daintily with a handkerchief. "Miss Sophia, you should be proud of your niece. She is a very talented girl, and her English is impeccable."

"I always knew Ipatia was a bright girl," said Aunt Sophia, smiling benevolently at Ipatia.

"Now that you are present, I would like to ask Ipatia something, with your consent of course."

"By all means, what is it?"

"I was wondering if Ipatia could spare three evenings a week."

"What would it be for?"

"My assistant just quit a few days ago and I need someone to help me out until I find another assistant. The classes are on Monday, Wednesday, and Friday evenings, from five thirty to about seven o'clock. Ipatia, what do you think? You will be paid for your services, of course."

"I would love that!" blurted out Ipatia. Then embarrassed by her outburst, she sheepishly looked at her aunt for approval.

"It appears to be fine with me," said Aunt Sophia slowly.

"So it is arranged. Ipatia, if it's not too short a notice, you can start tomorrow around five o'clock. We can go over things before the students arrive," said Mrs. Rodos, back to her brisk manner.

Ipatia nodded, rewarded by Mrs. Rodos' rare smile.

They chatted a little more, then bid Mrs. Rodos farewell.

CHAPTER 19

September 1988
My eighteenth year I found I must
My money earn without a trust

Wednesday morning, Ipatia and her aunt went to the pharmacy and placed the telephone call to her grandfather. He was there already and had been waiting for her call. He was relieved that she was with her aunt and that her aunt was all right. It was a very brief call, and it wasn't long before Ipatia and her aunt were walking back home.

"Ipatia, I've been meaning to talk to you about wearing your black clothes tonight for your English class. You've been wearing them since you came here, and those sandals don't quite go, do they? You can't go to class dressed like that."

"I started wearing black clothes in mourning for my parents and it's become a habit," said Ipatia simply.

Her aunt was staring at her with a perplexed look on her face.

"I also wear the sandals because I fell on my foot the other day and it is still a bit swollen."

"Then that settles it, young lady! Today, we go and buy you some clothes more suitable for you, and a new pair of shoes, too!"

"Thank you Aunt Sophia, but wouldn't it be better if we sewed my clothes? I mean, I'd like to learn how to sew, like you, and it'll probably cost a lot less money to do it ourselves."

"Of course, my dear, but you do need clothes to wear for your class tonight, and what about shoes?"

They took the bus downtown, and Ipatia's exuberance was obvious. The bustle of the city was invigorating. There were all kinds of shops, with all types of people. Aunt Sophia expertly guided her through the busy streets to where there were several clothes shops. The first shop was small and dark, filled with clothes racks everywhere. A young clerk was attending a customer while another one stood at the cash register.

"Miss, would you happen to have clothes for her age, around eighteen or so?" asked Aunt Sophia the woman at the cash register.

"Yes, Madam." She guided them to the section and waited politely.

Aunt Sophia looked at the clothes, then lifted up a skirt from the rack, showing it to Ipatia. It was a mini-skirt. Ipatia's tall height would make the skirt appear even shorter on her than on an average size girl.

"That looks like it was made for a younger girl," whispered Ipatia.

Aunt Sophia put it back. After a few minutes of searching, she realized all the clothes in the shop were geared towards shorter women. She shook her head, muttering, "Let's go somewhere else." She politely thanked the woman and left.

Eventually, they found a store that suited their taste and budget. The shoes were also difficult to find, since Ipatia's feet were larger than normal. Finally, they settled for a pair of brown, leather walking shoes. After they finished shopping, they stopped off at the fabric store and bought some fabrics and supplies.

They arrived home early afternoon. Ipatia took a light nap and afterwards, started to get ready for her class. She hummed as she put on her new white blouse and blue skirt.

"Ipatia, just so you know, it's almost five o'clock, dear," said Aunt Sophia, knocking on her door.

"Come in," said Ipatia. "How do you like it, Aunt Sophia?" She twirled around the room in her new outfit.

"Splendid choice!" laughed Aunt Sophia, clapping her hands. "You do look like a schoolteacher, I may say. All you need now, are those spectacles Mrs. Rodos wears"

They both laughed at the picture.

"By the way, what have you decided to do with your parent's clothes?" asked Aunt Sophia. "You'll probably be needing drawer space for your new clothes."

"I've been placing them in my trunk."

"Good idea."

"I've been meaning to ask you...if you were going to come with me to class."

"I'm afraid I can't. I have a client coming soon and I won't be able to leave," said Aunt Sophia. "You do know the way, don't you?"

"Yes, Aunt," said Ipatia, nodding her head. "What about after class?"

"What about it?" asked Aunt Sophia, starting to wonder what the girl was getting at.

"Well," began Ipatia, becoming nervous. "Grandfather didn't like it if I was still out when it became dark. He used to escort me."

"Oh, I see now," said Aunt Sophia, smiling knowingly. "It's different here. It's quite common to see young women your age walking alone in the evenings. I've done it for years."

"Really?" said Ipatia, feeling slightly uncomfortable with these new rules. "Then you mean it is all right if I come home alone?"

"Yes, my dear, perfectly all right!"

The walk to Mrs. Rodos' house was a brisk one, as Ipatia was mindful of the time. She quickly immersed herself in her new job. She was responsible for handing out the materials to the children and in aiding them with their lessons if they needed help. The class session flew by quickly and Ipatia enjoyed herself immensely.

❦   ❦   ❦

Tony arrived in Kifissia earlier that day. Katina answered the door. "Greetings, Katina. Is my father home?"

Katina nodded fearfully. "Yes…he is…in the verandah."

Just then, Melissa rushed out to greet him.

"Tony, I'm so glad you're home!" said Melissa, kissing Tony lightly on the cheeks.

"Hello, Melissa. What's going on?" asked Tony, studying her tear-stained face. It was not like her to greet him at the door. Something had happened. There was yelling coming from the direction of the verandah. "Is everything all right?"

"How can it be?" burst out Melissa, sobbing uncontrollably. "I broke up with Michael this morning and Father's upset about the whole thing!"

"One would think that he'd be happy instead," Tony remarked dryly, remembering his father's preference for Chuck Daras. He was about to ask her why she broke up with Michael when she cried out "Ohhhh," fleeing to her room.

"Melissa, Melissa!" said Tony, immediately regretting his words, but she had already vanished. He shook his head. Melissa had a habit of falling in and out of love quickly and this wasn't the first time she had broken off an engagement. What made it troublesome this time, was that the person she broke it off with was his best friend.

Tony found his father sitting outside, moving his arms about in an agitated fashion, while Christina was apparently trying to soothe him.

"In the end, she will have no one!" growled Gregory.

"Hello, Father. Hello, Christina," said Tony, settling into a seat after kissing them.

"Tony, you returned just in time to hear the good news!" said his father sarcastically.

"I heard."

"Your father is upset because Melissa didn't want to marry Chuck in the first place because of Michael…and now she broke off with Michael because she felt he was too cheap. Your father thinks Melissa will become an old maid and have no one to marry! I was telling him she is still a young and pretty girl and—"

"She is not so young at twenty-seven!" interjected Gregory. "I'm a sick old man, Tony. My years are numbered. I don't have the stamina I used to have before."

"Don't worry, Father. Everything will be all right," said Tony, patting him on the back. "Melissa is your daughter…a true Plakis…and will not let you down."

Little did Tony know how true his words would prove to be.

Early Sunday morning, Ipatia and her aunt decided to go to church.

Dressed in their Sunday outfits, they walked down the stairs, ready to leave.

Aunt Sophia stopped in front of Marika's door and knocked. "Let me see if Marika is ready. I usually go with her."

Marika was already dressed for church. They walked up and down a steep hill that eventually led them to the great church with the round dome. After service, they stood outside, munching on their *antithoro*. Aunt Sophia chatted with some ladies from the church. One happened to be a client of hers and she introduced her to another lady who wanted to have something sewn for her.

Aunt Sophia had found out a long time ago that happy clients were the best advertisement. She arranged an appointment with her.

"Why don't we go down to the Mikrolimano?" asked Aunt Sophia. "We can take a taxi."

They found the popular harbor teeming with people. As they walked towards the restaurant section, Ipatia enjoyed watching the white picturesque boats docked along the way. They contrasted well with the azure canvass of water. They strolled for awhile, enjoying the view of the blue water below, surrounded by the enticing smells that emanated from the restaurants. It seemed like everyone else had the same idea. People of all ages and nationalities, from singles and couples, to families, were strolling everywhere.

Marika turned out to be a pleasant woman, laughing frequently at Ipatia's cheerful words. Ipatia asked her about her teaching and Marika talked merrily about her classes. Ipatia mentioned her own plans for the university.

"The University of Piraeus might not have the program you are looking for. It's geared more towards industry rather than medicine," informed Marika.

"Oh, I didn't know that."

"I'm afraid so. Why don't you stop by sometime and I'll tell you more about it," Marika said. "I have some materials that may be useful."

They stopped at a restaurant and ate warm souzoukakia, fresh bread, and feta-topped salad, conversing and laughing.

Afterwards, they continued their walk, going towards the teeming harbor. It was a bittersweet moment for Ipatia. The sights and smells brought back memories that had been buried for years in the recesses of her mind. Her aunt and Marika were having a conversation, while she quietly gazed around her.

Ipatia spied a large ship docked at the harbor that resembled her father's ship. She wondered who the captain was. She wondered if he also had a family waiting for him when he'd return from his trips. Just then, she spied a man getting out of a cab and walking towards the ship purposefully. It looked like Tony. Her heart raced as her eyes followed his tall frame. He disappeared into the ship.

"Ipatia. Ipatia…is everything all right?" asked Aunt Sophia.

Ipatia blinked at her aunt. "What?"

"Is everything all right? You look like you just saw a ghost!"

Something held Ipatia back from telling her what just transpired. "I…I remember when we used to come here often with my parents when I was a young girl."

"Let's go and have some ice cream at the café. I know it will perk you up. Come on," said Aunt Sophia, hooking her arm in Ipatia's arm.

She was right. Soon, they were chatting and laughing away, and the rest of the day turned out pleasant enough.

❦   ❦   ❦

The next day was Ipatia's eighteenth birthday. That morning she peered into the mirror and saw the same face she had been seeing all her life. The same almond shaped green eyes, the same straight nose. Her lips were too full, especially after she ate. She pursed them together, trying to make them thinner. She laughed at the image in the mirror. She picked up the comb and began combing through her thick curls. Tony had said that he preferred it to be long.

"Ninety-nine, one hundred! There, that should help it grow faster!" she said smartly, going out of the bedroom.

The day went by quickly, and it wasn't long before Ipatia returned from the English class. She was surprised to see Marika when she arrived home.

"Happy eighteenth birthday, Ipatia," said Aunt Sophia, hugging her. "I have something for you."

A few minutes later she returned with the chocolate torte. Candles were lit on top.

"Thank you, Aunt Sophia!" exclaimed Ipatia, touched by her aunt's thoughtful gesture. "I don't normally celebrate my birthdays!"

"I know, Ipatia!" said Aunt Sophia. "But since you don't celebrate a name day either, I thought a birthday would be appropriate."

After Marika left, her aunt presented her with a wrapped package. Ipatia emitted an exclamation of joy when she removed the white cotton summer dress from the package. She proudly held it up in the air. "Aunt, it's beautiful!"

"I'm glad you like it," said her aunt, receiving her niece's enthusiastic hug.

"When did you find the time to sew it?" asked Ipatia.

"You should have seen me!" chortled Sophia. "Every time you went to class, I stopped whatever I was doing just so I could finish sewing it. I used every shortcut I could make to get it done in time. I'm glad you like it!"

Ipatia tried the dress on. The straps and open neckline showed off her slim neck. It fit her well, hugging her waistline. After she tied the sash in the back, she noticed how her small waist made her look fuller in other places.

"It looks great! Now I have something to wear for the summer!" she exclaimed, showing her aunt.

They spent the rest of the evening with much laughter, as Ipatia shared funny stories from the English class.

At some point, Sophia brought up the discussion of Ipatia's trust fund. "Ipatia, in the letter your grandfather wrote me, he mentioned that when you turned eighteen, he wanted me to take you to the bank to see about the trust fund. I believe I sent you all those papers after your father died?"

"Yes. Grandfather gave them to bring with me."

"Also, I just wanted you to know that your father loved you very much...and he wanted you to have the best." Sophia paused. "Now that you are eighteen, this upstairs suite will be your wedding dowry when you decide to marry. He told me so."

"Really?" asked Ipatia. She was surprised by the revelation. "But I don't have plans of marrying."

"It won't go away. Whenever you decide to marry," said Sophia. "What do you say we go to the bank tomorrow morning to take care of the trust fund?"

The next morning, they entered the large bank, their footsteps echoing on the marble floors. They presented her papers to the trust manager, Mr. Prasinakis. He was a thin man, balding, with large glasses that threatened to fall off his thin nose. He reviewed the papers, then excused himself. He was gone for several minutes. When he returned, he was holding more papers. He sat down behind the desk and peered at Ipatia from above his spectacles.

"Miss Kouris, you were correct in saying that your father opened this trust fund and that it was to be available once you turned eighteen. He formed it fourteen years ago. It's in American dollars, and the balance on the account now totals twenty-six thousand, seven hundred twenty-three dollars, which also includes the interest it has accrued over time."

"That's very good news!" exclaimed Aunt Sophia, satisfied with what she heard. "When can she be able to withdraw funds?"

"Let me see here. I thought there was one condition that had to be met before she could access it," he said, reading the papers carefully. He cleared his throat. "Ah, here it is. Ipatia needs to get married first."

"What?" sputtered Ipatia, looking back at the manager with a puzzled look.

"This money is to be used for your dowry, and it requires the signature of your husband before it is released."

"My father wrote that?" asked Ipatia incredulously.

The manager presented her the paper with her father's signature. She read it carefully, noticing it was dated two years after the account had been opened. Apparently, her father had added this as an addendum to the original paper and she hadn't received a copy of the addendum. She read where it said that her husband sign also before the moneys were to be released. She handed it back and nodded silently, biting her lip.

On the way back home, she sat quietly next to her aunt in the taxi, musing about everything.

"I know this was a surprise to you, as it was to me," admitted Sophia. "Maybe your father felt that this money would be better used as a dowry, which is not a bad thing to have. What amazes me is his foresight in setting up your dowry when you were so young!"

"I don't need that money," muttered Ipatia. "If a man loves me, he loves me for myself, not for my money. It can stay there for all I care!"

"Ipatia, your father worked very hard during his lifetime and I believe he was doing what he thought best for your future."

"I don't care about any dowry," repeated Ipatia. "It can't bring my parents back, and I don't want it to buy me a husband."

"One day, when the right young man comes along, you will think differently."

Shortly after they returned home, a woman came to pick up her clothes. Ipatia excused herself and retreated to her bedroom. She sat in front of the mirror, combing her hair, thinking about a number of things. She thought about her aunt, an old maid sewing for women for the rest of her life. Ipatia did not look forward to the same fate. *Let's face it, I'm confused.* She shut her eyes, picturing her parents, trying to communicate with them. *I've always loved you and obeyed you, but I hadn't known it was that important for you that I marry. I want to ask for forgiveness for going against your wishes, but I do want to go to school first. Then I promise that one day I will marry.*

For some reason, the image of Tony Plakis came to her. Her heart quickened. She went and found Tony's notes and reread them. She wondered what was happening with him and Bonnie. She wondered what it would be like to be married to someone like Tony. She fell sleep with Tony's notes in her hands.

❦   ❦   ❦

Tony rubbed his eyes. He had been in the office since early morning and was beginning to get tired. He looked out into the room, his eyes resting on the small table next to the window. The ancient vase with the geometric designs from the island was on it, but not for long. Arrangements had been made to have it copied, then it was to be placed in the museum, in a safe place.

He had been curious about Ipatia's father's accumulation of expensive items and had spoken with one of the older captains in the company a few days ago. He inquired how easy it would be to get a hold of a vase or item of worth.

"Why, would you be interested, Mr. Plakis?" asked Captain Sardelis. "I know someone who deals in those things. He likes to collect vases and items of value."

"Is that right?" asked Tony, quickly deciding not to reveal his real interest. "I am more interested in the process rather than acquiring anything. You see, my background is in economics, and I used to talk about this stuff at the university."

"It is common for those traveling at sea to make such purchases. We travel to so many different countries, so we take the opportunity to buy and trade," said Captain Sardelis, grinning. "What is cheap in one country has value in another. You do understand."

"Yes, I do."

"If you want more information, just ask Don Mcsweeny. He would know more. He's the expert on those things. His ship should be coming in today. You could find him at the harbor tomorrow."

Tony visited the harbor the following day and met McSweeny.

"Yes, I do a little of that whenever the opportunity arises," grinned McSweeny, his red nose matched his red hair. "I have quite a collection, if you'd like to see it."

"Maybe some other time," said Tony. "You knew Captain Kouris, didn't you?"

"A very good man," said McSweeny more solemnly.

"He used to dabble in buying and trading?"

"Well, yes, just like everyone else. He was always talking about getting something for his family."

Looking at the vase again, Tony realized that the girl's father had made some good choices in his travels. Just then, the image of Ipatia running away from him, with her long tresses flowing behind her, flashed in his mind. He was startled and rubbed his eyes once more.

Tony then thought about his father's health. The verdict had been that the tumor was located in a location of his brain that was very dangerous. It needed to be removed if he was going to live. However, the procedure to remove it may cost him his life. There was a specialist in Chicago, who had a good reputation for this type of tumor, but his father, always cautious, said he wanted to see if there were any other options available first.

CHAPTER 20

September–October 1988
No matter how much we try
Our hearts cannot keep a lie

September arrived and Ipatia began helping her aunt with her sewing projects during the days. One day, after the last client left, Ipatia and her aunt put the sewing accessories away.

"Ipatia, you have become quite adept at sewing," said Aunt Sophia, folding a piece of fabric. "I think you are ready to begin working on some of your mother's clothes. They are of good quality and are suitable to wear to church and to your English class. It's a shame to have them waste away in the closet."

That day, Ipatia's mourning period officially ended when she took down one of her mother's dresses from the closet. It was a pale green silk dress with a white lace collar. She held it up, picturing herself in it. It was as if her mother were there by her side encouraging her to wear it.

When she walked into the living room a week later, wearing the finished dress, her aunt's pleased expression was rewarding to see.

Ipatia wore it to class that day and received compliments from the children. After class, she talked to Mrs. Rodos about her dreams of a higher education. When Mrs. Rodos asked her what her aunt thought about it, she said that her aunt had the same philosophy as her grandfather, that a woman's goal in life was to marry. To Ipatia's delight, she found a staunch supporter for education in Mrs. Rodos.

"You see, Ipatia, I received a degree in languages from Oxford University in England where I had specialized in the Greek language. After that, I came to Greece to visit some friends and to practice my Greek. It was here that I met my husband. He was a cook in a restaurant and had the habit of singing loudly while cooking. So loudly, I might add, that it was impossible to ignore him! I went a couple of times to that restaurant before I got the nerve to tell him I liked his singing. Well, from then on, whenever I went there, he sang a special romantic song just for me, and the rest is history," said Mrs. Rodos, starry-eyed.

"That sounds so romantic," said Ipatia.

"Yes, but one cannot live on love alone. He did not make that much money, and we struggled the first few years," said Mrs. Rodos, nodding her head sadly. "I helped out by teaching English here and there. We lived with his parents at first. Then our son was born two years later, and we moved into a small apartment. A friend of the family found him a job as a cook on one of those cargo ships that travel long voyages. They were paying very well, so he took it. Then the following year, the war started and, one day, an enemy ship struck his ship. That is when I lost him."

"I'm sorry to hear that," said Ipatia, biting her lip. That was the very thing she had feared.

"Please don't feel sad, Ipatia." Mrs. Rodos smiled, patting her on the hand. "I do miss him, but I know he's up there somewhere watching over me. We all have to go someday. Some people go sooner than others. Anyhow, I am thankful for my education, because I supported myself and my son all those years with my teaching."

"Where is your son?"

"Robert is in England with his family," said Mrs. Rodos. She picked up a picture and proudly showed it to Ipatia. "I visit them during the holidays."

"They look like a nice family," said Ipatia, smiling as she gazed at the young couple and their two children. Although the son wore spectacles like his mother, he had a dark, Greek look to him, probably from his father's side. "So what made you remain here in Greece?"

"Greece is my second love, as one might say," said Mrs. Rodos. "I studied the Greek language and the Greek culture, and became fascinated about ancient Greece. The Acropolis and the Parthenon are such great architectural wonders. They continue to excite me when I see them. I've also read the works of Greek philosophers like Aristotle and Socrates, with their wisdom and logic. I could not help but fall in love with Greece."

"You know, I would love to visit the Acropolis and the Parthenon," said Ipatia wistfully.

"Then so be it!" said Mrs. Rodos. "We can plan an outing to go there soon! I've been meaning to visit them again, and this is just as good an opportunity as any."

"That would be wonderful!" said Ipatia, surprised by Mrs. Rodos' response. She had never seen her so excited before.

"Before I forget, let me show you some other books I think will be useful to read for the university exam," said Mrs. Rodos.

"Thank you, Mrs. Rodos," said Ipatia. "You are very kind."

As Ipatia was walking back home, she reflected upon Mrs. Rodos' story. Her husband had died and that was the very thing Ipatia dreaded. Yet, she was doing fine. Ipatia started thinking about Tony, wondering what it would be like if he were a cook singing romantic songs for her in a restaurant. For some reason, she could not see him doing that.

A car was honking in the distance. Her heart jumped. Could it be him? She turned and saw Dr. Michael waving to her from his car.

"Hello, Ipatia!" said Michael, pulling over to the side to speak to her. He was not surprised to see her there. He had learned her whereabouts from Tim.

"Hello, Dr. Michael," she said, smiling shyly, surprised to see him. She had mixed feelings as she walked towards the car, holding the books close to her chest. She was disappointed it wasn't Tony, yet somehow, his presence reminded her of Tony.

"How have you been?" he asked, smiling at her, appraising her.

"Fine, thank you," she said politely, remembering the last time she had seen him. It was when he and Melissa had stood outside her bedroom window, talking about Tony and Bonnie.

"Do you need a ride?"

"No, I'm fine. I live just down the block with my aunt," she said, gesturing towards the house.

"You are probably curious to see me here," he began. "A colleague of mine, Dr. Demetrios just retired and I have taken over his practice. I came by today to have a look at the office. You probably know where it is, on the second floor of the building right over there, next to the pharmacy."

"Oh, yes!" blurted out Ipatia impulsively, looking in the direction of the building. "I remember Dr. Demetrios! We visited him a few weeks ago because my aunt needed to refill a prescription."

"So now you and your family can come to see me instead. By the way, how is your ankle these days?"

"It has healed nicely, thanks to you!"

"Good. I see you are carrying books. Are you taking courses?"

Ipatia hesitated, once more feeling cautious. She was not quite sure why he was asking all these questions.

"No, actually, I'm helping to teach English at a school down the road," she said awkwardly, "and Mrs. Rodos, the English teacher, lets me borrow her books. I am reading them for the university entrance exam."

"That's wonderful!" he said, "Come to think of it, I remember you asking me about topics in medicine that day you came to my office. If you ever want to read any more medical journals, you can come by the new office anytime, and I'd be delighted to loan you some."

She thanked him and he left, waving to her. After that day, she played with the idea of going to his office to get the medical literature he mentioned, but didn't feel comfortable enough to do that.

Tony sat in the airplane, gazing pensively out the window. They were about to land in Greece. Yesterday at this time in England, he received a telephone call from his father. His voice sounded weak and fearful over the telephone. He complained about his deteriorating health. This prompted Tony to leave England immediately and return home.

His father's offices in England and New York made it necessary to travel to these sites often to ensure everything was in order. He was beginning to get tired from all that traveling. Then Tony's thoughts wandered inevitably to Ipatia. A gentle smile graced his face. There was a strong urge to seek her out, to laugh with her and feel good again. Yet she was not someone he could dally with. He found out quickly that day in the study when he kissed her. This girl had values, which were redeeming qualities, yet at the same time served as formidable barriers. Even if he wanted to seek her out, he was too busy these days to do anything other than work and travel. When would he find the time to woo her?

Hours later, when Tony arrived home, he met Melissa and Christina waiting for him. They appeared worried.

"Where is Father?" asked Tony, looking around. He noticed the dark rings under Christina's eyes, a sign that she hadn't been sleeping well.

"He is napping," said Christina wearily. She explained how his father was becoming weaker and his limbs were becoming spastic. "It's as if he doesn't have control over his movements."

"We have to do everything for him now," said Melissa.

"Then we need to do something…before it is too late," said Tony firmly.

"There is a doctor in Chicago," said Melissa hopefully. "Father has agreed to go there to be seen by him. He is supposed to be the best for this type of brain tumor."

After much discussion, Tony was convinced that this was the best option for his father. The next morning, he telephoned the physician's office in Chicago. The physician was available and they covered the pros and cons of surgery. Tony hung up the telephone, deep in thought.

When he walked into the living room, his father was sitting on the couch, waiting for him. Christina and Melissa were by his father's side, holding on to him.

"Well, what did he say?" asked Gregory, gesturing feebly, unable to control his movements.

"The doctor spoke very frankly. He needs to see all your tests and records before promising anything."

"That can be done easily enough," said Melissa.

"Did he say anything else?" asked Gregory.

"If he operates on you, he cannot guarantee you will be totally well from the operation," said Tony slowly, trying to put it more gently to his father than what he had heard from the doctor.

"That's what the doctor here told us. What can this doctor do for me that's better?"

"As you know, the location of the tumor is dangerous. In the past, these types of operations were risky, and they still are. He states his method uses state-of-the art technology, which has helped a number of patients live who would have died otherwise. The operation may give you a fighting chance of living a decent life. If you don't do anything about it, then you forfeit that chance."

"I've made up my mind. I'll take my chances and go to America to get rid of this thing once and for all! I'm tired of being sick," grumbled Gregory, striking his hand forcefully on the table. Christina and Melissa jumped at the sound.

Tony shrugged his shoulders and said, "So be it. We are coming with you."

Two weeks later, they left for America.

❦   ❦   ❦

It was a gray, rainy Monday in October. Ipatia hoped the rain would stop, but it did not. Upon the insistence of her aunt, she took an umbrella with her to class that evening. She forgot it in the classroom when she left, and by the time she reached the house, she was soaking wet.

Tuesday, she woke up with a sore throat and felt tired all day. By Wednesday morning she was coughing and had an earache. She slept most of the morning, waking up just to eat some warm *avgolemeno* soup that her aunt had made. She fell promptly asleep again.

Midday, Aunt Sophia said, "Ipatia, I think you need to see the doctor. You feel very warm and may have a fever. We need to take care of it."

Ipatia coughed, then said hoarsely, "But I need to be in class tonight!"

"I don't think so, young lady!" said Aunt Sophia. "Let's go to Dr. Michael, the one who replaced Dr. Demetrios."

Ipatia resisted at first, but after her aunt persisted, she finally agreed.

In the office, Ipatia continued coughing, causing the other patients to stare at her. She felt embarrassed from her coughing, but she and her aunt didn't have to wait long. The doctor took them in as soon as he saw her.

"Open your mouth wide. That's good," said Michael, examining the inside of her throat, then touching her jaw and neck area. "Your throat is red and swollen."

Ipatia was feeling shy with all the attention he was giving her. He was standing close to her; examining her and pressing his fingers on her neck. She could feel his breath on her cheek. Without notice she coughed in his face. She apologized.

Michael stepped back, smiling at her. "Don't worry." He waited for her to finish coughing. "Your body is trying to get rid of the phlegm."

He checked her ears next. She winced when he touched her left ear. "You also have an ear infection." He gave her a thermometer to put in her mouth, then took her pulse. It was beating too quickly. He smiled, realizing the girl's nervousness.

"She wanted to go to class tonight, but I felt she needed to see you," explained Aunt Sophia.

"You did the right thing, Miss Sophia. Ipatia has a fever, which is probably the result of the ear infection. It'll take about a week to get over this," said

Michael, reading the thermometer. He prescribed antibiotics and told Ipatia to get plenty of liquids and rest.

There was a knock on the door. He opened it and spoke with a patient. "Please wait here," he said to Ipatia before leaving the room.

Ipatia wondered if she should ask him about Tony, but decided not to. It would seem too bold.

Michael returned a few minutes later, holding a couple of medical journals in his hands. "Ipatia, if you still are interested in reading medical topics, I saved some to give you."

Ipatia's face lit up. "Oh, yes, Dr. Michael! I would love to read them!"

"When you are finished reading these, bring them back…and I'll loan you a whole set of new ones to read."

"Thank you, Dr. Michael!" exclaimed Aunt Sophia, surprised at the young man's generosity. She secretly wondered if he was still engaged to Melissa. He seemed to be treating Ipatia with special attention.

When Ipatia and her aunt left his office, they stopped at the pharmacy to get her medicine.

"Ipatia, as soon as I give you your medicine and get you in bed, I'll go and let Mrs. Rodos know you are sick and won't be coming to class for several days," said Aunt Sophia.

When Ipatia awoke later that day, her aunt greeted her, holding several books in her hands. "Mrs. Rodos sends you her best wishes. Look at all these books she gave for you to read!"

The next day, her aunt made it a point to say nice things about Dr. Michael. Ipatia agreed and thought nothing of it. She stayed inside, resting and reading most of the time. A few days later, she felt well enough to sit and watch her aunt sew.

"Ipatia, I haven't heard you cough at all today! Dr. Michael is a wonderful doctor. He knew just what to do to make you well!" said Aunt Sophia, handing her the medicine and a glass of water.

"Aunt Sophia, a day doesn't go by without you mentioning Dr. Michael's name!" laughed Ipatia.

"Really? I didn't realize I was doing that. I never had a young, eligible doctor treating my niece before," she chuckled. "He is handsome, isn't he?"

"Aunt Sophia…really! Even Tom Tsatsikas is more handsome than Dr. Michael is. Anyway…Dr. Michael is engaged to Melissa!" exclaimed Ipatia. She was beginning to feel annoyed at her aunt.

"My dear, I was only making an observation," said Sophia, suddenly becoming very intent on her sewing.

After that day, Sophia made it a point not to mention him.

A week went by before Ipatia was well enough to go to the English class. She stopped by the doctor's office on the way to the class. Although the waiting room was empty, she could hear the doctor in the examining room with a patient. She scribbled a note and left it with the literature she was returning. In the note, she thanked him for the material and stated that "*the homemade baklava was a token of appreciation from Aunt Sophia for everything you have done.*"

With the note, she left the box of pastries.

The next day, Sophia received a letter from John Stavrakis, the man she met in America. With trembling fingers, she eagerly tore open the envelope and read the letter silently in front of Ipatia.

Ipatia noticed her aunt's excitement. "What does it say?"

"John wants to pay me a visit. He'll be in Greece during the holidays to see his parents," replied Aunt Sophia, starry-eyed. "Isn't that wonderful?"

"Is that the man you met in America?"

"Yes, and you know what? Something tells me he's serious."

CHAPTER 21

November–December 1988
My father's health took up my time
I returned to Greece, my love to find

Tony and his family returned to Greece in early November. He immediately went to work in the office the following morning.

"Good morning, Mr. Plakis," said Rita, the secretary, arising to greet him as he entered the office.

"Good morning, Rita," Tony said, flashing a handsome smile her way. He had his hands full of gifts. He placed the packages on her desk. "These are souvenirs from America. Can you please have them distributed to everyone? Please keep one for yourself."

"Good morning, Mr. Tony, how was your trip?" asked Aristotle, coming out of his office.

"Hello, Aristotle!" replied Tony. He shook hands with the bookkeeper. "The trip was better than expected, thank you."

They walked towards his office.

"And Mr. Gregory, may I ask?"

"He's doing better, thank God. However, he is not well enough to attend to his normal duties, so I will continue taking his place for now."

"I am happy to hear you will be with us. Best wishes to Mr. Gregory."

"When you get a chance sometime today, I'd like to go over everything that has happened since I left."

"Certainly, Mr. Tony," replied Aristotle. "I'll be free in an hour, if that would be fine with you. Oh, and the vase you ordered has arrived. It is in the office."

Tony walked over to the vase, studying it. He couldn't tell that this was a replica of the vase from Lipsi. It looked like the original. He nodded, pleased with the results. The images of Ipatia swept before him. *Sweet, innocent Ipatia, this vase belongs to you.*

"Did you take care of the original?"

"Yes, I did everything the way you asked," said Aristotle. "It is now in the archaeological museum."

After Aristotle left, Tony sat down, staring out into space. It had been a turbulent time in America, with many questions unanswered. The brain surgeon had not guaranteed anything. He had stated bluntly that his father could die during the operation and that there was a possibility he could remain a cripple for the rest of his life. His father did not die, but it was to be seen in the future if his father would be able to walk again.

That very same moment, Ipatia and Mrs. Rodos were visiting the archaeological museum.

Ipatia walked slowly around the rooms, stopping to observe each artifact, moving on to the next object. "Just think. People thousands of years ago were making these objects!" she exclaimed, fascinated by the ornaments worn by women in ancient times.

They reached a room that held vases. There were so many different shapes and sizes. At one point, she spied a familiar looking vase. She pointed to it. "This looks just like the vase my father had given my grandfather! It has the same lines and figures!"

They went closer and read the inscription below the vase. Ipatia's heart began to race. The inscription read, "*Gift from Dr. Antonios Plakis. In loving memory of Captain Manolis Kouris.*"

"He remembered my father," whispered Ipatia, letting the tears flow.

"That was very nice of Tony," said Mrs. Rodos. "It seems that he not only has a good eye for beauty, but the logic to know what to do with it."

It was the end of November when Ipatia finally received a letter from her grandfather. Excited, she ripped the envelope open, her fingers trembling. It had been a long time since he had written her. She eagerly read his news.

"What does it say, Ipatia?" asked Aunt Sophia.

"Grandfather is doing fine," began Ipatia. She continued to read. "He apologizes for not having answered my letters...but he's been very busy. They have had a good crop of olives this season. Tom and another boy helped him. He says he misses me because I could pick olives quicker than both those boys could."

They both laughed.

Ipatia excused herself and went to her room. She finished reading the rest of the letter. Mrs. Tsatsikas came over with food periodically, and things were quiet now that Ipatia was not there. The horse Tony had given him was helping him tremendously. She reread the letter several times. Then sat down and wrote to him about her news, particularly the news about the vase.

❦   ❦   ❦

It was a week before Christmas, and Sophia was expecting John to visit her any day. He had written to her saying he would be stopping by to see her that week. Earlier that day she had gone to the hairdresser's, then the grocery store. She stocked the refrigerator, intending to make a special meal for him.

On the way to class, Ipatia stopped first at Dr. Michael's office, carrying the medical journals he had loaned her. When she arrived, she found him locking the door.

"Hello, Ipatia!" he said, looking surprised. "You made it just in time. I was closing the office early today."

"Dr. Michael! Here are the journals you loaned me," she said breathlessly. "It was very interesting reading. Also, my aunt and I made some *Vassilopita*. You can freeze the bread until the New Years." She presented him with a wrapped package.

"That's very kind of you and your aunt," said Dr. Michael, nodding his appreciation. "Why don't you keep the journals, as my gift for the holidays."

"Thank you," said Ipatia, starting to blush. "I need to be going now. I have the English class tonight."

"Here, let me walk with you downstairs," he said, touching her lightly on her arm.

For the first time, she noticed he was the same height as her, if not slightly shorter. They walked down the steps.

"How did you like the reading this time, Ipatia?" he asked.

"It was a little difficult to understand at times," admitted Ipatia. "Some of the words were technical, but it's amazing all the medical research being done on leukemia and cancer. I found it fascinating."

"Yes, isn't it?" he asked. "There is still a lot more to be discovered in those fields. We are just beginning to scratch the surface."

They had arrived outside.

"Before you leave, I would like to wish you the best for Christmas and New Years. Will you be spending them with your aunt?"

"Yes. Are you going to spend your holidays with Melissa?" blurted out Ipatia. She had been curious about Melissa all this time, for he had not mentioned her name once.

"I'm afraid not," he said, looking slightly amused, putting his hands in his pockets. "Melissa and I are no longer engaged. We just had too many differences that couldn't be resolved."

"I'm sorry to hear that. I didn't know!"

He was looking at her intently; in the same way he had studied her the first time there in the yacht, in an analytical and dissecting manner. Suddenly she knew why he had been interested in giving her the journals. She blushed, shifting uneasily away from him, ready to bolt, not wanting to face the dawning reality of his intentions.

"By the way, the office will close for the holidays and will reopen in three weeks. If there is any medical emergency, here is my telephone number where I can be reached."

She took the piece of paper, afraid to look at him. "Have a Merry Christmas, Dr. Michael." She sped on before he could say anything.

He stood there, gazing at her wistfully. He had been toying with the idea of courting her openly, but she didn't seem to be ready.

Sophia rested on the sofa, reading a magazine. Just then the doorbell rang. She looked at the clock. It was six thirty, too early for Ipatia to have returned from class. She jumped up excitedly, fixing her hair, knowing instinctively who it was. When she opened the door, John stood there, handsomely dressed in a dark navy suit, white shirt and maroon colored silk tie.

"Hello, Sophia!" John said warmly, taking her hands in his and kissing her lightly on her cheek. "It is good to see you again!"

"John! I'm glad you could come!" she replied just as warmly. She caught herself gazing into his eyes, then looked down, abashed at the emotions she was experiencing.

John stepped to the side to reveal a young man standing behind him. "This is my nephew, Stellios."

"Welcome," she said, shaking his limp hand. She gestured inside. "Please come in."

John entered the suite with his nephew. "I thought you lived downstairs, but Miss Marika told me otherwise."

"Yes, I've rented the downstairs to her," said Sophia, leading them into the living room. "This used to belong to my late brother. I like it better up here. It's roomier and has a nice view from the balcony." She pointed to the sofa. "Please have a seat."

"Thank you."

"Would you like some coffee?"

"No, no, some other time," said John, smiling. He gestured for her to sit down. "Tonight, I am treating. I'd like to invite you and your niece out to a nightclub."

"A nightclub?" asked Sophia.

John looked at his nephew. "Actually, it was Stellios's idea. He says good things about it. Right, Stellios?"

"It's sort of new and quite popular," said Stellios. "I've gone there several times, and they have good entertainment and a lake in the back."

"That would be lovely, but my niece hasn't returned from school. I'm expecting her any minute."

"Your niece is going to school?" asked John.

"Yes, she helps teach English classes three times a week."

"Interesting," said John. "English is a good language to know."

Meanwhile, the class had just finished. Ipatia and Mrs. Rodos were giving books as gifts to all the children; an annual tradition that dated back to when Ipatia was a student there. To Ipatia's surprise and delight, several children presented her with their own small gifts. She thanked them all as they left. As soon as Ipatia finished straightening the room, she gave Mrs. Rodos her own gift, a poem she had stitched on canvas. It was in a frame.

"Thank you Ipatia. The poem you wrote about me and the English class is lovely! I will hang it here in this room so that everyone can read it. I hope you enjoy the book I gave you," said Mrs. Rodos.

Ipatia thanked Mrs. Rodos in turn for her present, then chatted with her a little longer, wishing her a safe trip to England where she was going to spend the holidays with her family. Then Ipatia saw the time and left quickly.

"Aunt Sophia, sorry I was late!" said Ipatia, bursting into the house as soon as the door opened.

"Hello, Ipatia," said Aunt Sophia, interrupting her niece's next words. She whispered into her ear. "We have guests."

Ipatia looked at her aunt questioningly. By her aunt's glowing demeanor, Ipatia immediately realized who their "guests" were. She placed the children's gifts to the side, then followed her aunt into the living room. Her aunt introduced her to two male visitors. John gave her a hearty handshake and flashed her a boyish grin. She smiled cheerfully back, immediately feeling comfortable with him. The younger man, who was quite pale in color, gave her a cold, limp hand to shake.

"Ipatia, John has invited us out to a nightclub," said Aunt Sophia, glowing.

"Oh!" said Ipatia, taken by surprise. "Thank you for the invitation…but I've heard about night clubs, and I don't think Grandfather would approve of my going."

Aunt Sophia, appearing mildly flustered, explained to John, "She was quite protected on the island with her grandfather, you know. I must admit, the young ladies don't generally go to the nightclubs there."

"Oh, I see," said John, winking knowingly at Sophia. "Ipatia, the nightclub that I'm taking you to is suitable for families. There will be a show, with singing and entertainment, and there's even a lake with boats in it."

"That sounds very nice," said Ipatia, beginning to like what she heard.

"Good, then," said Aunt Sophia. "Why don't we go and get ready?"

"Will you excuse me, please?" asked Ipatia, to the gentlemen, who nodded respectfully back.

Aunt Sophia excused herself also and followed Ipatia to her bedroom.

"What should I wear, Aunt Sophia?" asked Ipatia, gesturing towards the clothes in her closet.

Aunt Sophia went to the closet and pulled out a black, sequined evening gown. She handed it to Ipatia. "How about this dress? I sewed it for your mother. It should fit you," she said. "It was tight on her and she hadn't really had many occasions to wear it."

"I'm doing this just for you, Aunt!" said Ipatia, chuckling, as her aunt left the room. She hummed a cheerful tune as she undressed and changed into the dress. The neckline was low, making her feel exposed, and she pulled on the thin straps trying to make it go higher. Then she put on the nylons the way her aunt had shown her and the black pumps she had bought recently. Her hair had grown since she had cut it and was now just below shoulder length. With the help of a few hairpins, her hair was pulled up. She put on her mother's long, diamond studded earrings, appreciating the way they sparkled. Her aunt came back, also wearing a dark blue evening gown with a shawl on her shoulders.

"You look very lovely, my dear. Worth a million drachmas!" said Aunt Sophia approvingly. "It's a little cool outside, so here is a shawl."

"Thank you Aunt Sophia. You look quite lovely yourself!" said Ipatia, observing how her aunt's elegant evening gown was becoming on her. She placed the black lace shawl over her bare shoulders.

John appeared pleased at the transformation of the two women, and his face showed it.

❦   ❦   ❦

It was close to nine o'clock by the time they reached the nightclub.

"There is parking down the street," said Stellios. "Why don't you wait here."

Aunt Sophia conversed with John, while Ipatia stood quietly nearby, appreciating the exceptionally mild temperatures for December. There were tall swaying palm trees lining the perimeter of the property. Plush landscaping with scented flowers added beauty to the place. Stellios came soon thereafter, leading them into the carpeted lobby.

"Why don't we have something to eat first?" asked John.

"That's a good idea," said Stellios. "The entertainment isn't until later, but we can get good seats now and watch the show from there."

They went into a large ballroom that had a stage extending out into the center of the room with tables encircling it. A wet bar was stationed in the corner.

John ordered appetizers and drinks for everyone.

Then the show began. Singers, dancers, and acrobats took their turns on stage. Large balls hung from the ceiling, spinning different colors over the performers, making them appear magical. It was quite entertaining. When the show finished, the floor was open to the public for dancing. It became noisy after that, so they strolled outside.

A walkway led to the large, oblong lake and circling its perimeter were soft lights, illuminating it romantically. Ipatia could see couples standing on a bridge that stretched across the lake. Soft romantic music was coming from somewhere above their heads.

"Oh, look over there!" exclaimed Aunt Sophia. She pointed to the boats that were gliding slowly down the lake.

John convinced Sophia to go with him on one of the boats. Stellios asked Ipatia politely if she would like to go also, but she declined. She pulled her shawl around her, shivering slightly as they walked slowly. It was a little cooler than she had anticipated. They found a bench and sat down, watching the people glide by on the lake. She listened to him talk about his last year at the Poly-Tech Institute.

Time seemed to go slowly, and Ipatia was becoming worried about her aunt. "I wonder what happened to my aunt and your uncle," she said.

He looked around, then pointed them out to her. "There they are, underneath the bridge."

Although the couple was not clearly visible, Ipatia was able to make out her aunt's height and her shawl. Suddenly, Ipatia saw a familiar looking man, sharply dressed, standing on the bridge, talking to a woman. She strained her eyes desperately trying to catch a better glimpse. It couldn't be, but it was! Tony Plakis had come to the nightclub with his sister!

❦   ❦   ❦

"Melissa, are you sure you want to continue to wait for this Daras fellow? We've already been here over an hour and I have to get up early tomorrow morning for my flight to England," said Tony, checking his watch. It was ten o'clock.

"I'm positive he's here somewhere! Now don't be a sour face! He said he'll be here, and he will!" said Melissa, smiling back at her older brother. She continued to look for Chuck Daras.

Tony's eyes searched the area once more, noticing a young couple sitting on a bench across the lake. What caught his attention was that the woman was taller than the man. On closer inspection, the young woman was quite attractive and oddly familiar. He stared for a moment and his heart quickened as he realized how her features were similar to Ipatia's. He shook his head. Ipatia wouldn't be dressed in a sophisticated evening gown, sitting alone on a bench with a young man. Not the Ipatia he knew!

"Oh, there he is!" said Melissa, pointing with one hand and tugging on Tony's sleeve with the other.

Tony looked in the direction she was pointing and saw Chuck waving back to them.

"See, I told you he'll be here. Look, he's waving to us to go there. Come on, Tony, let's go meet him."

"All right," said Tony. He smiled down at his sister. He had never seen her so excited before, not even with Michael. As they walked slowly off the bridge, he glanced across the lake once more at the bench where the girl had been sitting, but she had disappeared.

CHAPTER 22

December 1988
There she stood, elegantly dressed
A dream unfolding, he confessed

Ipatia became excited when she saw Tony. She got up nervously, saying shakily to Stellios, "Can we go and wait for my aunt and your uncle at the boat dock?"

"All right."

The small boat area was located close to the back entrance, near the walkway. Ipatia furtively glanced behind her, to where Tony had been standing. She felt slightly disappointed when she saw he was no longer there.

"Here they come!" said Stellios, interrupting Ipatia's thoughts.

They watched as her aunt and John returned from their excursion.

"Ipatia, you should have come!" said Aunt Sophia, laughing, as she got out of the boat with the help of John. "It was so much fun!"

"You both looked like you were enjoying yourselves," said Ipatia, smiling.

They walked around for a few minutes more, while Aunt Sophia chattered about their little adventure. "We almost fell into the water when another boat bumped into us!" she said. Then she noticed the time. "Oh, look at the time! It's been a lovely evening, but I think we should be going, since the trip back is close to an hour."

John nodded and said, "Whatever you'd like."

They reached the front of the club. John said, "You two ladies wait here and we'll go and get the car. It's parked down the road."

They were gone before Sophia could protest.

"Aunt Sophia, I wanted to tell you…," began Ipatia, intending to mention Tony's presence.

"I'm sorry, Ipatia. Can it wait?" interrupted Sophia, touching her arm briefly. "I need to excuse myself one minute. It is a long trip back to the house and I don't think I can wait. Do you want to join me?"

"No, thanks. I think it would be better if one of us stays here, in case they come back looking for us," said Ipatia, laughing.

Her aunt left hurriedly and Ipatia stood there, daydreaming of a tall, handsome young man who had saved her from a snake once. Then she suppressed a yawn, feeling somewhat sleepy. It was later than she had thought. She strolled down the sidewalk, enjoying the evening breeze, the palm trees and the quietness after all the loud music inside. There was no one else in sight. She wondered where Tony was now. Seeing his sister there with him had dampened her excitement. The memory of what she had said to Michael, regarding Bonnie and Tony, was still fresh in Ipatia's mind.

♦   ♦   ♦

Tony strolled through the double-glass door, his hands in his pockets, thinking about his trip tomorrow. He left his sister and Chuck behind momentarily to discuss things. It appeared that their relationship was becoming serious and Tony didn't want to be in the way.

He wondered what it would be like with Chuck Daras as his brother-in-law. He had a premonition that if allowed, Chuck could easily take over his father's business. He was just that type, and it would be just like Melissa to promise him that position.

Tony's thoughts wandered towards his own future. He should start thinking about what to do next if Chuck joined the agency. He could either stay, or return to his former position at Oxford. He had requested a one-year sabbatical. He could always return there.

He stopped abruptly when he saw the girl. She had her back turned to him, walking slowly, as if she was deep in thought. Her shawl had slipped down her shoulders, revealing her slim neck and bare shoulders.

He stood there, studying her, not quite sure whether to risk approaching her or not. If it wasn't Ipatia, he could get in trouble with the girl's family. He got his answer as soon as she turned around. At first, she appeared not to recognize him, but as she walked closer to him, her eyes focused on him and began to show recognition.

"Hello, Ipatia!" said Tony, walking towards her, admiring her. His father had been right about her beauty. She was like a walking dream in that shimmering black dress. Her long legs, slim hips, creamy white shoulders and graceful neck all were exposing an elegance and sophistication that had been hidden in her black garb from the island. This was not the peasant girl he remembered. This was a princess.

Ipatia was mesmerized by the pleasantly rich voice. That very same person it belonged to was now looking deeply into her eyes, into her soul. "Hello!" she managed to say. Her cheeks felt flushed. It was as if time stood still and they were in a vacuum, sucked up by a force greater than themselves, inevitably pulling them together.

"I thought I saw you by the lake, but when I looked for you, you had vanished! You always seem to be vanishing on me, Ipatia," he said, taking her hand. "Now I'm going to hold your hand so you don't run away this time."

Tony's action caught Ipatia off guard. She trembled slightly from his touch. *You must not let him get so close!*

"You know, Mr. Tony, where I come from, it's not considered proper for a young man to be alone with a girl at a nightclub, and even more so, to hold the girl's hand," she said firmly.

"Is that right?" asked Tony. There she went again, putting distance between them. He realized she was in earnest. "Then I will respect your wish, Miss Kouris, as long as you promise you won't run away."

They both laughed nervously.

"But now that we're on the topic of what is proper, may I ask, how is it that you were sitting with a young man all alone on the bench?"

"Oh, Stellios? Let me explain. It's…it's…not like it seems," said Ipatia, stammering lightly. "He's the nephew of John Stavrakis, the man who invited us to come with them here. My aunt and John went on a boat ride and left us alone, and I didn't feel like going on the boat because I get sick on boats…so Stellios stayed behind with me. Now they went to get the car and my aunt went to the lady's room."

"Then I came at a good time," he said. "What would your dear grandfather say if he learned you were out here this late hour, all alone at a nightclub?"

Ipatia knew he was teasing her, yet she still blushed, realizing how true his words were.

"He wouldn't like it," she admitted. She had been so caught up in knowing that Tony was there, she hadn't thought at all about what was proper.

"No, really, don't take me seriously," he said, laughing at her guilt-ridden demeanor. "How have you been, Ipatia? You know the house felt empty after I returned home from Thessaloniki, with everyone gone. I had been hoping to see you still there."

"I apologize for my impulsive behavior. Grandfather always scolded me for it. I just didn't feel comfortable staying there any longer while your father was in the hospital and you were about to leave."

"Is that the only reason?" he asked gently, gazing into her lovely eyes. They were slowly turning into a dark, green hue. He liked what he saw.

"No, but that was the main reason," she managed to squeak out, unable to move.

"You're forgiven," he said, his voice husky, as he bowed. "I hope some day you will trust me enough to confide in me what the real reason was."

Ipatia stopped, frozen, unable to continue, unable to say what she really felt inside. *He had said some day for me to confide in him. That means he wants to see me again.* She had the odd feeling he was about to kiss her, but the feeling vanished as quickly as it came when he stepped back slightly.

At that moment, Sophia made her presence known. She had been standing on the side, observing the young man talking to Ipatia. There was something familiar about him. Ipatia introduced him to her.

"Tony, do you know who I am?" Sophia said, excitedly shaking his hand.

"Yes, I surely do! You are Sophia, the nice lady who sewed for us when we were children, and who always gave us candy when you came over."

"How have you been, Tony? You have changed so much since I last saw you!"

"I'm doing fine," said Tony. "You look much younger than I remember you."

"You were always one for saying such nice things!" Sophia replied, smiling fondly. "What have you been doing lately with yourself? Last time I heard, you were somewhere in England, teaching at a university."

Ipatia was amazed at the familiarity between her aunt and Tony.

"Actually, I am staying with my family in Kifissia for the time being. Father's shipping business is keeping me very busy, traveling to different cities."

"You're working for your father?" asked Sophia.

"Yes. My father's recuperating from a surgery he had, and I am helping him with the business. My sister, Melissa, is somewhere around here with her new beau, Chuck Daras."

Just then, the car with John and Stellios arrived and honked at them.

"I'm sorry to hear about your father. Please give our best wishes to him and your sister."

"We'll have to talk another time, I see your escort has arrived," Tony said, somewhat dryly. "Have a pleasant evening."

Ipatia bade him farewell, disappointed that they were leaving. She watched him walk away, his hands in his pockets. He was not his usual, carefree self. Something had changed.

"Why don't you two women share the back seat," suggested John, opening the door for them.

Ipatia settled in the back with her aunt, and the car drove on into the night.

"Tony has turned out to be such a handsome young man," remarked Sophia.

"He's engaged," said Ipatia dryly. She knew what her aunt was thinking. *Yes, but where was Bonnie tonight?*

"Oh, I didn't mean it that way, you know…having known him when he was a child…and everything," explained Sophia, appearing flustered. "I was just noticing the difference."

Then everything became silent and the sound of the car's tires droning on the pavement made Ipatia feel sleepy. She began to doze off.

"Ipatia, did Tony say Melissa had a new beau?"

"Yes," murmured Ipatia, half-asleep.

"Wasn't Dr. Michael engaged to Melissa?"

"Oh, that's right, I forgot to tell you!" exclaimed Ipatia, bolting up from her sleep. She rubbed her eyes. "Today when I went to drop off the *Vassilopita*, he was closing the office for the holidays. I asked him if he was going to spend his holiday with Melissa, but he said he no longer was engaged to her."

"That makes Dr. Michael available," observed Sophia.

"What do you mean?" asked Ipatia, drifting off to sleep, unable to stay awake.

After that evening, John visited them almost daily, and there was much gaiety and laughter when he was around. He had a good sense of humor and his boyish charm was appealing to Ipatia. She felt her aunt's happiness every time he visited.

One day when she arrived from class, she found her aunt alone in the living room, sewing.

"How was your day?" asked Ipatia, joining her aunt on the sofa.

"Oh, fine, fine. John stopped by later this afternoon and he was his ever charming self," replied Aunt Sophia, smiling. She threaded a needle. "He had something to do, so he couldn't stay that long, but he invited us to his parents' house for New Years. Do you know what that means?"

"It means he likes you," said Ipatia simply.

"Not only that, I think it's more serious than that," said Aunt Sophia, beginning to sew a hem on a skirt. "I like him very much. I just hope his parents like me."

"They will!" exclaimed Ipatia, hugging her aunt. "You are such a lovely and kind person. They will be lucky to have a daughter-in-law like you!"

"Ipatia, whatever gave you that idea?" asked Aunt Sophia, appearing pleased.

The days seemed to whiz by and New Years eve came. Aunt Sophia fussed with her hair and clothes all day. Ipatia helped her bake a *Vassilopita* for the occasion, kneading the dough and making sure she placed a coin in it. John came by and picked them up later that evening. His parents turned out to be very nice people who embraced Sophia and Ipatia as if they were family. Ipatia and her aunt had such a good time that they didn't get home until early the next morning.

Ipatia woke up late the next day, feeling tired and groggy. She found her aunt already in the kitchen busily preparing breakfast and humming. She was in an unusually cheerful mood.

"Good morning, Ipatia! I hope you slept well. I hardly slept at all! I was going to tell you the good news last night, but you were so sleepy, I thought I'd wait until today to tell you!" said Sophia, her eyes shining.

"Yes?"

"John proposed to me last night. Your aunt is going to be married!"

Ipatia jumped up with joy, hugging her aunt with all her might. "Congratulations, Aunt Sophia! I'm so happy for you!"

"Thank you," said Sophia, hugging her back. "I know this is quite sudden, and at my age! But when God gives me an opportunity like this one, I must take it."

"Isn't that wonderful! So, tell me, dear Aunt, what are your plans? When are you going to be married?" asked Ipatia, settling back down in her chair. Amidst her happiness, a small doubt entered her mind and it began to nag her. How was she going to fit into this new couple's life?

"Last night, we didn't have much time to discuss all the details, but we did manage to agree that the wedding should take place in about two months. That will give us time to prepare for it, don't you think? I need to order my wedding gown and send out invitations, and do a number of other things that one needs to do when one gets married."

"Oh, yes, it'll be a lot of fun! I can just picture you looking dazzlingly beautiful in a long, white wedding gown, standing at the aisle with uncle John handsomely dressed in a tuxedo. You will make the perfect couple!"

"Thank you, Ipatia, that's so sweet of you!"

"Where do you plan to live after the wedding?"

Sophia cleared her throat and looked Ipatia squarely in the eyes. Her voice trembled slightly as she said, "Ipatia, as you know…John lives in a suburb of Chicago, and his house sits right next to Antonios' house. Once we are married…he wants us to go back to America and live there."

"America?" asked Ipatia, her voice ending in a high pitch. She stared at her aunt. She had mixed feelings about the idea. She was happy for her aunt's marriage, but going to America to live was another story.

"Yes! America!" replied Sophia, nodding her head. "Isn't that amazing…me go to America to live! I was up all night just thinking about it! Anyway, I thought about you and felt it wasn't fair I just get up and leave you. So I'd like you to know that you can come and stay with us. With your English, you'd get along just fine!"

Ipatia thought for a moment before replying, "What does Uncle John say about this?"

"Actually, I haven't discussed it with him yet. It came to me last night as I was thinking about everything…but I'm pretty sure he won't say no to the idea."

"I don't know what to say," said Ipatia slowly. "I did have plans to take the entrance examination in the spring, and the thought of going to America is exciting, but it's too far away from Grandfather. Although I love you very much, I do want to visit him in the summers, between classes."

Sophia hesitated as she thought about Ipatia's comments. She replied, "First of all, you can continue your studies in America. You understand English, so it will not be a problem. There are also plenty of universities there for your studies. You can still visit your grandfather. It'll just be a longer trip."

Ipatia was silent, digesting the information.

"Why don't you think about it for awhile? There's no rush," said Aunt Sophia, patting her on the back. "We have two months until the wedding anyway."

"Is it all right if I speak with Grandfather, to see what he has to say?"

Her aunt readily agreed. Later that day, Ipatia walked to the pharmacy and placed a call to speak with her grandfather the next morning. The rest of the day was spent thinking about everything her aunt had said.

The next morning, she spoke to her grandfather on the telephone. She told him about her aunt's wedding and her plans to move to America with her husband.

"So your aunt is getting married?" His voice sounded surprised. He paused. "That's very good news. Please give her my congratulations, Ipatia."

"Yes, Grandfather, I will. Meanwhile, what shall I do? She has invited me to go live with them in America, but I have plans to take the entrance examination in the spring."

"The idea of going to America is out of the question! First of all, you don't have the money for the trip and don't expect to live off of charity all your life, young lady!"

"I know," she admitted. "That means I could remain here. I won't be by myself, because Miss Marika rents the downstairs."

"Under no circumstances am I going to allow you to live there alone! If your cousins, George and Paula, are willing to have you, then you can stay with them. Otherwise, you come back here and stay with me."

"Grandfather, I tried going to the cousins before, remember? They weren't there. They like to travel."

"Try them again. I don't think they travel all the time," he replied firmly.

Ipatia walked slowly back home, deep in thought. She discussed her conversation with Aunt Sophia.

Her aunt listened, then said, "Although the invitation still stands for you to come and live with us, I understand you have your own life to live, and I wish you all the very best. We'll try and see about visiting your cousins one of these days."

After that day, her aunt was like a schoolgirl, excited about everything, glowing and happy all the time. John left for America a few days later, kissing Sophia and promising her he'd write often. He needed to go and prepare for his new bride to be.

CHAPTER 23

January 1989
Michael's story begins to unfold
Ipatia is seeing him I am told

One Saturday in early January, Tony was sitting in the study, conversing and joking with Michael, who had dropped by unexpectedly.

Michael said, "How long has it been? At least three months since I last saw you, ever since...."

"Michael, Michael," said Tony, laughing at his friend's complaint. "The reason why I haven't been by to visit you is not because of anything that happened between you and my sister, but because I have been very busy with our business...and with Father's health. Most of the time, I've been traveling back and forth to our various offices. There's always something that needs to be taken care of."

"You're telling the truth now," said Michael, half-jokingly.

"Of course! Just look at this pile of papers that still need to be read," said Tony, pointing at the stack on his desk. "I brought them here from the office."

"You know, Tony, I remember how you used to come back from England during your summer breaks and we'd go to all these different events so we could meet women," said Michael. "You've changed somehow."

"Things are different now," said Tony, nodding at his friend's description of him. "Life has changed so much since this last summer."

"All this work and no play, it's not healthy. I'm speaking to you as a doctor as well as a friend."

"You have a good point," admitted Tony. "But don't worry about me, old friend. I have a feeling that things will change after April."

"What do you mean?"

"Look, you've been such a good friend and everything, I don't want there to be hard feelings for what I'm about to say next. Melissa is engaged to Chuck Daras. Their wedding is planned for April."

Michael hesitated before speaking, "I wish them all the luck in the world. I had some time to think about everything that happened between your sister and me. Your sister had acquired expensive tastes and didn't want to give them up. I couldn't afford that lifestyle, not with the salary I was making."

"I understand," said Tony, nodding.

"What did you mean about things changing in April?"

"Actually, they've changed already," admitted Tony. "It seems Chuck Daras is not only interested in my sister, but in our shipping business. With her encouragement, he already started to manage the company while I was away on this last trip. Yesterday, when I returned, I found him sitting at my desk, with my sister there, going over papers!"

"Did you speak to your father about this?" asked Michael. "It seems Chuck doesn't waste time."

"Yes, this morning. I made it clear to him that I would only stay for a few more months, until Chuck took charge. My heart was never in this line of work, I'm afraid."

"Oh," said Michael, raising an eyebrow. "Where's your father now?"

"He's in Crete with Christina, and he'll probably stay there until he gets better. He doesn't want his old business associates seeing him so ill."

"Good luck with everything," said Michael, getting up. "By the way, I came by not only to see how you were doing, but to also ask if you wanted to join me and some cousins of mine. We're planning to go out to Diamond's nightclub tonight, you know, the one with the lake."

"Thanks for the invitation, but I'm afraid I'll have to turn you down, my friend. I'm meeting our attorney this afternoon. We have to go over some legal papers together."

"Don't say I didn't try," said Michael, laughing.

"It is interesting, though, that you would mention that nightclub. I went there with my sister, back in December," said Tony, leaning back in his chair with his arms behind his head. "The funny thing was, that I bumped into Ipatia, the island girl, and her aunt. She looked so different, so much older."

"Who, her aunt?" asked Michael with a twinkle in his eye.

"No, I meant Ipatia," said Tony. He smiled when he noticed his friend's teasing look.

"Tony, you've been away so much, I haven't had the chance to tell you the latest news. Ipatia's been coming to my office for several weeks now," said Michael, looking Tony squarely in the eyes.

Tony sat straight up in his chair, stunned. "How did this come about?" he asked cautiously.

"She visited me once with her aunt when she had the flu," said Michael nonchalantly. "I loaned her some medical journals then, and ever since, she periodically comes for a few minutes to drop off the old ones and pick up the new ones."

"She's a unique girl," said Tony, feeling odd about the whole thing, trying to picture her being interested in medical journals.

"I know, I know," said Michael, laughing. "That's what you say about all the women you meet."

"This one is different," said Tony, shrugging his shoulders.

"Remember, I'll be waiting for you to come and visit me in my new office," said Michael, at the door.

"All right, then, how about in a couple of weeks when I get back," said Tony, laughing, and bidding his friend farewell.

The attorney came a few minutes later, and Tony was busy with him. Then Melissa popped her head in the door to let him know she was going out on a date with Chuck and wouldn't be in until later that evening.

Afterwards, Tony sat alone in the living room. He gazed absentmindedly at the flames in the fireplace. He recalled the discussion he had with his father early that morning.

"Father, I need to speak with you," he said. "Yesterday I found Chuck Daras in our office, going over the papers. What's going on?"

"Let me explain," said Gregory. "Now that he will be part of the family, I think it best that he get involved with our company. Chuck has many years of experience in the shipping business and I think he'll make a good manager."

"I didn't go back to England because you wanted me here to help you out, but if Chuck is to take over, then it seems you won't be needing me much longer."

"No...please don't look at it that way! I want you to remain with the company, to oversee things."

Tony remained silent, digesting everything. "I'll stay for a few months, until Chuck Daras is ready to manage," he said before hanging up.

Tony noticed the fire was almost out. He arose and placed a few more logs in the fireplace, watching them feed the fire. He stood there, deep in thought, gazing at the flames.

His conversation with Michael had disturbed him. It seemed as if his friend had taken a fancy to Ipatia. It was unlike him to get involved with a female unless it was serious. *Why does that bother you Tony? Is it because you yourself were smitten the last time you saw Ipatia standing at the nightclub? Something stirred inside of you when you saw her and you could not forget it. Yet you did nothing. You were too busy with your father's business and all for naught, because after all is said and done, Daras is going to replace you and be in charge. But isn't that what you want? To go back to England and teach?*

"What would I be going back to? The university walls and dusty books that hide me from the world, that will keep me away from Ipatia?" muttered Tony aloud. Then he remembered his father's negative reaction when he learned Tony had spent time with her. "How could I get past his anger if I were to marry the girl?"

Your father never thought about your plans, or your dreams. All he cares about is himself and his business. That is why he chose Bonnie for you, to bring in more money for the business. You are letting your father control your life, Tony, and you are going to lose that girl if you don't do something about it.

Two weeks later, Ipatia and her aunt decided to visit her cousins, George and Paula. The taxi rolled to a stop in front of the building. The same lady was sweeping outside. It felt like it was only yesterday when Ipatia had come here with Tony. This time, the old woman nodded when Ipatia asked her if the Mastroyiannis family was home.

Moments later, Paula answered the door. Ipatia and her aunt introduced themselves, followed by hugs and kisses. They were escorted into the house. It was a cozy and comfortable place, with nice furnishings.

Ipatia liked the couple. George was a stout man, with a jovial nature. He laughed at everything, whereas Paula, although sweet, tended to be the more serious of the two.

"The lady next door, Mrs. Makroulis, mentioned about a girl coming here looking for us, but we had no idea it was you! Do you remember us, Ipatia?" asked George, smiling whimsically at her, as he observed her. "You were a little girl then, when you and your parents visited us that one time. I don't remember seeing Sophia then. Your grandmother and I were first cousins. My mother and your great-grandmother were sisters."

"Yes, you do look familiar," said Ipatia, shyly nodding her head. His nose was small and straight, like that of her grandmother's, but that was the only feature that had redeeming qualities other than his good-natured self. His large eyes bulged, and his mouth moved loosely, as if all the years of laughing had gotten it loose around the seams.

"I've had health problems, which have caused me to grow these white hairs and this stomach!" laughed George, his large stomach heaving with the laughter. "Ever since Dr. Hatzis left, we have had to deal with a young, inexperienced doctor who's always trying different medicines on me."

"Is that Dr. Michael Hatzis you are talking about?" asked Aunt Sophia, perking up.

"Yes, do you know him?" asked George, curiously.

"Yes! He treated Ipatia recently," replied Aunt Sophia, nodding her head emphatically. "I was so impressed with this young man. His new office is near our house. He is so kind, that he lends Ipatia medical journals to read."

"Dr. Michael had mentioned he knew you," said Ipatia.

"Ah, really? We need to pay him a visit one of these days," said George, nodding his head with pleasure. "What a good doctor! We had been going to him for several years. Now that he moved, Dr. Savas has taken his place. He is no good!"

"Now, now, George, give him time. When Dr. Michael first became our doctor, he was also fresh out of medical school, don't you remember?" said Paula, coming in to the room with a tray full of refreshments. "You see, we have a special place in our heart for Dr. Michael, because he and our Christos are the same age...thirty years old. They served in the army together, years ago. When Christos broke his leg during training, Dr. Michael helped treat the leg. They have been good friends ever since."

Paula picked up a framed picture of Christos in his captain's uniform and gave it to Sophia.

Sophia gazed at it, then showed it to Ipatia. "Christos is quite handsome, isn't he?"

"What? Yes, he is," said Ipatia, caught off guard. For some odd reason, the picture of her cousin had reminded her of Tony. Instead of Christos, she had pictured Tony dressed in the captain's uniform.

"Christos was studying at the University of Thessaloniki, where he met his wife, Tassoula, who was also a student there. After Christos received his degree, he served in the army. When he completed his service, he married Tassoula and has lived in Thessaloniki ever since, with his family," explained George. "We spend half the time there, so we can be near the other grandchildren."

"You also have a daughter?" asked Sophia, showing the picture to Ipatia before handing it back to Paula.

"Yes, she's four years older than Christos. Popi lives in Athens with her husband and two children," said Paula, getting the picture of her daughter and showing it to them. "Her husband owns an appliance store."

"Very lovely," murmured Sophia.

"Excuse me for asking, Sophia…but do you have family?"

"Actually, not yet," said Sophia, smiling inwardly. Greeks were notorious for asking nosy questions. "You see, I'll be getting married in a few weeks."

George and Paula congratulated her warmly, then Paula asked her how she met her husband to be. Sophia discussed the topics with enthusiasm and ended the discussion by inviting the couple to the wedding.

"Thank you for the invitation! We would be delighted to come," said George, nodding his head energetically.

"You said that John is from America. Will you be staying here after the wedding?" asked Paula.

Sophia replied, "I'm glad you asked that question. Actually, after our honeymoon, we will live in Chicago, where John owns a house and has a real estate business. Ipatia prefers to stay here and enter the university, but her grandfather doesn't want her staying here alone. Christos asked if it would be possible that she stay here with you."

"Ah, good old Christos! He was one for values! There's no one like him!" said George, guffawing and slapping his knee with enthusiasm. "I remember one year we visited your grandparents, Ipatia. My Popi was sixteen or so, and quite lovely, I might add. Anyhow, we had gone to a festival and she had been asked by a boy to dance the waltz. With our permission, she got up and danced with the boy. He must have been not much older. Christos wasn't too happy about that. We learned later that Christos went and reprimanded the boy's parents afterwards, just because their son danced with our daughter!"

"I can see that happening!" said Sophia, nodding emphatically.

"We'd love to have Ipatia come and stay with us. There's plenty of space," said Paula, smiling also. "When did you say that will be, my sweet?"

Aunt Sophia told them the date.

"February 12?" echoed George, scratching his head. "Just wait a minute and let me check the calendar. There's something about that day that reminds me of something."

He came back with his calendar and his reading glasses.

"Isn't this the week we're going to be in Thessaloniki for the baby's baptism?" asked George to Paula, pointing to the calendar. Paula studied it closely, then nodded.

"Christos will be baptizing his son on February 16, so we may be able to come to the wedding after all," said Paula. "However, we were planning to stay over their house for a few weeks after the baptism."

"Ipatia can come with us," said George, taking his reading glasses off and looking at the girl. "Ipatia, what do you think about that?"

"I'd like that very much!" said Ipatia. "I would like to meet my cousins."

"Now wait a minute, George," said Paula. "We need to check with Christos and his wife first before we go inviting. We don't know if they have anyone else coming there for the baptism that week."

"Ah yes," said George, stroking his fleshy chin thoughtfully. "I hadn't thought about that."

"Is it all right if we get back in touch with you first, before you make any concrete plans, Sophia?" asked Paula. "I don't want to make any promises until we hear from Christos first."

George and Paula promised to let them know as soon as they found out.

Later that evening, back at home, Ipatia decided to write her grandfather and let him know the news. She got some paper and a pen and sat in the dining room, writing what had just transpired. He had been right, the cousins were willing to take her in. She was sealing the envelope when her aunt entered the dining room.

"After you're finished, could you help me with the wedding invitations?" asked Aunt Sophia. "I've put them off for too long and I do need to get them out as soon as possible!"

"Of course I'd love to!" said Ipatia. "What would you like me to do?"

"Here is the list of the people I'm inviting to the wedding," said Aunt Sophia, handing her a bunch of envelopes, a piece of paper and an address book. "Could you write the name and address on the front of these envelopes for me? Then put our return address on the back. When you are finished, give them to me. I'll do the rest."

An hour later, Ipatia came across the Plakis name. She looked at her aunt curiously. "Are we inviting the Plakis family?"

"Yes. I thought it would be a good idea, since they were kind enough to take you in when I wasn't here," said Aunt Sophia. "Oh, and I also want to invite Dr. Michael, but we don't have his home address. Could you do me a favor and drop off the invitation at his office tomorrow, when you go to class?"

"You're inviting Dr. Michael?"

"Why not! He's done so much for us and that's the least we can do in return!" said Aunt Sophia firmly.

"I'll try and remember," said Ipatia, resigning herself to the task. She took the invitation her aunt gave her and placed it inside her handbag. Lately, she had been having mixed feelings about him. He was a nice man when it came to talking about medical topics, but she recoiled whenever she tried seeing herself getting close to him.

CHAPTER 24

January 1989
The invitation brought you to me
I walked you home and stayed for coffee

The next day, Wednesday, Sophia had several clients coming and going. Georgia Sarkidis came shortly after breakfast, then a few minutes later, Mrs. Vardis dropped by to pick up a finished dress. Aunt Sophia asked Ipatia to pin the hem on Mrs. Sarkidis' dress while she went to attend to Mrs. Vardis.

Ipatia enjoyed listening to Mrs. Sarkidis chat about her grandchildren.

In the hallway, Sophia was reassuring Mrs. Vardis by saying, "Yes, yes, it's just the right fit." Sophia saw her to the door, then went back into the living room.

Ipatia arose. "I finished the hem, Aunt."

"Good! Georgia, dear, if you can slip out of that dress, I'll have it sewn up in no time. There are refreshments in the dining room, please help yourselves."

Ipatia quickly finished her task and helped Mrs. Sarkidis out of her dress.

"I'll only stay for a little," said Mrs. Sarkidis, eyeing the refreshments.

They drank coffee and ate the sliced chocolate torte that Mrs. Sarkidis had brought, while Aunt Sophia sewed the hem of the dress, conversing with Mrs. Sarkidis.

"Ummm, this is really decadent chocolate!" exclaimed Ipatia, appreciating the chocolate torte.

"That's an interesting way to describe it, Ipatia. It's one of my favorite tortes," said Mrs. Sarkidis, nodding eagerly.

"Speaking of decadent, my dear Georgia," began Aunt Sophia, tying a knot. "Can you imagine my shock, when we went shopping for a skirt the other day for Ipatia and found the prices much higher than I ever remembered them to be, and the skirts so much shorter! I couldn't imagine my niece wearing one of those things! There is no decency in our society these days. The women are baring it all!"

"I've seen women wearing those short skirts, and it's disgusting! What about those bikini swimsuits one sees on the beach these days. They keep getting smaller and smaller. Some women aren't even wearing the top parts. Why, I remember when I was a young girl, we couldn't even show our ankles!" said Georgia Sarkidis, gesturing comically towards her plump legs.

"You know what I think?" said Ipatia. "I think people who do these things have something lacking in their lives. Maybe they feel they aren't pretty enough, or don't get enough attention from other people, so they show more skin, so someone would pay them attention."

"My philosophical Ipatia!" laughed Aunt Sophia. "In my days, even if someone had that idea in their silly head, they wouldn't think about doing it because it was unaccepted by society! People would shun them! Yes, my dear, times have changed."

Then they went on to the topic of Aunt Sophia's wedding. Georgia suggested having her grandchildren participate in the wedding ceremony.

"They would be perfect for the flower girl and ring boy," Georgia said, taking out photos of her grandchildren from her purse and showing them to Sophia. "Anna is four and Peter is five."

Aunt Sophia nodded, saying how lovely they were. She then asked if it would be all right with Georgia's daughter, and Georgia said that of course it would be all right.

"Oh, look at the time, it's almost twelve o'clock! I have to be back by two-thirty. I hope I make it," said Georgia, looking at her watch.

"How did you get here?" asked Ipatia.

"With the train and the bus," said Georgia. "Mind you, it took me over an hour to get here. But I just had to come, knowing Sophia will be leaving us soon, and this dress needed to be finished before she leaves."

Ipatia asked her where she lived and when Mrs. Sarkidis told her, Ipatia recognized the town. It was the same place where her cousins George and Paula lived.

After Georgia left, Ipatia discussed at length with her aunt about the commute from her cousins' house to Mrs. Rodos' classes. Her aunt agreed that it would be too far to be traveling back and forth in the evenings. With a heavy heart, Ipatia walked to class later that day. She didn't look forward to telling Mrs. Rodos she would no longer work for her after she moved.

After class, Ipatia straightened up the room, then waited for Mrs. Rodos to finish her writing. Mrs. Rodos looked up inquisitively.

"Yes?"

"Mrs. Rodos, I wanted to tell you some good news. My aunt is getting married and you are invited to the wedding," said Ipatia. "We mailed out the invitations this morning."

"How wonderful!" exclaimed Mrs. Rodos, clasping her hands together. "Weddings are such nice events! I love to attend weddings."

"Now, the bad news," said Ipatia, more soberly. "My aunt will be leaving for America right after the wedding, and I will have to move in with some cousins who live on the other side of town."

"Is that right?" exclaimed Mrs. Rodos, taking her glasses off and looking at Ipatia with wonder.

"Yes," said Ipatia, nodding. "At first, I thought I could continue coming here to the classes, but I found out today that I would need to take the train and a bus to get here. I won't be getting home until very late at night."

"I wouldn't have you doing that!" said Mrs. Rodos, shaking her head emphatically. "Although you've been an excellent help to me, and I will miss you… you need to do what's right for you!"

"Thank you."

Ipatia picked up her handbag as she was getting ready to leave.

"Before you go, let me give you your paycheck."

Ipatia thanked her and placed it in her handbag. At that moment, her fingers brushed against the white envelope inside. It was the wedding invitation. She exclaimed, "Oh dear, I forgot to pass by and give Dr. Michael his invitation! Good-bye Mrs. Rodos!"

Ipatia hurriedly made her way down the street, heading for the doctor's office. She knew it was late, but she could easily slip the envelope underneath the office door. The pharmacy's well-lit sign loomed up ahead, a signal that she was nearing her destination. She pulled on the door handle and was pleased when the door opened. She ran up the dark stairwell, stumbling on the last step as she entered the hallway. She winced, rubbing her foot and muttering softly. That foot always seemed to be sensitive, ever since she sprained it.

When she got to the office, she was surprised to see the light on and the door open. She stopped in her tracks, ready to leave, for inside were Tony and Dr. Michael, standing and conversing. Tony's tanned face contrasted well with the white, pressed shirt. His sculpted Grecian profile, with his firm chin, revealed a stunning likeness to an era in Greek history where gods and goddesses ruled.

Dr. Michael, standing next to Tony, for some reason looked even shorter and foxier tonight, with his brown mustache and pointed chin. Maybe it was because he had always been that way. It's just that she hadn't noticed it before.

"Hello, Ipatia," said Dr. Michael, looking pleasantly surprised, as he gestured her in.

Tony smiled tightly when he saw her. He was surprised to see her there at this late hour. He wasn't sure what the girl was doing here, but he was going to find out!

"Hello, Dr. Michael, hello Mr. Tony," said Ipatia breathlessly. "I had forgotten to drop this by earlier, so I came now."

She nervously handed Dr. Michael the invitation, mindful of Tony's eyes watching her.

"What is this?" asked Dr. Michael, his slim, pale fingers opening the invitation and reading it.

"My aunt is getting married and would like to invite you to her wedding, but she didn't have your home address, so she asked me to drop this off."

"I appreciate the invitation. What a pleasant bit of news," said Dr. Michael, peering at her from behind his spectacles.

Ipatia then turned and spoke to Tony. "We mailed your family an invitation this morning. Your fiancé Bonnie, is also invited, Mr. Tony."

"Thank you," said Tony slowly, caught by surprise at the girl's inclusion of Bonnie. "My parents are in Crete, and if I were to come, I would be coming alone. Bonnie is not and has not been my fiancé. When is the big day?"

"It's February 12," said Ipatia, feeling flushed again. He was not attached to Bonnie! Suddenly, he appeared different to her, nicer, as if the barrier that had been between them was no longer there.

"Ahh, just a few days from St. Valentine's day," remarked Tony. "I don't know if I'll be in town then, but if I am, I will try and make it. Thank your aunt also for the invitation."

"I must be going. It's late and my aunt is expecting me," Ipatia managed to say, although her feet did not want to move for some reason.

"You probably want this to take with you," said Dr. Michael, breaking the spell. He picked up a new medical journal and handed it to her. "There's a section there about a new treatment for cancer."

"Thank you, Dr. Michael! I almost forgot! Good night!" said Ipatia, regaining her momentum. She took the journal, and bidding the two men farewell, left quickly before they could say anything. She hurried down the hallway, mindful of the time, when she heard footsteps behind her.

"Here, why don't I walk you home," said Tony, joining her. "It's quite dark for you to be walking alone."

He took her arm gently and her heart soared at his touch. They walked slowly down the steps. She felt like she was living a dream, even as her heart's racing beat reminded her how alive this moment was. This time, she did not want to run away. This time, she just wanted to melt in his arms.

When they reached the ground floor, he opened the front door for her. The cool air smacked her soundly, bringing her back down to earth. She shivered ever so slightly.

"Are you cold?" asked Tony. "We can take my car if you're cold."

"No, thank you. I'll be all right, really," she murmured.

They strolled down the sidewalk. She noticed the other couples strolling by, and for the first time, she felt like one of them. Only he did not have his arm around her shoulder. She wondered what that would be like. The soft streetlights cast a magical glow around them.

"How have you been, Ipatia? The last time I saw you, it was when you were with your aunt at the nightclub," said Tony, breaking her concentration.

"Yes," admitted Ipatia, coming back to reality. "We've been so busy with the preparations for the wedding. Why this past week, I didn't even have time to read Dr. Michael's medical journals, and I don't know if I'll have time to read this one either!"

"I was curious to find out how you and Dr. Michael started this little exchange."

"Dr. Michael was driving his car one day and saw me walking home from English class. He stopped to say hello and told me about his new office. Then he noticed the books I was carrying and I told him they were books Mrs. Rodos let me borrow."

"Sorry for interrupting, but who is this Mrs. Rodos? I've come across that name before," said Tony.

"She was my English teacher. Her name was inside the book you found that day I dropped it," said Ipatia, nodding her head. "She has an English class down the street there and I work for her three days a week."

"Ahh, that's interesting," said Tony. So she was in need of money and had to work. The girl wasn't depending on her aunt to take care of her. That showed character. He continued, "But don't let me stop you. What were you saying about Dr. Michael?"

"What was I saying about Dr. Michael?" echoed Ipatia, starting to wonder why all this interest with Dr. Michael.

"You told him about the books Mrs. Rodos gave you?" prodded Tony.

"Oh, yes, sorry! Then he said I could also borrow his medical journals. I didn't go at first because I didn't think it was proper. Anyhow, when I had the flu, and we visited him, he gave me a medical journal. That is how it started! I had to return it and then he had another waiting for me!" Ipatia stopped abruptly, feeling she had spoken too much. She looked down bashfully, not sure what to say next.

Tony thought about what she said. The girl's story seemed plausible enough. His friend Michael was behind all of this, busily spinning his web, drawing the girl closer to him, and now her aunt had become involved. Why else would she invite him to her wedding?

"Do you often visit Dr. Michael at this time of hour?" asked Tony quietly, his body tensing up in anticipation. How far had this gone?

"Oh no!" retorted Ipatia, shaking her head emphatically. "Typically, I drop the magazine off before English class, when it is still daylight. Today I had forgotten the invitation in my purse and didn't see it until after I finished class. My aunt specifically asked me to hand deliver it since she didn't have his home address. Anyway, I thought I would just slip it under the door and leave quickly, but I did not expect Dr. Michael or you there."

"It's interesting you like reading medical journals and English novels on your spare time. Somehow I thought girls your age were not interested in such things," observed Tony. He was thinking of Melissa and her girlfriends when he said that.

"What do you mean?" asked Ipatia, beginning to get nervous, her fingers brushing back invisible strands of hair from her face.

"I mean, girls your age typically spend their time dressing up and going out with their friends, so that they can meet young men to marry," he replied softly.

"Yes, it's odd, isn't it? I was always different from my girlfriends," she said shakily, realizing how close to the truth he came. "Ever since I was a child, I have spent much time reading books and learning things. As I got older, I saw my girlfriends getting all dressed up for the boys and I would tease them about it. But do you know what?"

"What?"

"They all got married!"

"So why didn't you?" asked Tony, knowing he was treading on delicate ground.

"Why didn't I what?" asked Ipatia, swallowing hard. She was silent for a moment, wondering how much she should say on this subject. How much of her inner self did she want to reveal?

"Why didn't you get married?" asked Tony with a puzzled look. "It seems to me, there are plenty of young men that would be interested in you if you gave them a chance. Like Dr. Michael for example."

"Dr. Michael! Now you are beginning to sound like my Aunt Sophia," replied Ipatia, her voice shaking, troubled by Tony's astute observation. Was it that evident that Dr. Michael was interested in marrying her? He had never said a word to her that indicated he was. "I see him as a doctor, someone who treats people, and not someone to marry. Why haven't you married?"

"What?" asked Tony, caught off guard. She was throwing the ball back at him. He thought for a moment, then said, "I guess because I was too busy having fun to settle down. Besides, up until now, the right girl hadn't come along."

"Oh?" asked Ipatia, raising her eyebrows.

"So tell me, what's your excuse for not marrying?" asked Tony, enjoying this immensely.

"If I marry now, then I won't ever get the chance to go to the university! My husband would want me to stay home and have babies and take care of the house," she said firmly.

"Is anything wrong with that?" he asked, liking the picture of her surrounded by babies.

"No, not for most of the women...but I am different," she said defiantly. "I will always wonder what I missed if I don't do it now."

"I see," said Tony. "You think if you marry now, you would not be able to do all that. Hmm, that's interesting. So if the right young man came along today, this very minute and asked you to marry him, you would choose the university over him?"

Ipatia, baffled by his intensive probing, stopped to digest this new possibility he posed, wondering why all this interest in her life.

"I know this sounds ridiculous, but yes, I would!" said Ipatia forcefully. "If he truly loved me, he would wait until I finished my schooling. True love is patient and lasts forever, just like in that English novel you found and gave back to me."

"English novels don't always represent life the way it is," said Tony dryly, remembering the story in the book. The heroine had pursued a career and still had gotten her man by the end of the story. "I suppose you would do the same for him, if you had to."

"If I really loved him, I suppose I would," she said, hanging her head down. Tony had a way of being challenging at times.

Tony decided to change the subject slightly. "Don't get me wrong, Ipatia. I think what you are doing is admirable. I presume you are interested in medicine?"

"Actually, I was interested at one time in becoming either a doctor or nurse," she said, perking up. "But I found out I can't stand the sight of blood. It makes me sick to my stomach. So I've decided to get a degree in a health science, like microbiology, and work in a laboratory. This way I can help people who are sick get better."

"Yes, one's health is important," said Tony thoughtfully. It appeared she was determined to get an education. "We need people like you to study microbiology so they can fight diseases. Look at my father, for instance. He has all the money one could ever wish to have and it still cannot bring him back his health. He will probably depend on doctors for the rest of his life."

"How is your father's health?" ventured Ipatia, feeling mixed emotions of Gregory Plakis.

"Thank you for asking. He's had his surgery recently and is still recovering," Tony managed to say.

"If there is anything I can do to help, please let me know," she gushed forth, overcome by feeling sorry for Tony's father.

"Thank you," he said, touched by her kind offering. "Right now, he's getting all the help he needs."

They were both silent for awhile.

"By the way, how is your aunt doing?" asked Tony.

"Very busy preparing for the wedding! Last night we were up until midnight writing the invitations," replied Ipatia. "Next, there's the flowers to order for the wedding and the reception, the dresses to be sewn, and the photographer to be chosen."

Tony nodded, as if he wanted to hear more.

"Aunt Sophia is sewing her wedding dress, and everything has to be just perfect! I helped her sew hundreds of little pearls on the dress the other day! Now she has all this shopping still to do for her trip. I am afraid it won't all fit in her luggage. Already her suitcase is full, and she even had me sit on it while she closed it, trying to squeeze everything in. I almost fell off, because I was bouncing so hard on it!"

Ipatia giggled as she remembered the scene and was rewarded by Tony's burst of laughter.

"We're here," said Ipatia, as they approached the house. The walk ended too soon. She turned slightly towards him, ready to bid him farewell.

"I have been meaning to pay your aunt a visit, and this time is as good as any," said Tony, almost whispering, taking her hand, gazing ardently into her eyes. He had a difficult time holding back his feelings, not taking her in his arms. *You promised her you would keep your distance.*

Ipatia caught herself gazing back, relishing his nearness, not wanting this moment to end. His eyes were intense, so magnetic, so beautifully full of life. They were pulling her closer to him. She felt unexplainably happy, as if his closeness would always be there for her. Resigned to the task at hand, she found the strength to step back, pulling her hand gently away. She fumbled for the key in her purse and slowly unlocked the door. She turned towards him, and drumming up the courage, she said, "Will you please come in?"

They walked up the winding staircase. She was curious to see her aunt's reaction. Who would have thought that one day Tony Plakis would pay her and her aunt a visit?

CHAPTER 25

You took me home to visit my aunt
You offered me work, what more do I want

"Tony! What a pleasant surprise!" exclaimed Aunt Sophia.

"Hello, Sophia," said Tony. He lightly pecked her on her cheek. "I was visiting my friend, Dr. Michael, when Ipatia stopped by the office. I didn't want her walking home alone."

"That's right, Aunt Sophia. I went to Dr. Michael's after class to drop off the wedding invitation. I had forgotten to do it earlier. Mr. Tony asked if he could walk me home," said Ipatia nervously, not sure how her aunt would react, but her aunt seemed fine with the news. She was not at all like Grandfather, who would have been upset to see her walking home at night with a young man.

"How nice of you to do that," said Aunt Sophia, leading him into the living room. "Please come in and make yourself comfortable."

"Thank you," said Tony, immediately noticing the piano.

"How do you like your coffee?"

"Don't go to all that trouble," said Tony, smiling at her.

"No trouble at all!" said Sophia. "This being your first time here, shouldn't I offer you at least a coffee?"

"All right then, how about making mine sweet," he replied, knowing that a good hostess always served some refreshments, even if it was only water.

Sophia went into the kitchen with her niece right behind her.

"How did this happen? Tony Plakis here?" asked Aunt Sophia, in a hushed voice. She listened while Ipatia summarized everything in a few short sentences.

"He wanted to come and visit me?" asked Aunt Sophia, looking at her niece in surprise.

"Yes," said Ipatia, nodding resolutely.

"I'll find out soon enough! Now be a good girl and help me with the refreshments," said Aunt Sophia. She took the chocolate torte from the refrigerator and placed it on the counter.

"Can I cut this for you?" offered Ipatia. "Isn't it great that Mrs. Sarkidis brought this in today? It is now coming in handy."

"Yes, we do have her to thank, don't we? Oh, and remember, the good china and silverware are in that cabinet," said Aunt Sophia, pointing in that direction. "He wants his coffee sweet, just like we do, so make ours all in the same pot. We can pour the coffee at the table. I know I sound nervous, but I'm going back now. It's not polite to leave a guest alone too long."

Sophia found Tony at the piano, playing a soft, romantic tune, while gazing out at the balcony view. She sat down in one of the armchairs, admiring his fine playing. A sense of pride came over her, as if she were seeing him through the eyes of a mother. Even when he was a young boy, he held a special place in her heart. Maybe it was because his mother had died, that she felt that way. *No, that was not the only reason, Sophia. His sister was also without a mother, and you didn't feel the same way about her. She lacked the qualities he had.*

Whenever she would visit his home, the boy would be happy to see her, bringing his toys to show her. Then he would sit next to her, sharing all his news of the day, while she worked on her sewing. Melissa, on the other hand, was not accommodating at all. When Sophia arrived and wished to try a new dress on her, Melissa whined, wanting instead to go back to playing with her dolls. It was always a major task whenever Sophia attempted to fit a dress on her.

The music stopped and Tony turned around and saw her.

"Superbly done! You played a favorite tune of mine! It brought back fond memories of my youth!" said Sophia, clapping in admiration.

Tony came and sat on the sofa. "I haven't played this song for years, but it felt appropriate somehow."

"By the way, how is your father doing these days?" asked Sophia.

"Unfortunately, he's been in a wheelchair ever since his surgery and cannot walk or lift his hands. Although he speaks and thinks clearly, he needs help with everything. Christina feeds him and helps dress him."

"I didn't know that!" exclaimed Sophia, feeling shocked with the news. "Is he here in town, so that we may pay him a visit?"

"No, actually, he's in Crete with Christina. He felt it better to remain there. He doesn't want his old business associates to see him in the state he is in."

"Please give him my regards next time you talk to him."

"Surely," replied Tony, nodding. "By the way, what is this I hear? You are planning to get married?"

Sophia explained to him how she met John and how one thing led to another.

"Congratulations are in order. You do look happy," said Tony, smiling fondly at her.

"Yes, I feel happy. Everything has gone smoothly, almost as if some greater force is helping us. We did send you an invitation to the wedding. I hope you and your fiancé can make it."

"Dear Sophia, how did you ever come to the conclusion that I have a fiancé? Even your niece said the same thing earlier," said Tony, laughing aloud.

"I apologize for the mistake, but I think Ipatia had overheard someone mentioning it," said Aunt Sophia, afraid to reveal who it was.

"I see. Could that someone be a short blonde named Melissa? Anyway, I hope it will not disappoint you if I come alone," said Tony, raising an eyebrow. He wondered what else his little sister had said that might have caused Ipatia to leave their house so urgently.

"Not at all!" said Aunt Sophia, appearing flustered.

At that moment, Ipatia entered the dining room with a tray.

"Let's all come sit in the dining room for some refreshments," said Aunt Sophia, rising, appearing relieved. "Tony, why don't you sit here."

He sat where Sophia pointed to, and watched quietly as Ipatia poured the thick, sweet Turkish coffees into the small cups.

"Ipatia, thank you for all this fine preparation," said Tony.

"You are welcome!" replied Ipatia cheerfully. She handed him his cup of coffee. Was it her imagination, or did his fingers brush hers intentionally?

"By the way, Sophia, what are your plans after the wedding? Do you plan to remain here?" asked Tony.

"We'll be going to Chicago to live, shortly after the wedding," said Sophia. "John has a real estate business and he also owns a house there."

Tony's eyebrows rose; he was surprised with the news. "Real estate business?"

"Yes, he buys and sells homes," she said proudly. "He has done very well with his business. He told me he owns several houses and a few apartment buildings. Some he rents and others he remodels and sells them at a higher price."

"Very interesting," said Tony, stroking his chin, thinking about the idea. "And what does Ipatia plan to do?"

Ipatia's eyes opened wide. *He wants to know what will become of you!* She caught her aunt staring at her with a surprised look.

"I will be staying with my cousins, George and Paula Mastroyiannis, who live on the other side of town," replied Ipatia.

"Ah, yes, the cousins who like to travel," said Tony, gazing poignantly at her. "Will you continue to work for Mrs. Rodos?"

"No, it's too far to travel in the evenings," Ipatia said, shaking her head, looking puzzled.

"You are probably wondering why I am asking," said Tony slowly, toying with the new idea that just popped into his head. "I've been thinking about getting a personal assistant to help me sort through the pile of mail that has accumulated in the past few months. It's too much for me to handle, and it's difficult to find people who know the English language as well as you do."

"What are you proposing?" asked Aunt Sophia, putting down her cup, intrigued by this young man's suggestion.

"I'm offering Ipatia an opportunity to practice her English and to get paid for it," he said. "She could come and work for me...for my father's shipping agency."

"Thank you, Mr. Tony," responded Ipatia, perking up at the compliment. "I do need to find a job to meet my expenses." She looked expectantly at her aunt, who was silently digesting the news.

"Where is the shipping office?" asked Aunt Sophia slowly, a thoughtful look on her face. She had a premonition there was more to this than met the eye.

"It is close to my cousins' house, so I won't have to take public transportation."

"Is that right, Tony?" asked Aunt Sophia, raising her eyebrows.

"Yes," said Tony, looking amused.

"What about Ipatia's studies...the university?" asked Aunt Sophia.

"Mind you, it'll probably be only for the summer," said Tony quickly. "After that, things may change."

Aunt Sophia paused. "If Ipatia wants to do it, then I'll go along with it."

Ipatia's response was immediate. "Yes I would, Aunt Sophia."

"Stop by the office as soon as you can, Ipatia. I will have Rita, the receptionist show you what to do," said Tony, giving her his business card.

"Ipatia, one more request, if you may," said Aunt Sophia, somewhat nervously. She gestured to the piano. "Could you play a little music for us?"

Tony flashed a bright smile. "Yes, play for us. How about...Fur Elise?"

Ipatia granted their wishes, conscious of being watched as she went to the piano and started playing. It didn't take long for her to immerse herself into the music, forgetting everything around her.

After a few pregnant minutes of anticipation, Sophia spoke softly to Tony. "I appreciate what you are doing for my niece. However, I will be leaving for America in a few weeks and I want to leave with peace of mind that Ipatia will be all right. Ipatia's grandfather does not take lightly to men dallying after Ipatia without serious intentions...if you know what I mean."

"I was expecting that," said Tony, not surprised by her shrewd remark. "Don't worry, you have nothing to fear from me or any other young man. Your niece has made it clear she's not interested in any relationships at this time."

"Did she say that she wants to get her degree first?" asked Sophia, looking a little perplexed. This was not the response she expected to hear.

Tony nodded and said wryly, "Four years is a long time to wait." *Especially when one is in love.*

"Yes," said Aunt Sophia, wondering what he meant by that.

Tony gazed at Ipatia's willowy frame, moving rhythmically with the music. She was so delicate and at the same time, so strong, so firm in what she believed. "She plays very well and it's a shame to miss her playing. Let us listen to her." The music flowed into the recesses of his inmost being, filling him with a yearning feeling he could not shake off. They remained silent, listening to the music, and when it ended, Tony clapped, saying, "Bravo, Ipatia, well done!"

Ipatia arose and smiled at him, not knowing what to say. She was not used to all this praise.

"Now I'm afraid I must be going. I have an early appointment tomorrow morning. Thank you for your warm hospitality, Sophia...and your fine playing, Ipatia," said Tony, staring intently at Ipatia, rising to leave.

Afterwards, as Ipatia and her aunt cleaned up, their conversation inevitably turned to Tony Plakis. Aunt Sophia reminisced about him. "He was such a well behaved young boy," she said, "Look at how fine a young man he turned out to be." She also mentioned how handsome he had become and how nice of him to walk Ipatia home.

"Thomas, Mrs. Tsatsikas' son, used to walk me home many a time," said Ipatia, feeling slightly annoyed with her aunt's generous praise of Tony. Although she secretly agreed with everything her aunt said, she didn't want

Tony being discussed openly, especially by her aunt. She felt comfortable keeping him close to her chest where no one could challenge her views about him or try to change her mind.

"The funny thing is that he's not engaged to Bonnie after all," said Aunt Sophia, ignoring her niece's comparison with Thomas.

"That's right!" said Ipatia, perking up.

"He won't be a bachelor for long, though…mark my words," said Aunt Sophia, nodding her head knowingly. "I can't see him waiting around for any girl. He's a very good catch, and there are many beautiful rich girls ready to snap him up, just like that!"

Later in bed, Ipatia went over everything in her mind several times. She admitted she felt a sense of relief when she learned Tony was not engaged to Bonnie. The shadows of his playboy past seemed to disappear with that news. Maybe it was because Bonnie represented the type of woman a playboy would pursue.

However, when her aunt said he wouldn't be a bachelor much longer, Ipatia felt a knot form in her chest. Tony was handsome, intelligent, charming, and yes, very attractive to other women as well as to her.

Ipatia somehow wanted him to remain a bachelor forever, to remain single, so she could dream about him. *You silly girl. Your aunt was right! Stop living on dreams and face reality! He will probably be getting married soon, and you might as well accept that it won't be you! Besides, you still have to go to school and it'll be four years before you can even think about marriage! Do I really need to go to school if it means losing him? But he hasn't asked you to marry him! He hasn't even said he loves you! But I love him.*

George and Paula paid Sophia an unexpected visit two days later.

"We happened to be in the area and also had some good news for Ipatia," said Paula, smiling as she handed her a wrapped box.

Sophia thanked her and excused herself. In a matter of minutes, she had returned with coffee and a tray laden with refreshments.

"Is Ipatia here?" asked George, taking the coffee offered to him.

"You just missed her. She went to her English class. She'll probably be back shortly after seven."

"We wanted to let you know that Christos and Tassoula are looking forward to having Ipatia come to Thessaloniki with us," said George, sipping a cup of freshly made coffee. He took a bite of the baklava, savoring the honeyed dessert. He carefully wiped his hands on a napkin.

"Ipatia will surely be delighted with the news!" said Sophia.

"Unfortunately, we will need to leave early the day after the wedding. Thessaloniki is a day's journey with the automobile and the baptism will take place the following morning," said Paula apologetically.

"That is no problem," said Sophia. "Would it be too much trouble for you to come by on your way to the church and pick us up? That way you can also get Ipatia's luggage."

"It's fine with me," said George, nodding. He looked at Paula. She nodded back.

They discussed the details of their trip and Ipatia's preparations. Then Sophia told them about Ipatia's new job with the Plakis agency. With a little prompting from a curious Paula, Sophia confided that the son was a handsome, eligible young man.

"Oh!" said Paula, her eyes twinkling. "Maybe we'll be hearing some good news soon."

"I have my reservations," said Sophia, shaking her head. "I think because he knows our family, he felt comfortable in asking Ipatia to work there. Even if there was interest on his part, Ipatia stubbornly wants to go to college to get a degree. He's too good a catch to wait around all those years for her."

John came a few days later and things got busier. He visited them daily and they would stop everything they were doing so Aunt Sophia could spend time with him. One evening, he asked Aunt Sophia to go out with him. Her aunt invited her along, but Ipatia felt awkward and declined.

"Why don't you visit with Marika downstairs?" offered Aunt Sophia. "She would love to have company and she knows so many things. I think you'll like her."

It turned out her aunt was right. Marika had an encyclopedic memory and there were discussions on philosophy, politics, Greek archaeology and all kinds of other topics. Their discussion was still going on strong when there was a knock on the door.

"We're back," said Aunt Sophia at the door. John was standing behind her.

"We'll continue another time," laughed Marika as she bid Ipatia farewell.

Thus started a new friendship. Ipatia began looking forward to those evenings when her aunt went out with John.

CHAPTER 26

February–March 1989
Did you drop in to see me, dear?
A smile, a laugh, a dream to share?

It was two days before the wedding, and Ipatia was attending her last English class. It was an emotional time for her as well as the children. They came up to her to give her their best wishes. A few of them hugged her, their small bodies pressed tightly against her. Mrs. Rodos said she was coming to the wedding and asked her to keep in touch afterwards. When she heard Ipatia would be working for Tony Plakis, she even gave her an English dictionary, saying that she probably would need it. Ipatia thanked her and promised she would visit her in the future.

It was later than usual when Ipatia headed home.

Michael was standing outside the pharmacy, talking to Vassili, as he usually did when leaving for the day. But today he was late, having just finished seeing an emergency patient. He spied Ipatia walking on the other side of the street, carrying her books. She had stopped coming altogether, ever since Tony's visit a few weeks ago. He missed seeing her.

He must find out one thing from her before her shining image left his mind altogether. He hastily bade Vassili farewell and walked purposefully towards her.

"Greetings, Ipatia!" he said, as he approached her.

Ipatia looked up, surprised. She had not been expecting to see Dr. Michael.

"Hello, Dr. Michael," she said, looking at him shyly.

"Here, let me walk with you. My car is further down the road," he said, joining her. "What have you been up to? You haven't come by the office for weeks now."

Ipatia filled him in on the latest news, telling him about her impending move after the wedding.

"Will you continue working at the English class?" he asked, disturbed by the news.

"Today was my last day there," she said, shaking her head. "I'll be working for Mr. Tony…I mean…the Plakis shipping agency. Mr. Tony wants me to translate papers for him."

"I'm sorry to hear you will be leaving this area," he began, then saw her guilty look. *Don't be too hard on the girl.* He paused, struggling to find the right words. "But at the same time…I'm…happy you will be working for Tony. He is a good person to work for."

"Isn't he wonderful?" exclaimed Ipatia, looking starry-eyed. Then she realized how it must have sounded and said, "I mean…although I'm also sorry to leave this area, I am looking forward to working at his company."

They stopped in front of Michael's car. Michael's pleasant demeanor did not change, but inside, he felt as if a hot iron was pressing on his heart. It was evident that Ipatia was in love with Tony.

"Will you be coming to my aunt's wedding?" asked Ipatia, having come back down to earth.

He paused before answering. Should he tell a white lie? The conference in Italy wasn't until the following week but he simply did not want to attend the wedding, now that he saw for himself where Ipatia's true affections lay. "I'm afraid not. I am leaving tomorrow for Italy. I'll be presenting a paper at an important medical conference there and I could not get out of this engagement," he replied tensely. "Please give my apologies to your aunt."

Ipatia was taken aback by his response. She had expected his attendance at the wedding and was feeling sorely disappointed he wouldn't be there. "I guess this will be the last time I'll be seeing you," she began, feeling as if she was ending a friendship. "I would like to thank you for everything you've done for me. For all the reading materials and for all the times you were there when I was sick. I will always admire you and your profession."

"The pleasure has been mine," he said sincerely, taking her hands into his. It was difficult to be angry with her. "You also brightened many of my days with your youthful charm, intelligent questions and helpful comments."

She smiled at his compliment. "Please have a safe trip, Dr. Michael," she said, shaking his hand before leaving.

Ipatia awoke Sunday morning to the pitter-patter of raindrops on her windowsill. It didn't dampen her high spirits when she saw the rain, as she jumped out of bed and got dressed. *Today was the day! Her aunt was getting married!*

Her aunt was in the same high spirits, chatting about everything and giggling like a young girl. They spent the rest of the morning making last minute preparations for the wedding. George and Paula stopped by earlier than expected, apologizing for being early, but saying they wanted to make sure there were no delays because of the rain.

By the time they arrived at the church, the rain had stopped and sunrays began to peak through the clouds. It seemed as if time had stood still, as if everything was in slow motion. They entered the church and shortly thereafter, proceeded with the ceremony. Although Sophia had felt nervous all morning, that feeling was now replaced by a sense of calmness. She purposefully walked down the aisle towards the altar, towards her destiny. The priest stood there, smiling gently at her. Her husband-to-be was looking at her expectantly, poised and handsome in his tuxedo, waiting for her.

Ipatia walked behind her aunt, mindful of the people staring at them, and of the long dress she was wearing. She had almost tripped over it twice. Her steps became small and measured. It seemed forever before she reached the altar.

Ipatia went and stood to the side of the couple. The ring-bearer and flower girl, the grandchildren of Mrs. Sarkidis, stood by her side. She couldn't help but notice that the church was packed and Tony wasn't anywhere in sight.

Tony arrived late. He stood in the back of the church so as not to attract attention. He immediately noticed Ipatia standing next to the couple. She was a vision in that long, satin pink dress. She held a rose bouquet in her white, gloved hands. Her hair was pulled up, and curls framed her delicate face. He was pleased at the picture. He looked at the bride. Sophia could never match the beauty of her niece, yet there was a glow about her that revealed her happiness. There was a little girl and boy standing next to them.

After a few minutes, their *Koumbaro*, the nephew of the groom, moved towards them and placed two wedding wreaths, joined by a satin ribbon, on Sophia and John's heads. In the Greek Orthodox tradition, he crisscrossed the wreaths above their heads three times, leaving the wreaths on their heads when he was finished. The priest then gave the couple a cup of wine to share. This was followed by a procession with the priest, the *Koumbaro*, and children, three times around the small table. Their steps were slow and sure, almost like in a line dance, as the chanter's melodic strains set the pace. The priest blessed the couple shortly after that, and the wedding ceremony officially ended.

The couple kissed each other gently, then walked down the aisle and into the small hallway to receive their guests. Ipatia followed them, then kissed her aunt and uncle, congratulating them joyfully.

"Thank you Ipatia...now stay here and greet the guests with us," said Aunt Sophia, pointing to the space next to Stellio.

"What do I say?"

"Just nod your head and smile," said John, laughing. "The line tends to move quickly, so there's no time to chat with anyone."

As the guests trickled out of the church, Aunt Sophia and John greeted them with handshakes and kisses, receiving their well wishes. Ipatia was last in line, dutifully doing the same. People left packaged gifts along the side of the hall. Mrs. Rodos finally came by, and for the first time, Ipatia saw her not wearing gray, but a nice, beige suit. Then Ipatia pictured Tony, coming to her and kissing her cheek, and as soon as she pictured it, it happened. His fresh, manly cologne lingered on her cheek, as she looked up at him, her eyes shining brightly into his.

"Best wishes for your aunt and uncle. You looked very lovely standing there," he whispered, squeezing her hand, then moving on.

She sighed, her knees feeling rubbery. *He kissed me and I let him! So what? Everyone kisses you during this time. Yes, but he knew about our pact not to kiss. He could have shaken my hands, but no, he kissed me also! He kissed me!*

"Ipatia, come dear, we need to go back into the church to take photos," said Aunt Sophia, interrupting her thoughts.

The reception was held at a nearby restaurant, where only close family attended. There was live bouzouki music for entertainment. Some people got up and danced. The evening went by quickly, and it was soon after that Ipatia had to leave with her cousins. It was an emotional moment, as Ipatia hugged her aunt.

"I'll write to you," promised Ipatia, with moistened eyes.

"So will I," said Aunt Sophia, wiping her own eyes. "Ipatia, remember what I said about going to the house. You have the key. Just go with your cousins and check up on it once in awhile. You can also visit with Marika and play the piano, if you'd like. Also, please forward any mail that arrives to my address in America. We do plan to visit Greece in late summer, so we will see you then. But remember you are always welcome to come and stay with us if you ever decide to do so. Don't worry about the money, you can come sooner if you want. Just let me know, and we'll pay for your ticket!"

"Thank you, Aunt Sophia!" replied Ipatia. "Have a safe trip to America!"

Then Ipatia shook hands with her new uncle, who swept her up in a bear hug.

"Your aunt loves you very much!" said Uncle John, stepping back. "You are always welcome to come and stay with us!"

After the farewells were completed, Ipatia left with her cousins. Although she looked forward to the trip to Thessaloniki, her mind was constantly being bombarded by thoughts about Tony.

❦   ❦   ❦

Ipatia attended the baptism in Thessaloniki and enjoyed being with her cousins, who were a fun-loving group. The baby cried when the priest partially immersed him into the water, causing a stir in the church. Some people smiled, others cried, others giggled. Once he was placed into the dry towels, though, he quieted down. It was a noisy event and an emotional one.

The next two weeks were exciting times for Ipatia. Between George and Ipatia's natural knack for humor, they had everyone laughing at their antics. Ipatia became everyone's darling. Her cousins also took her on a couple of day trips. She enjoyed the sightseeing tremendously, which took her mind off of Tony, but in the evenings, when she settled into bed, the image of Tony would appear, beckoning her to hasten back. Every night, she thought about him before going to sleep.

It was not long before they were saying their good-byes to each other.

Ipatia and her cousins returned to Piraeus that evening. It had been a long ride, and Ipatia was exhausted. They had almost been in a car accident, when someone had cut into their lane abruptly. Her cousin had good reflexes and was able to swerve away just in time.

"Why can't they see where they're going!" shouted George, displaying a rare burst of temper.

Ipatia had been shaken by the incident, but Paula said, "Don't worry dear, your cousin is a very good driver."

As soon as they arrived home, Ipatia went straight to bed, feeling exhausted.

The next day, Tuesday, Ipatia was busy unpacking her clothes and settling into her new bedroom. Afterwards, she sat at the desk in her room and wrote to her grandfather. She wrote about the wedding, and how much fun she had in Thessaloniki. She sealed the letter and went to look for Paula. She found her in the kitchen with George.

"Hello there! I need to mail this letter to Grandfather," she said cheerfully, showing them the envelope. "Is there a post office nearby? I need to get postage stamps."

"Yes, there is," said Paula, wiping her hands. She had been preparing the evening meal. "All you have to do is go left on this street until you come to the intersection. There, you make another left and walk awhile until you see it. Oh, and here…let me also give you some money to buy stamps for us."

"Is it all right if I stop at some shops and browse? I feel like walking after that long trip yesterday."

"Surely! Now that I remember…take this extra key to the house in case we are out when you get back," said Paula, retrieving a key. "We also need to do some grocery shopping of our own!"

Ipatia enjoyed the walk immensely. It was a pleasant morning, sunny and breezy. She walked down the street, past the residential area, towards the shopping district. To her right, a tall building was being constructed. Men in work clothes were working there. A man working on the second floor was singing very loudly. It was a familiar romantic song, and Ipatia slowed down, enjoying the music. He was very good.

The man stopped when he saw Ipatia, saying, "Hello, my lovely girl!"

Ipatia walked briskly by, blushing furiously. Behind her, she could hear laughter coming from the workers, followed by the man's singing.

Spring was in the air and all around her. People were going about their daily business, shopping, conversing on the street corner, or waiting for a bus. There was a sense of anticipation, as if something new was about to happen.

As she approached the post office, she saw the Plakis building further down the block and started thinking about Tony. She hadn't seen him since the wedding. Her heart started racing at the idea that she would be working there soon. She entered the post office.

As Tony came out of the cab, he thanked Tim, then said, "There is no need to wait for me. I might be awhile. I'll call you when I'm ready."

As he stood on the sidewalk, getting ready to enter his building, he spied a girl going into the post office. There was something familiar about her. Could it be Ipatia? She must be back from her trip. He wasn't about to let her go so easily this time.

After Ipatia mailed the letter and bought the stamps, she slowly made her way towards the back door, attempting to place the stamps inside the handbag at the same time.

"Excuse me," she said, absentmindedly bumping into someone, dropping her stamps. She bent down to pick them up, then noticed the other person also bent down at the same time.

"Hello."

The deep voice made her knees feel weak. There was only one person she knew that this voice belonged to. She caught herself staring at the handsome, smiling face of Tony Plakis.

Tony handed her the stamps, then gently helped her up.

CHAPTER 27

March 1989
I changed into a business suit
Because now I will work for you

"Mr. Tony!" said Ipatia shakily. She tried to compose her racing heart. "We just arrived back from Thessaloniki and I was mailing a letter to my grandfather."

"I gathered it was something like that," said Tony, with a twinkle in his eye. "Can you wait here a moment? I need to mail something."

Ipatia nodded, then watched, as he went to finish his own business. He looked exceedingly handsome in the tailored beige suit and crisp white shirt. At one point, he turned and flashed her a warm smile, nodding at her, singling her out, catching her off guard. Ipatia blushed at his overture, nodding shyly back, noticing the women in the post office staring at her curiously.

"How was your trip?" he asked, moments later, walking outside with her.

Ipatia discussed the details of the baptism and her trip. She talked about how the baby began crying right before the baptism, and how they fed him a bottle of milk to stop his crying.

"And when the priest picked up the baby, he burped right there and then!" she finished, laughing.

Tony laughed with her.

Ipatia noticed they had stopped in front of the Plakis building.

"If you have a few moments, I can show you where the office is, and introduce you to Rita," said Tony, touching her arm lightly, not wanting to let go of her so quickly.

"All right," she said timidly. She followed him into the building. They took the elevator to the third floor. A mirror in the elevator made her look down, afraid to look at herself. She furtively glanced up, and caught Tony gazing at her steadily in the mirror. They went through two double-glass doors and entered the office.

A middle-aged smartly dressed woman was seated at a large desk in the middle of the room.

"Hello, Rita! This is Ipatia, the girl I was telling you about," said Tony proudly.

"Nice to meet you," Rita said, smiling warmly as she shook Ipatia's hand. Rita had been in the office for ten years, and had seen a number of beautiful females working for the senior Plakis. It seemed that the son took after his father.

Ipatia immediately liked Rita and the office. The office was spacious and tastefully decorated. Also, there were large beautiful landscape paintings on the wall. Tall windows allowed plenty of sunlight into the room.

Ipatia said, "Those are beautiful paintings!"

"I'll tell you a little secret. I'm not really a receptionist," confided Rita dryly. "I'm here to watch over the paintings so no one steals them!"

They all laughed.

"Will she be starting today?" asked Rita.

"Not today. I brought her here to introduce her to you," he said. "When can you start work, Ipatia?"

"I can start tomorrow," said Ipatia brightly.

"Good," he said, smiling at her. "We could use your help."

"The office opens at nine in the morning, and we close around two. Then we reopen in the afternoon at five, and stay open until eight. You will be working only in the mornings?" asked Rita.

"Yes," said Ipatia.

"Tomorrow I will show you around and introduce you to everyone, and we can go over your duties then."

"Thank you. I shall see you tomorrow morning," said Ipatia, heading towards the door.

"Wait a minute, Ipatia," said Tony quickly. He turned to Rita and said, "I won't be staying. Is there anything I need to sign before I leave?"

Rita raised her eyebrows. It wasn't like him to come and go so quickly. "Only these papers," she said dryly, picking up several documents and handing them to him. "If these aren't signed by tomorrow, Sarkalos will have my hide. He's been hounding me to get these purchase orders out."

He read them carefully, then nodded and retrieved a pen from inside his jacket and signed the forms.

"There, have a nice evening and I will see you tomorrow, Rita," he said.

They left shortly after that, and when they reached the front entrance, Tony asked, "Will you be walking home?"

Ipatia nodded, having completely forgotten her plans to browse the shops.

"Would it be all right if I joined you?" he asked softly, opening the door.

She nodded, feeling a surge of happiness with his request.

They strolled down the street together, and it wasn't long before he began discussing a number of topics. Ipatia became immersed in a world much larger than hers. She chimed in with her own ideas. Fresh from her talks with Marika, she expounded on the philosophical, political and archaeological history of Greece.

"I believe that there are two facets of Greece, the modern and the ancient. Everywhere you go, you see modern Greece with its bouzouki music, its souvlakia, its cars and buses. Yet, at the same time, right around the corner, there is ancient Greece staring at you, with the beautiful architecture of the Acropolis and the Parthenon, the pinnacles of that great society," said Ipatia dramatically.

"Which do you prefer, Ipatia…ancient Greece…or modern Greece?"

"Why, a little of both, I guess," she said, gesturing around her. "I admire what ancient Greece has offered us. Democracy, the Olympics, the philosophers such as Socrates, and the Hippocratic oath that the doctors use even to this day. But I also enjoy the wonders of electricity, modern medicine, and public transportation."

"It seems like you won't be needing to go to the university," commented Tony. "You seem to know everything already."

Ipatia laughed, explaining her discussions with Marika. "She knows so much. She's gone to the university. She also said that the food we eat now in present day Greece has been around for centuries. It was a way of survival for the Greeks for many years. It has been tested by time. Even the Americans are starting to look into our diet. They call it the Mediterranean diet."

"Speaking of food, I wonder if the loukoumathes were made in ancient times?" Tony asked, his eyes twinkling. "Remember the loukoumathes shop we went to?"

"Yes. It was so much fun," she said enthusiastically.

That was all he wanted to hear. "I'm feeling somewhat hungry. Why don't we go there? It's just down the road, and it's still early."

"You really should eat food first!" she lightly scolded. "The loukoumathes may taste good, but they're not very nutritious!"

"Yes, you are right," he said, enjoying her suggestion. "I know a place where they make the best food. It's around the corner. But we must go for coffee and loukoumathes afterwards."

"All right," she said. She felt giddy, as he offered her his arm and they strolled down the avenue slowly, browsing the shops and boutiques, discussing the items on display, heading towards the restaurant.

The rest of the day was like one long dream. They sat and ate souvlaki with Greek salad topped with feta cheese, talking about a number of things, amidst the bustle of people coming and going. She couldn't tear her gaze away from his. He was a good talker, and she enjoyed listening to him. She learned that he liked playing tennis, attending classical music concerts, studying archaeology, going to museums and traveling. He found out that she liked writing poetry, reading, cooking, swimming, medical topics, all kinds of music, and more recently, sewing.

Then they strolled to the loukoumathes shop, laughing and chatting. The little shops they passed were no longer a point of interest, for they had escaped into their own little world. They sat outside the loukoumathes shop, drinking iced coffee and biting into warm loukoumathes, enjoying the scenery and the sunset.

Tony began reminiscing about England and the way of life there. Ipatia nodded, feeling stimulated by the conversation, and at the same time comfortable, listening to Tony talk.

"I used to go to a restaurant owned by a Greek, not too far from the Oxford campus. I'd meet with a few colleagues of mine there. We'd joke around and have a laugh or two," said Tony. "The Greek food was exceptionally tasty, and the owner's company was even more so."

"Do you ever miss living in England?" asked Ipatia.

"Actually, I've been going to England often lately, because of the shipping business. But somehow, England doesn't appeal to me as it used to. Maybe the damp, cloudy weather is getting to me, or maybe the polite, cold indifference of the people I deal with," he said ruefully.

Tony became quiet after that, staring out into the distance, deep in thought. The truth of the matter was that he had been busy thinking about Ipatia lately, eager to get back to see her. He had truly missed her cheerful company these last few weeks. Today, he realized how much she meant to him, and how much he loved her. He didn't want to be without her and he didn't want to wait four years, and he didn't know how to get out of this dilemma.

Ipatia noticed his quietness. She wondered if she had said anything wrong. Maybe she had kept him too long and he had grown bored with her. "I truly must be going," she said reluctantly, getting up. "My cousins knew that I would be out shopping, but it's getting rather late, you know."

He touched her arm. "Please, don't go. You probably noticed I am quiet and I apologize for that. It is just that I can't ever remember having as much fun as I had with you today. Tomorrow I go back to the grind of the office...and sadly, I don't look forward to it."

"Oh," she said. She felt sympathetic towards him. She sat back down. "I had a very nice time with you also."

"So, Ipatia, tell me...how are your plans for the university coming along?" he managed to ask. *Why are you asking, Tony? Is it because you want her to deny her interest in school and admit her love for you instead, so you can claim her?*

Ipatia hesitated before answering. She was beginning to find the idea of school not so attractive these days. "I've begun studying for the examination...although I'm not sure which university I will attend yet," she finally said, deciding to say no more. "The job is going to be perfect, because I could work during the days and study in the evenings."

"I'm glad to hear it," he said briskly, abruptly getting up. Apparently, she was not ready. "Shall we go before your cousins become worried?"

The walk home was pleasant enough, with Ipatia talking about her cousins. Tony listened quietly, slipping his hand into hers, making her tingle inside. She wasn't sure if it was the proper thing or not, but it felt just right. He remained silent after she finished talking, causing her to wonder if everything was all right. It was not like him to be so quiet.

Little did Ipatia realize that Tony's silence was due to an internal battle, where his emotions were playing havoc with his heart and mind.

"Are we here already?" asked Tony, looking around.

"Yes," she replied. He was still holding her hand. "Thank you for a very nice time."

"You are welcome. I enjoyed it also," he said, bowing slightly, kissing the top of her hand. "I hope this little kiss didn't transgress the pact we made."

She shook her head silently. She knew he was going along with her wishes. But her wishes were changing. Somehow the memory of the day he kissed her in the study was no longer an anathema, but had transformed into a living promise, a promise of love.

"I shall see you tomorrow then, bright and early?"

"Yes, bright and early," she said breathlessly, slipping her hand from his and going quickly into the house.

Ipatia found her cousins waiting for her. She explained what had happened, and they were satisfied with her news, looking at each other knowingly.

Ipatia looked forward to starting work in the morning. That evening, she prepared her work clothes, choosing them carefully. She must portray a business-like character. She chose a beige jacket with matching skirt that used to be her mother's but had been tailored to fit her. The rest of the evening, although she tried to study for her entrance exam, her mind kept wandering toward the wonderful afternoon she spent with Tony.

❦   ❦   ❦

When Tony arrived home later that evening, he found his sister and Chuck in the dining room having dinner. He joined them and the evening was spent discussing the shipping business. Tony found a good resource in Chuck, who knew about the ins and outs of the business. The discussion led to the topic of computers.

"With your business reaching all parts of the world, you will need a better way of monitoring everything. Computers can do that, and more. They are the way of the future," said Chuck. "I've already got my business operating with computers."

They were going over a few technical issues, when Melissa interrupted them and said, "I hate to interrupt you two, but Chuck, dear, it's nine o'clock, and we're supposed to meet your friends down at the Club, remember?"

"Tony, would you care to join us? We can discuss it further at the Club," said Chuck.

"Yes," said Tony, pleased at the invitation.

It was close to midnight when Tony entered his bedroom. He had spent most of the evening discussing, with Chuck, the pros and cons of switching over from paperwork to a computer system. Ever since Tony began asking him for advice, the company's profits had increased considerably due to the cost-cutting measures Chuck had suggested. This could be one more idea worth pursuing.

❀   ❀   ❀

The next morning, Wednesday, Ipatia left the house, carrying the English dictionary. She enjoyed the brisk walk. The early morning coolness was refreshing. As she passed groups of children carrying their schoolbooks, walking to school, she fondly remembered the children at Mrs. Rodos' class. She wondered how they were doing.

When Ipatia entered the double glass door, Rita was speaking to two men dressed in business suits. She waited patiently for Rita to finish.

"Just go down the stairs to the second floor. There you will find Mr. Psaris' office. He is the person you need to see," Rita was saying.

After the men left, Rita rose and extended her hand to Ipatia. "Good morning, Miss Kouris. Let me take you to your desk."

"You can call me Ipatia," offered Ipatia.

"All right."

Ipatia was led to the end of the hallway, where she opened the door that had a sign titled *Gregory Plakis*. She was pleased with the size and airiness of the room. There was much sunlight coming in through the large window on the side, warming up the room. Two tropical potted plants were located on either side of the window. The room had a comfortable, yet professional feel to it.

"You will be working here," Rita said, pointing to the desk to their right. There was a sizeable pile of envelopes and papers already on it. In the back of the room was a large door.

"Is that Mr. Plakis' room?" asked Ipatia, pointing to the door.

"Yes it is," Rita replied, opening it.

Ipatia peeked into Tony's office and was surprised to see the Greek vase from the island standing by the window. The vase, the paintings on the wall, and the exotic objects that lay in the bookshelf, revealed an appreciation of art. The mahogany desk itself was a work of art, with feet shaped like an eagle's claws.

Rita said, "He usually doesn't come in until ten or eleven o'clock, and today he will be coming later, since he has a meeting to go to first. Once he is in, he works the whole day through until late afternoon. He goes by the English work day instead of the Greek…if you know what I mean."

Rita then went over Ipatia's duties and after she was finished, she said, "Before you get started on these papers, let me take you around and introduce you to everyone. You might be needing to contact people, so it's good for you to know who they are."

Ipatia followed her out into the hallway, stopping to meet Aristotle, the senior accountant, and Stamatis, a junior accountant. Afterwards, they went to the other two floors, where Rita introduced her to the people there. Ipatia couldn't keep track of all the names.

Sarkalos, the fleet manager, was seated in his office, speaking to someone when they entered his room. After Rita introduced Ipatia, the other man turned to stare at Ipatia.

"You are Captain Kouris' daughter?" he asked, appearing surprised.

"Yes?" asked Ipatia, looking puzzled, studying him. He was an older, heavy-set man with a thick mustache. His deeply tanned face was rough and rugged, and his eyes were lively. He was wearing a black Captain's cap over his bushy, gray hair.

"Come here, my girl," he said pulling her to him and kissing her lightly on the cheeks. "I am like an uncle to you. I am Captain Sardelis."

She could smell a hint of liquor on his breath. It was a familiar smell to her. Her father used to drink wine at his meals. She smiled shyly back.

"I knew your father well. We traveled the seas together. He was a good man. Many a time we sat down and shared stories over a bottle of wine. He was always talking about you to us."

"He was?" asked Ipatia, surprised at the revelation.

"Ahh, my darling daughter, he would say. She's written me poems. Then he'd share them with us."

"He did?" she asked, trying to remember the poems. It seemed so long ago.

"Just to get the record straight. I helped him pick out your gifts. You see I had more experience in that field, because I had five daughters I had to bring gifts back to." He spread out his hand, displaying the five digits.

They all laughed.

"Very nice to meet you," said Ipatia, blushing at the man's compliments. "By the way, I liked all my gifts."

"Welcome on board," he said, winking at her.

As they were leaving to go back upstairs, she noticed people entering the Sarkalos' office.

"Who are they?"

"They work for the company," said Rita. "Today they are coming to pick up their pay checks. Sarkalos will take care of their pay. Come, we need to go back to the office."

CHAPTER 28

My heart beats hard when I'm with you
This work I do, just suits me true

By the time they returned to the office, it was already eleven thirty. Rita showed Ipatia how to buzz her on the telephone, if she needed to speak with her.

"Oh, I almost forgot, Mr. Chuck and Miss Melissa are expected later this morning," said Rita, before leaving. "If they come while I am away, please let Mr. Tony know they're here by buzzing his office."

After she left, Ipatia looked around her once more, appreciating her work environment. Mr. Plakis' office door was still closed. She wondered what time Tony would be coming today. She also wondered how Melissa would react once she saw her there.

She began the arduous task of reading the first letter in the pile, painstakingly translating it into Greek. She was thankful for the English dictionary she had brought along, for there were several unfamiliar words. At one point, the telephone rang and Ipatia jumped at the sound. She had never had a telephone ring so close to her ear before. She answered it.

"Plakis Shipping Business, may I help you?" she asked, her voice trembling slightly.

"Hello, Ipatia!" boomed a pleasantly rich voice.

"Oh…hello Mr. Tony!" she replied cheerfully, surprised to hear him on the telephone.

"I am in the office and wish to speak with you. Can you please come in?" asked Tony. "Please bring some paper and a pen."

She hadn't realized that he was in his office. She was nervous when she went to his door and knocked.

"Please have a seat," said Tony, appreciating her professional attire. The light beige suit and creamy white blouse brought the highlights out in her green eyes. She was also wearing pearl earrings.

He caught himself gazing at her, wanting to take her in his arms, as he watched her take her seat. Slightly taken aback by his hungry feelings for her, he got up shakily. "I hope you don't mind if I shut the door. It helps me concentrate."

She did not know what to say in response to that. This was something new to her, being alone in a room with a man. *No, not just any man, but with Tony.* She tensed, sitting upright and remaining perfectly still, motionless, almost not breathing, not trusting her emotions which were sending all kinds of signals to her head.

He shut the door slowly, pausing to regain his composure before going back to sit down. She must not know how he felt about her, not yet.

"You are probably wondering why I wish to speak with you," he said softly, as he sat down.

She looked at him, her heart pounding. Was this his way of seducing women? She was ready to bolt.

He immediately sensed her fear, and chuckled. "I know this is all new to you, but we do this to everyone we hire. Rita probably took you to the different departments this morning, and now I will go over the operations of the business, how the different departments work together, and how you fit in all of this."

"Oh," she said. She felt better.

He began talking about the different departments, how they interacted with each other. She listened intently, and with shaky hands took notes along the way. She was mesmerized by the change in him. In front of her was not a seducer, not the man who kissed her hand the day before, but a man who knew his business, tough-minded and knowledgeable. Here, there was no softness, but a steely, single purpose of running a business, and doing it well.

"I admit I'm still learning about this business, as I've only been in it a few months," said Tony. "Do you have any questions?"

She looked at her notes briefly, shuffling the papers around. "It seems to me...trying to keep track of all the ships, their maintenance, and the cargo schedules...is quite a complex task. Is there an easier way of remembering all this? How do the departments do it?"

"The way I would do it, is make diagrams, like this," he said. He took the pad of paper from her hands. He wasn't aware that he had shifted into the professor role easily. "I would draw the departments, the cargo ships, put them in boxes, then connect them with lines. If the cargo ship needs maintenance, it goes to this department. If supplies need to be ordered, it goes here. Any papers needing to be signed come to me, here at the top. You can always come back to the diagram if you forget."

Ipatia watched his shapely hands, drawing broad strokes on her paper, enjoying the moment. After he was finished, he handed it to her.

She looked it over, nodding her appreciation. "Yes, now it makes sense. What happens when a ship breaks down at sea? How do they communicate, and what if the cargo schedule is affected?"

"Good questions," he said, nodding appreciatively. He answered as thoroughly as he could, making a mental note to ask Sarkalos more about that topic.

"I also had a few questions on the papers I am translating," she said, after he was finished.

"I am expecting some calls shortly. Why don't you bring them in tomorrow morning at eleven," he said, noting the time. "We can go over them then. Also, feel free to come and ask me if you have any other questions."

"Thank you," she said, getting up to leave, feeling slightly disappointed. Somehow, his impersonal lecture on shipping was not what she expected. *What did you expect, Ipatia? To be seduced? Get those silly thoughts out of your mind right this minute!*

"By the way, was everything all right yesterday when you got home?" he asked softly.

She nodded brightly, noticing the change in him right away. This was the Tony she knew.

"Good," he said, flashing her a wide smile.

Ipatia had a hard time working after that. She sat at her desk, in a daze. She thought about her meeting with Tony and her feelings while in his room. It wasn't long before she was daydreaming. At one point the telephone buzzed, shaking her out of her reverie. Her heart was racing as she picked it up.

"Ipatia, this is Rita, I'm going out for a snack. Do you want anything?"

"No, I'm fine, thank you," said Ipatia. Somehow, she wasn't very hungry. The only other interruption was when a young man came in the office, carrying a tray that held a cup of coffee and pastries. She pointed to Tony's room, and he took it in there.

She started working after that, forcing any intruding thoughts out of her mind. Several minutes later, she heard people talking in the hallway, followed by female laughter. The voices were coming towards her.

"Ipatia?" asked Melissa, looking surprised and annoyed to see her. Her brother hadn't mentioned that Ipatia was working for him. She wondered if Father knew.

"Hello, Miss Melissa," said Ipatia, forcing a smile and standing up. She didn't know how to react to Melissa's look of surprise. Ipatia noticed the man standing behind her. He was not much taller than Melissa, and his dark brown hair, graying temples, and small mustache gave him a distinguished air. Even though there were signs of overeating, he disguised it well with his tailored suit and tie. Dr. Michael was much better looking, Ipatia secretly thought. She wondered what Melissa saw in this man. She quickly got her answer.

"This is Chuck Daras, my fiance," said Melissa, somewhat reluctantly, hooking her arm around Chuck's arm.

Ipatia noticed he was gazing at her unabashedly and she looked down, bewildered. She never could get used to men staring at her. It didn't feel right.

"My pleasure," said Chuck.

"I'll let Mr. Tony know that you are here," said Ipatia, trying to act professional. Her hand trembled as she picked up the telephone. She realized she didn't know which button to push.

"Don't worry, we'll let him know," continued Melissa, pulling Chuck towards Tony's office.

"Hello, hello," said Tony, coming out from his office, having heard his sister's entrance. He greeted Chuck with a handshake, then kissed his sister lightly.

"I'm ready to start if you are," said Chuck, smiling at him. He liked and respected Tony. At first, Tony appeared soft, even somewhat of a wimp, and Chuck had categorized him along with other spoiled, rich sons of ship owners that he knew. But one day, when Chuck challenged him about something, Tony quickly revealed a steely interior inside. Tony had a character that would not bend if he were sure about something, and Chuck admired that.

"Come, follow me, then," said Tony. As they began to leave the room, he turned briefly and said, "Ipatia, please join us. We will be going over different operations of the agency and you can see first-hand how things are done. This will be a good experience for you."

Ipatia glowed, as she followed the group silently down the hallway and downstairs to the second floor. He had asked her to join them! They went into different departments, as Tony and Chuck discussed issues, going over the pros and cons of using certain methods over others. Melissa seemed to know quite a bit, because she piped in several times, offering her own advice.

Ipatia remembered some of the people from her tour earlier that day, and greeted them. The time flew as they worked their way around the different departments. It was now two o'clock and the two men and Melissa were reviewing some sheets of paper with numbers on them with Sarkalos.

Ipatia listened, trying to decipher all the jargon they were talking about. She gave up after a few minutes. Suddenly her stomach growled. She cleared her throat, trying to hide her complaining stomach. The others were too caught up in their discussion to notice, but Tony noticed.

He smiled at her and said, "If you'd like, you can go now. These items are not that relevant for you."

Ipatia said, "Thank you," and made her way back to her desk. She was mentally exhausted from the sheer volume of information packed in so few hours. She quickly left and headed home.

At home, she found a note from her cousins. They would be back around three. They had gone shopping, and were expecting people over for dinner. She slept soundly until a knocking on her bedroom door awoke her.

"Ipatia, are you awake?" asked Paula.

"I'll be right there," said Ipatia, noticing it was six o'clock. She jumped out of bed and freshened up.

She greeted Paula and George in the kitchen and told them about her new job over a cup of coffee and a snack.

"No wonder you were exhausted, my poor dear," said Paula. "I hope you are feeling up to having company for dinner tonight. We will be having John and Sylvia over. They baptized our son and they are very nice people. We do a lot of traveling together and I think you will like them."

Ipatia did indeed enjoy herself. The couple joked with George and Paula, and Ipatia joined in the laughter. They asked Ipatia if she liked to travel, and she replied yes. They talked about the different places they had been with Paula and George, describing some funny situations they had gotten themselves into. Later that night, the couples sat down and began to play a game of cards. Ipatia watched for awhile, then yawning, excused herself and went to bed. She slept soundly into the night, unaware of the laughter and noise coming from the dining room.

❦   ❦   ❦

The next morning proved to be just as exciting and stimulating as the first. Ipatia strove to do a good job, and her interaction with Tony and the rest of the staff was positive. He called her into his office as soon as he arrived and asked her to go downstairs and pick up a few papers for him. She went dutifully downstairs to the department and was met by a woman who said that the person who had the papers had momentarily left.

"He'll be back in a few minutes."

Ipatia chatted with the woman, who started a conversation with her. Then the man finally arrived and Ipatia asked him for the papers. He was obliging and gave her the papers she requested. Then he started talking to her. After a few minutes, Ipatia excused herself, noticing the time, remembering Mr. Tony was waiting for her.

When she knocked on Tony's door, she found Chuck Daras talking with Tony in his office. She handed Tony the papers and greeted Mr. Daras, then went back to her desk. Melissa did not come. The rest of the day, Ipatia worked diligently on her translations, waiting for Mr. Daras to leave so she could go and talk to Mr. Tony about them. However, when two o'clock came, Mr. Daras had not left yet, and the door to the office was still closed.

Ipatia left at two, feeling upset with herself. If she hadn't spent that time talking to the people downstairs, she would have had a chance to spend time with Tony. Once Mr. Daras came, she realized that her chances were gone.

The next morning, she couldn't concentrate on her work as she began day-dreaming about Tony. She glanced at the time. It was nine thirty. She should get back to work.

"Good morning, Ipatia," said Tony, smiling cheerfully at her as he entered the room. She was like a beautiful painting, refreshing to look at. He found himself coming earlier these days to work.

"Sorry I didn't have a chance to go over the translated papers with you yesterday."

"That's all right," he said. "Why don't we do it now? I'm expecting Chuck again later this morning, so I'll probably be tied up after that."

She followed him into the office. He read each translated paper out loud. Oftentimes, he would nod his approval, and once in awhile, to her dismay, he would break out in laughter at some of her translations. He apologized, saying she had a creative way of looking at things.

"You are doing a good job with the translations," he said, after reviewing all the papers. "At this rate, it seems as if you'll be done with this work much sooner than expected."

"Thank you," she said, beaming. "What will happen next to the translated papers?"

"They will be distributed to the various departments and reviewed, depending on what needs to be done with them," he said.

They were interrupted by a knock on the door. Mr. Daras had arrived. Ipatia excused herself and spent the rest of the time translating more papers, and once more, Tony's office door was closed for the rest of the day.

❧   ❧   ❧

The days flew by and two weeks had passed. Ipatia was becoming more familiar with the operations of the agency and with its staff. When she arrived in the office Friday morning, she got her first paycheck from Aristotle. Later that morning, she peeked inside the envelope and was amazed to see the amount. She had never had so much money in her hands at one time. She would have to see about putting it in a bank.

She went to work with renewed energy, feeling a surge of pride at having earned so much money. The paper pile was slowly being whittled down.

Rita buzzed her later that morning. "Mr. Tony is going to have a meeting and he needs to have his office arranged for the meeting. I'll be there with some extra chairs."

Rita came shortly after that, carrying a chair. Ipatia helped her, steadily bringing chairs into the room.

When Tony arrived, he was not alone. An older man was with him.

"Good morning, Ipatia," said Tony. "Mr. Glaros, this is my personal assistant. Ipatia, we will be having our meeting in here and if anyone calls for me, please take a message."

Ipatia nodded, noticing how different, how aloof he appeared when he used his professional demeanor. She watched silently as they went into his office. A number of other people trickled in his office. The last to arrive were Melissa and Chuck.

Around twelve o'clock the young man from the coffee shop arrived, carrying several cups of coffee on his tray and several pastries. The office door opened and he delivered the refreshments. Then Mr. Glaros left, returning a few minutes later carrying a big box. The door shut behind him.

The door was still shut when Ipatia left at two o'clock.

❦   ❦   ❦

Tony was pleased with the computer demonstration. "Very good, Mr. Glaros. Your plan is well thought out and we will strongly consider it," he said, standing up. Seated in the room were Aristotle, Stamatis, Jimmy, the computer guru they had hired a few weeks ago, Chuck Daras, Melissa, and Sarkalos, their fleet manager.

"Can you project how long it will be before we are up and running?" asked Chuck.

George Glaros turned off the computer and packed it back into the box. "It all depends on what we find," he replied, shrugging his shoulders. "It will probably take a few months to assess your company's needs. After that, we can meet to discuss the implementation phase."

"I will contact you in a few days," promised Tony.

After Glaros left, Tony stood next to his desk, with his hands in his pockets. He looked at everyone expectantly. "Well, what did you think? Can it be done?"

"The computers are top of the line, Mr. Plakis," offered Jimmy, nodding his approval. "Once installed, I can start training the staff to use them properly."

"Good, that's the spirit," replied Tony.

Sarkalos said, "I am curious to see how all this comes together. Glaros said we would be able to communicate with each other and eventually with the outside world. That is very intriguing."

"By the end of this year, you will see for yourself what he means," said Tony, nodding. "Gentlemen, this is an important step forward for our company. Thanks to my future brother-in-law Chuck Daras, who suggested the idea, we will move forward in a capacity never done before."

"Thank you, Tony. The world is advancing very quickly in the technology sector. In order for us to compete successfully, we need to incorporate this new way of doing business. Not only will these computers aid the accounting department, but they will also improve efficiency in our offices, and provide quicker processing of transactions and data," said Chuck.

They continued their discussion for a little while longer.

"Mr. Plakis, is that all you need?" asked Jimmy, standing up.

"That will be all," said Tony, nodding. Everyone filed out of the office except for Chuck and Melissa. They continued their discussion.

Tony sat in his office afterwards, thinking about everything that transpired at the meeting with Mr. Glaros.

He was looking forward to the new way of communication via the computers. That would mean less business trips on his part. Then he thought about his father. When he first approached him about using computers, his father had balked at the idea, not wanting to hear about it. He said there was nothing wrong with the way things were working. After Chuck spoke with his father, his father reluctantly agreed with the idea.

CHAPTER 29

April 1989
You asked me out on a date
To test my love and our fate

Another week went by and Ipatia had settled into a pleasant routine. She would come into the office, work a couple of hours, then greet Tony as he arrived into the office. Around noon, she would be invited to go into his office to discuss her progress and her translated papers, and usually he would say something towards the end of the session that was more personal.

The days went by quickly and the weekend arrived, marking the first week in April. Ipatia and her cousins arranged a trip to Loutraki, located an hour away, near Corinth. It was a famous Greek spa and resort area, known for its healing waters. They had invited another older couple to come. Although Ipatia enjoyed the trip and had a pleasant time, she looked forward to Monday morning, when she would see Tony again.

Monday morning Ipatia had arrived at the office a few minutes earlier. She was not surprised to see Rita already in the office, speaking to another woman. Like a mother hen, Rita made it her business to know everyone else's business. Ipatia would often find other women from the building coming to her for advice.

Rita introduced the other woman as an old friend who dropped by to visit with her. The woman left shortly after that, leaving them alone.

"How was your weekend, Ipatia?"

Ipatia shared her experience with the trip to Loutraki. "The nice thing is that it's close by, so we didn't have to go far."

Rita said, "That is a lovely place. I used to enjoy going there often. But now with three cats, two canaries, and an aquarium full of fish, it's difficult to get away. Who will take care of them for me? They are my family."

The morning went by quickly. Ipatia continued to work on her translations, careful not to misinterpret anything. Her English vocabulary was growing daily, and she had written down some interpretations that she referred to often. She kept checking the time. She was looking forward to telling Tony about her trip to Loutraki. But it didn't happen.

At twelve o'clock, the telephone rang. Ipatia jumped at the sound. It couldn't be Tony. His office door was open and he was nowhere in sight.

"Rita here. I'll be going for a snack. Did you want anything?"

"No, thank you," Ipatia said. She hesitated, wondering if she should ask or not. "Did Mr. Tony have a meeting this morning?"

"Oh, didn't I tell you? Friday, after you left the office, he received news he had a business trip to go to this week. He won't be back until late Wednesday," announced Rita.

Ipatia thanked her and hung up the telephone, feeling at a loss. She had looked forward to seeing him today. She continued her work, but her heart wasn't in it. The rest of the day seemed to drag. She was catching herself making mistakes. Ipatia sensed something was wrong with her. Why was she feeling this way?

Tuesday morning she felt listless as she walked to work. She arrived slightly late. It was a cloudy day, prone to rain. She had taken her umbrella with her. Working silently at her desk, she did not feel like talking to anyone. It was very difficult to concentrate, as thoughts about Tony kept intruding all day.

When she arrived home, she found a letter from Aunt Sophia waiting for her. Eagerly, she tore it open, reading everything carefully. Her aunt was doing fine, although she missed her and her friends. She asked if Ipatia had visited the house yet, and not to worry about the mail because Marika was sending it to her. Ipatia bit her lip. She had been so busy at work, she had forgotten to go! She must talk to her cousins about it.

Aunt Sophia described her life, the daily routines, the people, and her struggle with the English language. At the end of the letter, she wrote she had some important news for her, but wanted to wait a little more before confirming it. She said they had a telephone and asked if Ipatia could call her in a few weeks. The telephone number was written at the bottom of the letter.

"Ipatia, how is your aunt doing?" asked Paula, hovering around her. George came in at that moment.

"Fine," said Ipatia. She read the letter aloud.

"It sounds as if she's enjoying herself," said Paula, nodding appreciatively. "We could go and visit Miss Marika some time soon and check on the house. She seems like an interesting lady."

Ipatia said, "I would like that. Besides, I also haven't seen Mrs. Rodos for awhile."

"Why don't we go to the house this Saturday?" asked George.

❦   ❦   ❦

The next day, Wednesday, Melissa and Chuck Daras entered Tony's office later in the morning. They didn't shut the door behind them. Ipatia could hear their conversation. She couldn't help noticing how proficient Melissa was in the shipping business. It seemed that she knew all the answers to Mr. Daras' questions. Then Ipatia heard Tony's name and realized they were talking on the telephone with him.

Ipatia found it difficult to focus on her work after that. She wondered why he hadn't called her. *Why should he call you?* She caught herself daydreaming about Tony. She resumed her work reluctantly. The document she was translating was a particularly difficult legal document, as she was not familiar with the terminology. She managed to finish most of it by one o'clock, around the time that Melissa and Mr. Daras left. It was quiet after that, as Ipatia diligently finished the translation.

Thursday finally arrived and Ipatia felt excited. *Today Tony is returning!* She paid particular attention to what she wore. She chose a peach-colored skirt, which brought out the highlights of her hair, and a matching jacket with a white silk blouse. The suit made her body fuller in certain areas and gave her figure more curves. This time, she added her mother's pearl necklace with matching earrings. Notorious late-risers, George and Paula were still sleeping when she left.

Ipatia got off the elevator to the third floor and headed for the glass doors to the office. Her heart raced when she saw Tony standing in the office, talking to Rita. There were wrapped packages on Rita's desk.

"Ipatia, good morning!" said Tony cheerfully, kissing her on both cheeks, forgetting his professional demeanor for just a moment. He had purposefully stood there, waiting for her. He couldn't wait to see her. The days had felt empty without her. She looked even more beautiful than he remembered.

"Good morning, Mr. Tony!" she replied just as cheerfully, surprised at his warm greeting. The scent of his cologne lingered with her. Then she greeted Rita.

Rita smiled knowingly at the couple as they walked together down the hallway. It seemed like they were in their own little world.

"How was your trip?" Ipatia managed to ask, quite aware of his body moving in rhythm with hers.

Just then, Aristotle poked his head out of the office and greeted them, then retreated into his office.

"Somewhat tiring, I confess," resumed Tony. "But I did make it a point to meet with some old colleagues of mine, which made it more pleasant."

"Are these colleagues from college?" asked Ipatia, curious.

"Yes, and they keep asking me when I will return," he said. "But I didn't give them a date yet."

They reached her desk.

"Here is something for you," he said, retrieving a small wrapped gift from his suit pocket. "Straight from England." *Straight from my heart.*

She hesitated.

"It is customary for me to bring back presents for the staff."

"Oh?" she asked, surprised by his generosity.

"And you don't have to kiss me because I gave you a gift."

"Thank you!" she giggled, accepting his gift. She had never received a gift from him before.

"You're very welcome," he said, bowing slightly. "How is the work coming along? Are they keeping you busy?"

"It's going very well," she said. "I'll be finished with it in a day or so."

"Is that right?" he asked, looking surprised.

Ipatia watched, as his hand involuntarily combed his hair back. She realized he always did that when he thought. *Just like Grandfather, who pulled on his mustache.* She smiled. "Is there any more work for me?"

"Yes there is, as a matter of fact," he said. "Why don't I get settled first? I have a number of things I need to do today and I'll be very busy. How about coming into the office tomorrow…around noon. We can discuss it then."

❧   ❧   ❧

Later, in the privacy of her bedroom, Ipatia eagerly opened Tony's gift. It was a slim book of poetry by famous English poets, with beautiful artwork embellishing the front and back of the book. She stayed up late into the night reading it, inspired by the poems.

The next day, Friday, Ipatia entered Tony's office at the designated time. "Good morning, Mr. Tony. I'm here to talk about the work."

"Good morning, Ipatia. Please have a seat." Tony observed her quietly as she sat down. Sunday, he was leaving for Crete. He was going there to celebrate Easter with his family and was staying at least another week to attend Melissa's wedding. He wasn't going to be back in the office until the beginning of May. He needed an answer before then.

She looked at him inquisitively, asking, "What was it that you wanted me to do?"

"There are a number of issues relating to the business that I need to discuss with you. First of all, from what Rita told me and what I have seen myself, I am pleased with your progress and quick grasp of things."

"Thank you," she said simply.

"Now that you are finished with your work, I would like you to get involved in our new project," he said. "In the near future, I am planning to have computers added to our offices. Just like in England and America. We are very much behind, and we need to catch up with their technology."

"Computers?" she asked. "I've never used a computer before."

"Don't worry. You're bright. You will learn quickly."

He continued his discourse, explaining the usefulness of the computers. Ipatia asked a few questions and liked what she heard. He appeared to be well informed on the subject. When they were finished, she arose to leave.

"Did you get a chance to read the English poems?"

Ipatia turned, feeling flushed, recognizing the personal tone in his lowered voice. She had learned to listen for it. It had always made her feel warm inside. Now, it made her feel uncomfortably warm.

She blushed. "Yes! Thank you so much! They were very beautifully and nobly written." *There he went again, making you feel this way.*

"I'm glad you liked them. My favorite poem is the one written by Lord Byron," he said huskily. "She walks in beauty, like the night."

"I'll…look for it." Ipatia felt strong emotions as she went towards the door.

"Before you leave, I'd like to ask you something else."

"Yes?" Ipatia turned and looked at him expectantly.

"I would like to know if you are free...tomorrow...Saturday," he began. "We can go to a nice place, up in the mountain, where we can have a picnic. There is a beautiful view from there."

"That would be very nice!" she exclaimed, enjoying the image. "I mean, thank you for the invitation, but will it be just the two of us?"

"I can ask Tim to drive us there," he said dryly. Her grandfather had taught her well. "Can you be ready by eleven? I'll come...I mean we will come and pick you up then."

"Thank you. That would be fine," she said, as she slipped out of the room, almost running.

That evening, she talked to Paula and George about Tony's invitation and they looked at each other before nodding their approval. Paula said that they could visit her aunt's house on Sunday instead. Ipatia thanked them, then excused herself and went into the privacy of her room. She picked up the book of poems that Tony gave her and eagerly leafed through the book, searching for Lord Byron's poem.

She found it, and with hushed voice, read the title aloud, "She walks in beauty, like the night."

She continued with the rest of the poem until she reached the end, saying, "A heart whose love is innocent."

She sighed, gazing off into the room. Was it possible that Tony was trying to tell her something?

At that moment, there was a knock on the door.

"Ipatia, could I talk with you a minute?" asked Paula.

"Sure, come in," said Ipatia, putting the book aside and sitting upright.

Paula sat on the edge of the bed, looking at her. "George and I feel responsible for your welfare, and we promised your aunt and grandfather that we would take care of you. You see, Ipatia, when a young man asks a girl out on a date...it's either one of two things. He either is serious about her...or he isn't."

"What do you mean?"

"Simply put, has this young man said anything about his intentions towards you?"

"No," said Ipatia, blushing and shaking her head.

Paula looked at Ipatia intently. "If he tries anything, you just smack him with your purse and come home right away."

Ipatia laughed at the picture.

"Are you in love with him?"

The question fell like a bombshell.

Ipatia shut her eyes, contemplating her feelings. After a moment or two, she nodded. "Yes. To be honest, I'm a little confused. I mean...at first, I did want to go to the university, but now I can't stop thinking about Tony. He's on my mind all the time!"

"Of course! You're seeing him every day now," said Paula simply. "Are you sure it's not infatuation that you are feeling? Do you think he feels the same way about you?"

"I honestly don't know. Tony gave me this gift when he returned from England," Ipatia said, lifting up the book. "Now he's asked me out on a date. I don't know why he's showering me with gifts and all this attention, except that…"

"Yes?" prodded Paula, remembering her own conversations years ago with her daughter.

"I do know as a fact, that he's dated a number of girls and he hasn't gotten married yet. I've thought that maybe he might just want another girlfriend. On the other hand, Aunt Sophia said that he's an eligible man, and that he wouldn't be waiting long to get married," blurted out Ipatia.

"I see," said Paula. "So you are confused about his true intentions. Let me help on that issue. Before your aunt left for America, she confided in me that she had spoken to the young man."

"She did?" asked Ipatia anxiously.

"Yes, and he said his intentions were honorable," said Paula. "However, he had also mentioned that you were more interested in getting a degree than in marrying."

"He did?" asked Ipatia, stunned by the revelation.

🍁   🍁   🍁

That night, Ipatia dreamt that she was with Tony. *They were holding hands and he was leading her through a green meadow, toward the trees. Once they passed the trees, they stopped. Just ahead was a cliff, and beyond was a spectacular view.*

"I can see the sea," she said, pointing beyond. "It is beautiful here, just like Lipsi Island." Then she looked around her and said, "Are we the only ones here?"

"Don't worry," said Tony, smiling charmingly. "You can trust me, Ipatia."

Ipatia felt happy, as they placed a tablecloth on the ground and started preparing the lunch. Tony whistled, as he helped her remove the food from the baskets. At one point their fingers touched and she felt electricity run through her. Then he got up, saying he would be right back.

Tony returned with a bouquet of fresh flowers. "For you," he said, presenting them gallantly to her.

"How pretty!" she said, taking them and smelling them. "Let's put them here." She placed them in an empty glass and set it in the middle of the makeshift table.

"Your plate is ready," she said, handing him a plate full of food. Then she prepared her own plate. "This is delicious, Tony. You know…I feel very happy all of a sudden. As if we were in heaven."

"I know what you mean," he said, gazing into her eyes.

"You do?" she said, stopping to look at him with her large eyes.

"Umm hmm," he said, munching.

They were silent awhile longer, enjoying each other's presence and their meal.

"How long has it been since you came to Piraeus, Ipatia?"

"Seven months and two weeks," she said simply.

"Seven long months and two long weeks," he said.

"What do you mean?" she asked, not knowing what else to say.

"I mean, my little darling, that I love you and I can't live another day without you. I'm asking you to marry me," he said softly, taking her into his arms.

"I love you too," she whispered back, melting into his arms.

He kissed her passionately. She returned his kiss, and clung to him, feeling safe in his arms. He looked deep into her eyes.

CHAPTER 30

We drove into the mountain road
No clue of what the day would hold

Saturday morning, Ipatia arose bright and cheerful. She opened her window, enjoying the breeze. She decided to wear her white cotton dress for the occasion. After she dressed, she sat in front of the mirror, humming, as she combed her hair. It had grown long again. Her bangs had also grown long and were beginning to tickle her eyebrows. She blew them away. Just then, Paula entered the room, carrying a white shawl.

"I thought you might need this," said Paula, handing it to her. "It might be cool where you're going."

"Thank you," said Ipatia, placing it on the bed. "Before you leave, can you tell me if this looks too formal?" She pulled up her hair in a bun, revealing her long, slim neck.

"It does look a little formal," said Paula. "Why don't you leave it down and maybe just pull this towards the back a little."

"Good idea," said Ipatia cheerfully, as Paula left the room. She pulled the strands behind her ears, looking at herself in the mirror. That did look much better. She picked up the shawl to leave, when she noticed a spider on it. She dropped it, recoiling. Her heart started racing. She never liked spiders, or snakes, or scorpions. Last time she had seen the scorpion, it had been right before she found out that little Nick had cut his arm. Was this another sign? Determined to fight her fear, she took the shawl to the window and brushed the spider off. She watched in silence as the creature sped outside.

"Ugh!" she shuddered, shutting the window. "Stay away!"

Just then the doorbell rang. *It must be Tony.*

She picked up her scarf, then opened the door, hesitating. *Calm down, Ipatia. Everything will be all right. Don't let your imagination play games with you. It was just a silly little spider.*

❦   ❦   ❦

George answered the door. Tony introduced himself. He chatted with Ipatia's cousins, liking the older couple. He was not surprised to see Ipatia appear flushed when she came out to meet him. She looked appealing in that summer dress and lace shawl. He flashed her a warm smile, complimenting her.

"Thank you. The dress was a gift from Aunt Sophia," she said, smiling back. "I also brought the scarf along in case it gets windy."

"That's a good idea," he said, nodding his approval.

"Don't forget to take these sweets!" said Paula, handing Ipatia a box as they left. "Have a nice time!"

"We will," said Tony, smiling.

Once outside, Ipatia looked around for the car. Tony saw her puzzled expression, and with a twinkle in his eye, he said, "The car is over there." He pointed up the street.

"Oh," she said, having a strange feeling that he could read her mind.

When they reached the car, Ipatia noticed it was Tony's car and Tim wasn't there. She looked at Tony, confused. She didn't know what to do. A part of her held her back, but another part of her wanted to go wherever he went.

"I thought Tim would be here," she said flatly.

"I apologize that Tim is not here, my sweet," said Tony gallantly. "But, the truth of the matter is, when I went looking for Tim, I didn't find him."

"You couldn't find him?"

"My dear little sister decided to do her last minute shopping today. She borrowed him very early in the morning before I even got up. Gilda informed me. You see, Melissa is planning her wedding, and will be leaving tomorrow for Crete, so you know how busy that can be."

Ipatia nodded, remembering her own aunt's wedding preparations. So there was a good reason, and oddly enough, she felt good it turned out that way.

"Besides, my car needs to be driven," he declared, opening the door for her.

Ipatia smiled, then sat in the car. She noticed the picnic basket in the back.

He drove through the city streets, stopping and going slowly, cruising through the various neighborhoods, heading towards Athens and beyond. The weather was pleasant and the sun shone brightly.

"Have you been up there yet?" Tony asked, pointing to the Acropolis.

"Yes, I went there with Mrs. Rodos," said Ipatia. "It's amazing how the various parts of the columns are positioned so perfectly, one on top of the other. They form one straight line from top to bottom. Mrs. Rodos pointed that out to me."

"Did you get a chance to visit the archaeological museum?"

"Oh yes!" she replied, becoming excited. "I'm glad you mentioned it! I saw the vase from the island…the one Father gave to Grandfather. Thank you very much for the gesture. It was kind of you."

"You're welcome. I made a replica of it before giving it to them," he laughed. "The original is too valuable for me to keep. It could be stolen or even broken. It's safer in the museum, and besides, it should be shared with the public."

"You are right," she said nodding appreciatively.

He became silent as they drove through busy streets, past honking cars. Minutes later, they were on a large road, speeding along.

"Is that the mountain?" asked Ipatia curiously, pointing towards the large shape looming ahead.

"Yes. It is called Mt. Hymettus."

"Can one see everything from there? The city, the sea?" she asked.

"Yes, but the picnic area is much lower and doesn't have the same view," he said, gazing at her. "We need to go up much higher in the mountain. Would you like that?"

"That would be nice," she said, nodding her approval. "Where is the picnic area?"

"It's near the foot of the mountain. There is a monastery there, the Monastery of Kaisariani. It was built around the eleventh century and has some nice frescoes inside. There is also a spring there, on a hill above the monastery. You know, at one time, it used to be the sole source of water for Athens."

"That's very interesting," she murmured. "Is it still there?"

"Yes, we can go and visit it later. I think you will like it."

As they made their way towards the mountain, Ipatia was lost in her own little world, one in which only she and Tony existed. The breeze started to ruffle her hair. She tied her scarf loosely around her head.

"Tony, I've been meaning to ask you something," Ipatia said. "What is opportunity cost?"

"Where did you learn that?" he asked amazed. "It's an economic term."

"I know. Miss Marika mentioned it during our conversations and I didn't have a chance to ask her what it meant," she replied proudly. She didn't want to tell him the truth, that she had been reading economics books at the public library. She had browsed their pages trying to understand the world he had come from. The world he had chosen over shipping.

"Take this ride, for example," he began. "We decided to go on this trip rather than do something else. We are forfeiting other activities for this one. That's called an opportunity cost."

"Ahh, I see now. There's a cost for everything," she said, becoming stimulated from their conversation.

"Yes, and time is considered a cost," he said. "Like the time it takes to get an education versus getting married." He glanced at her, trying to gauge her reaction. She was quiet. *She understood.*

"Time," she said, relishing the idea. "Time controls so much of our lives."

"Yes, and efficiency is one way of getting an edge on time," he said.

"Is that why computers are so important?"

"Yes. They can do so many things in the same amount of time as someone who just does only one thing."

"And what does that gain you?" she laughed, knowing the answer.

"Why, more time to do other things, like go to picnics!"

They both laughed.

"How is your medical reading these days?" he asked lightly.

"I was reading something recently about the cells in our bodies. Researchers have found out that the cells replicate only so many times in one's lifetime, and then they stop reproducing."

"Our lives are finite," remarked Tony. "Which makes time so important."

Ipatia said, "Yes, but the good thing is that life doesn't end when we leave this earth. When we pass away, we move on to a new life, a new level, where time is no longer a factor."

"If we were to die, Ipatia, would our souls meet again someday?" he asked softly.

They were both silent.

He turned the radio on. In a short time, he was singing along with the music. Ipatia enjoyed listening to him sing. It was a love song

"You know, Mrs. Rodos, the English teacher met her husband in a restaurant. He was a cook who sang songs, just like this one," she said dreamily after he finished.

"Really?"

She continued, telling him about Mrs. Rodos falling in love with his voice and then marrying him.

"And they were happily married after that, right?"

"Yes," she replied, leaning her head back, listening to him as he continued to sing other love songs.

"Do you like my singing?"

Ipatia jerked her head up, surprised by his question. "I think you have a very nice voice!"

Does that mean you'll marry me, Ipatia?

They reached the mountain and began the arduous climbing of the winding road. She noticed how narrow the road was. There wasn't much room for error here. He honked right before turning a bend.

"Why do you honk?" she asked curiously.

"It's a safety precaution. There might be someone coming down from the other side, and I want them to know I'm here," he replied.

"Oh, so they can slow down?" she asked, tensing slightly.

"Don't worry," he said, laughing. "Ipatia, how long has it been since you came to Piraeus?"

Ipatia swallowed when she heard the question. It was just like in the dream.

"Seven months and two weeks," she said, almost whispering.

"Yes, that's right," he said. "That's how long we've known each other. But in fact, I feel I've known you much longer than that. You see, I took a trip once, with your father, years ago. On that trip, your father talked about you so much that I had to see for myself this bright, darling daughter of his. So when the ship arrived at the harbor, I stood on deck, watching you and your mother reunite with your father."

"You did?" asked Ipatia, wondering when this had happened. "I don't remember seeing you."

"You were five or six then. That was the year your father bought you the piano, wasn't it?"

"Yes," she said, nodding. "How did you know?"

"When he told me how you liked to sing so much, I convinced him to buy you a piano," he said, looking at her. "And he thanked me for it afterwards."

There was a honk and the screeching of tires, and that was all Ipatia remembered, for then she blacked out.

🍁　　　　🍁　　　　🍁

"Christina, quick, get Father for me. It's an emergency!"

Christina immediately went to Gregory's room and woke him up from his nap. "Melissa is on the telephone. She says it is urgent."

Christina helped him get into his wheelchair and pushed him to the telephone. He sat there and listened. Melissa received a telephone call from a hospital outside Athens. Tony had been in a car accident and was in the emergency room. He was in critical condition. They told her they were not equipped to handle such a severe case. She immediately arranged to have him flown by helicopter to the main hospital in Athens. Gregory was in shock when he heard the news.

"Father, please come," were Melissa's tearful words before she hung up.

Once she arrived at the hospital in Athens, Melissa was guided to the intensive care unit, where she saw several nurses and doctors hovering over her brother. She walked slowly towards the bed, afraid to look.

His face was bandaged up, and Melissa almost fainted when she saw him. She leaned against the wall for support. Gaining strength, she managed to squeeze in between one of the nurses, so she could get closer. There were tubes everywhere. She touched his hand. "Tony, Tony."

"It's best not to wake him, Miss," said the nurse to her left, sternly looking her way.

She walked to a chair and sat down, numbed by all the news. She stayed there awhile longer, gazing at her brother as if she were in a trance. A nurse nudged her awake and said that they didn't allow visitors to sleep in the intensive care unit. It was time for her to go home and get some rest.

It was almost midnight when Melissa arrived home. She got out of the cab slowly, then paid the driver. She unlocked the door and entered the dark house. There was no staff at the door to greet her, compounding the strange feeling. Where was everyone? Then she remembered. They all left this afternoon, and would be gone for the Easter vacation. The empty house echoed Melissa's loneliness, while her steps took her down the hallway and into the study. She must call Chuck. There would be no trip to Crete tomorrow. She telephoned him and told him the news. He said he'd be right over. She already felt better.

Ipatia found herself walking in a beautiful meadow. She was wearing all white. In front of her was a gate, and behind it stood Tony. When she saw Tony, she opened the gate and ran towards him, happy to see him.

"You're all right!" she said.

He took her hand and kissed it, saying, "Yes, my Love. You can't stay here though, you need to go back."

She felt sad, saying, "I don't want to go back, I want to be with you!"

"I'll try and come back," he promised. He turned around and walked away.

Ipatia woke up to the sound of voices above her. She blinked her eyes, trying to talk. Her chest felt heavy for some reason, and she had difficulty breathing.

"There, there, Ipatia. You'll be all right, my dear," said Paula, patting her hand. Ipatia looked a sorry sight. One side of her face was bruised, with one eye swollen shut.

"Where am I? What happened?' whispered Ipatia, looking around her. Light was streaming into the room from a window. Her mouth felt very dry. She licked her chapped lips.

"You were in a car accident, and were taken to a nearby hospital by some kind people who stopped to help."

"Ouch!" exclaimed Ipatia, as she tried to raise herself up. "What happened to Tony? Is he all right?"

"Now, now, try not to move," said Paula, helping Ipatia back down into her bed. "They said you have a couple of fractured ribs."

"Do you know what happened to Tony?" repeated Ipatia, concern written all over her face.

"We honestly don't know," said George, shrugging his shoulders apologetically at the girl's plea. "When we asked about him, we were told that no one by that name was admitted here."

"I hope nothing happened to him!" said Ipatia. Tears rolled down her face at the thought of Tony not surviving the crash. *Dear God, don't let that happen to him.* Her breathing became labored, and her head was beginning to throb. The pain in her ribs was becoming unbearable.

Paula saw the girl's difficulty in breathing and hurriedly left, bringing the nurse back with her.

The nurse helped Ipatia. She didn't leave until Ipatia was breathing better.

"Don't worry, everything will be all right," said George, trying to sound reassuring, but his voice cracked midway. "If you'd like, we can call Tony's home and find out for you."

There was a moment of silence. Ipatia thought it over, tears of relief wetting her face. "Thank you…. that would be wonderful! The telephone number is in a piece of paper…in my purse at home." She sniffled. "I forgot to take my purse with me."

"Don't worry dear, we'll call as soon as we get home," said Paula, patting her arm gently.

Ipatia smiled, feeling grateful, then brushed away the tears, wincing at the gesture. She delicately touched her closed eye, feeling its soft bulge. "What happened to my eye?"

"The doctor said that there is swelling in that eye, and that's probably going to be like that for a few days. Once the swelling goes down, then you will probably be able to see," said Paula.

"That's good!" said Ipatia, cheering up. "How did you find out that I was here?"

"When night came and you hadn't returned, we were very concerned for your safety," began Paula. She then looked at George as if waiting for him to continue the story.

"I have a friend who is a policeman, and so we contacted him around ten o'clock last night. We told him where you had gone, and he helped us find you," said George.

"I'm so glad you found me!" exclaimed Ipatia. "It must have been difficult, since I didn't have my purse with me and any identification on me."

"Yes, that was the hard part. Somehow, he learned about a car accident in the vicinity where you were going, and that a girl with your description had been hospitalized, so we took a chance and came here to see if it was you," said George.

"We were very worried about you," said Paula, nodding her head emphatically.

Ipatia started to drift off, feeling very sleepy.

"Dear, would you like for me to stay with you overnight, in case you needed anything?" asked Paula.

Ipatia's eyes fluttered open, she managed to whisper, "I'll be fine. I just feel sleepy."

Paula nodded, saying, "Don't be afraid to call for the nurse if you need anything."

Those were the last words Ipatia heard as she drifted off to sleep.

CHAPTER 31

Life is filled with lessons to learn
Some to keep, and some to spurn

The next morning, a nurse awakened Ipatia.

"My name is Maria. I will be your nurse today. I have come to take your vital signs. Is the pain medicine helping you at all?"

"Yes, and it's also making me sleep all the time," admitted Ipatia.

"Good, that's what we want. You need to rest," said Maria, as she put a thermometer in Ipatia's mouth.

"Can you tell me what's wrong with me?"

"Your x-rays showed you have two fractured ribs, and some bruising in your lung. That's why you have some difficulty in breathing."

Ipatia heard sounds of commotion and people talking in the background. The curtain had been drawn around her bed and she couldn't see them.

Maria read the reading on the thermometer. "Hmm, your fever hasn't gone away," she said, writing it down in the chart.

"Will I be needing to take antibiotics?" asked Ipatia.

"We already started you on them. You see that tubing leading into your hand?"

Ipatia looked at the thin tubing. She was surprised to see it entering her hand. She hadn't even noticed it before. The tubing came from a large plastic bag, filled with liquid. The bag was hanging on a pole.

"You're getting your food and medicine from here. By the way, I'll talk to the doctor about your fever. We don't want you to get pneumonia. Meanwhile, someone will be coming to draw your blood. Afterwards, you will be taken to the radiology room for x-rays."

"What are they for?"

"When you first came in, the x-rays showed a spot in your lung, so now they want to see if it's still there."

"Thank you, Miss Maria. Could you pull the curtains away from my bed as you leave?"

The nurse cheerfully complied, then left.

For the first time, Ipatia noticed her surroundings. Her bed was located next to a large window. She could only see the blue sky outside. She wondered what floor she was on. The room was cheerless, with its gray floor and low lighting. To her left, she saw one other bed, and across from her, two other beds, all containing women patients. They were talking amongst themselves.

She observed them quietly, trying to ignore the pain radiating from her rib area. Two of the women appeared middle-aged, and one looked to be around Ipatia's age. Ipatia didn't get a chance to find out more, because a young woman in white came towards her, carrying a box.

"I've come to draw your blood," she said, drawing the curtains slightly around them, then preparing her tubes.

When Ipatia saw the needle, she almost fainted. Looking the other way, she held her breath. She tensed up when she felt the pinch from the needle. "I'm afraid I'm not very good when it comes to seeing blood," she said, swallowing hard.

"Don't worry, we're almost done," said the technician brightly. "You can look now!"

Ipatia smiled apologetically as she watched the technician leave. A few minutes later, two nurses came into the room rolling a small bed with them. They lifted Ipatia up off the bed and unto the other bed, using the sheet that was under her to support her weight. She moaned lightly from the pain.

"We're going for your tests," said one of the nurses.

When Ipatia returned later that morning, she fell asleep. When she awoke, she was feeling better and took it upon herself to meet her fellow roommates. It didn't take long for her to become friends with them. Lula, the middle-aged woman whose bed was closest to the door, was there for some mysterious intestinal problem. The doctors couldn't seem to find the cause. Katina, the young girl to her left, had just gotten her appendix removed due to appendicitis. Across from Ipatia was Georgia, a young woman who was being treated for pneumonia.

Ipatia immersed herself in the other women's stories, forgetting her own pain. Sometimes she nodded sadly at their painful accounts, sometimes she offered a kind word. When she was asked why she was in the hospital, her short reply was that she had been in a car accident. She didn't go into further detail. She was quiet, contemplating on what to say next.

"The good Lord works in mysterious ways," said Lula, noticing the girl's pained expression. "Sometimes He puts us in situations because He wants us to learn a lesson, or because maybe we can be an example to someone else."

"Maybe He wanted us all to be here at the same time so we could become friends," said Katina, the youngest of the group.

Ipatia giggled nervously at the young girl's response.

Georgia said, "It is possible that the evil eye may have touched you."

"What?" asked Ipatia, surprised by the woman's suggestion. Georgia had been the quietest of the three.

"Sometimes when one has beauty and youth, and good things happening to them, there are people that may envy that," said Georgia importantly. "It can happen from anyone you meet, who looks at you and compliments you, or admires you. It's happened to me many a time."

"What did you do about it?" asked Katina, her eyes wide open.

"I had the spell removed," said Georgia. "My mother could tell if I had it or not. She would put water in a small bowl, then pour some olive oil into the water. She then made the sign of the cross in the oil. If the oil blended with the water, I had the evil eye. If it stayed separate, I didn't. Then she would say a special prayer to remove it. Within hours I was feeling better."

"Do you know the prayer?" asked Ipatia curiously. "I think I might have been affected by the evil eye."

Georgia made the sign of the cross, then began reciting the prayer. After she was finished, she began talking about the incidents when she had been afflicted by the evil eye.

The friendly discourse was interrupted when a group of people arrived. Ipatia watched curiously as Lula received her husband with their two children. The show of affection between the couple was unsettling for Ipatia. She looked away, unable to watch them. For some odd reason, that scene evoked a bittersweet feeling in her.

She began a conversation with Katina. She learned that Katina was fifteen, and that she would be leaving tomorrow. Their discussion didn't last long, for Katina's parents, grandmother and younger brother showed up. The area near Ipatia's bed became crowded and noisy as they all managed to settle themselves around Katina's bed. Katina introduced Ipatia to them, and Ipatia smiled sweetly back at them. She listened to their chatter for awhile, then she felt tired and shut her eyes.

Her thoughts inevitably turned to Tony; his smiles, the words they spoke before the accident, his gift, his kiss in the study; the scenes flowed together like one long movie. She began to pray silently. She prayed that he was all right and for her to have a speedy recovery. She fell asleep amidst her prayers.

A light tap on her arm woke her up. It was George and Paula. Paula brought some baked goods along with her smiles, and George made everything appear all right, sharing jokes with her. Ipatia introduced her cousins to Katina and her family, and they exchanged pleasant words for awhile. The room had gotten quite crowded by now, as more families had trekked into the room.

Paula said, "We contacted your grandfather. He was concerned about you, yet thankful that we were here to help you. He's happy that you are all right and doing better."

Ipatia thanked her.

"We also spoke with your aunt in America. The good news is that she is pregnant!"

"She is pregnant!" shouted Ipatia, clapping her hands together, lifting her body up. "I can't believe it!"

She winced from the pain. She eased back into her supine position.

"What is it dear?" asked Paula.

"I'm still a little sore," said Ipatia ruefully. More subdued, she then asked questions about her aunt's impending birth, but Paula laughed and said it was better if she talked with her aunt when she got out of the hospital.

"Your Aunt Sophia wants you to come and live with them in America as soon as you are well enough to travel," said Paula. "She said with the baby, she'll be needing your help. What do you think?"

"I'll have to think about it," said Ipatia. "Did you get a chance to call Tony's home?"

George shook his head sadly. "No one picked up the telephone," he said. "We tried two times."

They chatted awhile longer, sharing the latest news from their children in Thessaloniki, the national news, the weather, and their friends.

Ipatia's eyes were beginning to close. She felt sleepy.

"We better be going," said George, looking at Paula. "It looks as if Ipatia needs her sleep."

"I'm sorry, but I can't seem to keep my eyes open," Ipatia said. She drifted off to sleep.

The following day, the doctor visited Ipatia and examined her. He told her that there had been some internal bleeding, and that they were monitoring it. When she asked him about the black and blue areas on her body, he replied that the bruises were caused by the bleeding, and over time, should start to turn yellow, which was a sign of healing.

"All your internal organs are intact. The two fractured ribs will take several weeks to heal," he said. He ended the visit by saying if everything continued to improve, she should be ready to leave the following Monday.

✤   ✤   ✤

Gregory sat by his son's side, gazing sadly at the young man's bandaged face, waiting for the doctor's visit. Two days ago, he had arrived at the hospital in Athens, late in the evening, and was wheeled into the intensive care unit by Christina. There, he met with the doctor, who led him to his son. When he saw Tony, lying in bed, comatose, he began to weep uncontrollably, unable to contain his feelings. He hadn't slept these two days, worrying about Tony.

The doctor came into the room just then. "Good afternoon, Mr. Plakis."

Gregory asked heavily, "Doctor, tell me the truth. What are my son's chances of recovering completely?"

"Not very good," replied the doctor. "Surgery is needed, but it cannot be performed until his blood pressure is stabilized, and there's no guarantee he'll come out of his coma even after surgery."

Gregory collapsed right there on the spot. The nurses and doctors rushed to help him. As soon as he revived, he demanded in a raspy voice, "We must take him to the best doctors! Find me the best doctors! My son is not going to die!"

In what seemed like a miraculous show of renewed vigor, Gregory set out to find a doctor to save his son. He spoke with specialists in other hospitals, then, not satisfied with the poor prognosis, obtained names of top brain surgeons in other countries.

Finally, he contacted a top surgeon in England, Dr. Kildare, who was known for his high success rate in these special cases. He reached Dr. Kildare by telephone, and spoke to him at length, regaining hope after their conversation. Dr. Kildare suggested using a new surgical technique he had invented that he felt could help Tony. Gregory decided to take Tony to England.

At first, the doctors said that Tony might not survive the trip, but Gregory insisted that it would be even worse if Tony did not make the trip. With calls back and forth from the doctor's office in England, they were able to transport

Tony to England. As soon as they arrived at the hospital, Tony was wheeled off to surgery.

He was operated on seven different times before he was stabilized.

❦   ❦   ❦

Gregory looked up when he heard voices. The nurses outside in the hallway were speaking English in their crisp cool manner. Christina and Melissa entered the room.

"You need to get some rest, dear, before we admit you too!" said Christina. She kissed him lightly on the cheek.

"Why don't we go back to the hotel? Melissa will stay here and keep an eye on him."

He shook his head, muttering, "Not yet. I just have this feeling that any minute now, he will wake up. I want to be here when he does."

"I understand, dear, but it has been two weeks since he had his surgeries. The doctor said that it might take months for him to get out of his coma, if at all," said Christina, patting him on the shoulder.

"Tony means everything to me," said Gregory, brushing his wet eyes awkwardly. He rarely wept, but during these last few weeks, it had become a common occurrence. "Did Doctor Kildare have any word about his condition?"

"Once he performed the surgery, he says now it's up to Tony's body to recuperate and heal."

"Should we tell anyone back home or in the office?" asked Melissa.

"No, not yet," replied Gregory, shaking his head. "We will tell everyone in due time."

"What will happen if he doesn't come out of his coma soon?" asked Melissa. "I know this may not be the time to say it, but what about my wedding plans? What about the plans for the new house?"

Gregory did not respond right away, but instead looked thoughtfully at Tony. It was always the same story. As soon as he spent more time with Tony, Melissa's jealousy came forward, and she would start making demands.

After what seemed a long time, he nodded his head heavily and said, "Daughter, you will have your wedding and your house."

✤   ✤   ✤

Easter Sunday finally came. All the other patients had gone, and the room was now empty except for her bed. Time seemed to go very slowly with no one to talk to. Ipatia spent most of the morning reading the bible that Georgia had left her. She was able to read with both of her eyes for the first time without straining them. She read voraciously. Every word, every sentence she read seemed to have a deeper meaning, as if it were meant for her to read those passages. The bible was an escape from the thoughts that kept threatening to engulf her, and the stark loneliness that threatened to overwhelm her. Maria, the nurse entered the room, bringing in a tray of food.

"How about that…a nice meal for a change," said Maria, placing the tray down. "Here, let me take your temperature before you get started."

Ipatia placed the bible aside and complied by taking the thermometer offered to her. A few minutes later, she watched curiously, as Maria read the thermometer.

"Congratulations! You don't have a fever anymore!" said Maria brightly, as she shook the thermometer.

"That's wonderful!" said Ipatia. "Can I go home then?"

"Let me check with the doctor," said Maria. She returned after awhile and told her that the doctor wanted to be sure her fever was gone for at least twenty-four hours, so Ipatia had to wait one more day.

Ipatia picked up the bible and began reading more fervently. *Dear Lord, thank you for the blessing you bestowed upon me today, your day.*

Later that day, Ipatia's cousins paid her a visit. They brought a basket filled to the brim with red-dyed eggs, Tsoureki bread, roasted lamb, and other goodies.

Ipatia took an egg and held it in the palm of her hand, looking mischievous, exposing the one end of the egg. "Who will be first to try?"

Paula took her egg and tapped the end lightly on Ipatia's egg. "Ohh! Mine cracked!" she said.

They laughed together. Ipatia's egg also cracked George's.

"I'm afraid to eat it now. This one's a winner," said Ipatia, placing it down. She was beginning to feel better.

"Here, have my egg, and have some more bread," said Paula.

"No thanks," said Ipatia, rubbing her stomach. "You've stuffed so much good food into me today, I don't think I'll be able to fit through that door! By the way, did you hear anything from Tony's family?"

"Everything is closed for Easter, so we weren't able to place a call," said Paula. "We're sorry, Ipatia, but maybe we can try tomorrow."

"As soon as you get well, we're planning on visiting our children in Thessaloniki," said George quickly. "You can come with us, Ipatia. It might do you some good."

"Maria, the nurse, told me I no longer had a fever and I could leave tomorrow," said Ipatia hopefully.

"How wonderful!" exclaimed Paula. "I'll bring your clothes then, tomorrow morning."

After her cousins left, Ipatia took a nap, and later that evening, walked around in her room, remembering her conversation with her cousins and the talks with her new found friends. She wondered how they were doing. She then ventured out into the hallway, walking slowly and carefully. She didn't see anyone in the dimly lit hallway. It appeared that most of the nurses and medical staff had left for the day. She then returned to her room and lay in bed.

Her mind wandered to Tony, to their conversations before the accident, his thoughtful actions towards her, and all the kind deeds he had done. She wept quietly, brushing the tears away, feeling an inexplicable sadness. Deep down inside she was feeling the same pain as when her parents had died. The pain of losing a loved one. She thought she'd never experience it again. She thought she'd never love again. She knew she had been wrong.

She whispered softly into the night, "Tony, I love you. Where are you? How could you leave me alone like this?"

Inside her heart, a small voice whispered back, "*Do not fear, my love. You will never be alone again, because I will always be with you.*"

She fell asleep, feeling peaceful.

CHAPTER 32

April–May 1989
I cannot bear to think of thee
In Crete with your family

Ipatia woke up very early the next day in anticipation of her departure. She had been looking forward to this day. Her cousins arrived later that morning. Paula helped her get into her clothes. Several nurses came by to see her off, wishing her a speedy recovery.

Once home, they had lunch. Afterwards, Paula suggested that Ipatia take a nap.

"You don't want to exert yourself too much," said Paula.

Ipatia lay in bed, and before long, she was asleep. Afterwards, she found George and Paula in the kitchen, sipping coffee.

"George, could I ask you a favor? I need to go to the pharmacy to pick up my medicines, and I also want to call and see about Tony," she explained with a determined look on her face.

"Sure, sure," said George, putting his coffee cup down. "Paula, do you need anything?"

"Not right now, George. It's best to go now before the pharmacy closes for the afternoon," said Paula. "Here Ipatia, I have the telephone number."

George drove Ipatia to the pharmacy. When they reached there, George said, "I'll just drop you off and wait for you outside."

Clutching the prescription and her piece of paper, Ipatia slowly walked into the pharmacy, mindful of her sore ribs. She gave her prescription to the pharmacist and went to the telephone. She winced from the pain as she lifted the telephone. She was still experiencing some soreness in that area.

She made her call to the Plakis residence. Her heart was beating quickly. The phone rang several times and finally someone answered it. It was an older man's voice. It was the wrong number. Ipatia apologized and quickly hung up. She realized that her anxiety had caused the error. She paid more attention to the number as she redialed. This time, no one answered it. She let it ring several times before hanging up. She was feeling dejected as she slowly headed towards the door.

"Miss!"

She turned towards the pharmacist, a tiny thin man with a large nose and even larger ears. He looked distraught.

"There is a charge for using the telephone!" he demanded. "Also, your medicine is ready."

"I'm sorry," she said, blushing. She reached in her purse for the change. "I was thinking about something else."

She quickly paid, and left hurriedly out the door, still thinking about Tony.

"What's the matter?" asked George, as soon as he saw Ipatia's face.

"I can't get a hold of anyone at the Plakis house, and I'm worried about Tony," said Ipatia, slumping down, feeling miserable. "There's always someone at the house, either the housekeeper or cook. There must be something wrong."

At that moment, the pharmacist came running out the door with the medicine. "You forgot this!" he said, thrusting the small package towards her.

"Sorry," she said. "I just got out of the hospital and I'm not feeling too well."

"No problem," replied the pharmacist, his face softening. "Take care of yourself."

They drove away slowly.

"You really were affected, weren't you?" laughed George.

"I guess I was," she said solemnly. "I'm really puzzled about the whole thing and would like to know what happened to Tony."

"Maybe I can take you to the Plakis office building and you can ask there."

Ipatia perked up at the idea, and minutes later, George dropped her off in front of the Plakis office.

"I'll be waiting for you down here," he said, trying to sound cheerful.

For some reason the building seemed much larger today. Maybe it was because it was tiring to move around so much. She took the elevator upstairs, her heart beating quickly, as she thought about what she would find and what she would say. Should she act as if everything was all right if she saw Tony standing in the office talking with Rita? Or should she be quiet, so he would wonder why? She forgot her plan as soon as she saw Rita. She was simply happy to see her sitting at her desk. It seemed like everything was normal again.

Rita noticed her from the door and waved gaily to her as soon as she saw her. "*Christos Anesti!*" said Rita, greeting Ipatia with the Easter greeting, which was customary after Easter.

"*Alithos Anesti*," replied Ipatia, smiling fondly at her. She wasn't sure if she should mention her accident, because it would reveal the fact she had been on a date with Tony. A strong, gut feeling told her not to mention it.

"How was your Easter vacation?"

Ipatia paused before she spoke, trying to choose her words carefully. "It was nice and quiet. I spent it with my cousins. Did you spend your vacation with family?"

"I visited my younger sister and her family," Rita began. "Every year we go to her place because she has the biggest house and can accommodate all of the relatives." She rambled on about her holiday experience. Then she elaborated on each family member, describing in detail his or her life history. The telephone interrupted her chatter. It was a business call.

After Rita hung up, she said, "To be honest with you, Mr. Tony didn't leave any instructions for me to give you any work. He's in Crete celebrating Easter with his parents. Oh, and Miss Melissa and Mr. Daras went to Crete also. You know they're going to be married there. There's really nothing to do until they all return in a few weeks."

Ipatia was stunned by the news. So Tony was all right, and he and his family were in Crete! She realized now why her phone calls to the house were unanswered.

Ipatia managed to say, "Thank you Rita. I should be going then. Have a nice day."

Rita watched as the girl left. There was something about her that was odd. She looked as if she was ready to faint.

Ipatia entered the waiting car in a daze.

George asked, "Any news?"

"It seems as if Tony's all right," she said mechanically. "He's in Crete with his family."

"What?" sputtered George. "I can't believe it! These young men nowadays have no decency."

On the way back home, Ipatia remained quiet, puzzling over one thing. Why hadn't Tony tried to contact her?

She voiced her concerns with Paula later in the day.

"I understand how you are feeling, but maybe he had good reason to go to Crete," said Paula. "Sometimes there are things in life we don't have all the information for. You look at a person stealing a loaf of bread, and say he shouldn't be doing that. Then you find out that he has lost his job and has a sick wife at home and he wants to feed his children. His reasoning may be valid for him."

"I just don't understand it," said Ipatia, shaking her head. "One minute, he's giving me gifts, then asking me out on a date, and the next minute he's gone to Crete with his family for Easter without a word. It's not right to do that."

"I know, dear, it does sound a bit confusing," said Paula, nodding her head, looking puzzled. "Is it possible that he doesn't care for you?"

"I don't think so. I remember how concerned he had been when I sprained my ankle, and that was such a minor thing."

Later in the evening, Ipatia lay in bed thinking about Tony. Like a broken record, she went over everything in her mind once more; the days before the date, the day of the accident, and the days following the accident. Then she remembered the dream she had the night before the date. She now realized how her expectations had arisen. She had been expecting Tony to declare his love for her. *Maybe he really doesn't love you! Maybe he just sees you as he does other women! Just a friend!* That would explain his lack of interest the past week, and his leaving for Crete without a note to her. The spider was an omen after all.

Tears streamed down her face, soaking the pillow. Dr. Michael's words on the ship came back to haunt her. He had been right all along. Tony was a playboy, chasing one woman and dropping the next. Now she had become the next victim, just like Bonnie. He was probably busy chasing another woman. Afterwards, she resolved not to think about Tony ever again.

Melissa gazed at her husband's profile. They were seated in the back of the car while Tim drove them to her father's house. "You look tired, honey," she said. "Why don't you rest first before going back to work."

"I wish I could," he chortled. "I have to go back to the office and deal with some issues I found out about on the trip. If I wait until tomorrow, it may cost the company a lot of money."

They pulled up in front of the house. Melissa kissed Chuck good-bye before getting out of the car.

"I'll try not to be too long," he promised, before speeding off.

She waved to him. He had been very helpful these past three weeks, working hard at the agency, traveling on business trips, while she and her family battled with Tony's condition.

Planning her marriage had been difficult, but her persistence paid off. Her father didn't want to leave England, and Chuck didn't want to leave Greece. She finally managed to convince Chuck to fly over to England, saying how much she missed him.

It was a rainy spring day in England, when she exchanged vows with her husband. After their short honeymoon in Paris, they returned to England. In no uncertain terms, she told her father to bring Tony back to Greece, saying she could not stay there to help, now that she was married. She needed to be with her husband. Her father finally gave in to her wishes and they all returned to Greece in the middle of May.

Melissa entered Tony's bedroom. She wasn't surprised to find her father there in his wheelchair by the bed, reading a newspaper. He had become Tony's shadow, following him everywhere.

"Where have you been all morning?" demanded Gregory. "The nurse came already, and was looking for you. She needed to show you how to do some type of therapy on Tony. Since you weren't here, I had her show Christina instead."

"That's all right, the nurse will show me tomorrow. Chuck returned from his trip today, and I went to the airport to be with him!"

At that moment, Melissa's eye caught a movement coming from Tony's bed. She ran excitedly to the bed. "Tony! Tony!"

There was a flutter of his eyelids, and he slowly opened his eyes.

CHAPTER 33

May–December 1989
I leave Greece to be with my aunt
Your silence, dear, I can't understand

Ipatia became stronger over the next few days, but the painful memory of a betrayed love was to remain imprinted in her heart much longer. Determined to remove any reminder of Tony, she decided to leave for America.

Her cousins were reluctant to let her go just yet. George was concerned about her welfare. He suggested she remain with them awhile longer to let her wound heal more. But she wasn't swayed. She wanted to go as far away from Greece as she could. Her cousins eventually succumbed to her request, and helped her get her tickets and prepare for the trip. Paula also gave her luggage for the trip.

Then Ipatia telephoned Aunt Sophia to tell her she was coming.

"I'm so happy you are coming!" was her aunt's response. "We'll be waiting for you at the airport!"

Her grandfather received the news in a different manner. His silence spoke loudly and Ipatia's voice quivered, as she told him about her plans for the trip.

"Why did you decide all of a sudden to go on this trip when I specifically told you not to go?"

"Aunt Sophia is pregnant, Grandfather," she said. "She asked that I go there to help her with the pregnancy." She deliberately left out the real reason she was leaving. She didn't want Grandfather to know.

"And who paid for the tickets?" he demanded.

"I saved enough money from my earnings to pay for my tickets," she said proudly.

"And what did George and Paula say about all this?"

"They helped me buy the tickets," she said. "Aunt Sophia already knows and is expecting me there soon."

There was a long pause.

"If you feel well enough to go on such a long trip, then so be it," he said finally.

❦   ❦   ❦

Sitting in the airplane, Ipatia looked out the small window, gazing at the clouds absentmindedly, daydreaming; wondering what America would look like; wondering if she did the right thing. Her thoughts were interrupted by a female voice.

"We will be landing in a few minutes. Please fasten your seatbelts."

It was a beautifully smooth landing. Ipatia was shocked to see the airport buildings covered with a blanket of white snow. There was snow everywhere! When Ipatia arrived in the terminal, she looked around her anxiously, searching for a familiar face.

"Ipatia, Ipatia! Over here!"

Ipatia was relieved when she spotted her aunt and uncle waving at her from among the crowd of people near the entranceway. Her aunt was almost unrecognizable underneath the thick, winter coat and the woolen scarf circling her hair. They hugged and kissed and everything seemed so much better.

"We need to go to the baggage claim area," said Uncle John, leading the way. They took an escalator to the lower level and picked up her luggage.

They walked through the grand airport terminal, with its never-ending corridors, wall to wall windows, and streams of people. Ipatia was beginning to feel tired but she didn't say anything. It was a city in and of itself!

"This will take us to the parking lot," said Uncle John. He stopped ahead, placing the trunk on a moving belt, then stood on the belt, moving forward.

"Come on, Ipatia, we can go on this. It's less tiring," laughed Aunt Sophia as she walked onto the moving belt.

Ipatia jumped on and squealed, trying to balance herself on the moving floor.

"There, just lean on that rail," said Uncle John, looking back towards them, grinning.

After what seemed like a long time, they got off the belt. Outside, she could see the snow covered parking lot. She shivered in anticipation.

Uncle John said, "Wait for me here. I'll go and bring the car. I won't be long." He put on his hat and gloves, and was gone through the double doors, trudging through the snow, carrying her luggage.

"Can you believe this weather!" chattered Aunt Sophia. "They've never seen anything like this. It was a regular spring day, just a few days ago, then this snow blizzard hit us yesterday. It came out of nowhere! We called before coming, and heard there was a delay. We were afraid you wouldn't be able to come at all, what with all the snow. But you made it!"

"Actually, it worked out nicely. When I stopped over at New York, I had to go through customs, and the lines were long. I almost thought I wouldn't make the connecting flight," said Ipatia. "Luckily, it was delayed because of the weather, so I was able to catch that flight."

The conversation continued and after a few minutes, Uncle John pulled his large car to the curb and honked. Moments later, the car made its way slowly through the slushy city streets. Ipatia's eyes were large with wonder as she peered outside the frosted window. Everything looked white and so much larger. The streets were large, the buildings were tall, even the people looked like large bears, bundled up in their many layers of winter clothes.

They arrived at the house about an hour later and Ipatia immediately liked it. It was a red brick colonial with two white Grecian columns in the front. She watched in awe as a large door opened magically and the car slowly entered inside.

"Your car goes into the house?" she asked excitedly.

"Yes, it's one of us, you know," said Uncle John. "Here it's needed because of the snow."

Ipatia followed her aunt inside. The house felt cozy and warm, and there was a smell of fresh baked food in the air.

"Come, let me get you something to eat," chirped Aunt Sophia, leading her into the large kitchen.

"Is it time to eat yet?" asked Uncle John, entering the kitchen with the suitcases.

Aunt Sophia laughed, then went to the oven and opened it.

"You didn't have to go to so much trouble, Aunt Sophia," said Ipatia. "I could have helped you!"

"Don't you worry about a thing!" said Aunt Sophia. "We have cousin Stasoula to thank. She came by and prepared the roast beef for us."

Ipatia looked puzzled.

"Antonios and Stasoula live next door," explained Uncle John. "They have two sons, and own a catering business. They're very nice and friendly. You will like them. You have to watch the sons, though. They like to tease."

"They're expecting us at their house tomorrow for dinner," said Aunt Sophia.

"By the way, should I take these suitcases up to the bedroom?" asked Uncle John.

"Thank you. I almost forgot. I have a few gifts for you in them," said Ipatia. She picked up a suitcase. It was heavy. She winced from the pain.

"Are you all right dear? Do you need to sit down?" asked Aunt Sophia, looking concerned.

"I'll be fine, thank you. I'm still a little sore. I keep forgetting I'm not well yet," replied Ipatia, rubbing the sore area gently.

"You're also probably tired from the trip," said Aunt Sophia, looking sympathetic. "Here, let me show you to your bedroom where you can rest a little. You can show us the gifts later."

Ipatia followed her aunt meekly up the steep stairs, with Uncle John carrying the suitcases behind her. They went to the room at the end of the hall.

"This is your bedroom, dear," said Aunt Sophia, breathing heavily and laughing. "I have to catch my breath now. It's not the same as before, lugging all this weight around. It's like carrying an extra piece of luggage around all day."

They all laughed. Ipatia liked her room immensely. The bedroom was carpeted and had large, walk-in closets. There was a bathroom right next to it. Further down the hallway was another bedroom that served as her aunt's sewing room.

Ipatia rested after her aunt and uncle left. But she was too excited to sleep. After an hour, she went back downstairs and found her aunt and uncle in the kitchen, conversing quietly.

She helped prepare the table and serve the meal. They discussed her aunt's condition in detail during dinner.

"Since I'm forty-two, the doctors are keeping a very close eye on me," said Aunt Sophia proudly. "They don't want me to exert myself too much."

"Don't worry, Aunt Sophia, I'll help you around the house."

"You need to get well first," laughed Aunt Sophia.

After the meal they sat around the table catching up on news.

Ipatia stifled a yawn. "I can't keep my eyes open. Why am I feeling so sleepy?" She rubbed her eyes.

"You're experiencing jet lag," said Uncle John, nodding knowingly. "It's natural to feel this way after long trips. It'll take you a few days to get over it. Why don't you go and sleep it off?"

Ipatia helped clean up before excusing herself. It took her a long time to sleep that night. First it was too hot, so she changed into lighter clothing. Then it was too cold. She changed again. Finally, she was comfortable enough with the temperature. Outside her window there was enough light from the moon reflecting off the snow to make it appear almost as if it were daylight.

She lay awake, thinking about how it would be to live with her aunt and uncle and attend the university here. They seemed happily married, and the house was large enough for them all to live comfortably together. She also wondered what Tony was doing in Greece, replaying all sorts of scenes in her mind. A sad feeling descended upon her as she recalled hearing the news from Rita. It wasn't long before she began to weep. She wiped her eyes and rolled over. Maybe she was tired. She slept fitfully into the night.

The next morning she found her aunt in the kitchen reading a magazine. The clock on the wall showed eleven o'clock.

"Good morning! Hope you had a good night's sleep."

"Yes, thank you. The bed was so comfortable that once I fell asleep I had a hard time waking up!" said Ipatia.

"You must have been tired also from the trip. By the way, breakfast is already made. There's toast, eggs and sausages, and the milk and juice are in the refrigerator. Help yourself."

"Thank you!" said Ipatia. "Is Uncle John going to join us?"

"You just missed him. He already had his breakfast and then had to go see about a house," explained Sophia. "His business in real estate is such that he has odd hours. I'm still trying to get used to it."

Ipatia chatted with her aunt as she ate her breakfast. Then she talked about the women she met in the hospital and their stories.

"They had all these problems and were still happy," said Ipatia. "They helped me quite a bit with their stories. I felt as if my problems were nothing compared to theirs."

"Ipatia, if you need to talk, I would be more than happy to listen," began Sophia.

"Don't worry, dear Aunt," said Ipatia, laughing nervously. "Things are fine, I was just trying to make a point."

"By the way, I've been wanting to learn about how you got into this car accident. George and Paula didn't tell me the details, except that you were with some friends."

"It's a long story, and I'd rather not talk about it, if you don't mind," said Ipatia hurriedly. She didn't feel comfortable relating the story, reliving the pain. She just wanted to forget it.

"All right," said Sophia. She secretly wondered if this had to do at all with Tony and noticed there had been no mention of him at all by Ipatia.

Ipatia met her cousins the following day and was swept up by their good-natured behavior. Antonios and Stasoula were warm and generous people, and gave of themselves freely. The boys, Nick and Chris, were older than Ipatia. Nick, who was twenty-two, was finishing his last year of college, while Chris, who was twenty, had decided to work with his parents in the catering business. The boys quickly took Ipatia under their wing and planned an outing to take her downtown the following weekend to visit museums and other sites of interest. With their help, Ipatia was able to put aside the painful memory of a lost love and forge ahead to a new beginning. It wasn't long before her usual joking and laughter began to show.

The weeks flew by quickly, and Ipatia's ribs healed just as quickly. She submerged herself into her new role, helping her aunt with the chores and cooking. Her aunt was beginning to show signs of pregnancy, and either spent most of the day getting over morning sickness, or lying in bed, fatigued. Ipatia also visited her cousins' house often, becoming good friends with Nick and Chris.

One day, she asked Nick about the universities in the area, and the discussion led to Chicago State University, the university he was attending. Seeing her keen interest, he took her the following day to the campus and showed her around.

"This is a beautiful place," she said, walking alongside him. "What do I have to do to become a student here?"

Nick took her to the admissions office where she obtained helpful information.

"I need a thousand dollars to attend," she said woefully, having read the application form.

"I have an idea," said Nick. "Why don't you work with us in my father's business? You have two months left. You can earn that much, if not more."

Ipatia agreed, and with Nick's guidance, applied to the university.

Antonios' catering business was booming. There was always room for more help. Ipatia worked mostly on the weekends, when there were wedding receptions held at various places. She helped prepare the tables, serve the meals, and cleaned up afterwards.

She received a letter a few weeks later from the university. The admissions office needed transcripts from her former school, and she had to pass the English examination. She had brought all the papers with her. With Nick's help, she had her transcripts translated, then submitted the required documentation.

The next step was to overcome the task of taking the English examination. After a considerable amount of time and effort, she managed to pass it. Each day, she anxiously searched the mailbox for the acceptance letter from the university. It came one day in early July.

"Aunt Sophia, I got accepted to the university!" she shouted, waving the letter at her aunt.

Sophia looked at her niece's beaming face with pleasure. She had not seen her this happy in a long time.

"Ipatia, you were determined to get your education," she said. "And it looks as if you'll make it!"

After Ipatia received her acceptance letter, she worked even more hours at her cousin's catering business. She was determined to save every dollar she earned. The work was hard, and often she would come home too exhausted to do anything else except go to sleep. There was white linen to be folded, plates to be placed on the tables, and silverware to wipe clean. There were dishes of hot food to serve and cold drinks to pour. She was reminded of the work she did on the island. She'd catch herself having negative thoughts while peeling potatoes or stirring a stew. *Is this what you came here for, Ipatia? No, but this will help me get my education!*

When she received her paycheck and deposited it in the bank, the balance continued to grow, fueling her efforts, pushing her forward, closer towards her goal, and further away from the memory of a broken heart.

Even with her hectic schedule, she was able to attend the local Greek Orthodox church with her aunt and uncle on the Sundays she didn't work. The first time she visited the church, she noticed the Byzantine choral music wafting down from somewhere above her head. She looked up towards the balcony.

"That's the choir," replied Aunt Sophia proudly. "Why don't you join? They're looking for new people."

Ipatia was moved by the choral music. She joined the choir that very same day. Later, she wrote a poem describing her experience.

Woven together with the incense-laden air,
These beautiful, soulful melodies
Echoed within the church walls,
Permeating into the recesses of my heart.
Here it was I found peace.

🍁   🍁   🍁

On Ipatia's nineteenth birthday, she had to work for a wedding banquet. She came home later in the day, feeling tired. When she went to rest on the couch, she found an upright piano sitting against the wall in the living room.

"A piano!" she exclaimed. She touched the keys affectionately. "This is a wonderful surprise!"

"Happy Birthday! We were hoping you'd like it," explained Aunt Sophia, smiling proudly.

"How did you manage to get this? It must have cost a fortune!"

"Actually, it was quite simple. Your uncle found it in one of the houses he was selling. The sellers didn't want to take it with them. They said he could have it for free…so he took it!"

Ipatia hugged her aunt, thanking her again. She sat down on the bench, and began playing cheerful Greek tunes on the piano. She was transported back to Greece, to her grandfather, to the island.

After a few minutes, she switched to classical music. At one point, she began to play Beethoven's Fur Elise. As her fingers glided over the keys, the memory of Tony playing this very same song in his father's study intruded her thoughts. The scene that followed, when he kissed her, was hard to ignore. She stopped, unable to continue, as strong emotions threatened to overwhelm her.

"Don't stop! It's beautiful," said Sophia.

Later that evening, her cousins joined them for dinner and they celebrated Ipatia's birthday. After the meal, her aunt invited her to play for them. She played her favorite songs. She was brought back to reality by the sound of clapping.

"We didn't know you could play so well, Ipatia!" said Stasoula, clapping her approval. "We must see about getting you to play at some of the banquets. They are always looking for someone."

It didn't take long before Ipatia was playing the piano for special events. She started wearing a long black dress for the occasion, pulling her hair back. Her elegance and graceful playing didn't go unnoticed. She was becoming popular and in demand, and she started focusing her energies on her music, playing the piano rather than serving the meals.

The semester finally started, and because of the heavy classload, Ipatia stopped working altogether. On the first day of classes, she took a bus to the university and quickly got lost finding her way in the large, sprawling campus. That day was the hardest, as she tried to locate her classrooms. Her courses included Biology, English, Calculus, Physical Education, and Introduction to Philosophy. It took her several days before she finally knew where to go without asking someone.

The most difficult parts of the courses were the professors' lectures. Even though her English was quite good, it did not prepare her for the terminology spoken in the classrooms. Sometimes the professors themselves didn't speak clearly, or oftentimes spoke too quickly for her to comprehend what they were saying. Whenever Ipatia had free time between her classes, she went to the library and rewrote her notes, trying to decipher what the professor had said. Many a time, she came home frustrated, asking for help from her Uncle John or cousin Nick. They turned out to be great resources. A few weeks passed and Ipatia finally settled down to a comfortable routine.

One day in late October, Ipatia had finished her last course for the day and was walking briskly across the campus heading for the bus stop. A cool breeze ruffled her hair and she tugged her jacket closer to her, noticing for the first time the crisp fall air. She stopped and gazed around her, breathing deeply, enjoying the changing color of the leaves in the trees. The sun was brilliant, bathing every color brighter, bolder than before. There was color everywhere. Even the windows of the school buildings were splashed with reds and yellows as they reflected the color of the leaves.

Just then a man passed in front of her resembling Tony. Ipatia stared at him, her heart beating wildly. He looked her way. She lowered her eyes when she realized it wasn't him. He quickly disappeared into a building.

She resumed her walking. An odd thought occurred to her. She pictured the cat's eye stone with its changing colors, just like the changing leaves, sitting in Tony's large warm palm. She wondered where he was and what he was doing.

She also remembered he had been a professor once. *Just like the professors here, who teach your classes, with students looking up to them, admiring their knowledge, power, and prestige. He was one of them.*

She liked this new image of Tony, which lifted him from the low ranks of a rich spoiled playboy and into the ranks of a professor. It seemed to bring Ipatia a sense of satisfaction. *Your eyes have been opened by the books you read, by the knowledge you are gaining, day by day, just as the knowledge he once had at his fingertips.* Suddenly she felt much closer to Tony, as if by this process of being a student, she gained insight into his own soul that also thirsted for knowledge. *If only he hadn't left me.* She brushed the moisture from her eyes and hurried towards the bus stop.

That evening, just before going to sleep, she searched for the little poetry book…his gift. She had stuffed it in her luggage the last minute before leaving for America. It wasn't long before she found it in the small bookshelf, buried among her textbooks. She sat on her bed, leafing through it, remembering Tony's words, desperately searching for some clue as to her true feelings for him. As she read Byron's words aloud, the strong emotions that ran through her body brought tears to her eyes. She knew just then that he could never be erased from her mind. She slept with it clutched to her bosom.

❦   ❦   ❦

"Tony, it's time for your therapy," said Melissa, bending over and nudging her brother, who was sleeping. She stood up and felt faint all of a sudden, taking a step back to compose herself. Trembling, she went over and opened the window, allowing the cool winter breeze to enter the room, ruffling the window curtains. She took deep breaths as she tried to compose herself. She had confirmed her pregnancy with the doctor a week ago and was not surprised to be experiencing this spell. She heard footsteps in the hallway. It must be Suzie, the housekeeper. She went to the door to call her.

"Hi, Melissa!" said Bonnie.

"Bonnie! Weren't you in Paris or something?" asked Melissa, surprise written on her face. She hugged her best friend.

"I just got back last night. I passed by your father's house, but no one was there. Then I remembered you had moved. I looked up your new address in a letter you wrote me recently."

"It's so good to see you!"

"I have some good news!"

"What is it? Did you meet the designer you talked to me about, you know, the one you wanted to work with?"

"Yes, and it turned out I didn't go with him, because he had idiosyncrasies. Anyway, he introduced me to another designer, Pierre, and one thing led to another, and we fell in love. Melissa, I'm going to be married!" said Bonnie, lifting up her hand to reveal an engagement ring.

"How wonderful!" exclaimed Melissa. "Now I also have some good news to tell you." She told her about her pregnancy.

"Isn't that grand!" exclaimed Bonnie. "Now we can go shopping for the baby's new clothes."

They talked about Bonnie's wedding plans and Melissa's pregnancy. There was a chiming of a clock in the distance.

"I forgot all about Tony," said Melissa, fretting. "I need to wake him up. He has to get up for his physical therapy and he's already late."

She went back into the room and bent over Tony, speaking to him softly at first, then seeing it didn't work, raised her voice. Melissa looked down at Tony's handsome profile. The accident hadn't marred any of his handsome features, except for a telltale scar in the upper left corner of his forehead, which was hidden by his locks of hair. Yet he was changed inside.

His head injury left him with amnesia and he had recognized none of his family when he had awakened from his coma. Tony had to relearn everything. Her father, shocked with Tony's condition, began in earnest to help in his physical rehabilitation. It was as if he were on a mission to restore his son. He hired physical therapists, nurses, and doctors to come and treat Tony. He even paid private tutors to teach Tony how to read and write again.

Only now, months later, was Tony just beginning to understand things and starting to communicate. But he still needed to be guided in his activities, reminded gently of his appointments.

"Hello?" he asked.

Melissa looked at Tony, trying to keep her composure. He said it as if he did not recognize her. She said pertly, "I'm Melissa, your sister, remember? You need to get up because you have to go to therapy, for your walking."

She helped him get up in bed, trying to remind herself to be patient.

Bonnie looked at him, pitying him, pitying his weakness and his helplessness. He looked so pathetic. He was so different from strong, charming Pierre.

Tony sat up in bed, looking at Bonnie with a puzzled look.

"Hello, Tony," said Bonnie awkwardly.

He nodded his head silently, then stared at Melissa.

"I think he wants to be alone," said Melissa, finally realizing her brother's reluctance to be dressed in front of Bonnie. They went outside the room.

"I must be going," said Bonnie. "I still have a number of things to do."

"Before you go, I just wanted to let you know we'll be going to Switzerland after the holidays. Father felt it would be good for the whole family to get away."

"How long will you be gone?"

"I won't stay long because Chuck has to be back at work, but Tony will probably stay there much longer," said Melissa.

After Tony came out, Melissa helped him get into his coat and led him to Tim, who was waiting outside to take him to his therapy session.

CHAPTER 34

December 1989–May 1991
An independent man I want to be
To let go, and to build a family

One day in December when Ipatia returned home from classes, she found her aunt clutching her stomach, looking pale.

"Are you all right, Aunt Sophia?" asked Ipatia, rushing to her side.

"I think the baby is coming," said Sophia. "Can you call your uncle to come right away?"

Ipatia rushed to the telephone, dialing the number to her uncle's office.

Twelve hours later, Sophia gave birth to a beautiful healthy baby boy named Alexander. A few days later, she returned home with the baby. That day was a trial for everyone. The baby kept waking up in the wee hours of the night, crying and sputtering. The next day, he slept straight through, giving his mother a chance to catch up on her sleep. Then, again, he woke in the night. It took several weeks before the baby's sleep schedule was synchronized with everyone else's.

"Can I hold him?" asked Ipatia, one day after she came home from school. She received the bundled baby, holding him carefully. She was fascinated by his small features, his uniqueness, his vulnerability. He trusted her completely. He smiled when she teased his lips with her small finger. He then opened his mouth wide.

"He looks like he's hungry!"

"I just fed him! How does it feel?" asked Sophia, beaming proudly.

"It's a wonderful feeling!" said Ipatia. "He looks so small and fragile!" She touched the baby's cheeks lightly, playfully. He stretched delightfully and gave her a wide grin. "There he goes again!"

"I hope your studies aren't suffering because of the baby," said Sophia.

"Don't worry," Ipatia said. "Upstairs, it's really quiet when I close the door to study."

❋   ❋   ❋

Ipatia's duties were twofold now. Not only was she studying, but she was also spending much time helping take care of the baby. Even with all her workload, Ipatia did well in her courses. She passed them successfully, amazing both her aunt and uncle.

The spring semester went by quickly and around the corner, the summer came with all its glory, hot and muggy. Ipatia looked forward to working for her cousins once more with their catering business. There was laughter and joviality with her cousins, and she was saving money for college. She also continued to play the piano at the banquets, whenever there was a request for music.

It wasn't long though, when single, young men, eager to make her acquaintance, started surrounding her after each piano performance. At first, she was flattered by all the attention, but it quickly turned into annoyance when she realized it wasn't her playing that attracted them to her, but her looks.

"These aren't men...they are wolves," she complained to her aunt afterwards. "They expect you to say yes if they ask you out on a date, and if you don't, they act like you are their worst enemy."

"It's not like on the island," warned her aunt. "Here, there are different standards."

Ipatia began wearing a wedding band to fend off potential admirers.

❋   ❋   ❋

Ipatia's twentieth birthday marked the beginning of the next school year. As a sophomore, she was familiar now with the campus, and her English had improved considerably. She was able to understand the majority of the lectures. That year, she also signed up for a computer course and enjoyed it tremendously.

Besides the formal education she was receiving from her courses, the university also taught her another kind of education, one which did not need books, but came from experiencing life.

The students at the university were from heterogeneous backgrounds, ranging from Americans to foreign students from other countries. She also learned not everyone had the same beliefs as she did. There were different religions and different cultures. There were liberal thinkers, as well as conservatives.

One day in December, Sheila, a classmate she met in her philosophy class, asked her to join her and some other friends to go to a party on the university campus. "It's the end of the semester and kids just want to party," said Sheila, tossing her long brown hair and shrugging her slim shoulders. "Come on, don't be so prim and proper. You're living in America now."

The party was on a Friday night and Ipatia attended more out of curiosity than anything else. She made plans for her uncle to pick her up at nine o'clock. It was in a large banquet room on campus and a band was playing rock and roll music. She stood around with the girls at first, watching other students arrive. Ipatia greeted a few classmates she knew. Afterwards, they found a table, sat and ate refreshments, and listened to the music.

Eventually, Sheila invited some young men over at the table, and they sat there for awhile, chatting with them.

Ipatia watched silently. She smiled when the young men looked over at her, but did not offer to speak. She felt different from them, as if she was much older, as if she were their chaperone. After awhile, one of the young men stood up, as if getting ready to leave.

"Let's go over to my apartment. There is better action there," he said.

Her friends complied, but Ipatia did not go with them, giving the excuse that her uncle was going to pick her up. She avoided spending time with the girls after that day, giving excuses of having much studying to do.

The winter sessions went by quickly and the days rolled over into spring semester. Ipatia's openness and cheerfulness was assumed to be a sign of availability by the male students, and they began showing interest in her. One male classmate asked her out on a date one day in March. She didn't know how to answer and simply said "No!" Another one in another class asked her if she would like to go to Florida for spring break and she flatly refused.

These overtures happened enough times to shake Ipatia's naïve assumptions about people. The code of conduct she learned on the island did not exist here, and she learned to be more cautious around the college men and women, and not expect them to think like she did. How could they? They were raised in a totally different environment. Her cheerful, outgoing personality was replaced with a cautious, reserved outlook towards the young men and women on campus, waiting to see what their character revealed before she opened up to them.

Spring break came and Ipatia spent it quietly with her relatives, enjoying the baby and playing the piano.

One evening, after a session of playing the piano, she rested her hands on the keyboard, thinking. Her aunt was busily sewing while the baby lay nearby in its cradle.

"I don't know, Aunt Sophia," she said. "I've been trying to do well in my studies, and the boys in my classes are trying to get me out on dates. It is hard to concentrate in class, knowing they're sitting in the aisle next to me. I don't look forward to going back to school because of what may happen."

"I know what you mean," said Aunt Sophia sympathetically. "You're an attractive young girl and probably exotic to these American boys, with your looks and Greek accent. You are doing the right thing by not going out with them. Here it is different from Greece. The men and women often date to have a good time, not necessarily to get married. You don't know what their intentions are."

"Besides, I can't do well in my studies if I'm in any relationship now," Ipatia complained. "I know a girl who recently dropped out of philosophy class to get married. I don't want to be like that."

"You mean Sheila?" asked Aunt Sophia.

"Yes, how did you know?"

"I remember that party she took you to, was it last December?" said Aunt Sophia. "Anyway, she never was into her studies. I think she went to college to meet boys. There are girls like that, you know. Why don't you try making friends at our church?"

Ipatia continued to sing in the church choir on Sundays, and made several friends there. It wasn't long before she became involved in other groups at the church as well. She had opportunities to volunteer at different church functions, participate in the church festival, and help out at the outreach programs.

It was a different world from the small island, more complex, more varied, and even more tiring. She wrote letters to her grandfather, and to her cousins, describing her life. She wrote about the holidays and how they were different from those in Greece. For Easter, not all the businesses were closed, as in Greece. She had to attend classes on Good Friday. Then there were new holidays, like Thanksgiving and Labor Day.

Her grandfather responded infrequently, but when he did, they were long letters. Sometimes she would get a letter from Mrs. Tsatsikas, tucked inside his letter.

❈   ❈   ❈

Ipatia passed through her second year with very good grades, and soon, May loomed ahead, marking the end of the school semester. One weekend, Ipatia was in the living room, studying for her final exams. Aunt Sophia was sitting nearby, sewing.

"Tia. Tia."

Ipatia looked up from her studies. Little Alexander was trying to get her attention. Being a little over a year old, he was teetering, holding on tightly to the side of the couch, trying not to fall. His pudgy face was scrunched up and his large eyes were pleading with her. She laughed at his antics, encouraging him to come to her with her outstretched arms. He held on to the couch as his feet fumbled their way to her. He looked so proud at his accomplishment, giggling joyfully. She picked him up, hugging his chubby body.

The addition of little Alexander in everyone's life was a joy to experience. His playfulness and joy kept everyone laughing.

"Come, let's go for a walk," Ipatia said, taking Alexander's chubby little hand and walking slowly around the room with him. He teetered, almost falling, and she patiently helped him correct himself.

"Ipatia, you would make a good mother," said Aunt Sophia, smiling.

CHAPTER 35

May–August 1992
Now that I'm well again
A new life will I begin

"Come in," said Tony, buttoning his shirt.

Christina opened the door and peeked in. It was a Friday morning in May and she was glad to see Tony awake. Before she could speak, he smiled and said, "Thank you for the reminder, but you don't need to wake me up anymore. I know Jon is here. I know you have an appointment to go to with Father, and I also know that my birthday is today. I am thirty-three years old today, am I not?"

"Yes to everything," said Christina, pleased at his progress. She kissed him lightly on the cheek. "Happy birthday, Tony."

He thanked her. After she left, he thought about her and how helpful she had been the past two years. She was his father's right arm also.

Tony walked down the hallway, whistling. He met Jon in the front, waiting for him. Jon was a physical trainer, one of the best in Switzerland. He greeted him and they went together to the gym room. The gym room, built for Tony, had tall windows surrounding it, allowing plenty of sunshine into the room and breathtaking views of the mountains. Exercise equipment placed all around the room had aided him in his rehabilitation. He sat on the padded bench, listening to the trainer's suggestions, then began his exercises. After several sessions, Tony arose, feeling a little sore, yet content.

He took a towel from the rack. "I wanted to tell you that this will be my last session." He wiped the sweat from his face with the towel.

"It was my pleasure," said Jon, smiling, as he put away the equipment.

"I also want to thank you for all your help this past year. Now I can do just about anything...is that right?"

"You are not only officially healthy, but I think ready for the Olympics, as far as I'm concerned. You've worked hard, and we have seen great improvements."

"Thanks to you," said Tony, rubbing his biceps.

"What do you plan to do after this?"

"I plan to go back to Greece. Maybe go into business for myself."

"Good. Meanwhile, continue to do your exercises on your own," said Jon. "And don't forget to stretch before and after the exercises."

After Jon left, Tony took a shower, then dressed into something casual. A year ago, he couldn't do these activities without the aid of a nurse. This affected his sense of dignity, and his pride stepped in. Instead of the twenty exercises he had to do, he would force himself to do thirty, then forty. Pushing himself to the point of pain, he kept telling himself that the daily exercises and routines were his tickets to freedom.

It had been a laborious process, relearning everything, but he was motivated and very determined to improve. He had impressed his doctors and nurses with his phenomenal improvement this past year.

He started whistling as he combed his hair. There was still some soreness in his movements, but he learned to tune it out.

In the afternoon, he found his father sitting outside in his wheelchair with a blanket over his knees. The chalet was nestled high on a mountain, and the view was spectacular from here.

"Ah, here you are," said Gregory, looking up from his reading.

"I need to speak with you," said Tony, joining his father.

"Yes?"

"Today was the last session with Jon, the therapist. I've more than accomplished all my goals."

"That's good," said Gregory, lifting his eyebrows. "Then you will come to Crete with us next week?"

"I am telling you this, because I don't want to go back to Crete with you."

"What?"

"Father, you must listen. I appreciate all you've done for me ever since my accident," said Tony. "I have had many hours to sit and contemplate things, about life, about where I am going. I feel like I've been a burden to you and Christina. I need to go on with my life, as you need to go on with yours."

"Are you planning to join Chuck in the business?"

"Chuck is doing very well with the shipping company. Now that he has the computer system up and working, it is helping him out. I don't really want to go in and upset that," said Tony.

"So you will be going back to your teaching?" asked Gregory, resigning himself to his son's wishes.

"At first, I toyed with the idea of going back to teaching, but it seems too arduous at the moment. I want to remain in Greece, invest my money, the money I earned from teaching to buy property."

"Property?" asked Gregory, bewildered.

"Yes, buy a few villas or a few commercial buildings, fix them up and sell them or even lease them out."

Gregory looked keenly at his son as he expounded his idea. They discussed the pros and cons. It appeared as if Tony knew what he was talking about.

"You can do all that in Crete."

"I know, but you see, Father, you want me by your side all the time. I can't do that any more," said Tony more firmly. "I want to be my own man. It's impossible to accomplish that as long as I have you making decisions for me."

❦   ❦   ❦

A week later, Tony left Switzerland for the first time on his own. He traveled to Greece and visited his sister in her home in Kifissia. That morning, he found Melissa busy feeding her baby and Chuck gone away on a business trip.

He spent some time with Melissa, discussing things.

"You want to buy villas and properties, and rent them out?" she asked, looking incredulous. This was not at all like Tony to go into business for himself. "What about working with Chuck, or teaching at the university?"

He nodded, munching on a crisp *koulouraki*. "I've had a lot of time to think this past year, during all those days when I sat in bed. I realized that all my life, I had depended on Father to help me, and even more so these past few years. Now, I decided that I want to remain in Greece, yet not depend on Father anymore, or anyone else, for that matter. I want to be my own boss."

"Is it so bad that Father wants to help you?" she asked. "He'd do anything to see you get ahead."

"No, but by being dependent on Father, one loses one's freedom, and then Father gets to pull all the strings, little sister," he said sadly. "Father won't always be here, and I've got to prove to myself that I can stand on my own two feet."

"Do you have the money for what you want to do?"

"Yes. I checked at my bank and found that I had a considerable amount of money. Both from my earnings at the university and in some investments I had dabbled in," he said. "I have enough to get started, and plenty more in case it is needed."

"Where do you plan to live?"

"I haven't thought about it."

"You can live with us," began Melissa, wiping the baby's face with a napkin.

"Thank you," he said, pecking her playfully on the cheek. He enjoyed watching Melissa play with little Gregory. He joined them, laughing at their antics.

That evening, when Chuck came home from work, he spent time with Tony, discussing many different topics. Tony found out that Chuck also had property, and that he had considerable knowledge of that topic.

"That is how I was able to get started in the shipping industry," said Chuck. "Real estate."

The next few days, however, the house did not provide Tony any peace. The baby cried often, causing all kinds of commotion. Also, Melissa's next door neighbor, Marina, and some other friends kept popping in for coffee. Soon they were bringing their daughters with them. He quickly found out they were trying to marry their daughters off and that they considered him quite eligible. He listened with amused ear as Melissa talked about the eligible girls over dinner one night.

"The only one who is interesting enough to spend time with is Sara," he said, after she finished. "And I'm afraid I can't see her beyond just being a friend."

"It's amazing, but that side of you hasn't changed!" laughed Melissa. "You were always one for having many female friends and never settling for one to marry! It's not a bad idea for you to get married! Look at me! Chuck, don't you tell me you look forward to seeing me and the baby after a day's work?" She turned towards Chuck expectantly.

Chuck nodded, "Yes, and if I don't, I'll hear about it!"

Everyone laughed.

"I do plan to marry one day," Tony said thoughtfully.

*   *   *

Tony toyed with the idea of driving a car, but a fear inside his chest would come out of nowhere every time Tim drove and a car honked at them. Slowly, the fearful feeling faded away, and one day, drumming up enough courage, he asked Tim if he could take the wheel. At first, he felt overwhelmed by the nervous, aggressive drivers who impatiently honked at him. He persisted though, and practiced his driving faithfully, with Tim sitting in the passenger seat. In a short time, he mastered the technique and felt confident driving in the streets alone. The next thing to do was to buy a new car.

His new car gave him even more freedom to move around. He was beginning to feel more in control of his life, driving around to several real estates properties, developing his business plan.

He also noticed that Sara was dropping by the house more often lately. She was attractive and charming, bringing him many a smile, brightening up his days. There was something about her that reminded him of his past. Maybe it was her smile or impish look. Whatever it was, she was filling a void in his life. He had not been with a woman for a long time.

Yet, just as he was beginning to feel comfortable with her, he noticed she had two sides to her, the charming happy side and the moody quiet side, as if she was hiding something. Her moods began when she started hinting about marriage. He told her he needed time to establish himself first in his business before he could commit himself seriously to marriage.

As the weeks passed, Tony felt he could no longer live in his sister's house. The baby's noise, the interfering mothers and daughters, left him no peace. He began in earnest looking for a new home, trying to find the idea of marriage and family more attractive. Even if he had no wife, at least if he had a home, maybe a wife could come later.

He finally decided to build his own house. He purchased a piece of property on the outskirts of Glyfada. The land was on a hill, overlooking the sea. He hired a construction company, and worked out some floor plans with them. Month by month, he watched, as the villa slowly took shape.

In early August, Melissa received word from her father that he was returning to Athens. He wasn't feeling well.

"Father, Christina, it's so nice to see you again!" exclaimed Melissa, greeting them at the airport with her son.

"How's my little Gregory doing?" asked Gregory, planting a kiss on the toddler's rosy cheek. He was rewarded with a bright smile.

They drove home talking about everything.

"How have you been, Father?"

"Not well," he admitted. "I feel like I'm deteriorating. My right hand is shaking all the time. I can't write, or hold a spoon anymore. Anyway, I want you to make an appointment for me in Chicago so I can go and get tested."

"All right, Father."

"How's Tony?" asked Gregory.

"He's doing very well with his business. He's building a house for himself in Glyfada."

"That sounds promising," said Gregory, nodding. "Is there a bride in the picture?"

"You remember my mentioning to you about Sara, the banker's daughter? She lives next door. Tony's been dawdling with her, just like he did Bonnie. She's been talking about marriage, but he's been slow in going to the altar. I don't know what his plans are with her."

"He's like me," said Gregory thoughtfully. "I was stubborn like him when it came to marrying, but when the right girl came along, there was no holding me back."

As soon as they arrived home, Gregory arranged to take a trip to the hospital in Chicago, where he was tested. Although his tests came out normal, upon his return to Athens two weeks later, he consulted with his lawyers. The result was the writing up of a will. The attorneys also suggested putting some of that money towards a foundation. He balked at the idea at first, then he decided he would talk with his son first. Gregory called Melissa's house and spoke with Tony. They arranged for Tony to go over that evening to see him.

"What is it you wanted to talk about?" asked Tony, sitting in the living room across from his father. His father seemed tired and his one hand was shaking uncontrollably.

"I feel like I'm losing my strength, son. Day by day it's a struggle for me to get things done," he began heavily. "I don't know how long I will last. I want to see my grandchildren before I die."

"You will, Father," said Tony cautiously. Whenever his father brought up the discussion of death, it was always to make one feel guilty, and then to ask for something.

"Now that you're building that house, don't you think it would be a good idea to marry?" asked Gregory. "You know, what about that Sara? The one whose father owns several banks."

"I've been thinking about it," said Tony slowly, wondering how much he should share with his father. "But I'm not sure yet."

"At least you're thinking in the right direction," said Gregory. "I've been wanting to talk to you about something else."

"Yes?"

"What would you think if we started a foundation?" asked Gregory, looking at his son. His son had changed so much. He was more independent, confident, more respectable now. He admired his determination to become his own master.

"It sounds interesting to me. What made you decide on it in the first place?"

"Actually, it was not my idea," said Gregory, chuckling. "My attorneys thought of it. They said it would be a good way to use some of my profits towards a good cause."

"You mean get a tax break?" laughed Tony.

They both laughed.

"All joking aside. I truly am for it," said Tony.

"I knew you would, with your philanthropic nature," said Gregory. "You were always one for helping others."

They discussed the foundation further, deciding on its mission and where they would allocate the resources. Tony contacted the attorneys later that day and started the legal process.

After Tony left, Gregory was sitting alone with Christina, contemplating on what had just transpired.

"He's a good son," he admitted. "After his accident, I realized how much he meant to me. I couldn't bear to lose him. Now he's running his own business. I knew he had it in him."

Christina took a sip from her coffee, smiling.

"Isn't that something," he said, looking out into the distance.

"What, dear?"

"You work all your life making all this money, and in the end, you can't take it with you."

❧   ❧   ❧

CHAPTER 36

December 1992–March 1993
A memory, so sweet and fair
A mystery unfolds, do I dare?

The foundation was named Kalkinon Foundation, and its goal was to fund cancer research and help cancer patients who were unable to pay for their cancer treatment. By the end of the year, the foundation was finally formalized. Upon the guidance of the attorneys, Tony became its president officially on December 10. His sister became the treasurer. A storage room in their office building was emptied so that the foundation now had a physical location. They then hired a secretary and bookkeeper to help its operations. Once all of this was done, he telephoned his father in Crete.

"Father, I have good news," said Tony. "The Kalkinon Foundation is up and running and I am now the president."

"Good. The first place I want to make a donation is to the hospital in Chicago, where I had my surgery."

It wasn't long before Tony was receiving thank you letters from the hospital for their contributions. The foundation also began receiving newsletters from the hospital, informing them of the hospital's projects. In addition, monies were periodically sent to the hospital whenever a cancer patient required financial assistance.

One day in February, Tony read about the hospital's plans to build a new cancer center. The hospital was desperately seeking funding for the center. He called his father and spoke with him. His father agreed at first, yet balked when he heard Tony's proposed amount.

"What do you think, ten million dollars grows on trees?" growled Gregory.

"Don't worry," laughed Tony. "I've been doing very well with my business, and am offering to pay half of that, if you pitch in the other half. I know this is a drop in the bucket for you."

"A very large drop at that! Let me think about it," said Gregory before hanging up the telephone.

It took his father a couple of weeks before he agreed to do it. The contribution was dutifully sent out after that to the hospital.

❦   ❦   ❦

By the end of March, Tony's house was finished. It was a spacious villa that sat high on a hill. It had cool marble floors, Grecian columns, a fireplace in almost every room, a large swimming pool, and a verandah with a view of the sea. The morning he paid the construction workers their final payment, he felt a feeling of relief. He finally accomplished what he set out to do.

After the workers left, he walked inside the empty rooms, his footsteps echoing loudly against the marble floors. The large rooms, high ceilings and open floor plan gave him a sense of open space. Sunlight filtered into the rooms, giving it a warm, pleasant feeling. It was beginning to feel like a home.

Afterwards, he sat outside, looking out at the sea, listening to the sound of the waves lapping rhythmically against the rocks. He started to feel melancholy, as if something was missing. Maybe it was because the house needed to be furnished. Melissa could help with that part. She was good with those things. He went inside and telephoned his sister.

"Hello, Melissa?"

"Good morning, Mr. Tony."

"Oh, good morning, Suzie," he said, recognizing the housekeeper's voice. "Is Melissa there?"

"No, she's over at her mother-in-law's with little Gregory, sir, but she'll be here a little later."

Tony thanked her, then left, heading for his father's house. He had to shake off this feeling of melancholy. One way to do that was to gather his belongings together and start preparing for the move to the new house.

He walked into the empty house. It had been deserted ever since Melissa moved to her home on the other side of Kifissia. His father spent most of his time now in Crete. Gilda only came when his father was visiting, and Tim was Melissa's chauffeur now.

He went into his bedroom and started rummaging through his closet. There were custom tailored business suits, designer shirts, and expensive silk ties. He piled them all on the bed. They seemed foreign to him, as if another Tony had worn them once.

The closet was now empty, except for a bag stashed in the back. Curious, he removed its contents. The shirt was tattered and had dark stains on it. They looked like dried bloodstains. *They must have been worn on the day of the accident.* The shirt was beyond repair. He stood there, trying to recall the accident, but he couldn't remember anything. He tossed it aside. He was about to toss the pants aside also, when he noticed something bulging from inside one of the pant pockets. It was a small jewelry box. Inside was a gold ring with a large beautiful green gemstone.

"Whew!" he exclaimed, gazing admirably at the jeweled ring. His heart started racing. Who was this ring for? Why was it in his pocket the day of the accident? He shook his head, touching his forehead, feeling a headache coming on. His family had not mentioned anything about an engagement, nor did any female come forth.

He still couldn't remember the details leading up to the accident. Questions that he had been unable to answer were now coming back to haunt him. Why was he going up the mountain that day, right before the trip to Crete, and why hadn't his family known about it? Prompted by the mystery of the ring and his curiosity, he went through the drawers, taking everything out, mindful of any clue that could help him solve this puzzle. His movements were like that of a thirsty man searching for that single glass of water that would satisfy his thirst. At one point, a piece of paper fluttered out of some clothes. He stooped to pick it up.

He stood still as he read the note. The person who wrote it had lovely delicate handwriting, thanking him for everything he had done. It was signed by Ipatia. That was an unusual and pretty name. Who was she? Why did she say that she had to leave? Why didn't her name strike a memory chord in his mind? He didn't remember any Ipatia. He folded the paper and placed it in his pocket. This will have to wait. His headache had gotten worse.

The bookshelves were next. All kinds of books, ranging from economics to art to philosophy were there. He wondered if he had read them all. Once he was settled, he was going to go through them and read them. He diligently stacked them together, then carried them to the trunk of the car.

He worked steadily, filling the car slowly with books and clothes. When he was finished, the bedroom appeared like an empty seashell deserted by its occupant, a hollow reminder of another time. It held no memories for him.

Something spurred him to look underneath the bed. He found a pile of letters from old friends, held together by a rubber band. He didn't recognize anyone's name. He will have to go through them another time. They will help him juggle his memory.

It was already mid-day when he drove back to Glyfada.

❦   ❦   ❦

Tony returned to his sister's later in the evening to find Melissa and Chuck having dinner.

"You came just in time," said Chuck, wiping his mouth. "We got hungry, so I hope you don't mind that we started before you."

"No problem," said Tony. "I admit I'm a little hungry myself." He sat down and joined them.

"How's your villa coming along?" asked Chuck.

Tony talked about his villa, and Melissa cheerfully piped in, advising him on what type of furniture he should buy.

Then he talked about his discovery when moving his belongings from their parent's house to the villa. "Tell me, Melissa, do you know of a person by the name of Ipatia?"

"Ipatia?" she asked, staring at him, surprised by his question. She had hoped he would have forgotten about her. Father had specifically asked her not to mention the girl's name.

"I found a note written to me by an Ipatia," he said, becoming slightly agitated. His little sister wasn't making it easy.

"Oh, yes! She was just an island girl you met in Lipsi Island the one summer we got stuck in a storm and had to stay there."

"There's one other thing your sister didn't mention," said Chuck wryly. "Ipatia knew English, and you had her working at the office, translating your documents for you into Greek."

"Is that right?" Tony asked ruefully, shaking his head. "I don't remember her."

Melissa smiled sweetly at him. "There probably wasn't much to remember." She wasn't about to offer any more information.

Tony suddenly realized now why he hadn't been told about Ipatia. He became cautious. He decided not to mention the engagement ring. His intuition told him they wouldn't know about it. Instead, he changed the topic. "Did Sara come by today?"

"She did stop by and was asking about you," said Melissa lightly. "Sara is a good catch. She's not only pretty but she's rolling in money. Her father owns several banks!"

"Melissa, I don't think you should interfere in Tony's personal life," interrupted Chuck, somewhat jokingly.

"That's all right, Chuck," said Tony, laughing. "Melissa probably thinks that money will buy me happiness. For your information, I need to find out more about what happened to Ipatia before I continue any relationship with Sara."

That evening, Tony sat in his room, thinking. He thought about the note written by Ipatia and the gemstone ring. He racked his memory, trying to come up with answers, but to no avail. *What happened to Ipatia? If she was so important in my life, why haven't I seen her? Why did I keep the relationship secret from my family? Why did she leave? Why hasn't she tried to contact me or find out what happened to me?*

He thought about Sara, and how Melissa had subtly pushed this relationship upon him. It dawned on him that Sara's wealth was probably the reason why Melissa had her as a friend. During these last months, as the relationship blossomed, and construction of the villa was becoming finalized, Sara had hinted that there was more to their relationship than just friendship. He had entertained the idea of sharing the rest of his life with Sara.

But how could he promise her or anyone else anything if he had bought the engagement ring for someone else? Apparently, his heart had not revealed itself yet. He needed to find answers.

The next day, Sara visited Melissa. She had brought with her a nail manicure set and was filing her nails while talking with Melissa.

"I'll do your nails after I finish mine," she promised.

They began talking about Tony.

"I need to tell you something about Tony," said Melissa. "It's important."

"Yes?"

"You know that he had amnesia once. Well, there's an old flame in his life, Ipatia Kouris, whose name he recently came across. I don't know how much he remembers, but it seems he's interested in finding out about her," said Melissa. "I just don't want to see you hurt."

"Ipatia Kouris?" asked Sara. "Somehow that name sounds familiar. Was it serious?"

"I can't say, but apparently he's interested enough in finding out more about her. Her father, Captain Manolis Kouris, used to work for my father," said Melissa importantly.

That evening, Sara mentioned the name to her father, asking him if he could check up on it, maybe see if any accounts were with any of his banks.

❦   ❦   ❦

A few weeks later, Tony walked into Michael's office, wondering if it was the right thing to do. He got his answer quickly.

"Tony!" exclaimed Michael, greeting him wholeheartedly. "How long has it been? Three years?"

"I'm sorry I didn't visit you sooner, Michael, but I was too busy rebuilding my life," admitted Tony, studying this person who supposedly had been a very good friend of his. He seemed friendly enough.

Michael began to reminisce about the past, but Tony stopped him.

"It's no use talking to me about the past," said Tony apologetically. "You see, I had amnesia as a result of the accident. I have no memory of what happened before the accident, of you or any one else. I came across your name accidentally the other day, when I was going through a pile of old letters."

"I didn't know that, my friend," said Michael, sobered by the news.

"When I asked my sister, she told me where I could find you. She didn't seem happy when I asked her."

"It's understandable. Your sister and I were once engaged to be married. But that's in the past now. I married a year ago."

"Congratulations!"

"You had an excuse because of the amnesia, but now it's my turn to apologize for not coming to see you."

"Why do you say that?"

"After I found out that Ipatia was in love with you, I decided not to come between you two, so I simply kept away. You see, I had been interested in her for myself."

"Ipatia?" asked Tony, shocked. He sat there, looking stunned. "Ipatia, the island girl?"

"Nobody told you about her?" said Michael, looking surprised. "I guess the amnesia was severe."

"Michael, tell me about her. How did I meet her? What did she look like?" asked Tony eagerly. His emotions were mixed. He was excited to hear about her, but perplexed why she had become such an enigma.

"Let me remember. She was tall, with long, golden brown hair, and large, green eyes. She was quite beautiful, although tending to lean towards the thin side. She came from the island of Lipsi, where we met her. She moved here and lived with her aunt right around the corner from here, but last I heard, she had moved to the other side of town with her cousins."

Tony thought for a moment, shutting his eyes. "If only I had known sooner."

"I suppose no one in your family told you," said Michael dryly. "Are you seeing anyone?"

"Yes," said Tony, nodding his head heavily. "She lives next door to my sister's house and she's been pressuring me for marriage...but something has held me back."

"Ah, I see now," said Michael. "Maybe you aren't in love with her."

"Michael, I was in love with Ipatia, wasn't I? I can just feel it," said Tony, looking helpless. "The problem is, I don't know what happened to her. She just vanished."

Michael nodded thoughtfully, saddened by his friend's fate. "I distinctly recall that she talked constantly about going to the university," he said. "She had been reading medical journals of mine, showing interest in the medical field. I gather, if anything, that she may be at some university, studying towards her degree."

"Oh, I seem to remember now!" said Tony, juggling his memory. The girl had been more intent on an education rather than marriage. He still felt fuzzy in his mind about her, but it was beginning to make sense to him. Her going to school could be the missing piece to the puzzle.

Just at that moment, a young, attractive woman came in to the office. Michael hugged her, then introduced her. "Tony, I'd like you to meet my wife, Betsy."

The conversation shifted to the newlyweds.

A few hours later as he made his farewell, Tony invited them to visit him at his villa the following Sunday.

That evening, Tony rested on his off-white couch in his villa, thinking about the conversation with Michael. Soft, classical music from the stereo system drifted through the house, competing with the sound of the waves outside, as he searched in his mind, going over all the events, trying to piece the puzzle together. The notes that spilled into the room caressed his mind, stroking it, kneading it, coaxing it to come forth with the answers. He stopped thinking for a moment, enraptured by the music. There was something familiar about this composition that reminded him of something. After it finished, the radio announcer said that it was a piano composition by Beethoven, called Fur Elise.

Tony felt as if something just struck him. He stood up and began pacing the room excitedly. Images started flowing through his mind, of Ipatia with her long hair dancing in the wind, running away from him; images of a beautiful girl who wrote poetry and for whom he played Fur Elise on the piano at his father's house. Other images soon followed, surrounded by more intense feelings. Then he paused, staring out as if in a trance, remembering her gift and how he had made it into a ring. Suddenly he felt a surge of happiness, and he knew why. The ring had been meant for her, a promise, and a seal of love.

He continued pacing, troubled by disturbing questions that still needed to be answered.

❦   ❦   ❦

The next day, Tony drove to the same mountain where he had his accident. Maybe by coming here, he could remember what happened. It was late afternoon, when there was the least amount of traffic. He parked the car further down the road to the side, where it was safe.

Walking towards the edge of the road he stopped and gazed at the scene below him. The police told him that he had swerved his wheel to avoid headlong collision with the other car, and had careened down the slope and into the woods. His car had rammed into one of the trees in the woods, causing his injuries.

He made his way carefully down the steep slope, then looked around, hoping to remember something, anything. He found the tree that had the marks from the car on it, and even a few pieces of glass nearby, evident signs of the car accident. He then combed the area, searching for any clues of Ipatia, maybe a purse or a wallet. An hour later, he came up empty-handed. Just as he was leaving, he spied a flash of blue color among the bushes ahead, then it disappeared again. He moved closer to have a look.

It turned out to be a woman's silk scarf caught between the branches of the bush. His trembling fingers managed to untangle the tattered scarf from the bush, his heart racing with anticipation. Was it possible this was Ipatia's scarf? He touched it reverently, stroking it, picturing her wearing it.

He clutched it tightly as a searing fear pressed in his chest, a fear that Ipatia may have been in the car with him and may not have survived the accident. He must find out! He placed it in his pocket and continued his search with renewed vigor, but didn't find anything else.

CHAPTER 37

March 1993–June 1993
My love for you, a door that closed
The truth unlocks the door once more

Tony decided to pay a visit to the shipping office. Someone there should know what happened to the girl. He remembered where the office was. Tim used to point it out to him whenever they'd pass by. He never had returned since the accident, feeling awkward not remembering anyone and having to explain everything. But this time it was different. He was determined to find out what happened to the girl.

Rita greeted him warmly, chattering away as if they were the best of friends.

"I know this may be awkward for you," he said interrupting her midstream, "but I had amnesia from the car accident, and I don't remember you at all…or any of the people you are talking about."

Rita nodded understandably, as tears moistened her eyes. She had spoken a number of times with Melissa, who had complained about her brother's amnesia.

Tony listened while she explained to him what her role was in the agency, and how he used to bring back gifts from his trips for all the staff. He thanked her, then admitted the real reason he came there was to find out about Ipatia.

"The last time I saw her was the day after Easter Sunday, about the time of your accident," said Rita, shaking her head apologetically.

Tony said excitedly, "Are you sure?"

"Yes," said Rita emphatically. "She came to the office, and I remember we talked about Easter. She mentioned she spent it quietly with her cousins. I assumed she had come back to work that day, and I told her you had gone to Crete, so there was no more work for her. I told her to return in a few weeks when everyone was back from Crete. She thanked me and left, and didn't return after that."

"Didn't you know about my accident?" he asked incredulously.

"No, I'm afraid not," sighed Rita. "I learned about it afterwards. Mr. Gregory didn't want us to know right away."

"One more thing. How did she look?" he asked. He had a gut feeling that he was about to find the truth.

"What do you mean?"

"Was she limping or did she look sick in any way, maybe a bruise here or there?" he asked.

"Let me think," said Rita, looking thoughtful. "You know, now that you ask me, at one point, I remember thinking that she was going to faint on me. She looked as if she were in pain, and it seemed like one side of her face, around the eye, was a little swollen."

He was stunned by the revelation. He stood there, shocked. It was beginning to make sense now. He was beginning to see the true picture.

"I'm sorry if I said anything wrong," said Rita, becoming anxious at his far away look.

"No, actually, you just helped me tremendously," said Tony, bending over and planting a solid kiss on her cheek.

"Are you coming back to work here?" she ventured to ask. "Everyone here's been asking about you."

"Thank you for your interest, Rita," he said. "But Chuck is in command now. I've got my own business now."

He whistled as he went down the stairs. Ipatia was alive! It was beginning to make sense why she hadn't come to see him. If she hadn't known about the accident, she would have returned to work when she was supposed to. But since she had been in the accident, and once she heard he was in Crete, she had been upset enough to leave and not return.

"I tell you, it's true, Father!" stated Melissa, pacing the kitchen, talking on the telephone. "Captain Kouris had accumulated quite a bit of money. He had a dowry in the way of a trust, now worth over thirty thousand American dollars in Ipatia's name, to be withdrawn only in the case of marriage! Sara's father told me himself!"

"Why is money so important to you?"

"Father!"

"Now you listen here, Melissa! Tony knows what he's doing, and it's about time you stopped meddling into his affairs. If he's in love with the girl, whether she has one dollar or thirty thousand dollars, it won't make a difference to him. I married your mother because I loved her, not because of her money, and if I hadn't married her, you wouldn't even be here today! Never forget that!"

❁   ❁   ❁

The following Sunday marked the beginning of April. Tony had been awaiting his dinner guests, having prepared for the occasion by hiring a cook, when there was a ringing at the door.

"Michael, Betsy!" said Tony, greeting his friends.

They sat down to a pleasant dinner. After the meal, the couple shared their happy news.

"Congratulations! When are you expecting?" asked Tony.

"Sometime in November," said Betsy, smiling.

"We just learned this morning, so you're the first to know, old friend," said Michael. "We'd like you to be the baby's godfather."

"Thank you for the honor," said Tony, beaming. "I'd be more than happy to do it."

The conversation continued for awhile, then Betsy said, "If you'll excuse me, I'd like to rest a little. I get these spells lately."

"It's quite all right," said Michael, seeing his friend's puzzled look. "It's a phase of her pregnancy she's going through."

Tony showed her to the living room, where she thankfully lay on the couch. After he returned to the dining room, he conversed with Michael, putting the pieces of his past together. He then took the opportunity to learn more about Ipatia. He began by asking, "Have you heard anything about Ipatia recently?"

"Now that you reminded me of it, there is some news. George and Paula Mastroyiannis paid me a visit recently," said Michael.

"Who are they?"

"I guess you don't remember them. They are Ipatia's cousins, and had been prior patients of mine. Typically before trips, they would come and get prescriptions filled by me. This time they were on their way to Spain, and came to see me for a prescription."

"Did they say anything about Ipatia, where she lives?" asked Tony, surprised to hear the news.

"Yes, as a matter of fact, they did mention that she now lives in America, in a suburb of Chicago, with her aunt and uncle, John and Sophia Stavrakis."

"Chicago?" asked Tony incredulously. "Did they mention an address, a telephone number?"

"I'm afraid not. I wasn't thinking along those lines, now that I'm a married man," said Michael apologetically. "They did say that she will be graduating soon from a university in Chicago, with a degree in microbiology."

"Ah yes, the infamous degree that she chose over marriage," sighed Tony.

"One more thing that might be helpful."

"Yes?"

"Mrs. Rodos, the English teacher might know more about Ipatia. She lives right down the block from my office."

A few days later, Tony received a letter from the hospital in Chicago. He read it aloud, "We are very grateful for the ten million dollar donation, and invite you to a banquet to be held in honor of the Kalkinon Foundation, on June 26, 1993. Dignitaries will be present."

This was just the thing he needed. He had spoken to Mrs. Rodos and had found out where Ipatia lived. It was a simple matter of finding her house and knocking on the door. Or was it that simple? How would she react after all these years? Would he recognize her if he saw her?

It was a memorable day in June when Ipatia walked up on stage, dressed in her black robe and hat, to receive her bachelor's degree in microbiology. Her aunt and uncle, along with Alexander, proudly attended the graduation ceremony. The speaker was a judge who had graduated from the university years ago. His speech was inspiring, and it left Ipatia with good feelings.

She was exhilarated the rest of the day, enjoying the attention she received from her relatives. Aunt Sophia held a small graduation party for her, and Ipatia graciously played her part as the hostess. She helped serve drinks and talked to people, answering their questions, and joking with them. Her cousins were there to congratulate her, as well as her friends from church and some friends of the family. Her uncle even invited a couple of young men from his real estate business.

After all the guests had gone, and she finished helping clean up, she excused herself, feeling exhausted. Yet that evening when she retired to her room she could not fall asleep. She lay in bed thinking about her life, and her recent accomplishment. She admitted that she had focused all her energies these past four years on getting her degree and had thought of nothing else.

She remembered the questions that people asked her today. Where was she going from here? Was she going to continue her education and get a graduate degree, or apply for a job instead? She admitted that she had faltered in answering them. She wasn't sure what she was going to do next. She tried to think about the future, but didn't feel happy when she imagined herself doing any of those things. *Why not? Why are you feeling this sad yearning all of a sudden? Did you want Tony to be there, to witness your moment of happiness, like everyone else? Did you want him gazing at you lovingly, the way your aunt and uncle gazed into each other's eyes?* She buried her face into the pillow, sobbing.

After a few moments, she wiped her tears. *This couldn't be happening. I achieved what I wanted, and yet I'm not happy.* The people that she saw on a daily basis, her aunt and uncle, her cousins, and now Nick and his wife, all seemed happy with their life, and they were all married!

Oddly enough, no one asked her if she had plans on getting married. How could they, if all these years she had shunned even the mention of marriage?

❦   ❦   ❦

Sunday morning was filled with church services, followed by the social hour in the church hall. It wasn't until one-thirty when they returned home. After lunch, Aunt Sophia sat in the living room, finishing a dress she was sewing, while Uncle John read the Sunday newspaper. Ipatia sat down on the floor playing with Alex, helping him set up his new toy train set that his father had bought recently. After awhile, two of Alex's friends were knocking on the door, and he went outside to play with them. Ipatia stayed awhile longer, chatting with her aunt, then excused herself and went up to her room.

The recent letter of her grandfather came to her mind and she wanted to write back. She had already bought tickets for the trip to Greece. She reread the letter. He looked forward to her visit this summer, and if she hadn't found a young man yet, he had a few picked out for her. She knew it wasn't Tom Tsatsikas, because he was already engaged.

She smiled at her grandfather's matchmaking efforts, then paused, realizing how insightful his remarks were. Did her wise old grandfather know more about her than she did herself? To marry now, after having accomplished her goals, was not so terrible anymore. Yet the nagging thought hidden all these years in the back of her mind came back with full force to haunt her. How could she ever love so deeply any another man as she had loved Tony?

Ipatia's writing was interrupted by the sound of children's laughter outside. She removed her reading glasses, gazing out the window. Beyond the green leaves of the maple tree, she saw three children playing in her cousin's back yard. They were laughing and shouting with youthful abandon on this Sunday afternoon.

The loudest of the children was Alex, and the other two were his friends. He looked tall for his four years. She smiled as she was reminded of her carefree years back in Greece.

She put her glasses back on and finished writing the letter to grandfather. There, it was done. She let him know what day she was planning to arrive on the island. She sealed it and placed a stamp on it. The sunlight streamed in from the half-opened window, bathing her in its afternoon glow. She arose, stretching luxuriously. It felt good not having to study for any more exams.

She yawned, then caught her image in the full-length mirror, and smiled. She had gained enough weight so that a bust and hips were evident. With her slim waist and long legs, her voluptuous body was always attracting attention, particularly from the opposite sex.

She picked up the comb and began combing her hair slowly, looking at herself in the mirror. Although her hair was once golden from the sun, it now had turned into a rich golden brown. When she finished, it fell gracefully below her shoulders. She looked at her face, noticing her jaw for the first time. It seemed a little fuller. Humming a tune, she walked out of her bedroom, skipping down the stairs into the living room. There, she found her aunt sitting on the couch, reading the Sunday newspaper. Her uncle had gone to an open house.

"Ipatia, my dear, can you read this?" asked Aunt Sophia, handing over the newspaper. "My English isn't as good as yours."

"There's going to be a banquet in three weeks, hosted by the University Hospital. It appears some foundation has given ten million dollars for a new cancer center that's going to be built there. The banquet is in their honor," said Ipatia, skimming the article. She handed the newspaper back to her aunt.

"Is that right?" asked Aunt Sophia absentmindedly. "Didn't Stasoula say something about a banquet you needed to play in around that time?"

"Yes, I believe so," said Ipatia. "With all my classes, I had forgotten all about it."

"When is your trip to Greece?" asked Aunt Sophia.

"June 27. It's the day after the banquet," said Ipatia.

"Do you think you can still play?"

"Why not? I only play for a couple of hours, then the rest of the evening I'm free," said Ipatia, shrugging her shoulders. "I'll be packed by then anyway."

"Why don't you ask Stasoula tonight when we go over for dinner, just to make sure. It'll be a good way to meet people," said Aunt Sophia hopefully.

Ipatia smiled. Her aunt was always trying to get her to meet eligible young men. "I'll ask her."

"By the way, do you have to wear those glasses when you play?" asked Aunt Sophia. "For some reason, they make you look different, much older than your age."

"I know, I know. You've told me several times, dear Aunt," said Ipatia, twirling around and making comical faces with her glasses on. "Just be happy that I don't have a mustache and a big nose!"

They both laughed.

Later that evening, over dinner, Ipatia asked Stasoula about the banquet.

"Oh, yes, my darling, we are catering for that event, so of course we will need you to play," said Stasoula breathlessly, her short, plump body moving with her words. "Would you be able to make it?"

"Sure, why not?" said Ipatia brightly. "What kind of music did they request?"

"They would like some dinner music. Why don't you play the same music from the last banquet?"

❧   ❧   ❧

"Seats one through twenty are now boarding."

"Here, let me take him," said Melissa. "You must not be late for your flight."

"Bye, sweet one," said Tony, planting a kiss on his nephew's chubby cheek before handing him over to his sister.

"Bye-bye," said little Gregory, giving his uncle a wet kiss.

"Tony, there is something I've been wanting to tell you. I.., I feel like such a heel for not mentioning Ipatia to you sooner," began Melissa, stammering slightly. "I'm sorry. I hope you'll forgive me."

"Don't worry, sis," he smiled, patting her on the back. "You helped me in your own way."

"What do you mean?"

"You didn't push Ipatia on me like you did your other girlfriends," he smiled. "Maybe that was all I needed."

"Tony!"

"Good-bye, sis," he said, hugging her. "You know that I love you."

"I love you too," choked Melissa, her eyes moistening. She brushed away a tear. "We'll see you in Crete in a few days?"

He nodded, waving to her as he left through the door.

CHAPTER 38

The banquet was a huge success
I played piano in my black dress

Sunday morning, the day of the banquet, Ipatia was at her cousins' house by ten o'clock. The family packaged all the foods and equipment in the back of the van, then everyone got sandwiched in and drove off to the banquet facilities. There was much laughter and singing, as there always was with the family.

When they arrived, Ipatia helped unload the van, then followed Stasoula into the large dining hall, where she helped prepare the tables. Stasoula oversaw the table setting. Five other female servers arrived shortly after. The glasses had to be just right, and the plates and silverware positioned a certain way. Ipatia made sure the glasses were spotless and the silverware didn't have stains on them. Fresh cut flowers were placed in vases filled with water, and these were placed on the long table that would seat the honorary guests. Bottles of wine were added to each table. Everything was now in order. Ipatia went to the piano and practiced some excerpts from the music. She was rewarded by smiles from the other workers.

The hospital committee started filtering in. One lady of the committee began handing out brochures. She handed one to Ipatia, who thanked her, then placed it in her purse. She didn't have time to browse. It was now one hour before the banquet, and there were still a number of last minute things that needed to be done.

Later, Ipatia went inside the kitchen, where her cousin Antonios and Chris were busy preparing the meal. She helped place the appetizers in large trays. There were meatballs, and broiled shrimp, stuffed grape-leaves, and small pastry shells filled with different kinds of cheese fillings. Ipatia was beginning to get hungry.

"Here, have some of this, Skinny," said Chris. He handed her a plate of appetizers.

"Thank you, Potato," she said, teasing him with his nickname. He was always looking out for her and teasing her about being too thin. She sat down in a corner to eat the food. She watched as Antonios took the stuffed chicken breast from the oven. He then started preparing the salmon, his big body swaying, as he squeezed the lemons with a flourish over the fish.

Chris was busy cutting the vegetables to be steamed. Next to him sat a huge salad bowl filled to the brim with cut lettuce and sliced tomatoes. The desert trays were to the side. There were bowls of chocolate mousse dotted with chocolate sprinkles, Ipatia's favorite desert, and in another tray, small plates of the rich baklava.

Stasoula came into the kitchen hurriedly with bags of fresh rolls.

"Ipatia, my love, as soon as you are done, get ready to play, because people are coming already," said Stasoula, appearing flustered. Then she told Antonios, "We are ready to serve the appetizers."

Ipatia put her plate aside, and picked up her black outfit that was hanging on the rack near the door. She went out into the hallway, checking first to see if anyone was coming. It was empty, so she quickly made her way to the restroom.

Tony entered the banquet room just then and was escorted to his table at the front of the room, by one of the ladies of the hospital committee. She chatted about being delighted that he was able to make it. He graciously thanked her, then sat down at his table. It contained all the dignitaries, the mayor, the president of the university hospital, and members of the hospital committee. After the introductions, he spoke with the mayor, who was interested in having contributions made to his political campaign. Then the president of the university hospital talked to him about funding. Tony invited them to visit him in Greece.

"It's a different experience," he said, describing Greece, his eyes shining. "Once you go there, you'll always want to go back."

❈   ❈   ❈

Ipatia quickly dressed into her long black skirt and blouse. The outfit reminded her of her days on the island, when she wore all black. She pulled her hair back, forming a small bun at the nape of her neck. She skillfully fastened it with bobby pins. A few strands came loose, curling oddly, and she wet them, trying to smooth them out.

She decided to wear the glasses tonight, not wanting to encourage any ardent beaus. Her ring was on her finger. Ipatia was ready. She went out into the ballroom, noticing that people were already arriving. In the middle of the room was a row of tables, filled to the brim with steaming appetizers. Two vases filled with fresh flowers sat in the middle of each table.

Ipatia walked slowly and regally to the piano, focusing on her task at hand. She had learned a long time ago not to look at the people in the audience, so she wouldn't lose her concentration. The piano was situated to her left, at the far corner of the room, away from the tables. When she sat down at the piano, she began to play softly, trying to pace herself with the sounds in the room. She appeared oblivious to the different people arriving with their tuxedos and long, sequined dresses, yet she was sensitive enough to the ebb and flow of the noise in the room to adjust her playing.

The clanking sound of glasses and silverware alerted Ipatia that dinner was being served. She expertly shifted to dinner music, mindful of the rising tide of voices. This usually happened around this time. Stasoula waved to her from the back of the room. It was time to finish. She began playing the last song, Fur Elise.

❧   ❧   ❧

Although Tony appeared to be listening to the committee chairman speaking, his mind was on the pianist. He had noticed her the moment she entered the room. There was something about her that was so familiar, he could not erase the notion that it might be Ipatia. Maybe it was her height, or maybe it was her playing. Whatever it was, she had caught his attention.

"What do you think about that, Dr. Plakis?" asked the chairman.

"What? Can you repeat that again?" asked Tony, forced back into the conversation.

Ipatia finished playing the last song. As her fingers rested on the keys, she sensed someone staring at her. She looked up and saw a tall, handsome man sitting with the dignitaries, gazing at her. He was wearing a black tuxedo with a white shirt that contrasted well with his dark handsome looks. As she studied him more, Ipatia's heart started to race. Whenever she saw someone that resembled Tony, it had to happen to her. She would tremble. The memory of Tony could never be erased from her thoughts.

Just then her cousin tapped her on the shoulder. "The speakers are getting ready to go on stage," whispered Stasoula.

Ipatia quietly followed her to the back of the ballroom.

She stood in the back of the ballroom, opening the kitchen door for the servers as they wheeled the carts laden with dirty dishes, back into the kitchen.

One by one, the speakers went on stage. They talked about the ten million dollar donation and how it would help in building the new cancer center. Then there was a slide presentation of a model of the building. They displayed a picture of the plot of land where the building was to be built, followed by diagrams of the facilities to be constructed. The images looked impressive. Then there was a speech by the president, on how the center would benefit cancer patients.

The last speaker was a young girl in a wheelchair. Her hair was all gone. She spoke about her illness. She was a leukemia patient undergoing chemotherapy. Ipatia's eyes filled with tears at the girl's plight. Ipatia clapped heartily with the rest of the people after the girl ended her speech.

Just then, Ipatia was nudged from behind, as the door of the kitchen opened behind her. She moved forward to avoid the door and inadvertently bumped into one of the carts. The sound of the dishes crashing to the floor was so loud, that people turned and stared with annoyed looks. Ipatia hurriedly helped pick up the broken pieces, placing them blindly on the cart. Stasoula came to her side, lifting her up, whispering to her to go to the restroom and clean up. Ipatia noticed her soiled skirt and disappeared to the restroom, ashamed.

Tony's thoughts were interrupted by the commotion in the back of the room. He glanced in that direction. It appeared that the piano player had bumped into some cart and had spilled everything on the floor. He felt like laughing aloud at the comic scene. Instead, he chuckled inside.

"At this time, I'd like to ask Dr. Antonios Plakis, President of the Kalkinon Foundation, to come forward and accept this award," said the chairman, looking at him, beaming.

Tony arose and walked on stage.

"We thank you very much for this generous donation," said the chairman, shaking his hand. There were several flashes of light, as someone took pictures. Then the chairman stepped back and the girl wheeled herself forward.

"This plaque is for the generous ten million dollar donation that the Kalkinon Foundation has given towards the cancer center," said the girl. She handed him the plaque.

Tony took the plaque, and kissed her lightly on the cheek. The girl's pale face glowed in return.

Then he turned slowly and faced the audience. "On behalf of the Kalkinon Foundation, I am deeply honored to accept this award," said Tony. "For those of you who don't know the story, my father, Gregory Plakis, was diagnosed with a brain tumor almost five years ago. The doctors in Europe were pessimistic about his future, giving him only a few months to live. We heard about Dr. Bernard, and came here to Chicago where my father had a successful operation at the university hospital. Thanks to Dr. Bernard, my father has been alive five years longer, and the way he's going, plans to outlive us all!"

There was laughter, followed by clapping. He stopped, waiting for the clapping to die down.

"But, more research is needed to fight this disease. The Kalkinon foundation was formed to help the medical establishment continue to research the causes and cures of cancer. In addition to this donation towards the cancer center, there will be others in the future. The foundation is also focused on helping towards costs of health care for individuals with cancer, who do not have health insurance."

He bowed, as the applause filled the hall. He walked slowly back to his table. The mayor rose to shake his hand, and so did the other people at the table. Suddenly everyone was standing up in the room, as the clapping continued. Slowly, the people sat back down in their seats, and the noise in the room returned to a low hum.

"We'd like to thank everyone for coming here tonight, and also many thanks to the hospital committee for their help in making this banquet a success. All proceeds will go towards the cancer center. Have a good evening," said the chairman of the committee. The award banquet was officially over.

Within a few minutes, people began rising, starting to leave. The mayor asked Tony politely if he was staying after the evening.

"Yes, for a few days," said Tony. "There is some unfinished business I need to attend to, and I don't know how long it will take."

"We'd like to invite you to my house tonight," said the mayor. "We've invited some important guests for a small party and would be honored to have your presence."

"Thank you," said Tony, nodding.

The reception ended soon after that. He spoke and shook hands with a number of people who congratulated him personally, then he stood around with his hands in his pockets, waiting for the mayor to finish talking to some people. He kept glancing towards the back, hoping to get a glimpse of the piano player. He felt slightly disappointed that she hadn't shown up again. He wondered what happened to her.

"Dr. Plakis, please come with me," said the mayor, interrupting his thoughts, gesturing to him.

❦   ❦   ❦

The next day, Tony didn't wake up until early afternoon. It was cloudy and raining outside. He rubbed his forehead. He hadn't returned to the hotel until four o'clock in the morning and now he was beginning to feel a slight hangover. He lay back in bed, going over in his mind what he was going to do today.

He was going to call Ipatia's house and introduce himself. Just like that. Then he would ask to speak to Ipatia. If she invited him over, then he would visit them and go and find out for himself if the girl still had feelings for him after all these years. *Yes, but what if she already has someone? I will soon find out.*

Tony arose and washed. After dressing, he found the telephone number Mrs. Rodos had given him. It was the number of Ipatia's aunt and uncle. He would have to find a way to get there, but first, he needed to call.

"Hello?"

It was a woman's voice. It sounded familiar. "Hello, this is Tony Plakis," he began, then stopped when he heard the woman excitedly interrupt him.

"Tony Plakis, how is it, after all these years?" Aunt Sophia exclaimed.

"It's a long story," he said, laughing. "I am in town. I came for a banquet given by the hospital."

"The banquet, you mean the one given in honor for some foundation?" she asked, surprised.

"Yes, the Kalkinon foundation," he said. "My father and I formed it about a year ago."

"I'm surprised Ipatia didn't tell me about it."

"Ipatia? Why, was she there?" he asked, his voice catching in his throat. Immediately the image of the young woman dressed in black, wearing those glasses, playing the piano came to him. If only he had known.

"Yes, she played the piano at the banquet," she said, puzzled at his response. "Didn't you see her?"

She had been right in front of him, playing the piano last night, and he had missed his opportunity to speak with her. "I'm afraid I didn't...recognize her. It's a long story...I had amnesia...from an accident several years ago."

"Amnesia? I'm sorry to hear that."

"Is Ipatia available to speak to me?" asked Tony. "I know this is unexpected after all these years, but I must speak to her...it's important."

"Oh dear. I'm afraid it will be impossible."

"What do you mean? Is she married?" he asked, fearing the worst.

"No, it's nothing like that," laughed Sophia nervously. "You see, she left for Greece two hours ago. She'll be visiting her cousins, George and Paula Mastroyiannis in Piraeus, then she will travel to visit her grandfather on the island."

"She left for Greece?" asked Tony, digesting the news.

"Will you be here for awhile? We would like for you to come and visit us."

"I'd like to, but I have a plane to catch. It was good speaking with you, Sophia."

CHAPTER 39

June 1993
Our love began five years ago
Now this ring to thee I bestow

Ipatia's flight was delayed an hour because of the heavy storm. The rain began as soon as she arrived at the airport. She sat around, waiting for her flight to be announced. Outside it was gray and stormy, and looked as if it was going to last awhile.

She rummaged through her purse, searching for her passport and boarding pass. She looked them over carefully. Everything was in order. She placed them back in her purse. Her hand brushed against something hard. It was the brochure from the night before. She had forgotten it. She started leafing through it absentmindedly, reading the different projects going on in the hospital, and the advertisements. She came across the name of the Foundation and its generous donation. As she read more carefully, her eyes opened in wonder. It couldn't be, but Tony Plakis had been at the banquet last night!

She continued reading. He was the president of the foundation. How could she have missed him? She ran over the events of last night in her mind. Then she remembered the tall, handsome man staring at her while she played, and her heart starting racing at the possibility that it might have been him. He had been too far away for her to recognize him.

She hadn't stayed because of the little accident with the cart. She had been so upset from the commotion caused by the spill, that she thought nothing else but to go and bury herself in the restroom. Stasoula had come shortly after to help her.

"I can't get these stains off of this skirt," moaned Ipatia, showing her the dirty skirt.

"Here, don't worry about it. The banquet is just about finished and we have plenty of help," said Stasoula. "We will be fine. Would you like for Chris to drive you home?"

That's what happened. Ipatia had gone straight home from there. Then she had been busy getting her luggage ready for the trip. She had dropped into bed exhausted.

Ipatia's thoughts were interrupted by the loud speaker.

"We are now boarding passengers in seats 20-30."

She pulled her boarding pass shakily out of her purse, got up and went to stand in line.

Eight hours later Ipatia landed in the Athens airport. It was a sunny day, quite a contrast from the stormy weather she left behind in Chicago. Her cousins were waiting for her and their warm reception was heartening. They whisked Ipatia away from the hub of the airport and transported her back to their home. There was much chatter and discussion along the way.

When they arrived at the house, they chatted awhile longer over lunch, then Ipatia excused herself and went into her bedroom to take a nap. It wasn't long before she fell into a deep sleep. *She dreamt that she was wearing all white, and Tony appeared next to her. He was kind and gentle and kissed her. She felt happy. Then he went and sat outside on the terrace, drinking coffee. When she went outside to join him, he had disappeared. She felt disappointed and sad. Then he reappeared, sitting in a new car and taking her to a palace, saying, "This is your new home."*

When Ipatia awoke, she lay there thinking about Tony. Something had awakened inside of her when she read the brochure with his name in it. Was it hope? Was Tony coming back into her life? *It was only a dream, stop fantasizing! He's probably married by now!*

She found Paula in the living room. "Hi, Paula…where's George?"

"He went to get me something from the store," said Paula. "He should be back soon."

They talked for awhile. The doorbell rang and Paula went to answer it. She returned a few minutes later appearing flustered. "That was George…he forgot to take the money. He'll be back soon. Anyway…did you get a chance to catch some sleep?"

"Yes, thank you, and very well!" said Ipatia. "I had this strange dream. Tony Plakis was in it."

"I've been meaning to tell you something. We visited Dr. Michael's office recently and learned that Tony had been asking about you."

"What do you mean?"

"Tony asked for your address," said Paula carefully. "We also spoke to your aunt on the telephone while you were napping. She said Tony telephoned her yesterday morning. He was in Chicago, at the banquet. He asked for you and she told him you were coming here."

"She did?"

"What are your feelings towards Tony?" asked Paula.

"What do you mean?"

"If he asked you to marry him, would you?"

Ipatia was stunned. It was too much to handle in such a short time. She had blocked him for so many years from her mind, and all of a sudden, there he was, still single, still trying to come back in her life. "It's not that easy to begin loving him all over again. I mean…after what he did."

"Do you love him still?" asked Paula softly.

Ipatia was silent for a moment, digesting everything. She felt as if a ray of light was shining on her. She nodded numbly. "Yes, with all my heart." The tears swelled in her eyes.

Paula got up. "Excuse me for a minute, dear…I think I hear George at the door."

Ipatia sat still, motionless, as if in a trance. She could not ignore anymore the deep-rooted love she had for this man.

"Ipatia."

Ipatia jumped at the deep voice. She could recognize his voice anywhere. The same voice that sang her love songs was now here, in the room. She turned around to face Tony.

She felt her knees buckle under her as she drifted into darkness.

Someone was holding her closely, talking to her softly, caressing her arm, and kissing her cheek, saying he loved her. She responded, saying "Tony", melting in his arms. It felt so good.

She slowly opened her eyes and found herself gazing into Tony's eyes.

"Tony Plakis, how dare you come here and mock me…after all these years?" she exclaimed angrily, scrambling up, trembling all over. She pulled back the loose strands of hair from her face and crossed her arms. Tears, four years worth of tears, welled up in her eyes.

Tony took her in his arms, and said softly, "I love you."

"How could you say that after what you did?" she persisted. This time, she did not resist. He hugged her closely.

"What did I do, my sweet one?" he asked, still holding her close, starting to nuzzle her cheek.

"You left me there, in the hospital and went to Crete," she said, afraid to look at him, afraid to reveal her true feelings.

"Before I explain, please do me a favor," he said, tipping her chin up so he could look deep into her eyes. This was the only way he would know if she really loved him after all these years. Her eyes were a passionate green.

"What?" she whispered. She got her answer, as he kissed her slowly, fervently. She did not fight it, but instead gave her heart and soul to him. All her illusions were shattered in that kiss. She knew no matter what happened next, that she loved him and would always love him.

"Tell me, Ipatia, exactly what happened right before the accident." He saw her puzzled look. "It's important."

She told him, and when she got to the part where she heard a honk and blacked out, she stopped.

"You blacked out?" he asked, interested.

"Yes. I remember waking up the next day in the hospital," she admitted. "I had two fractured ribs and stayed there through Easter. I had my cousins call your house every day…but there was no answer."

"I'm sorry my sweet one, if I could, I would have been there by your side," he said, moaning slightly. "I didn't wake up until a month later."

"What do you mean?"

"I was in a coma…and almost didn't survive. When I woke up, I didn't remember anyone, not even my own family."

Ipatia was stunned. "How could it be? I thought you had gone to Crete for the Easter holiday! Rita told me!"

"I'm afraid Rita didn't know what happened," he said ruefully. "Father didn't want anyone knowing about it. The doctors in Greece said I didn't have much of a chance, so my family took me to England, where I was operated on several times."

She touched his face lovingly. "Is everything all right, I mean are you fine now?"

"Yes, my love. Now that I am near you, everything is fine," he said huskily.

"I'm so glad!" she said, hugging him impulsively. She was swept up in his embrace. He kissed her once more, murmuring sweet words in her ear. Years of holding her emotions at bay now dissolved into a timeless, passionate moment. After what seemed like eternity, she spoke, "Oh, dear, what about my cousins!"

"Don't worry, they know I'm here," he said, chuckling. "When you were napping, I came and introduced myself. I told them what had happened to me and that I wasn't sure if you'd still want me after all these years. Paula asked me to wait in the kitchen while she talked to you first."

"So that was why she was asking all those questions."

"Before I go on, there's something else you need to know about me," he said solemnly. He had to do this. This was the final test. "I no longer work for my father's business. I have my own business."

"You do?" she asked timidly.

"Yes," he said. "And I haven't that much money. I got myself into debt trying to start the business."

"It doesn't matter! In my opinion, money does not make a man noble, but his character does! I am proud of you for trying to do something on your own, even if it means being in debt!"

That was all he needed to hear. His money was not the reason she loved him. He kissed her tenderly. He then took out the little jewelry box from his pocket. Inside was the engagement ring. He wanted more than anything in the world to make her his wife. "Do you see this, my love?"

She stared at it, surprised at its beauty. She nodded slowly, mesmerized by its glitter. "It has the cat's eye stone I had given to you as a present."

"I found this recently, when I rummaged through my clothes I brought back with me from the hospital. It was in one of the pockets of my pants...the day we were going to the picnic."

"It was?" she asked, trembling at the implications. *He had been meaning to propose to you, just like in your dream.*

"I like to finish what I start." He removed the ring from the box and slipped it on her finger.

"I wasn't worthy of it," she said tearfully. "I mean, I was so bent on going to school, thinking only about myself, and here you were trying to marry me. Maybe God didn't want us to get together then, that is why he separated us."

"It is our destiny," he said, interrupting her with another kiss. "We cannot fight our destiny. We were meant to be together."

"Yes," she said dreamily, leaning against him, feeling safe. She told him about the dream she had, where she had wanted to be with him and he had told her not to go with him.

"Do not fear, my love. You will never be alone, because I will always be with you," he said quietly, placing his face against hers. "It was only yesterday when I last saw you. Everything is coming back to me now, your face, your hair, your eyes, and even your stubbornness."

She laughed, feeling joyful.

"Will you marry me?" he asked charmingly, looking intently into her eyes. He got his answer.

She nodded, her eyes shining brightly in his. "Oh, yes!"

He picked her up, twirling her around. They laughed together. "The ring matches your eyes," he said appreciatively.

"It is beautiful!" she admitted, raising it to her face. "I'm glad you made it into a ring."

"Your happiness is mine doubled!" he said. "Now I have a confession to make."

"Yes?"

"I'm not as poor as I told you previously," he said. "Actually, I am doing very well in my business. I even built a villa in a suburb of Athens. It sits high on a hill and has a beautiful view of the sea. It is waiting for you. It will be your new home."

"Tony, how could you!"

"I wanted to see your reaction," he said laughing. "Your heart is richer than all the money I have. You just proved it to me."

"I hope your family will like me."

"My dear girl, my love for you will overcome any reservations anyone has about you!" he said. "Once they see you for who you are, they can't help but fall in love with you!"

"I love you so much!" she said before melting into his arms. Her happiness was complete.

THE END

TRANSLATIONS

Greek	English
Alithos Anesti	Truly He is risen
Ante!	Go!
Antithoro	Holy bread
Avgolemeno	Lemon and egg soup
Cafenio	Coffee shop
Dolmades	Stuffed grape leaves
Drachmas	Greek currency
Christos Anesti	Christ is risen
Koulourakia	Greek cookies that are crisp
Koumbara	Godmother's relationship to parents
Koumbaro	Godfather's relationship to parents
Leventi	Fine man or gentleman
Mizithra	The name of a Greek cheese
Nona	Godmother
Tiropites	Cheese pies
Tsoureki	Easter bread which is sweet and rich
Vassilopita	New Year's cake, with coin inside
Yiasas	Greetings

978-0-595-37572-1
0-595-37572-3

Printed in the United States
64626LVS00007B/16-69

9 780595 375721